TAMING THE
DRAGON
SERIES

THERE IS NO RAINBOW

HELEN WEBSTER

authorHOUSE®

AuthorHouse™
1663 Liberty Drive
Bloomington, IN 47403
www.authorhouse.com
Phone: 1 (800) 839-8640

Published by AuthorHouse   06/08/2016

ISBN: 978-1-5246-1319-8 (sc)
ISBN: 978-1-5246-1317-4 (hc)
ISBN: 978-1-5246-1318-1 (e)

Library of Congress Control Number: 2016909366

Print information available on the last page.

DEDICATION

This book is dedicated to all the children who are striving so hard to survive in a world over which they have no control and to everyone who believed in me and this book including my husband Paul.

Helen Webster, March, 2015

FOREWORD

In May 1982 the House of Commons in Ottawa officially adopted that, "One out of ten Canadian women were battered by their spouses." Prior to and following this acknowledgement that spousal abuse is indeed a major social problem in Canada, there has been much debate on whether or not this figure represents an accurate account of the number of cases whereby a woman suffers at the hands of her partner.

The one fact that is beyond dispute is the social and psychological impact abuse has on children growing up in violent homes. It is something they never forget. They carry the emotional and physical scars to their graves. In many instances, they perpetuate unto others--their own spouses, children and families--the very inflictions they have come to internalize as "normal."

In the story you are about to read, you will become a helpless bystander as you are taken into Jason's world--a world filled with violence and fear.

Although Jason and the other characters in *There is No Rainbow* have been fictionalized, his shocking home life and experiences at the hands of his brutal father are based on real people and events. They have been taken from hundreds of true accounts of individuals who have been similarly victimized and those who have done the abusing.

What happens to Jason is not unique in our society today. One only has to read about the thousands of women and children fleeing to emergency shelters to escape the violence to realize the magnitude of this social problem

Unfortunately, there are no easy solutions, no pat answers to effectively eliminate family violence. For most, the resolution remains as elusive as the proverbial pot of gold at the end of the rainbow. Governments cannot effectively legislate an end to the problem, and police departments cannot arrest and charge every person suspected of abusing his family.

"Then it is hopeless!" you say? *No!* With increased awareness and education, the violence need not be perpetuated from one generation to another. Anger management programs, as well as other preventative programs, can help stop potential abusers from using physical and/or psychological abuse to solve their problems. This book – There Is No Rainbow- can help with educating society as a whole.

It will mean that many individuals will have to examine their attitudes and change their thinking patterns. But it is possible, if society as a whole, wants to eradicate the violence presently being inflicted upon thousands of women and children.

Only then will the rainbow of hope appear.

CHAPTER I

Someone was crying.

Jason stirred in his sleep. The sound came from far away and wove itself into the heart of his dream. He rolled over, plunging his face into his pillow, but now the focus of the dream changed, taking on a frightful dimension. He was battling a terrible monster on top of a cliff while his sister stood on a far-away hill calling for him to help her. With her pleas ringing in his ears, he fought against the forces threatening to drag him over the edge and into the bottomless, black pit below.

He awoke with a start!

The dream-- It had been so real; so intense it sent shivers racing up his spine and he trembled. He pulled his quilt up around his chin, trying to still his pounding heart. Huddling under his covers, attempting to separate dream from reality, Jason listened. Had his sister really called for help? He didn't know.

"Jason..." a voice wailed out of the darkness.

There it was again. He wasn't dreaming. Someone was crying, and now the sound filled his room. Frightened, Jason pulled his quilt tighter over his head, afraid to face whatever was out there.

It's the monsters! They're in my room, he muttered. They're coming to get me!

He clamped his hands over his ears and curled up in a tight ball, trying to block out the noise. Still he could hear faint echoes and knew whatever was out there wasn't going away.

Unable to get back to sleep, Jason cautiously lowered one corner of the blanket and peered into the night. His eyes, unaccustomed to the darkness, failed and he rubbed them, afraid he had gone blind. His fear turned to terror as he strained to see, trying to distinguish the familiar shapes of his furniture. At last, he was able to peel away the night and the grey shapes of his dresser and night table became visible. He sighed and lowered his blanket until his head was fully exposed. Slowly, he looked around his room searching for the intruder.

He was so absorbed in finding the source of the noise that it was awhile before he realized the cries were coming from outside his room. Relieved that whatever was making the sound wasn't about to leap out and grab him, he relaxed in his bed and continued to listen. It sounded like his sister.

It must be Becky. What's her problem?

His younger sister didn't usually wake up in the night and, if she did, she didn't make any noise.

If she doesn't shut up, I'll never get back to sleep, he thought, rolling over and punching his pillow. He pulled his covers back over his head and tried to ignore her cries.

It was no use. His sister continued to cry and now he was wide awake. Angry, he threw off his blankets and laid in his bed, glaring into the darkness.

He glanced towards his window and saw a small shaft of yellow light coming in from the street below. A soft breeze rustled his curtains and the movement caught his attention. The moving curtains cast dark shadows on his far wall, and as he watched, the shadows became two monsters, twisting and leaping; engaged in a deadly battle. It appeared to him that they were fighting to see who would win the right to leap off the wall and devour him. They gouged; they ripped at each other with vicious fangs and long curled talons. It was too much.

Terrified by these unearthly specters, Jason shuddered, his body as rigid as a board. He wondered how he was going to escape, knowing it was only a matter of time before one of them leaped off the wall and clutched him in its deadly embrace.

"Go away," he moaned, "Go away."

It's Becky's fault. If she hadn't started crying, the monsters wouldn't have come. Why doesn't Mom get up and see what she wants? What time is it?

If it were almost morning, Jason was sure his mother would get up and go to her, but if it were still night--. He had to know; he had to face down the monsters and see what time it was. He rolled over and peered at this clock-radio. The red digital numbers swam before his eyes, but he stared at them until they steadied and he could read: 11:36 p.m.

I can't get up. I just can't. But I won't be able to fall asleep again unless she stops her bawling. Maybe if I keep my eyes fixed on the window, the monsters will go away. Staring at his window, Jason tried to analyze his reaction to the shadows on his wall.

This is stupid! There's no such thing as monsters and I'm not afraid.

He snuck a quick peek at his far wall. The dark figures were still there and they still looked like monsters about to leap out of a nightmare.

"I'm not afraid," he whispered. "I'm not afraid."

"NOooo...!" a voice screamed.

Startled, Jason bolted upright and his eyes flew to his door. He shrivelled inside when he heard his dad yell. From the tone of his father's voice, Jason knew his dad was mad! And, he also knew it was his mother who had screamed.

He shivered. Now he knew why his sister was crying; now, he wanted to cry too. His parents were downstairs, but his father's voice was so loud and distinct that it almost seemed like he was standing right outside Jason's door. Jason heard his dad shout--

"You know something, Linda? You're just like one of the Pit Bull dogs. You know the kind. The ones that get a grip on your leg and won't let go, no matter how hard you try to shake them loose. Always hanging on, until one day you get enough and you take a gun and blow their God-damn head off! But, when you look down, the head is still gripping your leg."

Jason didn't want to listen to the hateful words any longer. He covered his ears with his hands, trying to stifle his father's voice.

Dad must be in one of his "moods" again.

A chill passed over Jason and he reached to the foot of his bed until his fingers touched a familiar furry shape. He picked up his stuffed raccoon and hugged it tightly.

"Help me, Pookie," he begged his best-- his only-- friend. "Make him stop."

Crash!

Jason flinched. It sounded like his dad had broken something again. His father almost always threw something-- or someone-- when he was angry. Jason was glad that he was in his room, away from the fighting, but he knew he wasn't entirely safe-- nobody was.

I hope Mom's okay.

Whenever his parents got into an argument, she came out the loser.

Don't hit her, Dad, he silently pleaded.

"Please Nick... NOooo...!"

His mother's scream infuriated Jason. He clenched his hands into fists, and sat in the darkness cursing his dad under his breath. He bit his teeth into his lower lip, fighting the urge to scream out his own rage. Unable to openly vent his anger and frustration, Jason grabbed his pillow and pounded on it.

"I hate you!" he hissed. "Do you hear me?" I hate you. Leave Mom alone. Oh, why don't you just die? Why can't I kill you myself?"

Hatred washed over him like waves hitting a sandy beach and he didn't realize he had bitten through the skin of his lower lip until he tasted blood.

I should go downstairs and kick the shit out of you! He flung his pillow across the room. But, he knew he wouldn't go downstairs; knew he wouldn't confront his father. Nobody dared stand up to his dad; least of all, him. Everyone was too afraid.

Caught up in his silent condemnation of his father, Jason forgot about Becky until he heard her cry out again.

"Oh shit!" he exclaimed.

His anger, so quickly aroused, vanished, leaving him shivering in the night. He hugged Pookie tighter and took a deep breath. He wondered if his sister realized that she was putting all of them in danger. If only he could shut out Becky's cries; his mother's screams; his dad's anger-- If he could do that, then maybe, just maybe, he would survive this nightmare.

But how...?

His world was out of control and he felt himself drawn towards the bottomless pit in his dream, to be lost forever; left to drown in the noise that now, filled his room. The sounds were hateful and he felt threatened. What could he do to stop his father?

Jason pressed his fists against his forehead. He had absorbed so much, it seemed his head would split open. His stomach churned and waves of nausea washed over him. A scream of terror caught in his throat and he swallowed it, before it could erupt and alert his dad. He felt small; small and vulnerable in a world filled with violence.

Unable to cope with his emotions, the last vestiges of his self-control disappeared, and long, jagged sobs burst forth, and were muffled in Pookie's body. Scalding tears coursed down his cheeks and soaked into the soft grey fur.

"Stop it!" he sobbed. "Shit. I can't take anymore. Please stop. Please...."

When at last his tears had subsided and been replaced by the occasional sniffle, Jason fought to regain control of his feelings. He was exhausted. Slowly, he let his body sink back onto his bed, while he opened his fists and gently flexed his fingers. They had gone numb and the numbness hurt. When he had worked them till the circulation began to return, he turned his thoughts to his dad.

His father wasn't a tall man, but he seemed to tower over Jason, especially if he was angry. Then, it seemed liked his dad had to be at least seven feet tall. Another thing that fascinated Jason, was his dad's hands. His father used his hands to inflict punishment, and did so on a regular basis. Jason thought of these hands as a separate addition to his father. His dad's hands demanded respect, and that respect was obtained totally by fear. Jason had seen the hands punch, throw things and used to threaten, whenever his dad was angry. And, for as long as Jason could remember, he had tried to stay out of their reach. Sometimes he was successful; other times he was not.

He was also afraid of his father's eyes. Slate grey, they reminded Jason of a steel knife blade and were just as deadly. He had seen those eyes cut through a person's resolve, as easy as a knife went through butter, leaving that person a scarred, cut up, lump of quivering flesh. He should know; he'd been on the receiving end of his dad's stares often enough

I hate it when he looks at me, he thought fearfully, cautiously glancing around his room.

Thinking about his father's eyes jerked him back to reality and he was afraid that he might encounter them staring at him out of the darkness.

Man, if Dad heard me bawling, would I have been in for it!

He rubbed his face in Pookie's fur, trying to imagine what his father would do to him. At the very least, his dad would have ridiculed him for acting like a baby, but it was more likely, that he would have been severely punished.

He grabbed a corner of his blanket and blew his nose. Satisfied that no tell tale signs of his lapse remained, Jason began to admonish himself.

I shouldn't have started bawling. Dad doesn't like it when we cry, especially at night.

His thoughts were interrupted when he heard Becky call out to him. He know that sooner or later his dad would hear her too. Then what?

I better get up and see what's bugging her. If she doesn't stop, he'll come up here--

Jason didn't want to think about what would happen should his dad come upstairs and find them both awake. He slipped out of bed and searched the floor for his clothes.

At first, he couldn't find his jeans until he stepped on the zipper. "Ouch!" he cried hopping around on one foot and holding the other.

He put on his pants and reached down for his shirt. Only after he finished dressing did it occur to him that he didn't have to get dressed just to run to her room, tell her to shut up, and come back and climb into bed.

Gee, I'm dumb, he thought starting across the room towards the door.

He had to feel his way, while at the same time, keeping his eyes from straying over in the direction of the shadows. They were too real-- too menacing-- and, if he gave them the chance, they could still leap off his wall and grab him. Now that he had finally decided to leave his room, he was determined that nothing-- not the shadows and not his father-- would prevent him from going out into that hallway to Becky's room. He had to see her and tell her to stop crying before she got all of them into trouble.

He jumped back, startled! His head had bumped against something and he struggled to regain his composure before his imagination could take over. He reached up and his hand touched one of his model planes hanging from the ceiling.

I have to get hold of myself he said.

He felt foolish that he could be so easily frightened by a plastic airplane.

Jason stood for a few moments, staring up at them. Their grey outlines were barely visible, as the planes turned and swayed in the air currents. He gently ran his finger over the undercarriage of the model he had bumped into, wishing that it was real, so he could climb in it and soar away forever.

He moved alongside his dresser until he stood in front of the closed door. His courage vanished the instant his hand touched the door knob. His knees turned to jello, and he gripped the top of his dresser to keep from falling.

Now, he no longer wanted to leave his room; he was no longer interested in going out into the hallway. Despite the presence of the shadows, this was his haven-- his safety-- against the storm of violence waiting beyond his door.

"God give me the guts to go out there," he prayed, but when his prayer went unheeded, his fear turned to panic.

No one could help him now. He was alone.

He stood in front of the door, twisting one of his buttons, and argued with himself.

"I can't go out; Dad might be out there waiting."

"But you have to go," countered the little voice inside him. *"Remember last time?"*

"Yes damit! I remember but, I'm scared--"

His objection was cut short when the voice interjected, *"Are you going to remain a sissy all your life? Your dad's right, you know. You are just a big baby."*

"No I'm not. It's just--"

"Just nothing! Listen dummy,...Can't you hear him? He's still downstairs. Now, don't be such a wimp. Grab the handle, turn it, and get going."

"But what if he comes upstairs and catches me out of my room? You know Dad has a rule about us leaving our rooms at night. No excuse is acceptable-- not even if we have to go to the bathroom."

"But he's not up here, is he?" the voice persisted." *"And he won't catch you if you're careful. Now-- Go!"*

Jason knew that there was no point in continuing the argument and instead, tried to mentally prepare himself to face whatever he might encounter when he stepped out that door. He straightened his shoulders, gritted his teeth, and tried to still his fear. He couldn't stop thinking about what would happen to him should he be caught before he could get safely back. He clearly remember the "last time" one of his dad's rules had been broken.

They had all suffered. And all because supper was late. Getting caught out of your room in the middle of the night had to be a much worse offense. That time, it was his mother who had made his dad mad, but no one had escaped being punished for her offense.

The punishment had consisted of a long "lecture" administered by his father, to her, along with Jason, his sister Becky, and his little brother Nicky. He didn't want another lecture-- not now. Not ever again.

It had taken place over a year ago, but Jason would never forget. He had just turned eleven, and Becky would have been six. His baby brother must have been eight or nine months old; Jason wasn't sure.

They had been expecting it. For days, the air was filled with tension and they all knew it was only a matter of time before their dad finally exploded. Well, maybe Nicky didn't know, thought Jason, because he's only a baby, but the rest of them knew that things were building up to a climax.

Jason wasn't sure how they were able to predict exactly when his father was likely to explode in anger. They just knew. It was sort of like knowing a storm is coming, because you can smell the changes in the air. The only difference was, that with his dad, you couldn't smell the impending violence, you could feel its approach; just as deadly and all encompassing as a descending tornado.

If he closed his eyes, Jason could still see his father pacing back and forth, his eyes as cold as the stone statue in front of Jason's school. His dad waved his fist in their faces and they had sat, at the table, petrified with fear. When his father stopped in front of him, Jason had almost passed out from fright. He had felt like a mouse that had been caught in a steel-jawed trap while going after a piece of cheese. There had been no escaping what followed.

*   *   *

His father came home early that day and found everyone standing around the kitchen waiting for supper. Only, Jason's mom hadn't finished preparing supper.

She had taken Nicky to get his polio vaccine and was late getting home. As a result, the roast wasn't cooked by the time his dad arrived home from his dental office. That was all that it had taken for him to fly into a blinding rage.

His dad had a "rule" about meals: They were to be served at specific times, and supper was to be on the table and waiting for him by exactly 5:00 p.m. No excuse was accepted. If he thought his wishes had been thwarted, he would get angry and every member of the family would suffer because one of them had failed to comply with one of his demands.

But, Jason noticed his father could come home late, and no one would say anything to him. Not even Jason's mom dared to mention that he was late. They would simply have to sit at the table and wait for him, because his dad had another rule: No one was to start eating the food his money provided without him. Period.

As a result of this rule, Jason and his family had long grown accustomed to waiting for his dad to arrive-- not daring to touch the food on the table. Then, when he did arrive, the food often had to be reheated and served again. If it lost some of its original appeal, his father didn't seem to notice or, if he did, didn't care. The only thing that mattered was that his "rules" were being obeyed.

Although he felt guilty at the thought, Jason couldn't help but wonder if his father kept them waiting on purpose; that he liked to see them sitting at the table-- hungry, but unable to touch the food that was laid out. As he had gotten older, Jason had harbored this same thought more often, and had even mentioned his theory to his mother. But, instead of being interested, she had told him to "hush," unwilling to discuss it any further with him.

But, on the day the "Lecture" took place, his dad wasn't late for supper. He had come home fifteen minutes early.

Jason's mom scurried around the kitchen, trying to get the roast to cook faster, which was impossible.

Cooking a roast isn't like getting kids up and dressed in the morning, thought Jason. *It can't be hurried and even if she had been able to make it cook a little faster, it wouldn't have made any difference. Supper was still-- late.*

The look on his dad's face frightened him, and he ran over and picked up Nicky off the floor, scared that his father might step on him. His dad stomped around the kitchen, screaming at his wife. Jason set Nicky in his highchair, and ran to sit in his own chair at the table. Becky took her cue from him, and scrambled up on her stool. Together, they sat, still as mice, watching their father vent his rage. They saw him kick one of Nicky's toys, sending it skidding across the kitchen floor.

Jason's mom tried to apologize; tried to explain why she was late. Jason felt sorry for her; she stood in the center of the kitchen, nervously running her hands through her hair and picking at a spot on her apron.

But, his dad wouldn't listen to her. No excuse was acceptable; least of all, the excuse that supper was late because she had to take Nicky for his needle.

"Since when are these damn brats more important than me?" he screamed, waving his fist in front of her nose. She cringed and pressed back against the stove, trying to get away. She managed to push herself sideways and then, ducked under his arm, a bowlful of peas clasped tightly in her hands. She hurried towards the table, but he intercepted her, yanked the bowl out of her grasp, and hurled it at the wall.

In disbelief, Jason watched the bowl disintegrate, spewing peas all over the wall, the ceiling, and the floor. Stunned by the violence of this act, Jason cowered in his chair and watched the mess of squashed peas slowly slither down the wall. His mother rushed over, and bent down, trying to scoop up the mess with her hands. His dad delivered a kick to her stomach and she landed on her knees amidst the broken glass and ruined vegetables, retching and gasping for air.

His father planted his feet on top of her hands and screamed at her. "You lazy, good-for-nothing slut! I told you before I wanted you home when I got here."

Smack!

The slap sent her sprawling, and Jason watched helplessly as his mother struggled to pick herself up off the floor.

"I'm not so stupid that I don't know what goes on here all day when I'm gone," his dad yelled, grabbing her by the hair and yanking her to her feet. "Don't try and pull those lies off on me. Tell me, Linda, Who have you been screwing around with this time?"

He let go of her hair and she slumped against the wall. "You know something? You're just like that lazy bitch you've got for a mother-- always lying and sneaking around."

There was nothing Jason could do except grind his teeth together, clench and unclench his fists that were hidden from view in his lap beneath the table, listen to his heart pound like a drum in his chest, pulsate in his ears so loudly he was certain everyone in the room could hear. If he interfered he, too, would be sacrificed to the heavy wrath of his father's hands!

His mother slowly stood and walked past his father, her eyes on the floor. A red welt slashed across her pale cheek. She went to the stove, and there were tears in her eyes as she picked up a wooden spoon off the counter and slowly stirred the stew in a pot on the stove. Her shoulders sagged and it seemed like she was no longer listening, but was instead, concentrating on what she was doing. She bent forward and with a trembling hand lifted the spoon to her lips.

"Put that God-damn spoon down and listen to me!" his dad roared, coming from behind and shaking her. She lost her grip on the spoon and it clattered to the floor, adding its contents to the mess already there.

"My Dad was right when he said that all women are conniving bitches, if you give them a chance," he gasped, trying to catch his breath. "Well, Linda, you're not getting that chance with me. Is that clear?"

She nodded her head, unable or unwilling to speak. He released her and walked over to the doorway.

Jason was terrified.

There was no escape from his dad's anger and he wondered who would be next. What was to become of them if his dad's fury continued? He squeezed his hands between his knees and wished he could disappear-- could sink into nothingness. He turned to look at this sister. Becky's face was pale, and he saw her lower lip quiver.

She's as scared as I am, he realized.

Tears had formed in the corner of her eyes, and she was sitting rigid in her chair, watching their mother.

No one, not even Nicky, made a sound except for his father. His yelling was only interrupted by the sound his fist made when he hit the wall or the table.

Jason saw Nicky lean over the side of his highchair, his eyes as wide as saucers. When his brother caught him watching him, Nicky reached out his arms to be picked up. Jason turned away.

Don't look at me, kid, thought Jason, I've got enough problems of my own. We're all in this together.

Hurt that he had been ignored, Nicky turned his attention to his mother, and Jason watched as he went through the same motions of reaching out, silently begging to be picked up. His mother looked at Nicky but then, she too, turned away. The hurt in his little brother's eyes made Jason want to cry. It wasn't fair. It just wasn't fair.

We're all trapped by dad's madness!

Jason didn't dare look at his mom, for fear that she might silently appeal to him for help. Why couldn't they understand that he was as powerless against his dad's anger as they were? Why did they think he was different?

I have to escape. I can't stand this anymore.

Jason focused his attention on a speck of dirt on the ceiling. He squinted at it, turned it over in his mind, stared at it, and tried to remove himself from what was happening around him. Gradually, he felt his mind begin to take him beyond the kitchen walls-- beyond his dad's anger, to a warm, dark hole and finally...

But before he could completely slip away, he was drawn back to reality by his sister's sobbing. Once again, he was part of the action taking place around the table, and he turned to glare at her.

"Mommm...y," she wailed.

Jason's eyes roamed wildly around the room, trying to spot his father. What would his dad do? Jason saw him walking towards them, and he pushed himself back against his chair. But, his father wasn't after him-- He was after Becky. Jason watched him come over to her chair, grab her by the hair, and fling her across the room.

To Jason, it was like everything was suddenly taking place in slow motion. He watched Becky sail across the kitchen, hit the side of the cupboard, and crumble, seemingly lifeless, to the floor. She looked like a twisted, broken, rag doll.

Shocked, he tried to stand, but his body remained glued to his chair making it impossible for him to go to her. He needed to know if she was okay. If she was dead, then he would make that bastard pay for her death.

Move, Becky. Give me some sign that you're really not hurt. Sit up. Just sit up. he silently pleaded, but she didn't move-- didn't respond-- and he sank dejectedly back in his chair.

Nicky, frightened by the commotion, started to cry. Jason held his breath. Would his dad throw Nicky across the room, too? For a second, Jason thought his father intended to do just that, because he turned and stepped towards the highchair. Jason's stomach turned over and he felt sick when he saw his dad reach for Nicky.

I can't let him do it, he thought, struggling to stand up.

But, before he could get up and save his baby brother, his mother rushed to the highchair and threw herself over Nicky, shielding him from father.

"Please Nick," she pleaded, "not the baby... Not the baby too."

His dad stepped back and stood, staring at them. Jason found himself unable to look away. It was as if he had been hypnotised by his dad's eyes. He watched his father blink twice, and then close. Then, before Jason could look away, he saw his father whirl around, lift his arms, and slam his fists down on the table. Jason cringed. The force of the blow rattled dishes and sent the cutlery flying.

"God help us all," Jason murmured softly, turning his head and looking at Becky. He saw her move her arm and hoped she wouldn't do anything that might further attract his father's attention to her.

"You damn little bastards!" his dad screamed. "You're all alike: No respect for authority. Always bawling and carrying on. No one in this house can take their medicine like a man. Well, if you think that's going to work with me, you're sadly mistaken."

Instead of pacing in front of them, his dad was now walking around the table. When he stopped behind Jason's chair and rested his hands on the back, Jason flinched and moved forward.

13

"By the time I'm finished with you," his father continued, "You're going to learn the meaning of the work respect. That includes you, Linda. Is that clear?"

Jason looked over and saw Becky nodding her head. The rest of them were too frightened to even nod. They just sat there staring at his father and wondering what they should do. However, his dad didn't seem to notice their lack of response, because he didn't even pause. He just went on criticizing them... for their behavior or lack of respect, while he paced around the table.

"You know, Linda," he said, walking over to where she was standing, "if you were a better mother, these little bastards wouldn't always be snivelling and whining. It's all your fault! You're turning them into a pack of cowards and I won't stand for it. Do you hear me...? I won't stand for it!"

This time, Jason saw his mother slowly nod her head and he heard he utter an almost inaudible, "Yes."

Jason turned his attention back to the spot on the ceiling, wondering why she never stood up to his dad, why she allowed him to call her names and hit her.

If I were her, I'd tell him to shut up. It wouldn't be hard for me to do, not if I was as big as she is. I would silence dad for good.

He could visualize himself coming up behind his father and grabbing him around his neck. He could feel the power in his fingers as they pressed into his windpipe, squeezing, until, with a final shudder, his dad would go limp and slide to the floor. It would be so easy. He tore his eyes away from the ceiling and looked across the room at his mother.

Do it, Mom. Just stand up and grab him by the neck, he silently implored. *Don't be afraid. I'll help too.*

He couldn't understand why she ignored his silent message. Why she just stood there, her head buried in her hands.

Why are you such a coward; why can't you do something for yourself-- for us? he condemned, glaring at her. Don't you care what happened to Becky-- what might happen to me?

His mother raised her head and their eyes met. He could see the suffering and pain in her eyes, but he didn't care; he was past caring. He saw her wring her hands and heard her moan softly.

"Coward," he muttered and then glanced around fearfully, in case his father had heard him. No, his dad was too busy screaming at them.

Thank God, thought Jason, nearly collapsing from relief.

His thoughts returned to his mother. Why didn't she fight back; throw his dad across the room like he had thrown Becky? It wasn't fair. Becky was just a little kid and kids cried when they were scared, didn't they? But, from what he had just witnessed, Jason was certain that they didn't. He looked at Becky and saw that she had moved, and was now huddled against the cupboard.

Silence...

The sudden quietness alarmed Jason. When had his father stopped yelling? He couldn't remember. It was as if the screaming had become part of his life and now, that part was suddenly missing, leaving in its wake a feeling of impending doom. Looking around, Jason saw that the stillness had unsettled the rest of his family, too.

His mom, Becky, and even Nicky, were staring at his dad, their expressions frozen, as if they had been turned to stone. It was eerie and Jason felt the icy fingers of fear clutching at his heart, as if demons from a nightmare were tearing at him. The silence was worse than the screaming worse than the violence. None of them knew what to expect next.

It reminded him of the stillness that follows a violent thunderstorm, when all the noise and light suddenly stops and a rainbow appears.

Only here, he thought, *there is no rainbow; only Dad... and the storm has just begun.*

CHAPTER II

His father was standing beside the kitchen sink, his mouth slowly opening and closing. But, he wasn't making a sound. Fascinated by this unusual sight, Jason watched his dad's lips form inaudible words, and tried to read what he was saying. But, Jason couldn't make sense out of the unspoken dialogue. He had only seen him like this once before and knew that his father was too angry to be coherent. As such, Jason was careful not to let his dad's lack of speech break through his guard.

He looks like a fish, thought Jason. *A cold-blooded barracuda, just circling, waiting to get us.*

However, Jason wasn't prepared when his dad suddenly returned his stare. In the second that it took Jason to look away, his dad had conveyed so much hate and disgust, that Jason crumbled inside. It was as if his father had consumed him with his eyes, chewed him up, and then spat out the pieces. The look his father had given him, frightened Jason so badly, that for a minute, he thought he was going to wet his pants. Scared that his dad was going to turn on him next, Jason crouched in his chair, digging his nails into the plastic underneath. Alone and at his father's mercy, he tried to pray.

"The Lord is my shepherd..."

He couldn't remember the words! Why couldn't he remember? He needed to pray, but the rest of the familiar passage escaped him.

Why am I so stupid? I can't even pray right, he thought, angrily shaking his head. He was disgusted with himself and the rest of the world.

I must be going crazy.

He felt like he was crazy; felt like he had lost control and was now drifting, lost in the emptiness of his mind. Tears of frustration gathered in the corners of his eyes, threatening to betray him. He fought back.

I won't cry; not now, not every again.

He needed Becky; needed her to help him stay in control. He wanted to go to her, so they could console each other as they did when they were little and slept in the same room. Back then, whenever his dad started shouting, they would wrap their arms around each other and huddle together in the darkness until it was over. Now, it was wrong, all wrong. When he needed her, he couldn't go to her. Now, he was alone and had to handle his fear alone.

I can't go to her because I'm afraid. I'm too much a coward. A real man would at least go over and see if she's hurt.

His helplessness hung over him like a shroud, and he felt deeply ashamed; felt like a baby still sucking at this mother's breast.

Hell, I'm worse than Nicky. Dad's right!

He always said that I'm nothing but a coward. Why can't I be someone he can be proud of? I've always been afraid of something or other. I'm no good at anything; not in school and not in hockey. Let's face it. I was born a loser and I'll remain a loser. Nobody wants me around and nobody likes me; not even Dad. He's right. I am a momma's boy-- a worthless piece of trash.

His self-analysis left a vacuum inside him and he filled the emptiness with loathing.

I wish I were dead. The thought, at first a whisper, turned into a chant and then a roar that pounded at this temples like the bellows of a wounded, trapped animal.

He glanced over to his dad and saw him standing, his back to them, staring out the kitchen window. He kept expecting him to turn around and say something to them, but the minutes passed and his father remained silent.

Jason willed himself to relax. The roar turned into a chant, then a whisper that became only a faint hissing in his ears.

Maybe Dad is through with us, he thought hopefully. Someday... yes, someday I'm going to be rich and famous and then, watch out! Nobody, not even you Dad, is ever going to make me feel small again. Or want to die. Just you wait; I'm going to be so rich that you'll have to be proud of me. I'll make you...

As though he had heard his thoughts, his dad turned and headed towards him. Thinking that it was now his turn to feel his father's wrath Jason shivered, shrinking further down in his chair. But for some reason his father seemed to have changed his mind, because he stopped half-way across the kitchen, hesitated a moment, and then walked over to Becky. Jason saw his sister press herself against the cupboard, trying to back away. His father drew back his foot and Jason gulped, afraid he was going to kick her.

He wanted to scream, wanted to cry out to him to stop. But the sound died in his throat when his father turned his head and stared at him. It was as if he had suddenly remembered what he had intended to do. Jason clamped his jaw shut and clenched his fists, dropping his head to his chest. He could hear his sister pleading.

"Please, Daddy, no... I'll be good. I won't cry anymore, I promise.

Jason forced himself to look at his sister. Although afraid that his father might change and come after him, he had to know what was going to happen to her. His dad bent down, grabbed Becky by the front of her shirt, and lifted her in the air. She hung in his grasp like a puppet waiting for someone to pull its strings. Jason watched his father as he pulled her close to him until her face was only inches away from his nose. They stared at each other for a few seconds, then he packed her over to where Jason sat. Jason heard a crunching sound as his father slammed Becky down in the chair beside him, then strode to the end of the table.

Jason put his hand under the table, reached over, and squeezed Becky's knee. She never moved. in no way acknowledged his touch. He carefully moved his foot and pressed it against her running shoe. This time she turned her head and stared at him; her eyes were vacant, unseeing.

God, she looks awful, he thought, noticing her paleness. Why doesn't someone help us? he wondered, nervously fumbling with the top button on his shirt. *Doesn't anyone care?*

Then, the "lecture" began.

His dad motioned them all to sit at the table. "No one leaves here," he said sternly when they were all seated, "until I get a few things straightened out, once and for all."

Constantly circling the table while he was speaking, his dad's behavior gave Jason the creeps. Especially when he paused behind one of their chairs. And, if it were his chair that his father stopped at, Jason would sit ramrod straight, trying not to let the hands touch him as they rested on the back of his chair.

He's the cat and we're the mice, Jason thought, watching him pace around the table.

Intimidated by this constantly moving, stalking figure, none dared move in case he noticed. Jason tried not to squirm, but his bladder felt as though it would burst. *I've got to pee!* he thought frantically, pressing his legs together and stifling a moan. His urgency grew as he waited for his father to finish his tirade. Only it seemed he was never going to stop talking. In fact, it appeared to Jason that his dad was just getting warmed up to his favorite subject as he ranted about their ingratitude and lack of respect. His pacing increased in speed, as if his feet were attempting to keep up with his voice.

"Now, I want all of you to listen closely to what I'm about to say," said his father, stopping beside Jason and shaking his finger in his face. "In fact, if I were you guys, I wouldn't miss a single word. There's going to be some changes take place around here; some rules so I won't have to put up with anymore of this shit! First, in case any of you are still wondering-- supper is cancelled. No one eats tonight."

Big deal, thought Jason, discreetly giving his dad the finger from under the table. *Who cares? I don't want to eat anyway.*

Jason looked at his little brother and saw that Nicky was sucking on his thumb. For a minute he felt guilty, because he knew that Nicky must be hungry.

Better get used to it, kid, because it doesn't sound like Dad's finished with us yet.

"Next," his father continued, "no one leaves this table until I tell them to. Got that?"

Everyone nodded. Jason crossed his legs and silently moaned. He knew he dare not ask to be excused to use the bathroom, but if he couldn't hold it... he shuddered at the thought of what his dad would do if he pissed his pants.

"Now, if everyone's nice and comfy, we're going to have a little chat."

His "little chat" lasted four hours!

Jason cast a quick look at the clock over the door: 5:50 p.m. He was surprised that it wasn't later. Only an hour had passed since his dad first exploded; but it seemed like days, and he was tired-- bone tired. Would his dad never quit?

Jason tried to ignore him by staring at the food on the table. His mom had managed to set the potatoes and gravy on the table before his dad had squashed any further attempt to finish laying out supper. The gravy was cold and had congealed into a solid brown mass in the gravy boat. Jason wondered what would happen if he turned the dish upside down. Would the gravy plop out like jello? He wanted to try it; wanted to test his theory, but didn't dare. It would be stupid to do something that would, certainly, direct his father's attention to him. Still...

Bored, his eyes wandered over the empty plates, stopping at the little basket of buns, sitting in front of Becky. His stomach rumbled. He sucked in his gut, trying to stop it from rumbling.

Not now stupid; not now! He thought to himself.

Maybe looking at the food wasn't one of his better ideas. Jason wondered if the others could hear him. But, he didn't have to worry that his stomach would get him into trouble, because at that moment, Nicky started to cry.

Jason looked at his brother squirming in his highchair, sucking his fist, reaching out to be picked up. From the way Nicky was acting, Jason figured he must be sitting in a wet diaper.

Why doesn't mom put him to bed? Hell, Nicky won't remember all this shit anyway so why should he be punished?

Jason waited for his mother to do something, but she seemed unaware of Nicky's distress, as she sat with her face buried in her hands. Listening to his brother cry, Jason's stomach knotted in anger.

Why don't you do something; why doesn't someone do something?

If his brother didn't remember what his father was saying, Jason was just the opposite-- he would never forget. His dad droned on and on as the hours passed, repeating his list of "dos" and "don'ts" over and over again.

And, every time he stopped to take a breath, and Jason had thought he was done, his father would start over from the beginning. His words became a blur in Jason's mind. It reminded him of a scratched record that gets stuck half way through a song, ever repeating itself, until someone goes over and lifts the needle. He wished his dad had a needle. He wouldn't only lift it, he would break it off!

Jason tried to ignore him; tried to rid himself of the irritating, whining noise. But, no matter how hard he tried to shut it out, his dad's voice always managed to intrude, penetrate his mental block. Jason was sure the "rules" were engraved in his memory forever;

... Supper was to be served on time.
... His mother wasn't to leave the house
    unless she got permission first.
... The kids were to do their chores properly.
... Jason was to take the garbage out every day.
... They weren't to start bawling if punished.

The list went on and on....

Half-way through the lecture, Nicky fell asleep. It was only eight o'clock. Jason had watched his brother gradually drift off to sleep. First, Nicky's head began to nod, then his eyes closed, and finally, his body slumped forward and rested on top of his tray. Looking at him, Jason saw his brother's arms fly into the air and he heard Nicky whimper.

Even babies have nightmares, he thought turning away. *Well, he's not the only one who is tired. I wish I could got to bed. I wish I could go to the bathroom. I wish....*

But, he didn't dare fall asleep. Maybe Nicky could get away with it because he was a baby, but he certainly wouldn't try it. Putting his hands behind his head, he leaned back in his chair and stared up at the ceiling. His eyes locked onto the speck of dirt. He felt lifeless; felt like a dishrag that had been wrung out and thrown over a bar to dry. Unable to keep his eyes from closing, he tried to keep awake by forcing them to look around the room.

He focused in on Becky. He could tell from the way her eyes were flickering that she, too, was having difficulty remaining awake. Her head began to nod and she yawned. Afraid that his sister was about to fall asleep, Jason wanted to poke her in the ribs; wanted to do something-- anything-- to keep her awake.

He could see a long, blue mark on her cheek. It started at her eyebrow, ran down her left cheek, and ended at her mouth. He wondered if she'd have a black eye by morning. Her head dropped forward, resting on her chest.

Please stay awake, he silently pleaded. If you cause anymore trouble, God knows what he'll do to you-- to us.

Determined to keep her awake, Jason slowly moved his foot over until it rested against her shoe. Then, waiting till his dad's back was turned, he kicked her in the shin. She stifled a yelp and glared at him, pulling herself up straight in her chair. Jason grinned. It didn't bother him that she was mad. At least now, she was awake. Satisfied, he turned his attention back to the spot on the ceiling.

The verbal storm ended as abruptly as it had started.

Without any warning, his father stopped his lecture and told them to get to bed. It was 10 o'clock.

Before Jason could get up, his mother had already left her chair and run over to get Nicky. She lifted him out of his highchair, while at the same time, apologized to her husband. It appeared to Jason that she accepted complete responsibility for everything that had occurred during the past five hours.

He couldn't believe how his mother went on and on, telling his dad how sorry she was for not having supper ready on time; for not showing him the respect he deserved; for not being more industrious around the house. It made Jason sick!

How could you? he wondered, disgusted with her display of humility. *Why don't you just kiss his ass, too, while you're at it? What's the matter with you, woman?* his mind screamed.

He knew she wasn't disrespectful or lazy; none of them were. How could they be, with his dad always checking to make sure things were done properly?

Hell, she does everything around here except get down on her knees and bow, and she'd probably even do that, if dad asked.

Listening to her left a cold, burning anger in Jason, and he felt like spitting on her as he passed her and left the kitchen.

You don't even swear, he silently condemned, hurrying up the stairs to the bathroom. *How the hell can everything be your fault?*

As he stood in front of the toilet, Jason thought about the "respect" his father was always demanding.

Maybe it is Mom's fault. Maybe if she were a better mother, I wouldn't have to put up with all this crap.

He heard someone in the hall and quickly finished, zipped his pants, and opened the door. It was her! His mother was cradling Nicky in one arm, with Becky clinging to the other. His mother stopped and looked at him.

For the first time, Jason became aware that his mom was injured. Four ugly red welts ran down the side of her face. He tried to remember how she had been hurt, but all he could recall was his dad's screaming, the peas smashing against the wall, and Becky flying through the air. How the bruises got on his mother's face was a mystery, and he was too tired for mysteries. Besides, he was past caring. It was her problem, not his....

*   *   *

Slowly, the events of that evening faded into the recesses of his mind, and Jason found himself, one year later, once again standing alone in the dark in front of his door, his hand gripping the doorknob.

He could still hear Becky crying, but the sound was muffled by the noise coming up from downstairs. He hesitated, no longer sure of what he should do.

At last, he made a decision.

I have to go to her. I got to get her to quit bawling before Dad hears her. Jason didn't want another "lecture."

CHAPTER III

Jason turned the doorknob, opened his door, and stepped into the hallway, quietly closing the door behind him. He breathed deeply, glad to escape the memories he had left in his room. They were too painful, too confusing, and once resurrected, hung around his neck like a rock. If he was ever to make it to his sister's room, he had to rid himself of the past. His room, once a haven, was now a place filled with fear, forcing him to flee into the night.

His footsteps made no sound in the deep pile carpet, as he padded, down the hall, towards her room. When he reached the landing, he stopped and looked over the rail. Below, he could see a light in the kitchen. His parents were down there. And, they were still fighting. Cold sweat broke out on his forehead, as he listened to his father's shouting and cursing. Suddenly, Jason heard his dad yell, and drew back with a start!

"What the hell do you think you're doing?"

Jason thought his father meant *him!* Shivers raced up and down his spine, and he froze, expecting to feel a hand grab him. Minutes passed, before Jason realized his dad hadn't caught him; hadn't been speaking to him. But, by this time, the sweat was tricking, in a steady stream, down his forehead, and into his eyes. But he didn't wipe the salty droplets away. He was too frightened to move. Finally, he was able to get up enough nerve to cautiously, peek through the wooden rails and peek downstairs. His father was standing in the kitchen doorway, his eyes on the stairway.

Jason scrambled backwards, afraid that he'd been seen. When nothing happened, he pushed himself over to the far wall, and stood up, gasping for air. That had been close. What if his dad had seen him? Jason trembled at the thought.

Oh please, don't let him come up here until I've told Becky to be quiet and made it back to my room, he prayed.

A noise behind him made him spin around.

He listened. A soft whimper came from inside his brother's room. Was he awake too? Jason was beside himself.

Doesn't anyone sleep around here? He wondered.

When no more sounds came from behind the closed door, Jason allowed himself to relax.

Good, he thought.

All he needed right now was for Nicky to start crying, too. He already felt like the fate of all of them rested on his shoulders, and he was beginning to sag under the load. Why were they doing this to him? Why was Becky trying to get him into trouble?

"She better watch out," he muttered, "because when I get a hold of her, she's in for it! She'll be in more shit then she's ever been in before."

There. He had said it again; that word-- *shit*. When had he first started to swear? It hadn't been long, because he could still remember the last time his mom had bawled him out for saying shit. When he was little, she would send him to his room whenever she heard him use a dirty word. But lately, she would only give him one of her looks. He wondered why she didn't punish him anymore. Maybe, she no longer cared if she swore or not.

He found it difficult to drop this train of thought and, stood at the top of the stairs, wondering why his mother had changed. Why had she punished him then, but not now?

His dad swore. In fact, he was swearing right now, and the words he was using sounded a lot worse than shit. Jason couldn't recall ever hearing his mother correct his dad for using foul language. Why didn't she say something to him?

At least, I've never called her names, he thought, listening to the battle going on downstairs. *Why doesn't she give Dad one of her dirty looks, instead of ignoring his swearing? If she lets him do it, I can do it too.*

I'm sick and tired of always being the one who gets in shit around here. Well, no more; she can go to hell. I'll swear whenever I feel like it, and just let her try to stop me.

His father's swearing always frightened Jason because it usually meant that his father was going to go on a rampage again. But, not always. Sometimes, his dad would swear when he was talking; when he wasn't angry at all. Most of the time, his father's verbal abuse mad or otherwise, was directed at Jason's mom. Lately however, his dad had begun to swear more often around Becky. Jason was glad that his dad almost never called him names or, if he did, it was when his dad swore at all of them, and Jason was just part of the group.

Jason could visualize his mother's reaction whenever his father let loose. She would run around the house, trying to appease him. It didn't make sense. If it was wrong to swear, why did it get such immediate results? He decided to try it; to see how his mother would react if he swore at her. Would she get mad, or would she try to please him? He had to know.

Jason tried to imagine the look on his mother's face, when he tested her reaction. A thought occurred to him. What if she belted him in the mouth? No.... She'd never do that.

Hell, she acts like a mouse, and whoever heard of a mouse hitting anyone? Mice just scurry away and hide. Besides, so she gets mad, so what. Like Dad always says, "She's only a woman," and I know how to treat women. She can get mad if she wants to; I don't care.

He straightened up and was about to leave the landing, feeling more like a man than the frightened child he had been only minutes earlier, when his father's words caught his attention. His parents were engaged in a rather one-sided conversation, with his dad doing most of the talking. Well, not talking-- shouting.

"You don't love me, Linda," his dad yelled. "If you did, then you wouldn't always make my life miserable."

There was a long pause, before Jason heard his mother reply.

"I do love you, Nick." She hesitated a moment and continued. "It's just.... Well, you see, I want us to have a good life together and, I can't see that happening, if you don't learn to control your temper-- if you keep hitting me."

"I had a good life before I married you. You've ruined everything," his dad replied.

"But, honey--"

"Don't 'but, honey,' me, you miserable bitch!"

"Nick, I only asked you to try and control your temper. You scare me when you get so angry. Remember what happened the last time you lost control?"

"There you go again," he shouted, "Always throwing the past in my face. I told you I was sorry; that I didn't mean to break your God-damm leg! But will you let me forget? NOooo..., because now, I'm some kind of monster. Hell woman, you're living on easy street. I wish all I ever had to do, was sit on my ass all day and watch soap operas!"

"Please Nick, don't...."

Smack!

Jason flinched. From the sound, he knew his dad had either slapped or punched her, thus putting an end to the argument. Shocked, Jason unwillingly found himself being drawn back into time; back into another memory.

He could see his mother lying on her bedroom floor, her leg twisted underneath her. His mind filled with the sounds of her screams.

For now, he wasn't the Jason who was standing at the top of a darkened staircase; now he was only seven years old, and he was huddled in his bed, listening to someone crying. Only this time, it wasn't his sister, it was his mother who was sobbing.

Frightened, he had grabbed Pookie and crept to his parents' bedroom. The door was open a crack and he peeked in.

His mother was walking from the closet to the bed, her arms filled with clothes, tears streaming down her cheeks. As Jason watched, he saw her stuff the clothes in a large, blue suitcase, and return to the closet. His dad walked over to the bed, took out the clothes, and threw them on the floor. Jason thought that they must be playing some kind of game.

Were they going to Grandpa's place for a visit? he wondered. He was tempted to go in and help her pack. But why was his daddy shouting? Didn't he want to go visit grandpa?

As he watched, Jason saw his dad come up behind his mother and kick her in the back, sending her sprawling onto the bed, where she bounced once, and landed on the floor. Jason knew this was no game.

His mom was on her hands and knees, when his dad walked over and grabbed her by her foot. He gave her leg a savage twist. Her scream terrified Jason, causing him to break out in goose bumps. He scurried back to his room and dove underneath his bed, where he lay, curled up in a tight ball.

His mother kept screaming and Jason clutched Pookie tightly to his chest.

"Stop it," he whimpered, as the sound echoed throughout his room. "Please, stop."

After a while, he heard the front door, downstairs, slam shut. Had someone left the house? He listened. But, all he could hear was the noise from down the hall. His mother was no longer screaming, but Jason could hear a low, moaning sound. It sounded like his mom, so it had to have been his dad who left the house.

"If Daddy's gone, we don't have to be scared," he told Pookie. But, even with the knowledge that his dad wasn't in the house, Jason wouldn't get out from under his bed. He was safe there.

He was almost asleep when he heard his mother call to him.

"Jason..., wake up Jason; I need you. Can you hear Mommy?"

Jason tried to resist the lure of her voice and so, instead of answering, he pushed himself further under the bed.

"Jason," she called again. "Jason, if you can hear me, come here. Don't be afraid. Daddy's gone."

Cautiously, Jason squirmed out from his hiding place and crawled to his mother's room. He sat in the open doorway, staring at her, as she lay on the floor beside her bed. He heard her moan and call to him again.

I'm here, Mommy," he cried, jumping up and running to her. He dropped down beside her, and wrapped his arms around her waist, wanting her to comfort him-- to take away his fear. He burst into sobs and buried his face in her lap.

"Jason, please stop crying and listen to me," she said, hugging him close. "You have to help me. I want you to go downstairs and call the police. You have to pick up the phone and dial 911. Someone will answer and you tell them your mother needs help, that she's been hurt. Have you got that? Can you dial 911 and tell them to send someone to help me?"

Jason lifted his head and stared into his mother's face, his eyes filled with tears. He slowly nodded his head, but wouldn't leave her side.

"Now, now," she said, disengaging his arms from around her waist. "Be a big boy, and do as I've told you. I'm hurt bad, and I need a doctor." She pushed herself into a sitting position and gave him further instructions. "Do you remember our address?" she asked.

"Yes, Mommy."

"Okay then. Dial 911 and, when someone answers, tell them I've been hurt. Remember..., they'll need to know our address, so don't forget. Now go."

Frightened, Jason ran down the stairs, trying to remember what he was supposed to say. He picked up the receiver and dialed. 911

When a lady answered, Jason repeated his mother's message, making sure that he didn't forget to give her the right address. The woman on the other end of the line tried to ask him a question, but Jason hung up the phone without replying, anxious to return to his mother.

He ran up the stairs and to her room. But, when he arrived, he found his mother asleep. He shook her. She had to wake up so he could tell her that he had done exactly as she had asked, but she didn't respond. Disappointed that he couldn't make her listen to him, Jason lay down beside her and fell asleep.

He woke to the sound of someone hammering on the front door, downstairs. Then, he heard the door open. Afraid that his father had come back, Jason huddled against his mother.

"Make him go away," he whispered in his mother's ear. "Make him stop."

She stirred and opened her eyes. Propping herself up on her elbow, she listened for a moment and then said to Jason: "It must be the police. You have to go downstairs and tell them I'm up here.

Jason thought about his dad. What if it was his father who was downstairs, and not the police. "I don't want to go down there," he whimpered, "cause a monster might get me."

"Jason," she said, "there's no monsters downstairs; only police officers. Now go and tell them I'm here."

From the tone of his mother's voice, Jason knew that he had no alternative except to obey her command. With his feet dragging, he slowly made his way down the stairs and over to the front entrance, in time to see two men, dressed in white uniforms, burst through the door. Another two men, dressed in blue, were already waiting inside the porch and Jason thought that they must be the policemen his mother had told him about. He heard one of them shout.

"Police! Is anyone here?"

For a second, Jason was too scared to respond, and flattened himself against the wall, hoping he wouldn't be noticed. But, he had been seen, and one of the officers hurried towards him.

"Okay son, we received a call that a woman was hurt," said the policeman.

Jason was too afraid to speak.

The officer dropped to one knee and asked, "Was it you who called us?"

"Y...es," Jason squeaked. He was intimidated by this stranger with the gruff voice and black, shiny boots.

"Can you tell us who's been hurt?" asked the man.

"It's my Mommmmm...," Jason wailed, letting out all the fear and terror he had accumulated over the past hour. "She's got a sore leg," he blubbered. "Daddy hurt her and then he went away."

Jason found himself surrounded by the men in white, and the two policemen. He felt small, as he looked up at the faces peering down at him.

"Where is your mother now?" one of them asked.

Jason pointed towards the stairs, and was brushed aside as all the strangers, except for the officer who had first questioned him, ran for the staircase.

"It's okay now," the police officer said, scooping Jason off the floor and holding him in his arms. "We're going to help your mom." He carried Jason up the stairs and joined the others. The officer set him down on the floor and spoke to his partner.

"Did that Social Worker from the Children's Emergency Shelter say when she'd be arriving?"

The other officer checked his watch. "She should be here anytime now."

"Well, Ralph," he replied, "it looks like this kid's father has left the scene, but I'd like to you to go downstairs and keep an eye out for him in case he comes back while we're still here. If he's like the rest of these bastards, he'll be back shortly. Oh, and by the way, if that Social Worker arrives, send her up here."

"Sure Bill," said Ralph, turning to leave.

"Wait," said Bill. "Before you go, can you tell me if the woman said anything about how she got injured.

"No," Ralph replied. "The ambulance guys were too busy trying to immobolize her leg, for me to get a chance to talk to her."

"Never mind. Go downstairs and I'll question her before they take her out."

Jason stood beside the police officer watching the ambulance attendants, bandage his mother's leg. A few minutes later, a strange woman walked into the room and came over to where he was standing.

"I'm from the Emergency Shelter," she said. "Are you the little boy who called to say his mom was hurt?"

Jason nodded.

"My name is Darlene Smith. Can you tell me your name?"

Jason.

"Well Jason," Darlene Said, taking him by the hand, "I'm just going to ask your mom a few questions and then, you can come and stay at the shelter till your mother gets better. Okay?" She turned to the policeman and asked, "When can I speak to the boy's mother."

"It'll be a few more minutes before they're finished getting her ready to be moved." replied Bill.

Jason was confused. What was the woman talking about when she said she was going to take him away. He wasn't going anywhere! He heard one of the men in white say to his mother:

"We're going to take you to the hospital now."

"I can't leave my children," she said, reaching for Jason. "My husband might come back. He so angry--"

Darlene walked over to the stretcher and patted Jason's mom on the shoulder. "It's okay, Mrs.--"

"Winters."

"Mrs. Winters," Darlene said, "My name is Darlene Smith and I'm a Social Worker with the Children's Emergency Shelter. I'm going to take Jason there, and he'll be looked after, till you get out of the hospital."

"Okay," she replied weakly.

Darlene stepped aside to let the police officer question Jason's mom. "Can you tell me where your husband is?" he asked.

"No," she replied. He went out--"

"One more question. Did your husband do this to you?"

Jason saw his mother hesitate, and then listened, incredulous, to his mother's reply.

"No," she answered softly, "You see-- I fell. I'm so clumsy sometimes. My husband gets very upset with me. That's why he left tonight."

"I see," said the officer. He nodded to the ambulance attendants. "Take her away. If I need any further information, I'll question her at the hospital."

Mom didn't fall, thought Jason. *Why did she lie? You always tell me that it's a sin to lie.*

Jason watched the men lift the stretcher off the floor and walk towards the door.

"Wait!" said his mom, reaching for Darlene's hand. "My baby is in the far room at the end of the hall. Don't leave her."

"Don't worry Mrs. Winters," Darlene said, squeezing her hand. "We won't forget to take her too. I'll make sure both of your children are safe."

"Thank you."

When his mother had left the room, carried out on a stretcher, Jason suddenly realized that she was leaving without him. He ran after her. "Stop!" he shouted, from the top of the stairs when he saw them take her out of the front door. He raced down the stairs and out the door.

But, before he could reach her, someone grabbed him from behind. He fought to break free, kicking and screaming.

"Settle down," a voice said sternly.

Jason turned his head and saw that it was the policeman, Bill, holding onto him. "Let me go!" Jason screamed. "I want my Mom."

"You'll see your mom after she gets medical attention," Bill replied, shifting his position so he could get a better grasp on Jason.

Jason pounded his fists on Bill's chest until, exhausted, he slumped in the policeman's arms and lay still.

"Here-- I'll take him," said Darlene, walking into the porch, holding Becky in one arm. She stopped in front of them and bent down until she was on eye level with Jason. "Don't be afraid. You'll get to see your mom as soon as she gets better. See," she said, showing him Becky, "your little sister isn't crying."

Darlene held out her free hand and Jason, too tired to resist, took her hand and they left the house. They went out to her car and Jason waited, while she put Becky into a car seat and fastened and the seatbelt around the sleeping baby. Then, she opened the front door and he climbed inside. She covered him up with a blanket before climbing into the driver's side.

"We're off," she said, turning her head and smiling at him.

Jason didn't smile back. This strange woman was taking him away from his mother-- from his dad.

I'll never see them again, he thought, turning his head, straining to keep his house in his sight for as long possible. When they turned a corner, his home disappeared, and Jason fixed his eyes on the road in front of him. He didn't respond to Darlene's questions and soon, they were riding to their destination in silence.

She pulled up in front of a grey building and stopped the car. They got out, and with Becky tucked in one arm, she took his hand and they walked to the door. She pushed a button and waited.

"Who is it?" asked a voice from a little brown box on the wall.

"Darlene."

Jason saw a hand push a curtain aside, and a face peered out at them. A buzzer sounded and Darlene opened the door.

A woman came over to meet them and Darlene introduced Jason to her. "This is Jason and his little sister," she said to the woman. "And Jason, this is Mrs. Lanze."

Mrs. Lanze ushered them inside, taking Becky out of Darlene's arm. "Here, give me the little one," she said. "I'll take her and put her to bed."

"Great," said Darlene. "I'll show Jason his room." Mrs. Lanze called over her shoulder: "What's her name?"

Darlene looked at Jason. "Becky," he replied.

"Her name is Becky-- Becky Winters," Darlene called.

"Thank you."

Jason followed Darlene across a large living room and down a hallway. The size of the house amazed him. He had never seen such a large front room or dining area before.

Lot's of people must live here, he thought, hurrying to catch up with Darlene.

They stopped in front of a door, and Darlene opened it and walked inside. Jason followed her.

"You can sleep here tonight," she said, pointing to a single bed in the corner. "And tomorrow, I'll come back and tell you how your mother is doing. Okay?"

Jason looked around the room. "Are you going to stay with me?" he asked, afraid of being left alone in this strange place.

"No," she answered, "I have some paperwork to finish up but, I'll only be down the hall from you. You go to bed and everything's going to be fine when you wake up.

Jason went to bed. But, when he woke the next morning, nothing had changed from the night before. In fact, to him, things had gone from bad to worse. His mother was gone-- never to return; he had been taken away from his home; and he had been left here, alone and frightened, in this strange house.

How could things be fine?

Softly weeping, Jason lay in the bed, staring out the window. "Mom's gone forever," he sobbed in despair, sticking his thumb in his mouth and quietly sucking on it.

The time spent in the strange house, without his mother, was the loneliest and saddest period of his entire life. Unsure of what was expected of him, Jason stayed in his room, refusing to be coaxed out. Another strange woman had came in that first morning, to get him to come for breakfast, but he had refused-- had clung to the end of his bed and screamed. She had given up and left him alone. A few minutes later, she returned with a tray and set it on the dresser and, without glancing in his direction, had quietly informed him that he could eat breakfast in his room.

When she had gone, Jason went over to the dresser and took down the tray, and sat down, placing the tray on his knees. His despair gave way to hunger, and he gulped down the food. When he had finished, he wiped his hands on the pajama bottoms and carefully placed the tray back on top of the dresser.

That afternoon, the same woman came back, bringing some clothes with her for him to change into. When she tried to talk to him, he turned his back on her and stood, rigidly facing the wall.

After she had left, Jason walked over and examined the clothing. These weren't his things! They couldn't make him wear someone else's clothes. Jason went back and climbed into bed. Exhausted; his stomach full, he couldn't keep his eyes open and drifted off to sleep. When he woke again, he was that the empty tray was gone and another stood in its place.

For the next three days, Jason resisted any attempt to get him to communicate, or to change out of his pajamas into the clothes they had provided. They had taken his mother away-- they were the ones who had locked him up here. Nothing they said or did, would make him forgive them-- or speak to them.

On the morning of the fourth day, Darlene came in and sat down on his bed. Jason turned away, hoping she would leave. She spoke gently to him.

"Jason, you have to take a bath and get dressed today," she said, reaching over and touching his shoulder. He moved away.

"Jason," she continued, as if she hadn't noticed his rejection, "your mom's coming here this afternoon and you don't want her to see you dirty, do you?"

Jason spun around. His mother was coming? Here? Today? He searched Darlene's face to see if it was a trick.

Seeing his disbelief, Darlene said, "It's true. Now, I think we should get you cleaned up before she gets here."

"Really?" he asked, still skeptical. Too many things had happened to him lately, and he didn't trust her.

"Yes," she replied, "The hospital phoned and I'm going to get her. She should be here in less than an hour."

Jason followed Darlene down the hall to the bathroom.

"Here's a towel and washcloth," she said to him. "You'll find the soap in that little dish over there." She pointed to the tub. "I'll run the water, while you strip down. "We'll have you spic and span by the time your mom arrives."

35

Jason hesitated. He couldn't undress in front of a strange woman. He was seven years only-- no longer a baby. But, he didn't know how to tell her, so he just stood there watching the tub fill with water.

When Darlene turned around and found him standing beside her, fully dressed, a perturbed look came across her face. Jason dropped his eyes and felt himself blush. He stood there, rubbing the top of his left foot, with his right. The uneasy silence lasted only a few moments and disappeared, when Darlene asked: "How would you like to bathe yourself?"

"Oh, yes," Jason gushed, gratefully. "I can do it."

"Okay," she replied, "I'll leave you alone, but you have to make sure you wash all over. And," she added, "when you're done, I want you to put on these clean clothes." She plunked a pair of blue jeans, socks, a shirt and a pair of underwear on the counter.

"I will." He waited till she had gone, before going over to the door and locking it. He undressed and stepped into the warm water. Slowly, he lowered himself into the tub, enjoying the warm sensation as the water washed over him.

I could stay here forever," he thought, spreading his arms out. But then, he remembered what Darlene said about his mother coming soon. He reached for the soap and lathered it over his body. When he was sure that he was clean, he wrung out the washcloth and threw it over the side of the tub. Satisfied, he climbed out of the water and grabbed the towel off the back of the toilet. Quickly, he dried himself and reached for his clothes.

But, these clothes weren't his. He had come here in his pajamas. Why hadn't they gone to his house and brought back his own clothes? Now, what was he suppose to do? He thought about calling for Darlene to come, but he didn't want her to see him naked!

Maybe I can wrap myself in the towel, he thought, but when he looked around, he spotted it at his feet, lying in a puddle of water. There was nothing left for him to do, except put on the clothes Darlene had left for him. When he had dressed, he walked back to his room and sat on his bed, waiting for his mother.

A short while later, he heard her voice in the hallway. Overjoyed, he jumped up and ran out of the room. He stopped in his tracks! His mom was hobbling towards him, a wooden stick under each arm. And, what was that white thing on her leg?

"Hi Jason," she called to him.

Forgetting about her strange appearance, Jason threw himself into her arms, nearly bowling her over. "You came back," he blubbered. "I thought you'd gone forever."

"You know I wouldn't leave you forever," she said, ruffling his hair and smiling down at him. "How's your little sister?"

That was a good question. How was Becky? Jason hadn't thought about her since their arrival and now, he didn't know how to answer his mother's question. He hoped Becky was okay. Crossing his fingers behind his back, he smiled and said, "She's fine, Mom. She likes it here."

"I'm glad that both of you are okay," said his mother. "I missed you guys."

"We missed you too," said Jason.

"Well, as soon as I finish filling out a few forms, Darlene's going to drive us over to another place where I can rest for awhile."

"Aren't we going home?" Jason asked.

"Not right now," she replied. "I want you to play for awhile, and then we'll go."

"Sure Mom," said Jason, disappointed that they weren't going straight home. He wondered where they were going to now.

They left an hour later, with Jason clinging to his mother's arm. Even after they were in the car, and were riding towards their new destination, he stayed close to his mother's side. At last, they arrived at another huge house and Jason helped his mother climb out of the car. He reached inside the car and handed his mom her crutches. Darlene carried Becky, and they walked to the door.

Jason grew suspicious when he saw Darlene push a button, and heard a voice come out of a small box. Was this place the same as the one he had just left? He hoped not.

I won't be left alone again, he thought, moving closer to his mom.

A lady opened the door and led them inside. "We've been expecting you," she said to Jason's mom. "My name is Judy and I'll be one of your counsellors during your stay here."

What stay? Jason wondered. We're not staying here. We're going home. We only stopped here for a visit or something.

The woman led them to a bedroom. This time, however, the room had two beds and a crib in it.

"This will be your room," said the woman. "I'll get the key for it shortly."

"Thank you," his mother replied, "Would it be okay if I laid down and rested. I seem to have run out of energy."

"By all means," replied the woman. "Here, I'll take the baby and set her in the crib for you." The woman took Becky out of Darlene's arm and laid her in the crib.

Well Mrs. Winters, if you're settled in, I have to get back to the office," Darlene said, turning to leave.

"Yes," replied his mom, "And thanks."

"No problem," Darlene said. "Well, so long Jason."

Jason ignored her.

"Jason," said his mother. "Don't be rude. Say good-bye to Mrs. Smith."

"No."

"It's alright," said Darlene, "Jason has had a bad time."

"I guess so," his mother replied, too tired to argue with her son.

"Now you just lay down and rest," said the other woman, "and Jason can come with me. I'll show him where the playroom is."

"I don't want to go," replied Jason, glaring up at her.

"That's enough Jason," his mom said. "I don't know what's got into you. Go play for awhile and then you can come back and see me."

He went with the woman. She led him into another large room. A boy and two girls were sitting on the floor, putting a puzzle together. Jason walked over to them and stood, looking down at them. Finally, tired of being alone, Jason asked if he could join them.

"Sure," the boy replied, moving over so Jason could sit down. "Now, I won't have to sit next to these dumb girls."

One of the girls stuck her tongue out and Jason giggled.

"I don't think she likes us," he said to the boy.

The boy grinned. "Too bad. I don't like her, either. She acts like she owns the place, always bossing everyone around and telling them what to do. She's been bugging me ever since I got here."

"Have you been here long?" Jason asked.

"Oh, about two weeks now, but Mom and I are going home tomorrow. When are you leaving?"

That was a good question. When were they going home? His mother hadn't given him a straight answer. But, he didn't want to admit to the boy that he didn't know, so he ignored his question and said: "I have to go see how my mom is. She just got out of the hospital today." He got up off the floor, dusted his hands on his jeans, and went back to where he had left his mother.

"Mom! Mom! Are you awake?" he shouted, running through the doorway and over to her bed.

His mother opened her eyes. "I am now," she replied.

"Mom, are we going home today?"

"No."

"Well, are we going home tomorrow?"

She turned her face away and stared at the wall. "No Jason, we're not going home tomorrow," she whispered softly. "No today or tomorrow--"

His face fell when he heard this unexpected response, but he persisted. "Then, are we going home the next day after that?"

"Please, honey," she said. "Try and understand. I don't know right now when we'll go home; maybe never."

Jason's mouth dropped open, and he stared at his mother, speechless. What did she mean by "maybe never?"

"But Mom," he whined, "Dad's waiting for us; I know he is."

"Jason...please, not right now. I'm getting a headache."

"But, Jason didn't care if she had a headache or not, he needed to know when they were going home. He didn't believe his mom when she said that they may never go home again. He frowned and said, "But Mom, Dad's lonely. I want to go home. I don't want to stay here."

"Jason, I told you before that I don't know when we'll go home."

"I want to go home. I want to go home," he chanted, his voice rising.

A woman came running into the room and tried to grab him. "Stop it Jason!" she said to him, her voice commanding his attention. "Your mother just got out of the hospital and here you are, screaming at the top of your lungs, upsetting her." She glared at him and Jason backed away. "What's the matter with you?" she asked.

He ran over to his mother and grabbed her by the arm. Please, Mom let's go home. I'll pack Becky, so you can walk. Can't we go home?" he pleaded, tears filling his eyes. "I want Daddy...," he wailed.

"Yes..., Jason," his mom replied softly, "we'll go home. But, not today. We'll go home tomorrow. Now, will you go and play so I can get some rest?"

Jason stopped crying and gave the woman, standing in the doorway, a smug look. "We're going home tomorrow," he said, as he passed her and went out into the hallway. He heard the woman as his mother: "Are you sure this is what you want...?"

Jason headed for the playroom and found the boy, still sitting on the floor, working on the puzzle. He walked over to him and sat down. "I'm going home tomorrow too," he said.

"That's too bad," replied the boy, his eyes fixed on the puzzle in front of him.

Jason didn't understand. Didn't this boy want to go home? Puzzled, he asked, "Don't you want to go home tomorrow? You don't want to stay here, do you?"

"No, not here," the boy answered, "but I don't want to go home, either."

"Why?"

"Because Dad's there."

"Don't you like your dad?" Jason asked, thinking that this boy was getting stranger by the minute.

"Sure I like him, but I can't stand it when he beats on my Mom," he explained. "If we didn't go back, then he couldn't hit her." He gave Jason a knowing look. Jason didn't know what to say to that. His dad and mom had fights-- lots of them-- but he still wanted to go home.

You're weird, thought Jason, picking up a piece of puzzle and pretending to examine it. *I'll always want to go home.*

"Why did your mom bring you here?" the boy asked.

After what he had just heard, Jason was reluctant to tell him about the fight his parents had; his mom's broken leg, and his stay at the other place, so he replied, "Oh Mom hurt her leg, and she came here for a rest."

"Bullshit."

Jason looked at him in astonishment.

"I said bullshit," he repeated. "Your old man beat her up, didn't he?"

"No, he didn't!" Jason denied, vehemently. "She fell and hurt her leg. That's why we're here."

"Don't be a dope," the boy replied. "They don't bring someone to a battered women's shelter just because they've fallen and hurt their leg."

Jason didn't understand. He asked, "What's a battered women's shelter?"

"That's what this place is. Women come here when their husbands beat on them-- like my Mom," he said, then added, "and like your Mom."

"No, that's a lie," Jason shouted, standing up, his hands on his hips. "I told you, she fell and hurt her leg." He kicked the puzzle with his foot, sending the pieces flying across the floor. "You can stay here, I don't care," he yelled, "but I'm going home tomorrow." Jason ran out of the room.

The boy called after him: "You can run away, but I'm telling you the truth. Your dad beat up your mom and that's why she brought you here."

Jason stopped outside his mother's room, trying to regain his composure. His hands were clenched into fists, and he felt warm. He wanted to hit that kid; wanted to make him take back his words. The only thing that had stopped him, was his fear of being caught and punished. Maybe they would make him stay here for good. He waited a few minutes and then, went outside to the playground. He walked over to the sandpile and kicked at it, sending sand spraying into the air. "If you're so smart," he said aloud, "why don't you come out here? Then, we'll see who gets beat up."

He went to the swing, sat down, and thought about what the boy had said. What had he called this place-- a women's shelter?

It's not true, he told himself, pumping the swing higher and higher, until he could see over the top of the fence. *It's not true.*

Jason never told his mother what the boy had said. Instead, he kept away from the playroom and waited patiently, rarely leaving his mother's side, until they were ready to leave.

I'm never coming back here, he thought, climbing into the taxi. He sat beside his mother and sister. No one will ever make me come here again.

When they arrived at home, his dad came running out of the house to meet them. He threw Jason in the air and caught him coming down.

He set him on the ground and went over and took Becky out of his wife's arm. "I'm glad you're home," his father said to them.

"I'm glad too," said Jason, hugging his dad's leg and following him into the house. He ran up the stairs to his room. "I'm home, Pookie!" he shouted, throwing his raccoon in the air. "Everything's going to be great now. I'm home...!"

CHAPTER IV

But "everything" hadn't stayed great for long. In fact, from that point on, their lives had steadily deteriorated under his father's iron rule. Jason thought about the boy at the shelter-- the one who didn't want to go home. Jason no longer thought that the boy was strange. Now he thought that he, Jason Winters, was the one who was weird. The boy had been right....

Now, standing at the top of the stairs, listening to his dad scream, Jason wished he could live that part of his live over; wished he could go back in time and, instead of telling her to return home, he would convince his mom to stay away-- to take Becky and him and leave forever.

Why was I so stupid? he wondered, closing his eyes and burying his face in his hands.

Jason tried to rid himself of the painful memories; tried to store them in the back of his mind. But, once resurrected, they refused to be put away. He had taken them out and dusted them off, and now, he was being devoured by the images they manifested. Why had he made his mom bring him home?

Who was I trying to kid? he thought, recalling how it was him who had defended his father, when the boy accused his dad of hurting Jason's mom. *I was a fool to come back to this hell!* Would it never end? Would there ever come a time when his Dad wouldn't beat up on his mother? He desperately sought an answer to his dilemma, but could find none.

How will I survive a lifetime of this? he wondered bitterly.

He blamed Becky

If it wasn't for her, I'd never have woken up tonight and been forced to listen to this shit. It's all her fault. When will she learn to keep her big mouth shut?

Even now, he could hear her crying and it infuriated him. It didn't appear to him that she had learned anything from that other time-- the time his dad threw her across the kitchen because she had started bawling.

Women are so stupid, he thought, gripping the banister rail and squeezing, until his knuckles turned white. He looked down, but he couldn't see his father. *Grandpa George was right, when he said that the only reason women were put on this earth was to cause a man grief.*

His Grandpa George knew everything, and Jason liked him better than anyone else in the whole world. His grandparents lived on a small farm 150 miles away. The distance, coupled with his dad's busy schedule, limited the number of visits Jason's family made to the farm. The last time being, almost two years ago, when Jason and his sister were shipped to the farm when Nicky was born.

*   *   *

It was almost time for Jason's mom to go to the hospital to have her baby, and his dad said he wasn't going to be left to "baby-sit them damn kids." As a result Jason's mother packed their suitcases, and his dad took Becky and him to the farm, for a surprise, but welcome, visit with his grandparents.

His mother was upset about their going, but his dad had been adamant, and would brook no opposition, once his decision had been made. Jason remembered his mother crying as she kissed them good-bye, telling them to be good and to listen to grandma.

Jason knew the reason his mom didn't want them to go. She didn't like Grandpa George. Jason couldn't understand why, but he knew it was so, because his mother only went to the farm, when his father insisted. Then, while she was there, she would make an effort to stay out of Grandpa George's way. Jason had asked her why she didn't like Grandpa George, and she had mumbled something about his being a bad influence. Then, she abruptly ended their conversation by telling him to go and play outside and quit pestering her with so many questions.

Jason wondered why she was so reluctant to go to the farm when, in his opinion, having the chance to see his Grandpa was the best thing that could happen to him.

Grandpa George was an important person. As well as having the farm, he also owned the seed-cleaning plant on the edge of town. Between the two places, Jason was kept busy, travelling back and forth, with him. Jason enjoyed being with his grandpa. His grandfather didn't treat him like a kid when they were together. Grandpa didn't tease him or call him names-- just the opposite; he treated Jason like a man.

When they were together, his grandpa would take time to talk with him about the meaningful things in a man's life. Things like women and money, and what plans Jason had for his future. His grandpa also answered any questions Jason might have, and he never said they were dumb, or that Jason should spend more time on his schoolwork and less time dreaming. As such, Jason enjoyed being with him. He liked to go to the plant, or help with chores around the farm. When he was with his grandpa, Jason was free to make his own decisions, and he relished this freedom, unwilling to relinquish it when he had to return home.

But, it wasn't the same for Becky. His sister didn't like to come to the farm, and she didn't share the special feeling he had for their grandpa. Before they had come to the farm, she had told Jason that she was scared of Grandpa George. Jason was indignant! How could anyone be scared of his grandpa? That had to have been the most ridiculous thing she ever said to him, and she'd said a lot of stupid things.

She's just jealous because Grandpa never takes her with us when we go to town. Well, too bad. Girls don't belong at a feedmill, anyway.

Every evening, once the chores were finished, and they had eaten supper, Jason went with his grandfather for a walk down by the creek, flowing past the cow pasture. A narrow, dusty path wound its way through the trees and alongside the water. They would start down this path and before long, Jason would take off his shoes and socks, and walk along, enjoying the feel of the dust between his toes. It was so peaceful, just walking along, with not a care in the world, that Jason asked his grandpa why Becky and Grandma never came with them.

His grandfather stopped in the middle of the path and looked down at him. "Women belong at home in the kitchen," he explained. "Even small ones like your sister." He nudged an anthill with the toe of his boot and continued: "You shouldn't allow any woman to run your life. If you do, then she'll soon take right over, and before you know it, you'll find yourself standing in front of a sinkful of dirty dishes, all decked out in an apron and wondering what the hell happened."

That makes sense, thought Jason, smiling up at his grandpa. *I hate doing dishes.*

With his thumbs hooked into his belt and his chest puffed out, Jason strutted beside his grandpa, trying to show him that he was a real man. And, no woman was going to rule his life. When his grandfather kicked at a stone on the trail, Jason kicked a stone, too.

I'm going to be just like him when I grow up, he thought happily.

When they came to a bend in the trail, instead of turning right as they usually did, his grandpa turned left, and followed a less-visible path leading away from the creek. They walked a long time, and Jason's legs were beginning to tire, but he struggled to keep up. Finally, when they had climbed a small hill and walked down the other side, they entered a clearing. Jason was about to ask him if they could stop so he could rest, when he saw his grandpa point towards a spot in the bush less than fifty yards away. Jason looked where his grandfather was pointing and saw a small wooden cabin, nearly concealed from view by the surrounding trees. Jason forgot about being tired and hurried to catch up with his grandpa.

"Well, here it is," said his Grandpa, patting him on the shoulder. "It's a long walk from the farm, but I wanted to show it to you before you return home."

"Who owns it?" asked Jason.

"Why I do," he replied proudly. "I'm showing it to you, but I don't want you to mention it to anyone else-- especially not to your grandma. Only your dad and I know about this place. I finished building it shortly before your father was born, because I needed a place where I could come to when I wanted to get away from my old lady."

Jason waited while his grandpa searched in his pocket and pulled out a key. He unlocked the door and they went inside. The cabin smelled musty, reminding Jason of his grandparents' attic where Becky and he used to play, before he became a man. Now, he was too old for that sort of childish behavior. He walked over to one of the two bunk beds by the wall, sat down, and waited, while his grandpa opened the windows, trying to air the place out.

Jason looked around the cabin, admiring his grandfather's handiwork. The walls were constructed out of heavy logs and the plank floor was covered with cow hides. An assortment of miscellaneous pots and pans hung on nails, pounded into a log, over a make-shift sink. An old woodburning stove stood in the centre of the room, its crooked stovepipe winding over a large wooden beam and disappearing into the ceiling. Jason's admiration for this rustic setting grew, when he spied a large set of deer horns nailed over the doorway. "I like it here," he said to his grandfather.

"That's great," his grandfaather replied, pulling an old chair out of the corner and sitting down. "I wanted to bring you here before now, but I had to wait till you were old enough to enjoy this," he said, reaching under the bed and pulling out a case of beer. "Here, try one of these." He handed Jason a bottle and took one for himself.

Jason wasn't prepared for such an unexpected event, and gingerly took the bottle from the outstretched hand. He held it in front of him and stared at it in awe. He had never had a beer before. His dad drank Scotch.

Jason watched his grandfather walk over to the sink and come back with a bottle opener.

"Here, let me pop the cap off," he said, taking the bottle out of Jason's hand. He opened the bottle and handed it back to Jason. When he had opened his, he laid the opener on the floor by the box. He sat down, placed the bottle to his lips, and took a deep swallow.

Jason wanted to impress his grandfather, but he wasn't sure if he could take a deep drink without choking. So instead, he raised the bottle to his lips, but took only a small sip. He was glad that he hadn't followed his grandfather's example. The beer tasted funny and he wrinkled his nose. He wasn't sure if he was going to enjoy it or not, but he saw his grandpa looking at him, and all doubt fled from his mind. Jason lifted the bottle to his lips, threw back his head, and let the liquid pour down his throat. Some of it went down his windpipe, and he started to cough and sputter, trying to breathe.

His grandfather laughed. "This your first beer?" he asked.

Jason could only nod, tears streaming down his cheeks, as he gasped for air.

"Well then, take it easy until you get the hang of drinking," his grandfather suggested, leaning over and slapping Jason on the back. "We have plenty of time before we head for home."

Jason propped his back against the wall and drank his beer, while his grandfather talked to him, telling Jason how he came to build the cabin in the first place.

"It was when you grandma was expecting your dad. Yes..., it seemed like that woman was pregnant for years, instead of months, the way she carried on. And," he added, winking at Jason, "trying to make love to her was like screwing a wet blanket. I finally gave up and got my tail somewhere else." When he saw the puzzled look on Jason's face, he explained: "Well, she couldn't expect me to become a monk, could she? A man has needs."

Jason shook his head, not sure what his grandpa was talking about.

"So," he continued, "when she got knocked up, I built this cabin. You can't see it from here, but there's a road leading right up to the back of this place. If I want to bring someone here, I usually drive the truck over. I've used this place a lot over the years. How about you?" he asked, leering at Jason. "Have you had a piece of tail yet?" He took a swig from his bottle and waited for Jason to answer.

Something clicked inside Jason's head. Now, he knew what his grandpa was talking about. He shook his head and tried to overcome this deficiency, by taking another swallow from the half-empty bottle resting on his knee. It was getting warm in the cabin, and he felt relaxed. He wondered why his head felt light and his eyes wouldn't focus.

I must be tired, he thought, closing them. He felt like he was drifting on top of a warm, fluffy cloud.

Unaware that he was almost asleep, his grandfather continued to talk to him. "Never mind," he said, "you have plenty of time left for chasing women. I only hope you don't catch one as owly as your grandma. I never seen anyone so cold in bed. She's like a fish."

I have to stay awake, Jason told himself, shaking his head to clear the fog from his mind. He thought about his grandmother. There was something he wanted to ask his grandpa, about her, but he couldn't remember what he wanted to say. It was only after he had thought for a few minutes, that he was able to recall what was bothering him. For one thing, he didn't feel close to her, like he was with his grandfather, and he wondered why?

His grandma acted strange whenever his grandpa was around her; like a robot-- stiff and unfeeling; moving silently around the kitchen, staring in front of her.

And, during this visit, Jason noticed that she acted the same way towards him. She didn't seem to like him or was it that she acted like she was afraid of him? He didn't know why she gave him that feeling. It wasn't as if she had said anything to him; just the opposite. She was always waiting on him; always giving him what he wanted-- sometimes, before he could even ask. Maybe that was the reason that made him think she was acting pretty strange whenever they were together. Around her, Jason found he could do no wrong, and he knew that some of the things he had done the past few days were wrong-- even if she hadn't said anything.

For instance, just yesterday, he had pushed Becky off the porch into the rose bush when his sister refused to give him the kitten she was petting. Her dress was torn and she had scratched her face on the thorns. Crying, she called for their Grandma to come and help her get out of the bush. By the time their grandmother got there, Becky was carrying on like he had tried to kill her, or something.

Jason knew he was in for it now! He tried to make amends by handing the kitten back to his sister before his grandma reached the bottoms of the steps.

But, nothing happened.

She never even looked at him, as she helped Becky out of the rosebush and into the house. And, she had made Becky give him the kitten. Why?

He had sat on the step, the kitten on his lap, trying to make sense out of what had happened. When he had looked up, he saw his grandmother staring at him through the kitchen window. But, when their eyes met, she quickly stepped back and closed the curtains. What was that look on her face-- fear?

Puzzled by her behavior, Jason decided that now was the time to ask his grandfather about it. But he was careful how he worded his concern, in case having escaped punishment once already, he made his grandpa angry and was reprimanded for his behavior.

He was thinking about various ways to raise the subject, when he felt his grandfather tap his knee. Jason flinched.

"Hey Jason, are you all right," he asked.

"Oh sure... sorry..., I guess I let my mind wander," Jason replied, taking a sip of beer. "Dad always says that I spend too much time with my head in the clouds."

His grandpa set his bottle on the floor beside his chair, placed his hands on his knees, and looked Jason straight in the eye. "Well, I don't know about that," he said, and his eyes twinkled. "I used to do a lot of daydreaming when I was a kid but, as I recall, it was mostly about women!" He leaned back, erupting into gales of laughter. Then, he reached over and slapped Jason on the back, nearly knocking him off the bed. "No harm in dreaming about women?" he chuckled.

Jason giggled. He had almost finished his beer and now, he found everything his grandfather said to him hilariously funny.

Boy am I lucky to have such a great guy for a grandpa, he thought, trying to push himself back into a sitting position. Becky would be jealous if she saw me now-- sitting with Grandpa, drinking beer.

When he finished his beer, Jason carefully leaned over the edge of the bed and set it on the floor beside the beer case. He was about to stretch out on the bed, when his grandpa flipped a cap off another bottle and handed it to him.

"Drink up," he said, smiling.

Jason reluctantly took the bottle from him. He wanted to tell him that he didn't think he could drink another bottle of beer without getting sick. His stomach already felt queazy. But how could he refuse without having his grandpa think he wasn't man enough to drink two beers. "Thank you," he replied faintly. He tipped the bottle back and took a deep swallow.

"Well?" his grandfather asked, "Aren't you going to let me in on your daydream about that girl. You were so glassy-eyed, I thought you were going to come--right here and now."

Come? wondered Jason. *What did he mean?*

Baffled by his comment, Jason thought he must have missed something. "I wasn't dreaming about a girl?" he said, but when he saw his grandpa frown, he quickly added, "But I do-- lots of times."

His grandfather nodded, a smile on his face.

"Right now," said Jason, I was thinking about Grandma. She acts strange every time I come near her, and I was wondering why."

"What do you mean "strange"?

Jason tried to explain: "It's just that, whenever I'm around her, she becomes real quiet and she won't say anything to me; not even if I do something wrong."

"I should think she wouldn't," he replied indignantly. "She'd really be stepping out of line, if she was to start thinking she could tell my grandson what to do."

"What do you mean?" Jason asked.

"Jason..., the first thing you got to learn about women is that they need to be kept in their place, right from the start. Take your grandmother.... She wouldn't think of ever saying anything to me about my behaviour so why should she think that she has the right to tell you what to do. Or, correct you for that matter. If there's any correcting to be done, I'll be the one to do it in my house."

Jason thought about the episode with the rosebush. "But--"

"No buts about it," his grandpa replied. "If you don't show them who's boss right from the beginning, before you know it, they'll spend your money, ruin your life, and run off with the first Tom, Dick or Harry that comes along. You have to stay in control."

Jason tried to listen to what his grandpa was saying, but now, his mind seemed to have separated itself from the rest of his body and he felt like he was floating; felt weightless, drifting around the room. When he tried to speak, his tongue refused to help him form the words, and his speech was slurred. He decided to keep quiet and listen.

"As I was saying," his grandfather continued, "real men know how to keep their women in line. And, I'm not talking about those pansies who have a vacuum cleaner in one hand and a dishrag in the other, while their wives wear the pants in their family." He spat on the floor. "I have nothing but contempt for them! They make it damn hard on the rest of us men who are just trying to raise our families in a decent, respectable manner."

"I ain't no pansy," Jason slurred. He belched and then, added; "When I grow up, I'm going to be just like you."

His grandfather smiled. "Good," he said, leaning over and ruffling Jason's hair. "I didn't think any son of mine would ever raise a sissy. Hell, I

51

taught your dad everything he knows about handling women." He paused, took a drink, and added: "And I'll teach you, too." His arm swept through the air. "It was right here," he said, "in this little cabin, that your father had his first woman. Right on that bed you're sitting on."

Jason looked down at the bed, expecting to see some sign that would indicate that his father had used this bed with his first woman. But, there was nothing.

"Your dad was quite the little stud," said his grandfather. "After that, I considered him a man."

"Will you help me become a real man someday?" asked Jason. He wondered what becoming a real man had to do with women, but if that's what he needed....

"I sure will," he laughed, "but you'll have to do most of the work. I can't help you there!" He winked at Jason and then added: "I mean, I still could, but I shouldn't have to."

Jason was more confused then ever. "I don't understand," he confessed.

The amazement on his grandfather's face made Jason uncomfortable. He tried to redeem himself. "I mean, I understand about needing a woman to prove I'm a man, but what do I do with her when I get one?"

"Hasn't your dad taught you anything?" he asked. "If he hasn't told you what women are good for, he's sadly neglected your education. What I'm trying to tell you, Jason, is that if you're ever going to screw a woman, you have to be able to get it up first. You need a hard-on," he said, pointing to the front of Jason's pants.

Jason felt the blood rush to his cheeks and knew he was blushing. Embarrassed, he dropped his eyes to where his Grandfather was pointing and stared.

So that's what he means. God, he must think I'm a real dummy. I thought he meant I had to find myself a wife and start training her.

"What'ya say, Jason," his grandpa teased, "can you get it up yet?" He laughed and slapped his knee.

Jason didn't mind being teased, especially since he was able to tell him that he could "get it up." He remembered the times he had woken up in the night to find the front of his pajama's wet and sticky. Also, there were times when he was in the shower-- "Yes," he bragged, "I can get it up."

"Good for you," replied his grandpa admiringly. "I guessed the next time you come for a visit, I'll have to arrange a little entertainment here for us. We'll have a ball here." He laughed at the pun. "Just you and me together, and," he grinned, "a couple of the local ladies from town. But remember, I don't want you saying anything about this to your grandma or to your ma, either. Understand?"

"Sure," Jason replied dreamily. "I won't say anything." All this talk about women caused a warm, tingling sensation in his groin, and he shifted his position. Why did talking about girls make him feel so good? He decided that he would think about them more often, so he would be ready for his next visit to the farm.

What happened next was a blur in Jason's mind. He could remember feeling dizzy and the bottle slipping out of his hand but, after that, everything was a blank.

The next thing he knew, it was morning and he was lying in his bed, back at the farm.

When he tried to stand, his head pounded and he had to race to the bathroom and throw up. Why was he so sick?

I must have the flu, he thought, climbing weakly back into his bed. God, my head hurts.

He wondered how he managed to get here, when the last thing he could remember was sitting on the bed in the cabin, drinking beer and talking with his grandpa. What had they talked about? Something about women.... He was too ill to try and recall their conversation, and after a few more minutes, never gave it another thought.

*　　*　　*

Until tonight.

Now, Jason could remember exactly what his grandfather had said about women. And, in his fear, Jason had already broken one of Grandpa's rules: He'd let a woman get the upper hand. Anger flooded over him when he thought about Becky. Never again was she going to make him stand in a dark hallway, listening to his parents' fight. Not, just because she couldn't keep her big mouth shut.

I've been a fool, he thought, glancing down the hall towards her room. *Well, no more. From now on, there's going t be a few changes in this house. I guarantee it!*

He left the staircase and walked to her door. Giving the doorknob a savage twist, he entered his sister's room, pulling the door closed behind him. Silently, he stood by the doorway, allowing his eyes to become accustomed to the dark. He thought about his grandpa and the things he had said about women. Jason wondered if that was what his dad was trying to do now with all his screaming and yelling. Was he trying to stay in control? If so, it didn't sound to Jason, like his father was having much success.

"You know something, Dad," he muttered, "you didn't listen close enough to what Grandpa told you. He doesn't have to scream at Grandma to be boss in his own home, because Grandma knows her place. And, I'm going to teach Becky hers."

He walked over and stood at the foot of his sister's bed.

CHAPTER V

But, he didn't stand alone.

Jason could feel his grandfather's presence in the room, standing beside him; offering him support. Jason cocked his head-- listening. He could hear the old man's voice, and the advice his Grandpa George was giving him made Jason feel more secure; more in control: "The way a man survives in this world is by standing on his own two feet-- by taking control of his life. Don't let anyone push you around."

"I won't, Grandpa," Jason whispered, staring down at his sister's bed. He saw her rumpled blanket, her bedspread, dragging on the floor, but, he couldn't see-- her! Becky wasn't there! Confused, Jason reached down and grabbed her blankets, throwing them off the bed.

Where the hell was she? She had to be here, somewhere? He had heard her. He walked around the bed and stood by her pillow. A small impression in the pillow convinced him that his sister had been in her bed sometime that evening. He glanced around the room trying to locate her. She had to be here. He just knew it.

His eyes stopped on her bookcase, and he stared at Becky's stuffed animals, lining the shelves. Some of these toys had glass eyes that glowed in the dark. It seemed to Jason like these eyes were now staring at him, trying to recognize the intruder skulking around in the dark, disturbing their quiet domain. Jason was forced to look away. Where was his sister? He began to move quietly around the room calling softly: "Becky, Becky."

Still-- nothing.

Everything remained quiet. The sobbing noises he had heard earlier had completely vanished, leaving an eerie silence in their wake. Jason began to get nervous. Maybe his dad had gotten here first! Frightened, Jason's eyes flew to the door, expecting a trap. Had he been set up? Tricked into breaking a rule, so that his dad would have an excuse to punish him?

No..., he told himself, trembling. *Dad's downstairs. I saw him. Becky's just hiding somewhere, trying to make me believe that Dad's been here.*

The thought that his sister had almost gotten away with such a terrible trick made him furious.

"Women!" he hissed, spitting on the floor. "Always causing trouble. Well, just wait Becky, because your turn's coming!"

He heard a soft whimpering noise behind him.

Spinning around, Jason tried to pinpoint the location of the sound. His eyes fastened on Becky's closet, and he stood there, staring at the closed door. He took a step forward and then, stopped when a thought struck him. What if Becky wasn't hiding from him, wasn't playing a trick on him? What if one of the monsters from his room had followed him here and was now waiting, inside the closet-- ready to strike when he opened the door? Maybe it had already eaten Becky, and was now just waiting to eat him, too..

"Grandpa," he whimpered, now on the verge of tears. "Grandpa, help me."

Terrified, that he had somehow stumbled onto the truth and was now dealing with a monster, instead of his sister, Jason was paralysed with fear and couldn't move.

"Someone help me," he cried. "Grandpa, I need you."

Grappling with his fear alone, Jason tried to think of what his Grandpa would do, if he were dark, in front of a closet with a monster in it? Had he ever been so scared that he needed someone to give him a hug and tell him that it was only is imagination; someone to tell him that nothing was lurking in the shadows, waiting to devour him? No..., the more he thought about it, the more convinced Jason became that his grandpa wouldn't be frightened. And... instead of sympathizing with Jason, he would condemn him for being a coward.

Grandpa wouldn't be scared to look in a closet, he told himself, trying to build up his courage. *I bet if he was here right now, he'd just walk over to that door and open it. He'd say: "To hell with the monsters. I'm not scared."*

Grandpa's a real man and I'm a coward. I've always been afraid. Dad's right when he say I'm nothing but a big sissy. It's a good thing Grandpa isn't here, or he'd be ashamed of me, too. What's wrong with me?

Jason continued to talk to himself as he inched towards the door.

Grandpa doesn't need someone to hold his hand, and neither does Dad. They stand on their own two feet. If they could see me now, they'd laugh at me. What a disappointment I must be to them.

At last, he stood outside the closed door and slowly, reached for the door handle, his thoughts still on his grandfather.

I wish I could have stayed at the farm. Then, I would have learned how to be a real man. Grandpa George would have taught me. I thought that after I drank that beer I was a man, but I'm not. Maybe if I had a woman like Grandpa suggested.... Maybe that would have made a difference. Maybe then, I wouldn't be afraid.

*   *   *

The day before Jason had left the farm to go home, he had gone down to the milkhouse and sat on a milking stool, leafing through some old copies of Playboy Magazine. As he flipped the pages, looking at pictures of naked women, his penis began to tingle. He wanted to rub it, but his grandpa was standing beside him, so Jason resisted his urge. But, before he left, he slipped one of the magazines inside his shirt and that night, in bed....

The next morning, his dad came to take them home. Jason was coming out of his bedroom, when he heard his dad tell Grandpa George that his mom had a baby boy. Jason knew he should have been excited that he had a new brother, but he wasn't. If his mom hadn't had the baby yet, then he wouldn't have to return home.

"Why couldn't you have waited for at least another week?" he muttered, returning to his room to pack his bag.

Before they left, his grandpa called him aside and gave Jason some parting advice.

"Son," he said, laying his hand on Jason's shoulder and looking him square in the eye, "always remember to look out for Number 1, because if you don't there'll always be someone just waiting for the chance to walk all over you. You have to be in control if you're going to survive. Don't let down your guard for one minute. And," he added, "remember-- stay one step ahead of those bastards, or they'll do you in. Mark my words...."

Jason kept his eyes glued on his grandfather's face, while his grandpa spoke to him. When his grandfather scowled, or emphasized a particular point by shaking his fist, Jason felt weird. He had this strange feeling that if he closed his eyes, he could imagine that it wasn't his grandfather who was speaking to him, but his dad who was standing in front of him, giving him a lecture.

I must be dreaming, Jason thought, rubbing his eyes and staring at his grandfather's face. *They're not alike.*

Still, Jason couldn't rid himself of the feeling, that when his grandfather spoke, he looked and sounded much like his dad.

His grandpa smiled at him and Jason's suspicion vanished. *Grandpa isn't giving me a lecture, he's just teaching me how to be a man.*

"Do you understand what I'm trying to tell you?" his grandfather asked.

His grandpa's question caught him off guard, and Jason scrambled to remember what they had been talking about. He saw his grandfather looking at him, waiting for a reply.

"Yes," said Jason seriously, trying to give the impression that he'd been listening intently, instead of letting his mind drift off. "I understand perfectly, Grandpa."

"Good," the old man said. "And... before you go, I just want to say one more thing. Respect. It's important that people respect you. Demand it! If people are afraid of you, then they're going to respect you. You'll have the power, not them. But," he stressed, "you have to be strong to be in charge. No one's going to be around to wipe your nose or fight your battles for you, so you have to stand up for yourself. That is, if you're going to amount to anything. And," he winked at Jason, "next time you come, I'll take you back to the cabin."

Jason returned his grandfather's wink and ran to the car. Becky was already in the back seat, sitting in his place. "Move over," he ordered, punching her. She glared at him for a second, and slid over to the other door. Jason was kind of sorry he had hit her, because for the rest of the trip home, Becky stared out her window, refusing to speak to him.

*   *   *

The memories of his visit to his grandpa's farm, swirled inside his head, gradually fading away until he was once again, standing in front of Becky's closet.

"Becky," he growled, giving the door a rap with his fist. "Are you in there?" He waited, but when he heard no reply, he rapped again. "Listen here, Becky. If you're in there, you better answer me or I'm going to come in there and kick the shit out of you. Do you hear me?"

He heard a shuffling noise from the closet and then, a soft voice called out: "Is that you Jason?"

It was his sister who was in the closet-- not the monsters. But, the sense of relief he had felt at hearing Becky's voice, was now replaced by anger. Who did she think she was anyway, trying to scare him half to death?

"Yes, it's me," he hissed, trying to keep his voice down. "Who else would be stupid enough to get up in the middle of the night just to save your scrawny neck!"

"I thought maybe you were Dad...," her voice trailed off and Jason heard her start to sob again.

"Well, I'm not Dad and you can thank your lucky stars that it's me instead of him, or you'd really be in shit!"

Jason waited, but when Becky made no move to open the door, he yanked it open and found her sitting on the floor. She stared up at him, wrapped in a quilt, her arms encircling her doll. They looked at each other. Then, Becky threw down her doll and wrapped her arms around his knees.

Jason tried to extricate himself from his sister's grasp. "What's your problem?" he asked. "Are you trying to get Dad up here? Is that it?" When she didn't reply, he continued: "And why are you hiding in your closet, bawling your head off? Hell, I could her you from my room."

"Oh Jason," she sobbed, her grip tightening around his legs, "I'm so scared. Dad's yelling again and I heard Mom scream. Please Jason," she begged. "Please make them stop."

"I'm so scared," he mimicked, sneering at her. "Who the hell cares if you're scared or not? Not me, and certainly not Dad! Look kid, I have enough problems of my own, without you dragging me into yours. The only reason I came here is so that Dad won't come up here. Understand?"

Becky didn't answer and her silence infuriated Jason. He had an urge to kick her to make sure she got the message. "I don't give a shit if Dad comes up here and tans your ass for crying, but I don't want him to think I'm involved in this crap, too," he said, reaching down and prying his legs free from her embrace.

"I didn't mean to get you into trouble," Becky answered. "I only wanted--"

"Who the hell cares what you want?" he interrupted. "What you want is no concern of mine. You're just like Mom-- always sniveling and carrying on. Why the hell don't you grow up for a change? Because, I'm sick and tired of always getting blamed, every time you get some stupid idea in your head. Well, no more! Do you hear me stupid? I'm finished with you; you're on your own."

Becky's eyes filled with tears and she picked up her doll. But, instead of coming out of her closet, she pushed herself backwards until she was hidden from his view.

"Look, you dumb little bitch! I told you to stop your bawling and get to bed," he ordered, reaching forward and grabbing his sister by her nightgown. He jerked her out of the closet and stood, holding her in his grasp. "When I tell you to shut up, I mean shut up!" He shook her, snapping her head back and forth, hissing in her ear: "Shut up. Do you hear me? Shut up!"

When his anger died, he opened his hands and let her slide to the floor. Shocked, Jason looked down at his sister. Becky didn't move. "God," he moaned, "What have I done?" He didn't mean to hurt her; he only wanted her to stop crying. Was she dead? He knelt down and touched her shoulder. She flinched and moved away, as if his touch had burned her. Jason slowly stood up, walked over to her bed, and sat down. He buried his face in his hands and moaned softly.

"Are you satisfied now?" he asked, dropping his hands in his lap and looking over at her. "See what you made me do? I'm going back to my room and you better get in this bed and go to sleep. I don't want any more trouble from you." Jason stood up and walked over to the door. But, before he left, he turned to look at his sister one last time. She was in bed.

"Becky...," he murmured, "I'm sorry. I never meant to hurt you. I just--"

The terrified look his sister gave him stopped him in mid-sentence. Seeing her so afraid, Jason was reminded of the time he had caught a wild rabbit in a box. The rabbit had looked at him the same way.

"Don't look at me like I'm some kind of monster," he said to her. But, Becky didn't answer. She just sat there for a moment staring at him and then, she pulled her blankets over her head, leaving him once again alone in the dark.

"Go ahead and sulk. See if I care," he mumbled, opening the door and walking out.

He hurried down the hallway, not bothering to stop to see if his parents were still downstairs. He had to get away. He had to escape the scene of his disgrace. Only when he had reached the safety of his room, did he allow himself to think about the night's events. He walked over to his bed and sat down.

What a night! First, Becky starts bawling. Then, I have to listen to Dad scream at Mom. And now, I lose my cool and almost hurt her.

Jason turned and looked at the shadows on his wall. The monsters were still there, but he was no longer frightened of them. Because now, he could relate to them. He was a monster, too.

He slipped under his covers and stared at the ceiling for a few moments, before reaching for Pookie. He plunged his face into the soft fur. Soundless, heart-wrenching sobs racked his body, as he gave way to his emotions. He repeated the same phrase over and over: "I am not a coward; I am not a coward...," until he fell asleep.

CHAPTER VI

Jason stretched, yawned, and rubbed his eyes. He glanced around his room. Sunlight flooded in through his window and when he looked at the wall, the shadows had disappeared. He stared. Where had they gone? Where were the images that had frightened him so badly just a few hours ago. All that was on his wall now were his Motley Crue posters.

He rubbed his eyes again, expecting the monsters to suddenly reappear. Apprehensive, he continued to gaze at his wall. They had been so real last night that he now found it difficult to believe that they had simply vanished without leaving some sort of trace of their presence in his room. With trembling hands, Jason pushed his blankets aside and climbed out of bed. He walked over to his wall and stood looking at the posters. He lifted up the corner of the poster in front of him and peeked underneath. Nothing. Jason let go of the paper.

Maybe I was dreaming, he thought, walking back to his bed and climbing under his covers. *Maybe there never were any monsters on my wall.*

He rolled over and pushed a button on his radio. The familiar voice of his favorite disc jockey filled his room, and Jason began to feel calmer. He listened to the music and stared at his model planes, suspended from his ceiling by invisible plastic threads. It had taken him a long time to build them, and he couldn't look at his models without feeling proud of them.

He tried to imagine what it would be like to be a pilot and have a real plane to fly.

His reverie was broken when he heard the disc jockey announce, that, at the sound of the tone, it would be eight o'clock.

"Eight o'clock," Jason groaned. "Why am I awake so early? There's no school today."

He pulled his quilt over his head, hoping that somehow, he'd be able to fall asleep again. He was tired and tried to turn off the images that kept popping into his mind. As he fidgeted in bed, sleep eluded him, and he wished he had a button that he could press to switch off his mind. For instead of falling asleep, he was now wide awake, his mind filled with the night's events. And Jason knew that he hadn't dreamt them. They were real-- too real.

What a screwed up night, he thought, glancing towards his door.

Why had he gotten so angry with Becky? He couldn't remember. Hell, I'm used to her whining by now, so why did I shake her? I guess I was just too tired to think clearly.

Jason wondered when his parents had finally gone to bed. He must have been asleep when they at last, called it quits and came upstairs. He wondered if they were finished fighting for a while. Even now, he could recall the angry words-- the accusations. This fight had been worse than most of the others.

I wish they could get along, he thought unhappily. All they ever do is yell and scream at each other, or at us.

He reached behind his head for his pillow, but his hand failed to connect with it. Bending his head back, Jason looked at his headboard. Then, he remembered. He had thrown the stupid thing on the floor. Jason sat up and scanned his room until he spotted his pillow lying in a corner. For a second, he thought about getting up and going to get it, but then changed his mind. It wasn't worth the effort when he was going to get up pretty soon, anyway. That is, he was going to get up, if his dad wasn't home. Jason turned down the volume on his radio and strained to hear, trying to determine if the rest of his family were already up.

Faint noises were coming from downstairs and he heard the sound of dishes clattering. It must be his mom. She must be fixing breakfast. Jason wondered if she was as tired as he was; if she felt like she'd been run over by a truck.

Well, so what if she is tired? he thought unsympathetically. *Hell, no one gets much sleep in this house. Not with you guys up screaming half the night. So, what else is new?*

It would be great if just once, I could wake up in the morning and find out that I was adopted-- that I wasn't really part of this family. Then, my real parents could show up at the door and take me out of this zoo.

Jason didn't really think there was much chance of that ever happening, but he liked to dream about it. He even went as far as imagining what his "real parents" would look like, and where they lived. But, he didn't allow his imagination to take over today. Because, after last night, he knew that no one was going to come and rescue him. Today, he was on his own.

"I never have any luck," he grumbled, throwing his blankets off and stumbling out of bed. He picked up his raccoon and gave him a quick hug before placing him on top of his night table. "I guess we're both stuck here for good," Jason said to Pookie. "But, someday, yes someday, things will be different...."

Preoccupied, Jason reached to the floor for his clothes and then realized he was already dressed. He hadn't taken them off when he returned from his sister's room. For a few minutes he debated whether or not to put on clean clothes, or keep the ones he was already wearing. He sniffed his armpits. They didn't smell. The decision made, he headed for his door, hoping his dad had already left for work.

Please let him be gone, he silently pleaded. I can't face him-- not after last night. What if he knows I was up last night?

Jason shuddered. He tried to still the panic inside him, by rationalizing with himself.

Don't be silly. If Dad knew, he would have come up here long before now. Dad wouldn't let me get away with being out of my room at night without some sort of reaction. And even if he is downstairs, he's still no mind-reader. Calm down. Still....

Jason couldn't help but think that somehow his dad had found out and was just waiting for him to come downstairs before he pounced on him.

This last thought sent Jason scurrying to the door, where he stood, his ear pressed against the wood, listening to the noise outside his room. Ten minutes passed, before he was finally reassured that the only sounds coming up from downstairs, were being made by his mother.

And, as he listened, Jason was pretty sure that only she and his little brother Nicky were downstairs in the kitchen. He couldn't hear Becky, and he couldn't hear his father. Jason straightened up, opened the door, and walked to the landing. He leaned over the railing and looked downstairs. The coast was clear.

Good. I don't need any hassles today, he thought running down the last dozen steps and going into the kitchen.

The smell of bacon filled the air, and he breathed in deeply, absorbing the fragrant odor. God, he was hungry. His stomach, not satisfied with mere odors, lodged a protest by grumbling loudly. "Hush stomach, I'm going to feed you," he told it, as he walked to the table and sat down.

His mother was standing in front of the stove, her back to him, and Jason wondered when she didn't turn around, if she knew he was there. He watched, as she took two eggs out of the carton, cracked them on the side of the frying pan, and plopped them in the pan.

Yuck. Not eggs. She knows I hate eggs.

Ever since he was little, Jason had rebelled at the thought of eating eggs. Not that his rebellion did him much good if his father was around. But, his mom shouldn't expect him to eat eggs when they were alone. His aversion to eggs had occurred when his mother had read him a book titled, *Green Eggs and Ham*. Ever since then, every time he looked at an egg, he didn't see a small yellow yolk surrounded by a while mass; he saw an ugly green blob of slime, staring up at him from his plate. Which he was expected not only to eat, but to be grateful that he had something to eat. His dad had once said something about starving kids in Africa. Jason would have been more than happy to ship his share of the eggs to them.

Now to be served eggs this morning, on top of everything else that happened.... It was too much. He decided to ask his mother about the eggs, when he was interrupted by Nicky. His little brother leaned out of his highchair and dealt Jason a sharp rap on his knuckles with a wooden spoon.

"Ouch!" Jason exclaimed, rubbing the back of his hand. "What did you go and do that for?"

Nicky giggled and waved the spoon in the air. Jason pushed his chair out of his brother's reach. He was about to reach over and tweak Nicky's nose, when he saw his mother go to the cupboard and take down a plate. He remembered the eggs.

"Hey Mom, I hope you're not cooking those for me," he said, "because you know I hate eggs."

"No Jason," she replied, turning around. "These eggs aren't for you."

Jason was about to say, "Good," but the sight of his mother's face stopped him, and he stared at her, his mouth open.

The whole left side of her face was an ugly purplish-blue color, and one eye was swollen shut. Her bottom lip was split and, as he slowly looked her up and down, Jason saw purple marks running up both sides of her arms. Stunned by his mother's appearance, he had difficulty speaking. It had been a long time since he had seen her so badly hurt. Finally, he swallowed twice and, with his teeth clamped together, hissed: "Oh, shit!"

"Please Jason" she implored, "don't swear."

"Don't please Jason me," he retorted, getting up and walking towards her. "Not again, Mom?" Not again?"

She didn't reply. Instead, she turned around and set the plate on the counter. It was as if she was no longer aware that he was standing there, waiting for her to answer his accusation.

"Turn around!" he yelled. All the rage and frustration he had been holding back spewed forth in a torrent, not to be halted by her quiet acceptance of the blows that had been dealt her. "You really let that bastard put the boots to you this time; didn't you?" he exclaimed, grabbing her by the arm and whirling her around until she was facing him, again. "Why did you let him do it?" He continued to berate her. "What's the matter with you, woman? I suppose when he was finished beating on you, you just kissed his ass and thanked him for keeping you in your place! You're such a coward, you make me sick."

He saw her physically crumble under his attach. First she started to shake, and then she dropped her head to her chest and tears spilled forth. Finally, she just slumped to the floor like a deflated balloon. For a second, Jason was seized by guilt as he stared at the top of his mother's head. He hadn't meant to make her cry-- to hurt her feelings. But dammit anyway, he was hurting too. And it was all her fault. Her cowardice affected them all.

Never in his life had he despised his mother as much as he did at this moment. When she looked up at him, her eyes silently appealing to him to understand, he didn't hesitate. He drew his hand back and slapped her across the mouth. She reeled from the blow, her head cradled in her hands. Slowly, she began to rock back and forth, crying softly.

"You stupid slut," he screamed. "I hate you. Do you hear me? I hate you!"

She pushed herself away from him and leaned against the cupboard, her tears now flowing in a steady stream down her face, dripping to the floor.

"You're to blame for always making Dad mad," he accused. "If I'm such a big sissy, it's all because of you. I hate you and I hate this house!" Jason spun around on his heels and ran out of the kitchen, through the porch, and out the door; slamming it shut behind him.

He stood on the front step, his hands gripping the iron railing to keep them from shaking. "Life sucks!" he muttered angrily. "If you're big, then no one can hurt you.... Well, someday, when I grow up, I'll be big and then, watch out! Someone's going to pay. Yes...,

He felt a tear roll down his cheek and angrily wiped it away. But it was soon followed by another, and another and... Jason tried to stop crying but it was no use. Once they started, this tears poured out, until they ran freely down his cheeks and soaked into his shirt collar. He turned and laid his forehead against the door.

He pounded the door with his fists, moaning softly: "Coward..., coward...."

He stayed there until his anger had subsided and his tears dried on his cheeks. He pulled his shirt tail out of his pants, yanked it around, and wiped his face. Now, except for the occasional sniffle, he felt he was regaining control of himself. Then the enormity of what he had just done struck him, and his legs buckled. Jason gripped the rail to keep from falling.

Why did I do it? he berated himself. I hurt Becky and now, I've hurt Mom. What's happening to me? Why can't I control my temper? I didn't mean to slap her; I was mad, that's all.

He felt he should go back in the house and tell his mother he was sorry, beg for her forgiveness. But, something inside him prevented him from opening the door. What if she was too mad at him to accept his apology, what then? After all, he reasoned, it hadn't worked with his sister, so why should his mother be any different? They were both women-- well, weren't they?

Although he wasn't sure that no apologizing was the best course of action, Jason couldn't think of any other alternative. Maybe if he just gave his mom some time to cool off, he could come back and she would have forgotten all about it. And besides, he was sure that his mother must know that he was sorry. Women were suppose to know that sort of thing.

Satisfied that he had at least solved his problem for now, Jason took a deep breath and started down the steps. So what if the morning had gotten off to a shaky start? He didn't have to let it ruin his whole day.

Jason was almost to the end of their sidewalk when he looked down and saw that he didn't have on his shoes. Quickly, he ran back to the house, quietly opened the door and slipped inside. His runners were just inside the door, and he grabbed them and beat a hasty retreat back outside. He sat on the step and put them on, not bothering to tie the laces. He looked over into their neighbor's yard, hoping that nosy old Mrs. Sealton was in her house. If she had seen him bawling, Jason was sure she'd be over in an instant to see if she could help him. He didn't want her or anyone else asking him questions, or worse yet, trying to console him. He had enough of adults and their interfering in his life. Today, he wanted to be left alone.

Jason took a shortcut across the lawn and headed down the sidewalk. As he strolled along, his hands in his pockets, the image of his mother, sitting on the floor-- crying-- kept flashing through his mind.

I'm not sorry," he said aloud to the shadowy apparition, kicking a flattened pop can out of his way. He heard it clatter, as it skidded across the cement and landed in the gutter.

I'm through being a momma's boy. From now on, I'm going to stand on my own two feet. She can't tell me what to do, because I won't listen. She can go to hell! Jason stuck out his chest and strutted down the sidewalk, daring anyone to cross his path. When he came to the end of his street, he had to stop for a red traffic light. To Jason, it was just another obstacle, put there by grownups, to prevent him from doing his own thing. Impatiently, his anger building, he waited for it to turn green. He wanted to yell at it; wanted to smash it with a rock.

"That would teach you a lesson," he muttered angrily, shifting from one foot to another.

As if aware of what he was thinking, the light suddenly changed to green, and Jason ran across the street, yelling back at it: "I'm not stopping again. You can't make me."

And, after that episode, if a light were red, Jason ignored it and boldly stepped out onto the street. The sounds of squealing brakes and honking horns, made by angry motorists, gave him a sense of power. He could make them stop for him; instead of the other way around.

Two hours later, he found himself on a footpath beside the river, and followed it, until he came to a footbridge. It stretched across the river and ended up in a park on the other side. He climbed up the steps and looked at the vast expanse of lawn stretching before him. There was something vaguely familiar about this place. Then he spotted a sign and knew why he felt that he recognized this area. He had been here once before with his family. This was Elton Island Park.

His mother had brought him here along with his brother and sister for a picnic. His dad was out of town for the weekend and his mom packed a lunch and told them that they were all going out for the day. When they had arrived, his mom kept an eye on Nicky, while he and Becky explored their surroundings. It had been fun because for once in his life, Jason was able to think of his family as just another happy, carefree group, enjoying a picnic like all the rest of the people gathered there. For once, his family didn't seem any different than any other family. It made Jason feel like he belonged there.

He wondered if he could recapture that feeling today. If he could, then maybe everything would turn out right for a change. He started across the bridge, but stopped in the middle and leaned over the side, staring into the water below. The swirling, grey river seemed to be beckoning to him; seemed to be calling to him to join it on its way to the sea. It was offering him an unspoken promise that everything would then be okay. Never again would he have to feel scared or lonely.

I wonder what it would feel like to drown? he thought, as he watched the water flow under the bridge. *Would it hurt?*

With these thoughts foremost in his mind, Jason had to force himself to leave the railing and walk the rest of the way across the bridge.

Would anyone even miss me? he wondered, stopping to look back to the spot where he had stood, gazing down into the water. *Would anyone even care?*

Elton Island Park stretched before him, and Jason took his time as he strolled down one of the gravel paths leading into the interior of the park. He was still thinking about the river when a loud *snort* sounded behind him. Startled, he leaped to the side, turning sharply, and nearly ran into a large black horse carrying a policeman. The man and horse had tried to pass Jason by stepping off the path and walking alongside him on the grass.

"Morning," said the officer, stopping his horse. He looked down at Jason. "Sorry I frightened you, son. I thought you could hear us coming up behind you."

Jason glanced up at him and then, dropped his eyes and stared straight ahead. In a cold voice, he replied: "Morning, sir."

When Jason didn't make any further effort to engage in conversation, the police officer clucked to his horse and they moved down the path leaving Jason standing there, his eyes burning into the cop's back. Jason waited until they had disappeared behind a bend in the trail before spitting on the ground and muttering: "Stupid cop! Why don't you get lost and leave me alone?"

Jason hated cops. His dad always said that cops spend more time interfering in a man's home life, than they do out on the street catching crooks. Jason remembered the two policemen who had come to his house when his mother hurt her leg.

A few days after his mother had brought his sister and him home, his dad had accused her of trying to ruin him by calling the cops. This had led to another battle, and Jason could still recall how his mom had cried, promising his dad that she would never again call the police. Only then did his father quit shouting. Ever since that time, Jason hated cops, too.

When Jason was sure that the police officer wouldn't be coming back down the trail, he surveyed his surroundings. His eyes spotted a large fountain, spurting water high into the air. It reminded him of a whale he had once seen in the outdoor aquarium in Vancouver. He could have stayed there for hours, watching the huge animal swim gracefully through the water, sending up jets of water every time it surfaced. Jason remembered wishing that the whale was his, so that he could be its trainer and look after it. He hadn't wanted to leave the aquarium back then, and now, he felt the same reluctance about leaving the fountain. But, he felt a need to continue walking, a need to relive the day they had come here for a picnic.

He tore his eyes away from the sparkling water and moved in the general direction where he knew the playground must be located. But when he arrive, he was upset to find the place already occupied. A boy, about his own age, was sitting on a swing reading a book.

Great! Just great, Jason thought, walking towards the stranger meanacingly.

At Jason's approach, the boy glanced up and then, returned his attention to the book on his lap. Jason stopped by the slide and studied him, wondering if he had ever seen him before. Maybe in school.... No, the kid was a complete stranger to him.

Maybe if I ask him, we can take turns playing on the swing, thought Jason. *That would be fun. We could see who could pump it the highest.*

He took a few steps towards the boy and stopped, again. *No, it wouldn't work. If I ask him to play with me, he might want us to become friends. I don't need a friend. Having a friend only causes more trouble. Besides, what was the use of making a new friend when I couldn't even keep an old friend?* Jason remembered Gary Peters.

*   *   *

Gary's family had moved into the large stucco house at the end of Jason's block three years ago. The moving van had barely left the yard, when Jason arrived on their doorstep to see if the Peters had any kids his age. Gary had answered the doorbell and, minutes later, the two boys were happily exchanging greetings.

"Hi," he said to Jason. "I'm Gary-- Gary Peters. We're from California. What's your name? Do you live around here? Will you be going to my school?"

Immediately, Jason knew he was going to like Gary. Gary's open, carefree manner made Jason feel welcome and he hoped that he and Gary would become special friends. Friends that could share all their secrets and who would play together after school and on weekends. Jason returned Gary's smile, introduced himself, and then said: "California is a long way from here. I hear its always warm and you don't get any snow. I don't think I would want to leave California to come and live in here. Did anyone tell you that we get snow here? Lots of it."

"Yeah, I know," Gary replied. "My Dad told me. But, I'm going to like living here. Dad says he's going to take me to the mountains to go skiing this winter. Want to come with us?"

Jason was surprised by Gary's invitation to join his family when they went skiing. He knew that he would never dream of asking Gary to come with his family, unless he first asked his father for permission to invite his friend. "Won't your dad mind?' he asked.

"No, Dad won't mind," Gary replied. But, when he saw the look of doubt on Jason's face, Gary grabbed him by the arm and started dragging him into the living room. "Come on," he said to Jason, "We'll ask him-- you'll see."

When they entered the living room, Gary's parents were in the center of the room, sorting through a pile of boxes. Gary introduced him to his mom and dad, and then told them he had invited Jason to go skiing with them this winter.

"Well," Mr. Peters replied, "it's still a bit early to think about skiing, but sure. It's okay if Jason comes with us." He reached out and shook Jason's hand. "I'm glad Gary has made a new friend so quickly. He was feeling kind of lost without his old friends to play with."

"I know it's too early to go skiing," said Gary, "but I just wanted to check to see if it was okay to bring Jason with us. And," he added, "we've already decided that we're going to be best friends."

"That's great," said Gary's mom, standing up and coming over to give Gary a hug. "Jason can come with us whenever he wants." She looked at Jason. "I want you to think of us as family," she said to him, smiling.

Jason shyly smiled back at her. He had been afraid of meeting Gary's parents, but they seemed to be glad that he was going to be Gary's friend. Jason knew he was going to like coming over here to play with Gary. But, he wondered if Gary would like his parents-his dad? Or, better still, would his father like Gary?

Just then, Gary's mom invited them into the kitchen for ice cream and cake. Jason put aside his doubts, and joined them at the table where Mrs.

Peters gave Gary and him each a generous serving of ice cream. She pushed a box out of her way, and sat down.

"Everything is in total chaos," she said, looking around the kitchen. "I can't even find where I put the cake."

"I think it's in the fridge," said her husband.

She fought her way through the boxes to the fridge and returned with the cake. "Here it is," she said triumphantly. Now, If I can only find some plates for us to put it on." She reached and pulled a box over to her chair. "I think they should be in here."

They finished their snack, and Gary's parents left them sitting at the table while they went back to the living room to finish putting things away.

"Let's go in the backyard and do something," suggested Gary.

"Fine with me." Jason replied. He followed Gary out of the house and into his backyard. They played there until it was time for Jason to go home for supper. He went inside to thank Mrs. Peter's for the cake and ice cream. "I'll be back tomorrow, if that's okay with you," he said to her.

"That's just fine, Jason," she replied. "I'm glad you came over today and I know Gary's glad too."

When he got home, Jason was bursting with excitement. He couldn't wait to tell his family all about Gary. And, throughout supper, he sat at the table describing the Peters' family. He told his dad how Mr. Peters was going to help Gary and him build a tree house in Gary's back yard. And, that Mr. Peters had told him he could come with them when they went skiing this winter. Between each mouthful of food, Jason mentioned some new aspect of his visit. He told his family that Gary's dad had asked him to go with them to the car show next Saturday at Stampede Park. He was about to tell his dad that Mr. Peters was thinking about buying a Mercedes, when his dad interrupted him. Jason looked up and saw that his father was frowning.

"Jason," his dad said, "there's no way that I'm going to let you go skiing, or to a car show, or anywhere else with that boy and his family. In fact, I don't want you ever going over there again."

Jason was heartbroken. "But why?" he asked, biting his lower lip trying to fight back the tears forming in his eyes.

"Because they're black, that's why," his dad replied. He hit the table with his fist. "I don't know what this neighborhood is coming to, when a bunch of black immigrants can move practically next door, and everyone welcomes them with open arms. And," he added, "if that's not bad enough, the very first thing they try and do is start acting like they own the place. Imagine. They even had the gall to think that my son was going to start hanging around with their kid. You stay away from them," he ordered, pointing at Jason. "Do you hear me? I don't want to find out that you've been over there again. Understand?"

Devastated by his father's unexpected response, Jason could only nod his head. All his dreams and plans had evaporated, under his dad's verbal barrage, like whisks of smoke, leaving an empty feeling inside of him. Jason swallowed and replied, "Yes, Dad, I understand. I won't go over there again."

"Good," said his dad. "I'm glad we got that mess straightened out." He shook his head, a look of amazement on his face. "Imagine. They sure got nerve."

However, Jason didn't share his father's feelings about Gary and his family. And, just because he had said that he wouldn't go over there anymore, didn't mean that he understood why. He'd never understand. What did being black have to do with having someone for your best friend? Gary's family seemed like nice people, but now, after having heard the disgust in his dad's voice, Jason felt that he may have been deceived. That maybe, the Peters were bad because they were black.

I'm glad I wasn't born black, he thought, pushing his plate away. He had lost his appetite. For the remainder of the meal, Jason sat quietly, staring up at the ceiling.

Jason kept his promise and never went over to Gary's house again. He never told Gary why they could no longer be best friends, because he never talked to Gary again. At first it had been difficult avoiding Gary, but Jason kept out of his way as much as possible and, when they did meet, he would simply turn around and head in the opposite direction. After a while, Jason knew that Gary had gotten the message, because he no longer made any attempt to talk with Jason. In fact, after that first week, it appeared to Jason that Gary was going out of his way to avoid meeting him.

Jason didn't know why, but it bothered him when Gary openly ignored him. He tried to shrug off this feeling by reminding himself that "black" people could be real "uppity" if you gave them the chance. Jason wasn't going to give Gary that chance. And so, they had both gone their separate ways.

*   *   *

Jason still saw Gary from time to time and he no longer tried to avoid him. There was no need now. Their friendship had been over a long time, and Gary had a new best friend. But, from that time on, Jason had decided never to have another best friend. Having a friend was only asking for trouble, and it was far better to spend his free time alone than to risk being hurt again.

Why did Gary have to be black? he wondered, as he stared at the boy on the swing.

The boy looked up again and it appeared to Jason that the boy was going to say something to him. Jason frowned. The boy gave him a puzzled look, and then went back to reading his book.

Who does he think he is, acting like I don't exist? thought Jason angrily. *I'll teach him not to ignore me!* Jason puffed out his chest and swaggered over to him. "I want to swing," he said.

"Use one of the other swings," replied the boy, not bothering to look up.

Jason crammed his hands into his pockets and glared at him. "I want the swing you're sitting on," he demanded.

"Not right now," the boy answered. "If you want this swing, then you're going to have to wait until I've finished this chapter. I'll be going home then."

"I said I wanted it now!"

"No."

Jason was furious. He lunged at the boy, grabbing him by the arm and yanking him off the swing. The boy pulled free and pushed him backwards, knocking him to the ground. Jason scrambled to his feet and took a swing at him. Pain shot up through Jason's hand when his knuckles connected with the boy's front teeth.

"Take that, you sneaking coward." Jason stammered. By this time he was so angry that he couldn't speak properly.

"Leave me alone," the boy cried, holding his hand over his mouth to stop the blood from pouring out of his split lip. "I didn't do anything to you," he added, backing away from Jason.

Jason smiled when he saw the boy cringe- afraid. He took a step toward him and hit him again. This time, the boy fell to the ground, wrapped his arms around his head for protection, and tried to roll away. But Jason wasn't finished with him yet. He kicked him in the ribs and the boy screamed in pain.

"Get out of here!" yelled Jason. "You're nothing but a sissy-- a momma's boy. If you don't start running now, I'm going to kill you."

The boy looked at him, his face smeared with dirt and tears. Then he jumped to his feet and ran out of the playground. Jason could see him running down the path leading to the bridge. When the boy disappeared over a hill, Jason walked over to the empty swing and sat down. When he looked down, he saw the boy's book in the dirt at his feet. He picked it up and turned it over to read the title: *Moby Dick*. Beneath the title, was a picture of a large whale.

Interested, Jason leafed through the book, stopping every few pages and reading a passage.

Hey, this might not be too bad, he thought, turning to the last page so he could find out how the book ended. He always did that before he read a book because he had to know what happened in the end. He couldn't stand the suspense of not knowing how everything turned out. When he had finished reading, Jason slipped the book inside his shirt and looked around to see if anyone had seen him pick up the book, or had witnessed his fight. He thought about the cop and shifted uneasily on the swing. What would have happened if the cop had come along when he had the boy on the ground?

However, when Jason checked and saw that he was the only one anywhere near the playground, he knew his fears were groundless. His knuckles hurt, and he sucked them, as he slowly pushed the swing back and forth with his feet. He thought about the boy.

I guess I showed him who's boss. Next time I ask him for the swing, he won't be so damn smart.

Jason wanted to remain in the park for a while, but for some reason, the good feeling he had when he first came here had vanished. Even having the swing didn't lift the gloomy feeling that now filled the playground.

Why did that kid have to ruin everything? Jason asked aloud. Why couldn't he have just given me the swing when I first asked him for it?

Slowly, Jason got up off the swing and walked out of the playground. He took the same path the boy had taken, leading to the river. When he reached the bridge, Jason stopped and looked back, his eyes scanning the park.

This is a stupid place to come. I'm never coming here again, he decided, crossing the bridge and heading for home. *Only sissies come to parks.*

As he neared his house, Jason's stomach began to rumble and he thought about the breakfast he had missed. By now, he was so hungry that even the thought of eating an egg didn't seem quite as repulsive as it had before. He hoped his mom had at least saved him some bacon, so he could make himself a sandwich.

Jason wondered if his mother was still mad at him. He hoped not.

She must know that I never meant to hit her. It's just that I was so mad. Everyone gets mad once in a while. It wasn't as if he had committed some unspeakable crime by losing his temper. *She can't expect me to be perfect, can she?*

The more he thought about it, the more important it became to him that his mother should forgive him for his behavior.

Hell, even if she doesn't stand up to Dad, she's the only one in my family who gives a shit about me. Maybe I should tell her I'm sorry.

Jason was still wrestling with his conscience when he reached his front door. Should he apologize or keep his mouth shut and hope she had forgotten about it? If she was still mad at him, what would she say to him when he went inside? But then, maybe if he kept quiet, the whole thing would blow over and, in time, she'd forgive him anyway. After a while, Jason knew that there was no point in standing outside on the step, debating the matter forever, so he opened the door and went in.

Throwing his shoes in the closet, Jason went to the kitchen to find her, but his mother wasn't there. He was wondering where she was, when he heard the washing machine going, down the basement. He walked over and stood at the top of the stairs. "Hey Mom, are you down there?" he yelled. For a second, there was no response, and then he heard a faint reply. The noise from the machine made it impossible for Jason to hear everything his mother said, but he managed to get the gist of her message.

"...downstairs...laundry...hungry...make a sandwich...bacon in the fridge...."

He turned and went back into the kitchen. From what he could tell, she didn't sound like she was angry at him.

I guess she's forgotten all about it by now.

This made him feel a lot better because now, he didn't have to worry about it or tell her he was sorry.

No sense in looking for trouble, he thought, taking the bacon out of the fridge and fixing himself a sandwich.

While he was eating, Jason suddenly remembered his younger sister. Where was she? He hadn't seen her all day. He wondered if she had told their mom about last night.

She better not have; not if she knows what's good for her!

Jason could just imagine what his mother would say to him if she ever found out he had roughed up Becky, too.

She'd never forgive him!

The thought of getting in trouble again made Jason lose his appetite and he sat at the table, staring at the half-eaten sandwich in front of him. He had to know if his sister had said anything to her about last night.

Jason headed upstairs. Even before he reached Becky's room, he could hear her talking with someone, and he stopped outside her door to listen.

She's talking to that stupid doll of hers, he thought, disgusted, as he listened to the one-sided conversation. What a baby. He had an urge to march into her room and snatch away her doll, just to see what she'd do. He liked to tease his sister, but she usually started to cry and he didn't want her to start bawling now-- at least not today. He had enough problems already. He quietly opened her door, stepped into her room and went and sat on her bed. Becky was sitting on the floor, her doll cradled in her arms.

When she saw him, she pulled her doll closer to her breast. "What do you want, Jason?" she asked fearfully.

"I don't want anything," he replied, stretching out on her bed, his hands behind his head. "I just came in to see what you were doing."

When she didn't reply, he added: "I hope you didn't tell Mom about last night. Remember, I told you I was sorry. Are you still mad?"

"No..., I'm not mad at you," she said, standing up and walking to her window. "But I was scared of you."

"Good," he said, "I mean, I'm glad you're not mad. I didn't mean to shake you. It's just that you made me so mad that I lost control. Besides, It's not my fault, you know. If you hadn't started bawling, I wouldn't have had to come to your room in the first place."

Becky just stared out the window without replying. Her unwillingness to talk to him began to make Jason uneasy. Why didn't she tell him she was sorry for all the trouble she had caused him?" Was he the only one in this damn family that had to apologize every time something went wrong?

Jason felt like going over to her and shaking her again. But, he didn't want to get her going again, so he decided to try a different approach. "Well, if you're okay, then I won't bug you anymore," he said, his voice filled with humility and forgiveness.

Yes, why shouldn't he forgive her? He was in control now and she came under that control. He could afford to be generous with her.

He had been in three scrapes in the last twenty-four hours and had come out of them the winner. And now, he knew that he could do whatever he liked to both her and his mother and neither one of them could stop him.

They won't turn to Dad for help, that's for sure, he thought, relishing this new sense of superiority and power. He rose from her bed and walked over to his sister.

"What's out there, that's so important that you can't talk to me?" he asked. "Or, is it that you can only make a lot of noise at night? Is that it?"

Instead of answering him, Becky brushed past him and walked over to her bed. Jason watched, as his sister climbed under the covers and pulled he bedspread up over her head.

Now he was mad! Who did she think she was? Didn't she know that he could break her as easily as he did the boy in the park?

"You know something, Becky?" he said, "You're really starting to get to me. I'm sick and tired of you ignoring me when I talk to you. Well, I'll let you get away with it this time, but don't ever try and pull that shit on me again."

He turned and stomped out her room, slamming the door shut behind him.

CHAPTER VII

After Jason left Becky's room, he stomped downstairs and into the living room. He flopped down on the floor in front of the T.V. and flipped through the pages of the *T.V. Guide*. Preoccupied, the turned on the television and pushed the channel selector, randomly stopping at one or another of the stations, until he finally settled for a repeat of a He-Man show he had seen a few weeks before. Something was poking him and he shifted his position. He remembered the book. Reaching inside his shirt, he pulled out Moby Dick and looked at the picture on the cover. After a few moments, he opened it and turned to chapter one. He was still reading when he heard the front door open. His father must be home. Jason closed the book and slid it underneath the chesterfield.

Jason waited until his mother called him for supper, before he reluctantly left the living room. He hadn't bothered to seek her out after his run-in with his sister, because he didn't want to talk with his mom, or see her swollen, discolored face anymore than was necessary. It made him feel sick.

Everyone else was already at the table when Jason joined them, and he slid into his chair making sure to keep his eyes averted, so he wouldn't have to look at her. But, her condition didn't seem to bother his father. Jason heard him ask her to pass the rice, as if, sitting across from a battered, bruised woman was an every day occurrence. Jason raised his eyes and looked at him. His father picked up the plate with the roast on it, took a slice and passed it over to him.

"Thank you." Jason said, helping himself to a large slice of meat and handling the plate over to Becky.

While they were eating, Nicky managed to squash his carrots into his hair and rub them on his face. Jason looked disgustedly at his little brother.

That's gross, he thought, staring at the orange lumps sticking out of Nicky's hair. Jason looked down at the carrots on his own plate. Somehow, they weren't quite as appealing as they had been when he first dished them out of the bowl. He wondered if his dad would say anything about Nicky playing with his food, but it didn't look like his father had noticed.

He hasn't said one word since we sat down. I wonder if he's still mad or something?

Unwilling to be the one to question his dad's silence, Jason went back to eating his supper, taking care to push his carrots to the side of his plate.

"Would you pass me the gravy?" his dad asked him, and then added, "and quit playing with your food."

Jason quickly handed his father the gravy, miffed that his dad had reprimanded him for pushing his carrots aside, when Nicky had totally demolished his supper.

Must be nice being a baby. You can get away with anything.

Jason glared at Nicky, but instead of being properly chastised for his behavior, Nicky thought Jason wanted to play with him and threw his spoon across the table hitting Jason on the arm.

"That's enough Nicky," his dad said, tapping Nicky on the wrist. Then, he turned to Jason and asked: "What did you do in school today?"

But before Jason could reply, his mother interjected: "I mentioned to you last week, dear, that the kids were going to have today off from school because their teachers were having a professional development day."

"Oh yes," he replied, "I remember you saying something about it. Sure must be nice being a teacher. If I had been smarter, I'd have gone into teaching, instead of dentistry. They can find more reasons to get out of working than anyone else I know. It's just too bad that my taxes go to finance their paid vacations. It's no wonder that Jason's having trouble learning. His teachers are never in school long enough to teach him anything. I have a good mind to write a letter to the school board and lodge a formal complaint." He wiped his lips with his napkin and sat back in his chair, looking across the table at Jason.

Surprised by his dad's remarks about the reason for his poor grades, Jason mulled over what he had just heard. His dad usually blamed him every time he brought home a poor report car, but today it was different. Today, his teachers were to blame. It made sense, and Jason thought that it was about time his dad quit blaming him for his below-average grades. However, he didn't think that cutting out professional development days for his teachers would make a lot of difference to his grades. He hoped his dad wouldn't follow up with his threat to write to the school board.

His dad spoke to him again. "Well," he said, "I'm still waiting to find out what you did today, since you didn't have school."

Jason looked at his father's face, trying to determine if he knew about the fight in the park. If his dad thought that he was in school today, then it wasn't likely that he knew. Still, Jason could never be completely sure when it came to his father. He stared into the grey eyes, trying to read whether or not his dad was setting him up for a fall. He knew the penalty for lying, but Jason decided to take the risk.

He can't know about today. No one knows, not even the cop.

And so, he replied: "Nothing much. I just stayed home and did my homework." He kept his eyes glued to his father's face, trying to anticipate his reaction to the lie. Jason saw his mother give him a curious look, but he ignored her and waited for his dad's response. He was pretty certain that his mom wouldn't say anything about his story; wouldn't call him a liar in front of his father. She wouldn't dare! Not if she knew what was good for her.

Jason knew that everything was going to be okay when his father only grunted, "Good. It's about time you started spending more time on your schoolwork. Maybe you can pull up your grades if you work harder." He pushed his plate aside and stood up. "Now," he said to Jason, "if you're done eating, get out and cut the grass. You should have done that this afternoon."

"Yes sir," Jason replied. He was relieved that he had gotten off so easily, and welcomed the dismissal, cramming a last forkful of potatoes into his mouth. "Excuse me," he mumbled, and hurriedly left the table. He went outside to the garage and hauled the lawnmower out from behind the barbecue. As he filled it with gas and checked the oil, he thought about the lie he had told his father.

It had been risky thing for him to do, but he had gotten away with lying before, and was now a firm believer that his father would much rather hear a lie then the truth.

His dad almost never questioned his lies, but he had questioned Jason about some of the things that had been true. And, as long as Jason could escape being punished it didn't matter to him what method he used, as long as it worked. And lying did work. Besides, this way, both of them avoided a lot of hassles.

Whistling between his teeth, Jason pushed the mower across the lawn, making sure that he cut under the birch trees and right to the edge of the sidewalk. His dad wanted the lawn cut right and if Jason didn't do a proper job the first time, he knew his dad would send him back out again to do it right. One time he even had to go out and do it again in the dark!

As he mowed the backyard, Jason thought about his mother. He knew that she knew about his lies, but she never had said anything to his dad about them. He could only suppose that she was glad that trouble was being avoided. Of course, Jason knew that there was a good chance that someday he would be caught but, for now, he could relax and forget about it. His dad didn't know about the boy on the swing.

Maybe telling lies was okay, he thought, if it kept you out of trouble. Jason finished cutting the grass and carefully cleaned the lawnmower blades before putting it away.

It was almost dark before he came back into the house. Nicky was sitting on the kitchen floor, banging a wooden spoon against the leg of his highchair. His mom and Becky were sitting at the table, and Jason saw that his mother was helping Becky with her spelling. He walked over to the cookie jar and took out a cookie, munching thoughtfully, as he leaned against the cupboard, listening to them. When he finished the cookie, Jason went into the living room. His father was stretched out on the sofa reading the newspaper. He walked over to the sofa and stood beside his father.

"I'm all done," he said.

"Did you put everything away?" his dad asked from behind his paper. "Did you clean the blades?"

"Yes, and I filled the lawnmower with gas and checked the oil, too."

"Did you remember to cut behind the back fence?"

"Yes, Dad," Jason replied. "Now, can I go to my room? I'm almost finished a new model plane and I want to start painting it."

"If you're sure that you've done a good job on the lawn, then you can go," his father said. "But, I don't know why you're still wasting your time playing with toys. Aren't you getting a little old for that sort of thing?"

"No, Dad. I mean, yes, Dad, but it's only a hobby," replied Jason, unsettled by his father's remark.

"Building those stupid models isn't going to prepare you for the future," his dad countered. "All they do is hang from your ceiling and get in everybody's way. I don't know why your mom hasn't complained by now. I'm sure she must bump into them every time she goes in there to clean."

Jason lifted his eyes and looked at his dad, but he saw that he had already been dismissed. His face was turned to the newspaper in front of him and Jason could tell that his attention was absorbed in what he was reading. Jason wanted to knock the newspaper out of his hands; wanted to tell him that his models weren't stupid toys, but he didn't dare start an argument with his father. His dad would only get mad at him.

Why is it that everything I do is either stupid or dumb? he thought, walking out of the living room and heading towards the stairs. *Guess I was born a loser and I'll always be a loser.*

Up in his room, Jason worked quietly at his desk, with his radio tuned to his favorite station. When he finished applying the second coat of grey paint to the model plane in front of him, he carefully picked it up by the prop and set it on a newspaper on top of his dresser to dry. Then he stood back to admire it. The plane was perfect.

"Tomorrow I'll hang you up with the rest," he said aloud, glancing up at the ceiling.

He cleaned up his mess, taking care to wash each of his brushes in paint thinner to remove any trace of paint. Then, he stored his equipment in a brown paper bag and set it back on the top shelf in his closet.

When everything had been put away, he got ready for bed. The last thing he remembered wishing before he fell asleep was that he didn't have to get up and go to school the next morning.

Jason was sleeping so soundly, that he didn't wake up when his alarm went off the next morning. When he did finally open his eyes, he saw that it was already 7:45 a.m., leaving him only fifteen minutes to get dressed and make it to his bus stop, if he were going to get to school on time.

Scrambling out of bed, he grabbed a clean pair of jeans and a shirt out of his closet and hopped around on one foot, trying to pull on his sock. He didn't have time to stop at his closet mirror to check and see if his appearance was satisfactory. It didn't matter this morning. All he was concerned with, was getting to the bus stop before the bus left without him. He ran to the bathroom and brushed his hair, all the time wondering why his mom hadn't called him when he didn't come down for breakfast.

I knew she was still mad at me. This is her way of getting even. Now, I'm going to be late and it's all her fault. Where's my knapsack? Shit. It was here yesterday. Who the hell moved it?

Jason spotted his missing school bag standing beside his night table and threw it over his shoulder, as he ran out of his room and downstairs.

He stopped in the hallway, slipped on his running shoes and jacket, and ran outside and down the street. He could see the bus just pulling up in front of a group of kids. The driver opened the door and the kids started to go inside. Putting on a burst of speed, Jason raced down the street yelling: "Wait for me. I'm coming."

A small boy was just climbing into the bus when Jason arrived. Jason shoved him aside and pushed his way up the steps. The boy lost his balance and would have fallen, except that the bus driver reached down and grabbed him by his arm.

"Hey you...!" the driver hollered after Jason, but Jason ignored him. He could hear the angry murmurings coming from the kids around him, as he pushed his way to the back of the bus and plopped down on a seat.

Let them talk. I don't give a shit, Jason thought, ignoring the angry glances being cast his way.

He saw the boy he had pushed pointing him out to the driver. "Dirty little snitch," mumbled Jason, under his breath. "Just wait 'til I get you alone. I'm not finished with you yet." He rode the rest of the way to school brooding over the injustices in his life.

Some stupid kid blocks the way into the bus and I get in trouble because I give him a little push. It isn't fair. This is great, just great! The little bastard will turn me in to the principal, and I'll get called to the office. What else can go wrong today?

When the bus stopped in front of the school, Jason waited till most of the kids had left, before he got up and walked down the aisle towards the door. He could feel the driver's eyes boring into his back, but Jason ignored him and, once he was off the bus, hurried towards the school.

All through his Language Arts class, Jason kept expecting to hear a voice come over the intercom, requesting that he come down to the office. But, when class was nearly over and he still hadn't received a summons, Jason began to get nervous. His next class was Social Studies. Again, Jason waited impatiently to be called. The loudspeaker over his teacher's head, remained ominously silent. His anxiety reached a near panic stage. And as a result, by the time he got to Math class, the suspense was killing him. He felt like a condemned man sitting it out on death row; not knowing if he was going to be granted a reprieve or someone was going to pull the switch.

During his entire Math class, Jason fiddled with his pencil, chewed on his eraser and kept his eyes glued to the intercom. It was impossible for him to concentrate on what his teacher was saying, and he didn't try. The "waiting" began to remind him of his father.

Every one of his family knew when his dad was getting set to explode. They sensed it long before the explosion actually took place, and the waiting was worse in the long run than the violence that followed. Because, once his dad had vented his anger, the family could get back to normal. The stress would be gone and all of them could let down their guard for a while. But, before that happened, the house was filled with tension and fear. Jason couldn't stand it. That feeling of impending disaster could break him easier than the violence that followed.

And now, as he sat in his desk, waiting to be called to answer for his crime, Jason felt the same kind of hopelessness and anxiety. He didn't know how much longer he would be able to calmly sit there before he finally cracked. If something didn't happen soon, he would either end up screaming, or trying to escape. He thought about doing something-- anything-- that would bring this waiting to an end and would force his teacher to send him to the office.

He looked at the girl sitting in front of him. She was busy working out a math problem from her textbook, and Jason thought about lifting his own book into the air and hitting her on top of her head. That should be enough to get him set down to the principal. Slowly, he lifted his book and was about to hit her with it, when a voice interrupted him, causing his hand to freeze in mid air.

"Jason," said Mr. White, his math teacher, "have you been listening to what I've been saying?"

Jason lowered his book and looked up. Everyone of his classmates had turned around and were now staring at him, waiting for him to reply. His cheeks began to burn, and his humiliation was complete when he heard someone giggle. He felt like a caged animal in a zoo full of prying eyes. Jason wanted to run, to hide. Unable to cope any longer, he involuntarily felt himself rise up in his desk.

"Jason, you have been listening, haven't you?" his teacher asked again.

"Yes, Mr. White," he replied, sinking back down into his desk.

"Okay then," Mr. White continued, "if I wanted to find out how many kilometers are in 112 miles, how would I get the answer?"

All the tension and fear generated over the last few hours, coupled with the unexpected question now being posed to him, caused Jason's mind to go blank. He didn't know the answer. He didn't know how to calculate the answer, and, he didn't care about the answer. It wasn't important. Right now, he had other things to think about. Helpless, he silently stared at the top of his desk.

He wanted to tell his teacher to get off his case; to leave him alone, because he already had more problems than he could handle. But he knew Mr. White wouldn't understand. Jason slowly shook his head. His response caused another giggle to erupt somewhere behind him, making him cringe.

"Come now, Jason," Mr. White persisted, "we took metric conversion tables last week. Think....

Jason was thinking! He was thinking about how he could escape further humiliation by fleeing from this room and his taunting classmates. "I don't know," he stammered in a defeated voice.

"Jason..., I want to see you after school today," said Mr. White, walking back up the aisle and over to the blackboard.

Terrific! Is there anyone who doesn't want to see me today? he wondered, cradling his head in his arms on top of his desk. *What the hell is happening to me? Why is everyone picking on me? I haven't done anything wrong. I didn't hurt that kid. Hell, I only gave him a little shove, for Christ's sake. Now, everyone's acting like I tried to kill him or something.*

It took everything he had to remain in control, as he sat through the rest of the class. He wanted to shout-- to scream-- to do anything that would relieve the pressure building inside him. Quickly, his frustration turned to anger and he had to stifle urge to pick up his book and hurl it across the room.

Leave me alone, he silently screamed. *Just leave me alone....*

He sighed with relief when he heard the sound of the noon buzzer. Jason gathered up his books, stuffed them into his backpack, and headed for the door. On his way out, he passed by his teacher's desk and glared at Mr. White. Jason was surprised to see Mr. White look up from the stack of papers in front of him and smile at him.

Oh, so you're just waiting to get me alone, hey? You're going to enjoy punishing me; is that it? thought Jason, giving his teacher one last glance before he fled from the room. *Well, just wait. You might not have the last laugh. Because you can't make me come back here after school-- not if I don't want to. And... I don't want to come!* Jason ran down the hall.

When he reached his locker, he fumbled with his combination lock. His hands were trembling so badly that he had difficulty getting the proper settings. Just when he was about to give up, the lock sprung open and he was able to get inside his locker. He threw in his books and reached for his lunchbag. No lunch. Then, he remembered. He had left the house without stopping in the kitchen to pick up his lunch.

"Shit!" he muttered, reaching for his coat and checking the pockets to see if he had any money to buy something in the school cafeteria. He found a loonie, a dime and three pennies.

Well, so much for my buying something to eat, he thought disgruntedly, as he stared at the money in his hand. *But, at least I can buy a can of juice.* Jason slid the money inside his pants pocket and headed down the hall to join the crowd of students waiting to get into the cafeteria.

As he waited in line, he looked for a place to sit and noticed some of his classmates were already gathered around a long table at the back of the room. He watched them take out their lunches and spread the food on top of the table. Looking at the stack of sandwiches only increased his own hunger, and Jason wondered if he had the nerve to go over there and ask if he could join them. Maybe they would even consent to share a sandwich with him. But just when he made up his mind that he would go over there, he remembered what had just happened in Math class. These were the same boys who had laughed at him and Jason was certain that if he joined them now, they would tease him about having to go see Mr. White after school. He sucked in his stomach and turned away.

When it was his turn at the cash register, Jason handed the woman his two quarters for the can of juice and started across the room. He ignored his classmates and found himself a small table in the corner beside a window. Before he sat down, he pushed one of the two chairs over to another table so that no one could join him. He wanted to be alone; he felt alone.

Somehow, he managed to get through the rest of the afternoon without attracting further attention to himself. He fooled his teachers into believing that he was paying attention by spreading his books out on his desk and pretending to read, when in fact, his mind was far away from what was taking place around him. His mind was on Mr. White and he was wondering whether or not, he would go see him after school. What would Mr. White do if he didn't show up? How would he be punished for this act of defiance?

Maybe I'll be kicked out of school-- suspended. That wouldn't be so bad.... Then, I wouldn't have to come back here.

But, what would his dad say? The school would probably phone his parents or send a note home with him to be signed and returned to the school.

Jason tried to imagine what his dad would do to him if he ever found out that his son had been suspended. The very thought made Jason gulp, and he pressed his hands between his knees to still their trembling. Whatever punishment Mr. White inflicted couldn't be worse than what his dad would do to him. No..., getting suspended wouldn't be the thing to do. But, the question still to be answered was: Would he be suspended for merely failing to go see his teacher after school? Would the school be that mean?

Maybe, I'll only get the strap. I could handle that okay, he thought, taking his hands out from between his legs and looking at this palms.

Jason had talked with another boy who had got strapped and it didn't sound too bad.

I bet Dad hits harder than they do. I wouldn't care if I got the strap, but I don't want them to suspend me from school. Dad would really give it to me then!

He wished he could be sure what type of punishment would be meted out, so he could decide, once and for all, whether or not to go see Mr. White.

When he looked at the clock, he realized that he was running out of time. School would be over in five minutes and he still didn't know what he was going to do. He had to make a decision. And... he would leave that decision to chance. He fished in his pocket and hauled out the remainder of his money. He selected the dime and threw it into the air. Heads-- he would go see Mr. White; tails-- he would go home.

The coin dropped into his outstretched hand, wavered on its edge a second, and fell-- heads!

Jason didn't question the fairness of the decision made by the coin. When the buzzer sounded, he gathered up his books and headed to Mr. White's classroom.

The door to the room was open and Jason peered inside. The room was empty. Unsure of what he should do now, he walked down the center aisle and sat down in his own desk. He glanced up at the clock-- 3:10 p.m. If his teacher didn't come soon, Jason knew he would miss his regular bus home. "Well," he said aloud, his voice echoing in the empty room. "I'm here; where are you?"

As the minutes dragged by, Jason's nervousness increased. The empty room was spooky. He kept his eyes on the clock, and when fifteen minutes had passed and Mr. White still had shown up, he got up to leave. Where was his teacher? Why didn't he come and get it over with? Had Mr. White forgotten about him, or was he deliberately making him wait in order to instill fear into him? If the latter was his intention, then he had succeeded. Jason was on the verge of panic. Sweat was running down his forehead and his body felt cold and clammy as he stood beside his desk, uncertain as to what he should do.

He wiped his forehead with the back of his hand and slumped back down in his desk. He continued to wait.

Minutes passed and his fear took hold completely, filling his mind with wild, disorientated thoughts. His teacher's image kept floating in front of his eyes. His teacher was coming to get him!

Mr. White was carrying a large axe, dripping blood, as he moved towards him. Then Jason saw him smile! Jason tried to scream, but his vocal cords froze and he whimpered instead. He crouched down in his desk, shielded his body with his arms and groaned, "Please sir..., please don't hurt me. I'll be good. I'll pay attention. Please don't hurt me."

"Jason..." Jason. What's wrong with you?" Mr. White asked, reaching out and resting his hand on Jason's shoulder.

Jason yelped and pushed the hand away. "Don't touch me; please don't touch me," he whimpered.

"Hey old man, calm down. It's okay. No one's going to hurt you." Mr. White removed his hand from Jason's shoulder. "See," he said holding his hand up in the air, "no one's touching you. Try to get a hold of yourself."

Gradually, the red mist in front of his eyes disappeared and so did the axe. Jason was able to clearly see again. Mr. White was sitting on top of a desk across from him in the next aisle. His teacher looked worried. Jason looked around fearfully. What had Mr. White done with the axe? Finally, when he was sure that the axe was no longer in the room with them, Jason looked up at his teacher. Gone was the leering, fanged creature that only moments before had been walking down the aisle, coming towards him. Now, Mr. White looked the same as he had in class this morning. Was the axe and the monster just a dream? Disorientated, Jason tried to collect his thoughts.

Are you okay now?" Mr. White asked.

Jason nodded and sat up straight in his desk.

"You had me worried. I've never seen anyone as scared as you were. You were staring at me like I was some kind of monster or something. You weren't scared of me, were you?" asked his teacher, his voice filled with concern.

Jason was afraid of him, but he didn't know how to tell him without mentioning the monster and the axe. He didn't want to think about the monster; didn't want to relive the nightmare he had just had. So instead, he stared at the ceiling and shook his head.

"Well, that's a relief," said Mr. White, "because I wouldn't want to think that I was such an ogre that I nearly scared one of my students half to death."

Although he wasn't watching his teacher, Jason was aware that Mr. White had moved and was now standing beside him. He wondered what was going to happen now; how he was going to be punished? Jason remembered the axe and shuddered.

"Jason," said his teacher, "it's time you and I had a talk about your school work.

Jason shrugged and lowered his eyes until he was now staring at the top of his desk. He picked at a glob of glue with his thumb nail and waited for his teacher to continue. But, when a few minutes had passed and Mr. White remained silent, Jason was forced to look up at him to see why his teacher wasn't saying anything. His silence was threatening and the fear inside of Jason grew. He was relieved when his teacher at last spoke to him.

"Jason, ever since you started school last fall, I've become increasingly concerned about your work habits in class. But, more than that, I'm concerned about your attitude. You don't seem to care about school-- not about your grades and definitely not about your fellow students. In fact, I'd have to say that it almost appears to me that you go out of your way to either shun or torment the rest of the kids. What's wrong Jason? If you can tell me what's bothering you, maybe we can work together to fix it."

Jason didn't answer and the silence increased.

"Come on, Jason. Don't shut me out. I only want to try to help you; to understand where you're coming from. If you have a problem, we can work something out." He almost patted Jason on the shoulder, but the look Jason gave him stopped him, and his hand fell to his side. "Look Jason, won't you at least give me a chance? I know you've been wrestling with some kind of problem for a long time now and maybe, if you could just talk to me, we'd be able to come up with a solution."

A scream erupted inside of Jason and the repressed noise vibrated inside his head. *Why can't you leave me alone?* he thought, pressing his fists against his temples. *Why can't you just send me down to the principal and get it over with? I can't stand it anymore.* His head began to pound and he felt a stabbing pain behind his eyes. *Why are you doing this to me?* Despite his earlier resolution about taking his punishment like a man, tears of frustration gathered in the corners of his eyes. He angrily wiped them away. But, to Mr. White-- he said nothing.

His teacher tried again. "Please talk to me. Nobody's going to hurt you. No one wants to make you cry or even make you feel bad. There's no need for you to be afraid. We... I... only want to help."

Unable to copy any longer, Jason blurted out: "Well, if you're so concerned about me, why are you sending me down to the principal to get strapped or suspended from school? That doesn't sound to me like someone who gives a shit about what happens to me. Why did you ask me to come here?"

Mr. White was taken aback by Jason's accusation. "Good Lord, Jason, whatever gave you the idea that I was going to send you down to the principal? The reason I asked you to drop by after school was so that we could talk. Not to punish you."

"I'm not going to get the strap or get kicked out of school?' asked Jason, skeptical about his teacher's sincerity.

"No."

"I thought you wanted to see me because I screwed up in class and couldn't answer that question."

"Well, that's a concern, to be sure," Mr. White agreed, "but I'm more concerned about what is happening to you. You seem so alone; so cut off from life; so lost. It's like you're hurting deep inside, but you're afraid to reach out for help. You've shut all of us out. Jason, I want to help you, if you'll let me."

His teacher's words made Jason feel vulnerable and, if he didn't shut him out, he was sure that he would break down, lose control and be lost forever. He tried to withdraw from his teacher by closing off his mind; by retreating into his mind and the blackness that he knew awaited him. Gradually, Mr. White's voice faded and Jason found himself hurtling towards the darkness.

When his head quit spinning, he found himself alone in a large grey room, empty except for a stone staircase leading up to nowhere. The walls that surrounded him were so high, that he wasn't able to see the ceiling. Intrigued by this strange place, Jason looked around. Never before had he been able to travel so far-- or come to this place. He could hear a faint rustling sound, like distant waves striking a sandy beach and then retreating, pulling the sand with them as they returned to the sea. He wondered where the noise was coming from, then accepted it as part of his strange surroundings. For instead of disturbing the peacefulness of the place, it helped to soothe his ragged nerves.

When he had finished exploring the room, he knew that the only exit leading out of this place was a small wooden door beside the staircase. As impressed as he was with his new hideaway, Jason was glad that the door wasn't locked. Because, he didn't think that he would want to spend the rest of his life locked away in this room.

He was about to go over to the door and take a look at what lay beyond, when his dad's image begin to materialize in front of him. Jason watched the shadowy apparition float towards him. The eyes on the phantom stared back at him, accusing him of unspeakable crimes.

Jason screamed and ran towards the door. The room began to darken and the blackness now held more terror in it than the thought of facing reality. Jason raced through the door and slammed it shut behind him....

The next thing he knew, he was back at his desk, listening to Mr. White.

"... and, as I was saying," Mr. White continued, apparently unaware that Jason had left for a while and had just now returned, "If you have any problems you'd like to talk about with me, please feel free to come and see me anytime."

Jason couldn't stop shaking and he hoped his teacher wouldn't notice. *I have to get out of here before it's too late,* he thought. A chill ran up his spine. "Please," he asked him, "please can I go now? I'll do my homework from now on and I'll answer questions in class. I promise."

Mr. White looked at him. He had a sad expression on his face. "Why have you locked all of us out?" he asked. "I wish I knew what to do to help you. Don't be afraid of us, Jason; we're your friends. Like I said before, we're only trying to help. Can you understand that?"

But Jason couldn't understand. All he could see was his teacher standing over him, just like his father did, giving him another "lecture." He clenched his fists, fighting back the fear that had overtaken him again and was now on the verge of breaking him completely.

I mustn't lose control, he told himself. *I'm a man and I'm not afraid.* He bit his lower lip and waited.

"You can go now," said Mr. White, "but if you ever need someone to talk to, please come and see me. Even if it's not about school. I promise I'll try to understand. Okay?"

Terrified, Jason murmured a quick "Yes sir," grabbed his bag and bolted out of the room. He ran down the hall towards the exit. When he was outside, he stopped at the bike rack and sucked in deep mouthfuls of air. Still shaking, he leaned across the metal structure. He stayed there until his mind cleared and he was able to think properly.

"Why me?" he whispered. "Why did he pick me out for punishment?" Alone and safe from prying eyes, Jason allowed his emotions to run free. All the misery that was bottled up inside him, broke loose and ragged sobs racked his body. He buried his face in his hands. "Why can't they leave me alone?" he sobbed. "Why can't everyone just leave me alone...."

CHAPTER VIII

He didn't go home after school.

Once he had regained his composure, Jason left the school grounds and walked past the bus stop without stopping. He glanced at the kids standing on the sidewalk, waiting for the bus, but he didn't acknowledge their presence. The thought-- that some of them may have seen him crying- made him feel ashamed.

Now I've really given them something to laugh at, he thought.

His shame made him walk faster and he hurried past them, his eyes on the sidewalk ahead of him. He could feel their stares drilling into his back and he was sure they were talking about him.

"Go ahead and talk; I don't give a damn!" he shouted.

His pace steadily increased until he was almost running now. He had to get away. When he was sure that he was far enough away that they could no longer see him, Jason slowed down and stopped when he came to another bus stop.

He sat on the bench and waited until he saw a bus pull up in front of him. He climbed on, not bothering to look at the number on the front to see where it was going. If it would take him away from the scene of his disgrace, that was good enough for him. Jason flashed his bus pass at the driver and went to sit down at the back of the bus. He stared out the window as they passed through a few side streets and then turned onto a main road. When he spotted a sign saying "Memorial Drive" he pulled the cord and got off at the next stop. Jason looked around, wondering where he should go now. He crossed the street and came to a bike path alongside the river. He began to walk along the path, hoping that whatever was at the end of this trail would be better than what he had left back at his school.

It wasn't long before he spotted another sign that said: ZOO AHEAD. Jason checked his watch: 6:30 p.m. Between the bus ride and his walking, he had been on the move for over two hours.

While he stared at the sign, Jason wondered what he should do. Should he forge ahead or return home?

I've really screwed up this time. First Mr. White bawls me out; now, Dad's going to kill me for coming home late. What the hell am I suppose to do? I can't go home. Not this late. As far as he could see, his only other option was to continue walking till he reached the zoo. Maybe by then, he could think of something.

I could go see the animals, he thought, fishing into his pocket, hoping that by some chance he might have missed a loonie. But no, when he opened his hand, the dime and three pennies lay in his palm. Thirteen cents. How could he get into the zoo with only thirteen cents? Another thought struck him: What if the zoo was closed for the evening? What then? He wouldn't be able to get in even if he did have the money.

But, I could get in if I went around to the back.

Jason stared at the path in front of him. *I bet if I keep following this trail, it will lead right past the back fence.*

He remembered being able to see the river from inside the zoo and had seen people on bicycles by the fence. *I bet they were on this path,* Jason thought excitedly. *And, if I follow it, I'll get there. Then, all I'll have to do is climb the fence and I'll be inside.*

His problem solved, Jason hurried down the trail and arrived at the zoo thirty minutes later. He pressed his face against the wire, trying to see if anyone was around. The place looked deserted. Satisfied that he wouldn't be caught, he climbed to the top of the fence and carefully threw his leg over the three strands of barbed wire on the top. When he had successfully overcome this obstacle, he lowered himself to the ground. So far, so good.

Silently, he crept along the fence, taking care to keep out of sight. When he was sure that it was safe, he scurried across a wide expanse of lawn and hid behind a large building. The sign over the door said: Large Mammal Enclosure.

This is where the elephants live, he thought, looking for a way to get inside. He spotted a door at the far end of the building and walked over to it but, when he tried the door handle, it was locked. Disappointed, Jason walked over to the exercise yard, hoping that the elephants were outside. Their pen was empty.

Jason sat down on the grassy steps beside their pen and stared down at the empty yard. What should he do now? He thought about his parents. Did they miss him? Were they worried because he hadn't come home? He didn't think so. He could see the sun setting in the west and he looked at his watch. It was almost eight o'clock. Feeling chilly, Jason zipped up his jacket and got up to leave.

No use in staying here. I may as well walk around and see the rest of the animals before it gets too dark. I wish I had something to eat, he thought, heading down another pathway.

Something let out a loud shriek behind him. Startled, Jason spun around and stared. A large blue peacock stared back at him!

The bird's tail was spread out like a huge oriental fan and, as Jason watched, the bird moved slowly from side to side, never taking its eyes off of him.

"What are you looking at?" Jason demanded. He felt silly that he had been so badly frightened by a bird. "Go on. Get out of here!" he ordered, but the peacock didn't move. It just continued to stare at him with its beady yellow eyes. Jason thought about the kids at the bus stop. "Well, go ahead and stare! See if I care. Stupid bird!" he said to it before stomping off down the path, leaving a string of soft curses lingering in the night air.

Jason wandered aimlessly through the zoo, stopping at the various cages to talk to the animals. The sun had completely disappeared by the time he reached the polar bear enclosure. The trees waved in the breeze, their branches casting dark shadows across the path. The shadows made Jason uncomfortable, and he deliberately made a point of stepping on them, trying to crush them.

"You can't hurt me; no one can. I'm not afraid of you. Do you understand? I'm not afraid of anything anymore!"

He climbed the steps leading up to the observation deck and stared down at the polar bears. Three of the bears were stretched out-- asleep, but the fourth bear was pacing back and forth alongside its swimming tank. The huge animal neither looked left nor right as it walked to one end of the tank, turned, and walked back; never veering from its course or altering its speed.

Something about the bear reminded Jason of himself and he called down to it. "You know something, Bear?" he said. "You're just like me-- trapped! And, they're never going to let you escape from here. Oh, I know I've managed to elude them for a while, but I'll have to go back-- they'll make me. There's no place in the world for us to hide. They'd catch you, if you tried to escape, and they'll catch me."

Jason paused for a moment and stretched his arm out in gesture of friendship and understanding. He thought he heard the bear speaking to him in a raspy, gruff voice and he leaned over the edge of the rail to listen. It didn't surprise Jason that the two of them had somehow managed to break through the language barrier that separated them. It had been broken because of their mutual suffering. They had formed a bond.

"You say you hate it in there?" asked Jason. "Well, I can sympathize with you, because I hate it at home. Everyone's always fighting and screaming all the time. I don't want to go back there." The bear spoke to him again, and Jason replied: "No, I don't like people either. You can't trust any of them. They'll do you in, if you lower your guard. In fact, I'll tell you a secret, Bear. If you don't trust anyone, then you won't get hurt. You'll be able to survive. There's no way you can win-- no way at all. So, always be on your guard. Understand?"

The bear continued its ceaseless pacing and, just when Jason was beginning to think that the bear hadn't heard him, or if he had, hadn't understood what Jason was trying to say, the bear stopped and looked up. His eyes locked into Jason's and for a second, they stared at each other-- recognizing each other's pain.

It was Jason who dropped his eyes first. He couldn't stand to look any longer into the bear's eyes. It was as if he had seen his own soul mirrored in those eyes. The bear turned and started walking again.

"I have to go now, Bear," he said. He heard the bear answer him. "Oh yeah," Jason added, "good luck to you, too."

It was completely dark now except for the light from a few scattered lamp standards. Jason kept to the path, afraid of getting lost. He wandered up one path and down another until he spotted a sign post pointing the way to the Prehistoric Park. He moved in that direction, thinking that the Prehistoric Park might not be such a bad place to spend the night.

When Jason arrived the rocky, jagged landscape stretched out before him. There were no lights here and he wondered how he would find his way through the park in the darkness, using only the moonlight to guide him.

It's a good thing I've been here before, he thought, intimidated by his surroundings. He knew there had to be a cave somewhere up ahead and he hurriedly climb the lava-strewn path.

He passed the volcano and stopped at a pond to get a drink of water. The life-like replicas of the giants from the past seemed to be staring at him, appeared so real that these dinosaurs frightened him. Everywhere he walked, he encountered them lurking behind every shrub and curve along the trail. Jason kept his eyes on the gravel path in front of him. At last, when he saw the waterfall, he knew he'd reached his destination. The cave lay directly behind the flowing water. From past experience, Jason knew that he was going to have to get wet if he was going to get inside the cave. He climbed the slippery rocks and took a flying leap through the waterfall and into the darkness beyond. He landed on the dirt floor with a thump! He had reached the cave.

He was shivering and his teeth were chattering. He tried to get warm. Gathering himself up into a tight ball, he leaned back against the cave wall. Cold and hungry, Jason had never felt so miserable in his entire life. He thought about his family and his teacher.

I bet they're not wet and cold or sleeping on the hard ground, he condemned. He could see his room and the warm bed that awaited his return.

God, what a day! I wonder what Dad will do if I ever go back? Maybe he's glad I ran away; glad that he's finally rid of me for good. But, I bet mom will miss me. She can't stay mad at me forever.

His mother's image swam before his eyes, and he could see the same frightened, sad expression on her face that she had when he had struck her.

"I'm sorry, Mom," he cried. "I didn't mean it. Please miss me, because if you don't, no one will care if I ever come back." He wanted his mother now, but this time, she wasn't here to put her arms around him and tell him that everything was going to be okay. Jason reached out his hand, trying to touch his mother's shimmering image, but she disappeared, leaving Jason to face the darkness alone. He thought about Mr. White.

Dad hates me because I'm a sissy; Mom hates me because I hit her; and now, Mr. White hates me because I don't fit in at school. Is there anyone who doesn't hate me? He slid his hands inside his sleeves trying to get warm.

Well, Mr. White, I don't believe all your shit about wanting to help me. Why should you care what happens to me, when my own family doesn't give a damn if I ever come back? I bet everyone would be glad if I never returned; if I disappeared for good. Or, better yet, if I were dead. No more Jason-- no more problems!

His mind lost in thought, the cold no longer affected him. He wrapped his arms around his knees and sat in the dark, thinking about what his dad was going to do to him when he went home. And, although it was like sucking on a sore tooth, Jason tried to imagine how he would be punished.

Maybe I'd be better off dead, he thought, shrinking at the grim prospect that lay ahead. *At least then, I could choose a less painful way to go. Especially, if Dad gives me a beating like he did when I scratched the car.*

*   *   *

It had been an accident. But that had made no difference to his father.

Jason had left his bike leaning against the garage wall, even though he'd been told that the bikes were to be kept in the bike rack at the back of the house. His father had driven the car into the garage and the bike had fallen over and landed against the car door, scratching it. His dad was furious. He had come into the house screaming: "Where is that little bastard? I'm going to kill him when I get my hands on him!"

Jason heard the commotion and came out of his room, just in time to see his dad bounding up the steps two at a time. Jason ran back into his room but he couldn't escape. His dad followed him and cuffed him on the side of the head, knocking Jason backwards onto his bed. Then his dad picked him up by the scruff of the neck and yanked him to his feet. With his free hand, his father ripped the cord off Jason's lamp, folded it in half, and began to beat him. The whip struck Jason across his legs, stomach and back.

Jason screamed and twisted, trying to break free. But, it was no use. His body was on fire and he screamed in pain. He begged for mercy. The pain-- it was everywhere. Jason fainted, his dad shouts ringing in his ears.

When he came to, he was lying on his floor. He couldn't remember anything except the pain. He hurt-- every inch of his body was on fire and he couldn't move. He remained on the floor until his mother came in his room, picked him up, and put him to bed. She put some kind of salve on the long, red welts crisscrossing his body, and then washed the dried blood off his chest.

When Jason woke up again, it was morning. His legs were stiff and he gritted his teeth, trying to wiggle his toes. It took everything he had to lean over and pick up his stuffed raccoon. He hugged Pookie to his chest. Then he wept, burying his face into Pookie's soft head, until the hurt and pain were replaced by sleep.

It was three days before Jason could walk without limping and before he could return to school. His dad wrote a note explaining his absence and requesting that Jason be excused from gym classes for the next two weeks. His dad also warned Jason to keep his mouth shut. But, Jason didn't need to be warned; he already knew that he wouldn't say or do anything that might give his father a reason to punish him again.

*   *   *

And now, as he sat there wrapped in darkness, the ugly memory sent a cold chill down his spine. The memory was too fresh-- too real-- and he could still see his father's face as his dad beat him with that cord. The menacing image filled the cave and Jason's mind and body went numb from fear. He cried out in anguish: "What can I do? Where can I go? Please God, please help me..., help me...."

He heard an owl hoot and it seemed to him to be an omen of things yet to come. Alone-- his heart filled with fear-- Jason sat there, thinking about his dad until he fell asleep. His dreams reflected his fear. They were filled with hideous monsters reaching out, trying to grab him.

When he woke, Jason could see inside the cave and knew it must be morning. He rubbed his eyes and stretched, trying to get rid of the stiffness in his back and neck. It was time for him to go before someone discovered him. Jason looked around the little cave, reluctant to leave. Slowly, he crawled to the entrance. He wished he didn't have to get wet again. But there was no use in stalling, so he steeled himself and leaped through the waterfall.

Outside, the sky was overcast and he could smell rain in the air. He shivered.

That's all I need right now. I'm already wet, he thought, sliding down the rocks and making his way over to the path. He was thinking about going back into the cave when he heard someone shout at him.

"Hey you...kid...what are you doing in here?"

Jason turned and saw a man running towards him. Jason took off, racing along the path until he saw a fence behind some rocks. He scrambled over the rocks and when he reached it, scampered up the wire and over the top, letting himself drop to the grass below. In a split second, he was back on his feet and running towards the highway. He heard the man call to him to stop, but he ignored the command,

"You won't catch me," he gasped, putting on a fresh burst of speed.

Jason ran until his legs gave out and he collapsed on the grassy slope alongside the highway.

I have to keep going; can't stop now. Bent over, his lungs burning, Jason forced himself to continue walking. He had to get away from the zoo and his pursuer.

He stumbled along until he came to a bus shelter. Satisfied that he was probably safe now, Jason slumped down on the bench. He stretched out on his stomach and rested his head on the wooden slats. When his breathing had returned to normal, he looked up. In front of him was a newspaper box and he could see the front page of the newspaper inside.

He sat up with a start. He recognized the person on the front page. It was him! He scrambled off the bench and crouched in front of the box. The headline was printed in bold black letters and he read: SON OF PROMINENT DENTIST FEARED KIDNAPPED. Under the headline was a picture of him, and beside it was a picture of his mom and dad holding each other. His mother was crying. Jason read the article until it ended with a "Continued on page A2."

Jason when back and sat down on the bench, trying to comprehend what he had just read. *Kidnapped.... They think I've been kidnapped.* He turned his head and looked at the picture of his mom and dad again. *What a laugh. Who would want to kidnap me?* He tried to picture his dad handing over a suitcase of money for his son's safe return. Jason broke into gales of laughter. That would be the day!

Then, he sobered when another thought occurred to him. *If they think I've been kidnapped, then the cops will be looking for me.* For a moment, he felt like a bank robber trying to elude the police. *Maybe I could hide somewhere where they wouldn't be able to find me*, he thought hopefully. But where would he hide? Jason knew he was no bank robber; he was just a twelve-year-old boy who had run away from home. How could he stay lost forever when the city, once so large, now appeared to be too small to hide away for long. *Where would I run to? Where would I hide?* he wondered.

Jason already knew the answer-- Nowhere.

"Now, I have no choice. I have to go home," he said aloud, resigning himself to the inevitable. He glanced back towards the zoo. "I almost made it, Bear," he whispered. "I almost made it."

CHAPTER IX

They would be home waiting for him.

As he rode the bus home, Jason has an awful premonition that his parents already knew he was coming back and would be waiting at the house for him.

When the bus stopped to let him off at the corner, he had to force his feet to head in the direction of his house. Even when he reached the sidewalk leading up to the front door, he had to force himself to walk forward. And, by the time he reached the doorstep, he was shaking like a leaf. He had a sinking feeling that he might not survive whatever lay beyond that door. Slowly, he climbed the steps and went inside.

His intuition had been correct.

His parents and Becky were standing in the hallway when he came in. Lightheaded, his knees shaking, Jason stopped and stared at them. For a few seconds, no one said a word and then, Becky broke away from them and came running over to him, hugging him around the waist.

"Oh Jason," she cried. "I'm so glad you're home!"

Jason smiled down at his little sister. When he had thought about his family, and how they wouldn't give a shit if he came back or not, he had forgotten about Becky. Her hug meant a lot to him right now. However, his smile disappeared when he heard his dad order her back.

"Leave the boy alone," he said, his voice filled with disapproval.

Becky loosened her grip around his waist and backed away. His dad stepped forward and stood in front of him.

Jason was too scared to look up at his father, so just stared down at his feet. All the way home, he had tried to imagine how he would be punished and, with each possibility, his fear had increased. And now, as his dad stood towering over him, all his fears were about to come true. Jason, a bundle of raw nerves, could only stand there waiting for the sentence to be passed.

"Jason," his dad said, "I've told you before not to try to defy me. It would appear that you don't listen very well. Or, could it be because you think that what I say to you isn't important? Or maybe, you think that when I say something, it doesn't apply to you?"

Jason shook his head; unable to understand what he meant.

"Oh," continued his dad, "so you do think that I might say something worth listening to. Is that it? Well, if it is, it's obvious to all of us standing here that you don't listen closely enough, or you wouldn't have tried to embarrass me. Yes..., you're going to hear me when I talk to you!"

His father's voice was so cold and controlled that it terrified Jason. He shriveled under the scathing attack and stood cringing before his father. What was he going to do to him? Jason looked at his mom, but she had her face buried in her hands and was softly weeping. He tried to find Becky. He needed her; needed someone to tell him that this was only a nightmare. That he wasn't really standing here, waiting to be punished.

Someone...anyone...please take me out of here! he silently screamed, as his legs buckled and he collapsed on the floor.

"Get off the floor and go to your room," his dad ordered.

Jason struggled to his feet and leaned against the wall for support. "Yes, sir," he whispered.

"I want you to stay in your room 'til I tell you that you can come out. Is that clear?

"Yes, sir."

"Well, what are you standing around for? Get going. Now!"

Jason shuffled past his father, using the wall to help keep him from falling. Everything was strange. His dad hadn't exploded; hadn't screamed; hadn't hit him. What was going on here? It was all wrong. *Maybe I'm dreaming*, Jason thought, stopping at the bottom of the stairs and turning around to stare at his father. He watched his father walk over to the phone, pick up the receiver, and dial, his fingers drumming on the note pad sitting beside the phone.

"Hello, Nick Winters calling. Could I speak to Sgt. Blane?... Hello, Sgt. Blane, Nick Winters here. I just called to let you know that my son came home. What? Oh, about fifteen minutes ago... Stayed at a friend's house and didn't bother to call us-- Yes, isn't that the truth. Kids can be so thoughtless... Yes, I certainly agree with you there. When we were kids, it was a lot different. We knew better than to do something so stupid... I agree, more respect back then... I sure will. Well, thanks again for your help and I'm sorry for all the trouble. My wife and I really appreciate it. I can assure you, it won't happen again."

His dad hung up the receiver and glared up at him. Jason turned and stumbled up the stairs. By the time he reached the top of the stairs, he felt so weak and ill that he half-walked and half-crawled the rest of the way to his room. He opened the door and stepped inside.

In disbelief, Jason looked around his room!

Everything was in ruins! The whole room looked like someone had run through it with a bulldozer leaving total destruction in its wake.

Jason's mind refused to accept what his eyes saw. There must be some mistake. Somehow, he had come to the wrong house; the wrong room. This terrible mess must belong to someone else. He noticed his father standing beside him and Jason stared up at him, silently beseeching him to end this cruel joke; to show him where they had moved his real room. He had to find it. He had to get out of here. But, his dad only smiled and walked out, shutting the door behind him. Jason heard a soft *click* and tried the doorknob. It was locked.

He pounded on the door and screamed: "Let me out... Let me out!" His voice was hoarse when he finally realized that it was no use-- that no one was going to come and let him out. He was a prisoner; his cell-- this disaster area where everything he had once known and loved was now gone.

His eyes swept across the room, but his brain was paralyzed and refused to comprehend the damage around him.

His curtains hung in tattered strips from a bent curtain rod and his bed and blankets lay in a torn pile on the floor in the middle of the room. His mattress had been slashed and now lay underneath his window. When he tried to find his night table and dresser, Jason found only splintered chunks of wood, scattered everywhere.

Slowly, he walked around and around the room, stepping over broken boards and torn clothing. He felt something snap under his foot and looked down. Small splinters of grey plastic lined the floor. His eyes shot to the ceiling. His planes, his beautiful planes were gone.

Jason bent down and scooped up a handful of crushed plastic, moaning softly, "Not my planes... not my planes."

Everything that he loved was gone. The storm had destroyed it all!

Then he remembered Pookie!

Where was his stuffed raccoon? He ran around the room, searching through the rubble, trying to locate Pookie. He had left him on his night table, but now, he couldn't even distinguish what pieces of wood had once been his night table. Where was Pookie?

"God," he beseeched, "Please don't let Pookie be hurt." Jason had had Pookie for as long as he could remember. Pookie was the only thing Jason loved; or that loved him. "Please be in the closet," he begged, when his efforts failed to locate the raccoon.

He ran over and threw open the door. All his clothes were lying in shreds on his closet floor. Jason dropped to his knees and began to sift through the rags.

"Where are you Pookie?" he asked in desperation. "It's okay. You can come out now; Dad's gone. Don't be scared. I won't let him hurt you." Just when he was beginning to despair of ever finding his friend, he spotted the familiar grey tail poking out from the bottom of the pile. Jason grabbed Pookie's tail and pulled. But, all he found himself holding was the tail. Just Pookie's tail! Stunned, Jason stared at the bit of fur in his hand. Where was the rest of Pookie? Frantically, he began to throw his clothes out of the closet until he reached the bottom. Scattered over the floor, he saw small grey and black pieces of fur, along with clumps of white stuffing. He had found Pookie; or what was left of Pookie!

Carefully, Jason scraped the floor with his hands, gathering up the remains of his friend. Only when he was absolutely sure that he had collected every last piece, did he stop running his hands along the floor. He picked up the small pile in front of him and pressed it to his cheek.

Each tiny piece of fur and fluff meant more to him than life itself. He felt as if he, too, were now just bits and pieces of his former self.

Slowly, he began to rock back and forth, still holding Pookie tightly against his face. He felt himself begin to slide into darkness; felt the floor racing up towards him.

He screamed!

A low, heart-wrenching cry of desperation echoing all the pain and sorrow that could pour out of a broken heart burst from his lungs. He felt himself being drawn towards the edge of the black pit of his nightmares. He felt out of control.

Before he was swept away completely, there was a strange boy staring at him out of the full length mirror on his closet door. Jason reached for him, trying to save himself. He begged the boy to help him; to save him, but the boy just lay, curled up on the floor, sucking his thumb, while he stared back at Jason.

"Sissy," Jason yelled before the darkness descended, sweeping him away....

When he came to, Jason saw that the strange boy was still there in his mirror. Jason looked at the mirror. How did the boy get inside? Why wasn't the mirror broken, like everything else in his room? Maybe the boy had somehow saved it from destruction. Maybe he always lived inside the mirror, but decided only now to allow Jason to see him. Jason didn't mind if the stranger wanted to live in his mirror, but he did think that the boy should stop sucking his thumb.

"Only babies suck their thumb," said Jason.

The boy didn't answer, but gave him a long, knowing look. Then, he stepped out of the mirror and into the closet.

"Hey, watch where you're going," Jason said, afraid the boy was going to step on him. "There's not much room in here, you know."

But he need not have worried, because it was as if they boy had been inside the closet many times before. He carefully stepped over Jason, picked his way through the mess, and stepped out into Jason's room. Curious, Jason stood up and followed him, wondering what the stranger would do now.

As if he was aware of what Jason was thinking, the boy stopped and gave him a questioning look, as his eyes drank in the devastation surrounding him.

"Dad?" said Jason.

The boy slowly nodded his head and then, began walking around the room, touching one broken object after another.

His casual, unconcerned manner disturbed Jason. It was as if the stranger didn't care about the state of his room.

How can he be so cold? Jason thought, surveying the damage. *Sure, I know it's not his room that got sacked, but still....*

As Jason watched, he saw the boy stoop down and pick up a brown paper bag. He opened it and dumped the contents out on the floor.

"Hey!" exclaimed Jason. "Don't do that. That's my stuff for my models."

The boy looked up at the ceiling and then down at the floor. He picked up a piece of a broken plastic, turned it over in his hand, and let it drop to the floor. He looked at Jason, and his face was drawn and cold.

Taken aback by the intensity behind those eyes, Jason could only mutter, "Yeah, I guess you're right. It doesn't matter anymore...."

The boy walked over to him and opened the bag. It took Jason a few seconds before he realized what the boy wanted him to do. Slowly, he held out Pookie and dropped his remains inside the paper bag. The boy closed the bag, rolled it up, and walked back to the closet. Jason was overcome with gratitude. He tried to thank him; tried to tell him what his small act of kindness meant to him. But, the boy walked back through the mirror and disappeared.

The blackness descended once again, and Jason felt himself hurtling through space towards a blinding light in the distance.

When he regained consciousness, Jason found himself lying on the floor of his closet. He looked at the mirror to see if the boy was there, but this time, his own reflection stared back at him.

I'm a mess, he thought, dismayed at his disheveled appearance. His face was dirty and his clothes felt like they were sticking to his body. When he tried to stand, dizziness washed over him and he slumped to the floor. He crawled out of the closet and over to his mattress. A piece of broken furniture was sitting on top of the mattress and Jason reached over and weakly pushed it off. He climbed onto what was left of his bed and lay down.

He thought about Pookie and glanced at his closet. *Pookie's dead and the boy buried him in my closet*, he thought sadly. Jason wondered if he'd ever be able to force himself to go inside the closet again. He didn't think so.

He felt dead inside. How long had he been in his room? It felt like days had passed since he first stepped through that door. He wondered if it was still locked, but felt too weak to go and see. Besides, even if the door was unlocked, he couldn't leave here without his dad's permission.

I'm hungry," he whimpered, rolling over so that his back was to the door. "Don't let me die in here."

His thoughts returned to the boy in the mirror and he pushed himself up into a sitting position. His eyes retraced the boy's steps around his room, stopping to rest on certain objects that had once held meaning for him. It was hard for him to believe that the broken remnants were all that remained.

Nothing has been left alive in here, he thought. Nothing has been left alive-- except me. Everything is dead; including Pookie.

Feeling broken and dejected, his body weak from lack of nourishment, Jason slowly stood up and stumbled towards his closet door. He looked in the mirror.

Where are you? Why don't you come out so I don't have to stay here alone?

But it was his mouth that moved, his lips that were forming the words. The boy was gone. Jason looked at himself. His face was pale and he had dark smudges beneath his eyes. And, when he looked down, he was embarrassed when he saw a large stain on the front of his pants.

Hell, I've pissed myself, he thought disgustedly. He wanted to change his pants, but when he looked around he knew that he didn't have any clean clothes to change into. At least, not anymore. He stood in front of the mirror wishing the boy would come back; wishing he was here to tell him what to do.

Finally, Jason had to admit to himself that the boy wasn't coming back. And, this realization made the loneliness more unbearable. He asked the mirror: "Where is he; where has he gone? Wherever it is, I hope it's a better place than here." Reluctantly, Jason left the mirror and went back to the mattress, sat down and waited....

Hours later, he heard a noise outside his door. He watched as the door swung open and his dad entered. His father walked over to him and stood, looking down at him.

"I hope this taught you a lesson," he said, shaking his finger in Jason's face. "Don't ever try and embarrass me again."

Jason tried to reply, but his throat felt like sandpaper. He had to swallow a couple of times before he finally managed to croak, "No, sir. I won't do that again. I promise."

"Good. Now I want you to get in that bathroom and clean up. It's almost time for supper." He sniffed the air and gave Jason a disapproving look. "You smell terrible," he laughed, pointing to the front of Jason's pants. "Jason you're worse than Nicky. Maybe we should get you a diaper, too. Imagine, a big boy like you...."

His dad's taunting made Jason cringe and he looked guiltily at his pants. He wanted to tell his dad that it wasn't him that had wet himself--it was the strange boy. He had done it! He had pissed his pants and then, when Jason was asleep, had changed clothes with him. Jason wanted to tell his dad about the boy in the mirror, but held back. His dad would probably think that he was trying to make excuses and might change his mind about letting him come out of his room. Jason kept quiet.

After his father had left, Jason walked over to the mirror. He stared at his reflection. "It wasn't me that pissed myself or sucked my thumb," he said scornfully. "It was you."

When the boy didn't reappear, Jason left his room, walked down the hall to the bathroom and went inside. He locked the door. Stripping off his dirty clothes, he wondered what he was going to wear when he had finished his bath. It reminded him of the time the lady had come and taken him away to that other strange house. When he had finished undressing and was standing naked beside the tub, he looked down at his body. He felt light, as if he were now weightless.

I wonder if I'm dead and I've turned into a ghost? He pinched himself but he didn't feel anything. Frightened, he pinched himself again. This time, much harder and felt a small twinge in his arm. *No*, he decided, *I'm not a ghost*. He looked at the red mark on his arm. *If I were a ghost, Dad would have noticed, wouldn't he? Dad wouldn't waste his time talking to me if I were dead.*

Jason leaned over and turned on the hot water full blast, breathing in the clouds of steam rising up out of the tub. When he had added enough cold water to prevent him from getting scalded, Jason lowered himself slowly into the water until only his face was left exposed. The hot water felt so good that he couldn't resist letting out a long sigh of pleasure. His body began to relax and he felt the tension leave his muscles. First his toes relaxed, then his legs, until finally, his whole body felt like a warm, spineless jellyfish. He stayed, stretched out in the tub until the water began to cool. Then he reluctantly sat up and reached for the soap.

Jason began to meticulously scrub every inch of his skin to make sure that he didn't miss one speck of dirt. No one must ever know how dirty he had been. When he had finished with the outside of his body, he wished that there was some way he could scrub inside him, too. He felt that the filth he had collected in there was much worse than what had been visible on the outside of him.

If I could just turn myself inside out, I could get completely clean. However, he knew that it was impossible to clean his soul with soap and water so instead, concentrated on his hair. He washed and rinsed it three times before he was satisfied.

When he was done bathing, Jason pulled the plug and climbed out of the tub. He dried himself and looked around for something to wear. He couldn't very well come downstairs wrapped in a towel. Wondering how he was going to solve his problem, Jason went over to the door and opened it a crack. He struck his head around the corner. Where was his mom? She'd know what to do. Just as he was thinking about calling her, his eyes spied a pile of clothes sitting on the floor outside the door. Holding his towel in front of him, Jason reached down and pulled them inside.

The clothes were new and still had price tags pinned to the material. *I guess Mom has been shopping for me*, he thought, putting on the new clothes. He didn't bother ripping off the price tags. He didn't care what he looked like; he just didn't care anymore.

After he had finished dressing, he dared to look in the mirror. For a second, Jason thought he saw the strange boy staring back at him but, when he looked again, it was only his own reflection. Jason continued to stare into the mirror, glad that he was real-- that he hadn't turned into a ghost.

His family was seated at the table, eating supper, when he came into the kitchen. Jason glanced at his father, expecting him to say something about coming in late for supper, but his dad never looked up from his plate.

In fact, no one looked at him, as he slid into his chair-- not even Becky. His mom silently reached for his plate, loaded it with food and handed it to him. He was glad that she had filled his plate for him because he didn't think that he would have had the nerve to break the silence around him, by asking them to pass him the food.

Jason stared at this plate, trying to remember the last time he had eaten.

I didn't have breakfast that morning and I forgot to bring my lunch. I didn't eat at the zoo. How long was I locked in my room? He was afraid to ask. He scooped up some potatoes with his fork. But when he put them in his mouth and tried to chew, his stomach churned and he couldn't swallow. Jason took a sip of water, trying to wash the food down. This wasn't going to be easy. Maybe he wasn't hungry, after all.

He was about to set down his fork and ask if he could be excused, when he looked up he saw that his dad was watching him. the look on his father's face frightened Jason and he lifted another forkful of potatoes to his mouth. Throughout the rest of the meal, Jason continued to force himself to eat. He would chew each mouthful until it had turned to mush and then, would take a drink of water so that the food would slide down his throat.

Thank God Mom didn't give me too much, he thought, staring at the food remaining on his plate. He persisted, and when he looked down again, his plate was empty. He set his knife and fork on his plate and waited for his dad to tell them they could go.

"I've written you a note for school explaining your absence," his father said to him. "If anyone asks you why you were away, tell them you had the flu."

"Yes."

"Yes, what?"

"Yes, sir," replied Jason. "I'll tell them I had the flu."

"That's better." His dad wiped his lips with the corner of his napkin and pushed back his chair. "It's time you learned who's boss around here and started showing a little respect for authority. I should have put my foot down a long time ago." He turned his head and looked at his wife. "Just imagine, Linda, this little jerk thought he could run away, worry us half to death, and saunter in, as if nothing had happened. I guess we showed him a thing or two."

Jason stared at his mother. Did she help his dad wreck his room? This last act of betrayal left him reeling and he sat in his chair, barely listening to what his dad was saying.

"...and until we get your room refinished, you can sleep in the spare room in the basement."

Jason waited until everyone left the table before he pushed back his chair and stood up. He had seen his father go into the living room and Jason thought that he was probably stretched out on the sofa reading his paper. Becky was helping his mom clean off the table. His mother came over to him and picked up his plate. She squeezed his shoulder on the way back to the sink. Jason flinched. He didn't ever want her touching him again.

Traitor, he thought, his eyes filled with hate, as he watched her a few moments, before leaving the kitchen.

Jason went downstairs to his new room. He flipped on the light and looked around. *Guess, it'll have to do*, he thought. Then, he turned off the light and felt his way through the darkness over to the bed. He sat down on the edge and stared into the darkness, thinking.

He felt far away-- from life; from his family. His world was filled with blackness and he knew that now, he would never have a problem escaping to the grey room with the winding staircase again. Because now, his mind would take him there whenever he chose to go and no one would ever be able to bring him back. And, the next time he went, he just might close and lock the little wooden door leading back to this world.

He felt himself being drawn towards the blackness and he welcomed the journey.

CHAPTER X

For the next three days, Jason went through the routine of living as if he had been programmed. Each morning he was up before the alarm went off, dressed, and ready for breakfast by exactly 7:30 a.m. After eating, he would go to the bathroom, brush his teeth, put on his jacket, and head for the bus stop. After school, he would come home, do his chores, eat supper, do his homework and go to bed.

Only when he was safe in bed did his routine vary. He would sometimes explore the grey room, starting with the staircase. Other times, he would just lie back and stare up at the ceiling-- his mind blank.

At school, he never spoke to anyone, unless they spoke to him first, and then, he would answer with a polite "Yes" or "No." If a teacher asked him a question in class, Jason answered as briefly as possible and then, would sit quietly at his desk until the period was over. He caused no trouble; got into no fights-- either on the bus or at school-- and talked to no one at home, unless it was his father who spoke to him. Then Jason would politely and quietly answer him, and then fall silent again.

When he went to Math class, Jason made a point of being the first one to put his homework on Mr. White's desk. He also made a point of staying out of Mr. White's way as much as possible. He would be one of the first to arrive at class, so he could be in his seat before his teacher entered the room. Under no circumstances was he going to give Mr. White any reason to ask him to stay after school again. And, when class started, Jason would slouch down in his desk, out of Mr. White's sight, and stay in that position until he heard the buzzer, signaling the end of the period.

Jason had been afraid to go back to school; afraid that the other kids would ask about his "disappearance" or about his picture in the newspaper. But after three days had passed and no one had said anything to him, his fear turned into indignation. Didn't anyone even care that he had been away? Maybe kidnapped? He wondered if they would have cared if he had been killed. From the way everyone was acting, it was as if they didn't give a shit if he was alive or dead. He felt more alone now than he had ever felt in his life.

In an attempt to escape the loneliness, Jason retreated into the fantasy world he had created. He lost himself in his daydreams and would return to reality only if one of his teachers asked him a question. But now, he was prepared for their sudden intrusions into his life. If he was approached, he would politely ask his teacher to repeat the question and then turn to his notes in front of him. If he knew the answer, he would state it immediately. If he didn't he would shuffle his notes, scratch his head, and apologize for having missed some vital clue that led him astray. His respectful manner, coupled with his apparently sincere effort to correct his shortcomings, worked every time. His teachers wouldn't question him further, and he could return to his daydream, undisturbed, for the remainder of the class.

So far, his scheme worked perfectly, and none of them had wised-up to the fact that, for the better part of each class, Jason was far away. He had no difficulty retreating into his fantasy world, but returning was starting to pose a problem. It was as if his mind was beginning to rebel whenever he tried to return to reality. He had to fight to regain possession of his mind and these battles left him drained and irritable. But no matter the risk involved, he needed this method of escape. However, he also knew that someday, he would cease his struggle and never return.

Thus, he finished the week and had only forty minutes left in class before school would be over for the weekend, when he looked up from his desk and saw that Mr. White was looking at him. It made Jason nervous and he tried to hide behind the girl in front of him by slumping down and bending his head. However, even when he was sure that he was completely shielded from his teacher's prying eyes, his uneasiness remained. Why was

Mr. White looking at him? Jason tried to think of reasons for his teacher's sudden interest, and mentally ticked off a list of possible causes: Homework done-- check; in class on time-- check; answered that question-- check. He couldn't think of one single reason to explain why his teacher was staring at him.

Suddenly, a thought occurred to him: Maybe Mr. White was going to ask him to stay after class again. Well, if he did, too bad!

I don't want to talk to him. Why can't he mind his own business and leave me alone? He couldn't help me before, and he can't help me now: No one can! Besides, I don't want his help, because I finally have everything under control. Don't mess it up now, he begged, *just leave me alone.*

Jason wanted to be left alone, left to enjoy his fantasies in peace. He knew that he could no longer cope with the pain and disillusionment that filled his life. In his dream world, he was master of his fate; he was the one to decide what would happen to him. He had worked hard to build himself the perfect world-- a world where his dad couldn't enter. And now, that world was being threatened by Mr. White. For if his teacher was to somehow breech those walls, Jason knew his world would crumble, leaving him once again at the mercy of his father.

His anxiety increased as the minutes passed and he flinched when the buzzer finally sounded. It was a few moments before his vision cleared and he was able to see around him. The rest of his classmates were clearing off their desks and he hurried to do the same. He picked up his books and his pencil and shoved them in his knapsack. Then he followed the crowd out of the room and down the hall, stopping at his locker to pick up his coat. When he was finished in his locker he inserted the lock, gave the dial a spin, and headed down the hall leading to the exit.

The pressure he had felt all week began to subside as he neared the door. He thought about the weekend ahead. No homework, and his dad was going to be gone the entire weekend.

Maybe things are going to come together for me after all, he thought, as he approached the door.

A group of kids were standing around the door, laughing and chatting, as they made plans for the weekend. For a moment, Jason hesitated. He wanted to join the happy group; wanted to share their happiness, but he resisted the urge.

118

I don't belong and they don't want me, he told himself, drawing up straight and walking towards the group; his eyes straight ahead. The kids parted to let him pass and he walked to the door. But, before he could push it open, he heard someone call his name.

"Jason!" Hey, Jason! Wait."

Jason's heart sank. He recognized that voice. It belonged to Mr. White. Slowly, Jason turned around and saw his teacher running towards him.

"Hey Jason," he called. "Can you wait for a minute? I've got to talk to you."

The other kids looked at him, their eyes filled with curiosity, as Jason stood in the middle of them, waiting for his teacher.

Now what have I done? he thought, trying to recall everything that happened during the last four days.

Mr. White was out of breath by the time he reached him. He stood beside Jason, breathing heavily. "Let's go outside," he said to Jason.

They left the school together and walked down the cement steps. Jason followed him across the schoolyard to a bench. Mr. White sat down and indicated with his hand that he wanted Jason to join him. Jason sat down on the other end of the bench, trying to put as much distance between Mr. White and him as he could, without appearing rude.

"I need to talk with you," Mr. White said. "Can you spare a few minutes, or do you have to catch your bus right away?"

Suspicious about his teacher's motives for calling him aside, Jason hesitated before he replied. "I guess I can stay a few minutes, but I don't want to miss my bus."

"Great!" replied Mr. White enthusiastically. "I won't keep you long. I just wanted to tell you how glad we are that you're back safe and sound. We were worried when we read that article about you in the newspaper. What happened? Did you run away?"

So, someone had noticed his absence. Jason didn't know whether he should be relieved that at least they had noticed his absence, or be dismayed that he was now being questioned about it. Jason remembered his dad's warning. His teacher's inquisitiveness made him nervous. If he was so concerned about what had happened to him, why did he wait until now to say something? Was Mr. White trying to get him to break his promise to his father, trying to get him in trouble again?

If it hadn't been for you, Jason thought, *I wouldn't have run away. It's all your fault.* However, he couldn't tell his teacher this without revealing to him that he had run away from home.

Afraid, Jason replied, "I didn't run away. Who told you I ran away? I stayed at a friend's place overnight and forgot to tell my parents. That's all. It was a very inconsiderate thing for me to do, but I learned my lesson. Yes, I learned my lesson and I won't ever do that again."

"Oh...," said Mr. White, leaning back against the bench and studying him. "I see. Well, I guess all of us have forgotten to do something important at least once in our lives. The main thing is that you're back. Your mom and dad must have been pretty worried."

"Yeah."

"You certainly have had a rough time of it this past two weeks," continued Mr. White. "You probably got in trouble with your folks and then, you came down with the flu. I bet you're glad that the weekend is finally here, so you can just stretch out and veg."

"I didn't say that I got in trouble when I got home," replied Jason, immediately on the defensive. He wondered if his teacher suspected something.

"No, you didn't, but I just assumed that your parents must have been pretty upset when you showed up. I know if you were my kid, I'd have been so worried, that when you came home, I'd have made sure that you were all right, and then, I'd have probably sent you to your room to reflect on the error of your ways."

"That's what Dad did," said Jason, taking a deep swallow. "He sent me to my room." He felt a lump inside his throat. Why did Mr. White have to mention his "room" when he was trying so hard to forget about it? Why was he being so mean? Jason had to force himself to speak to his teacher, again. "Yes, he continued, "Like I said before, it was a stupid thing to do and I deserved to be punished. But, it won't happen again; it'll never happen again!"

Mr. White looked at him, surprised by the tone of his voice. "Well yes, I imagine you've learned your lesson, but I want you to know that you're not the only one who has ever made a mistake. We all have..." He paused, and then added: "As long as we learn from our mistakes, things can sometimes work out for the best in the long run. Anyway, I won't keep you. I just wanted to tell you that I'm glad to have you back in class and back to your old self again."

"I'll never be my 'old self' again," replied Jason coldly.

"Oh, I know it's difficult when parents lay down the law from time to time, but that's what parents are for. Take my Mom, for example. Here I am-- a grown man-- and she still gets after me to wear clean underwear, in case I'm ever in an accident and end up in the hospital. Jason, even if your parents did get mad at you, It's not the end of the world; it doesn't mean that they don't love you."

Jason lifted his eyes and stared at his teacher. He couldn't believe that Mr. White could be so stupid! How could he talk about it not being the end of the world or say that his parents loved him? He wasn't there; he hadn't seen his room-- or the strange boy in the mirror.

For once, Jason didn't care what his dad would say, or even, that by talking to his teacher, he might disclose his "secret" place. He had to set Mr. White straight. He had to tell someone how he really felt.

"I told you," he repeated, "I'll never be the same again."

"Jason, I don't understand. Are you in some kind of trouble at home?"

"That's my whole problem!" Jason replied sarcastically. "Nobody understands!" Pookie's dead! Do you hear me? He's dead, dead, dead...." His voice trailed off, and he sat on the bench, gasping for air. "There's nothing you or anyone else can do that will make him alive again. "I've lost him forever," he wailed.

Jason didn't wait for Mr. White to reply. He rose from the bench, walked over to the fence and leaned against the wire. Why had he broken down? He had nearly told his teacher about his room and the consequences would have been devastating. He had to escape. The blackness was beginning to descend but Jason didn't want to use this method to get away. Not in front of his teacher.

Mr. White got off the bench and came over to where he was standing. "Are you all right?" he asked, putting his hand on Jason's shoulder.

Jason shook his hand off and returned to the bench to sit down. "I have to get control," he said, fighting against the darkness swirling around him. He felt faint and his head began to spin. by the time his teacher came back and sat down, Jason was too weak to move. Afraid that Mr. White might try to touch him again, Jason drew his knees up to his chin and sat there shivering. He didn't want anyone to ever touch him again.

Maybe his teacher had read his mind, because he kept his hands in his lap and sat there, quietly watching him. When minutes had passed and Mr. White still remained quietly sitting beside him, Jason wondered if his teacher was waiting for him to begin the conversation again.

Finally, Jason couldn't stand the silence any longer and blurted, "You know something, Mr. White? This world stinks. I try and be the man my Dad and Grandpa expect me to be, but no way; I always screw up. I can't do anything right and I'm no good. Can you understand? I'm no good!" Hearing no response to his disclosure, Jason continued, "If you don't believe me, just look around. I don't have any friends and none of the kids like me. Everyone is just waiting for me to make a mistake so they can jump on me. And," he added, "if I dropped dead tomorrow, no one would even know I was gone. Life would just go on as usual--minus Jason!"

"You're wrong Jason-- terribly, terribly wrong," his teacher replied.

Jason saw him reach in his back pocket and pull out a handkerchief. Mr. White blew his nose and wiped his eyes. Jason didn't understand. Was Mr. White crying?

"Wrong?" Jason asked softly.

"Yes, wrong," said Mr. White, blowing his nose once more before he stuffed his handkerchief back into his pants pocket. "I care what happens to you and I'd miss you if you were gone. And, I wouldn't be the only one either; a lot of people would be devastated, if anything happened to you."

Jason looked at the tears in the corner of his teacher's eyes. Why was he crying? Was it because of him? No. Jason dismissed the thought. He must have an allergy, thought Jason. Still.... Confused, Jason dropped his gaze and looked at his feet. His teacher sounded sincere; sounded like he did, in fact, care, but Jason knew that unless he told Mr. White everything, he wouldn't be able to know for sure. And, he couldn't do that.

He had already said too much and if he continued this conversation any longer, he would end up telling Mr. White everything about Pookie, his room-- his dad. If he opened up any further, he would be swept away by the flood of emotions that would be released. His whole being would be torn up by the roots and he'd be lost forever. Jason stood up and looked down at his teacher.

"I have to go now," he said, "or I'll miss the bus. I don't want my Mom to worry."

"Okay," Mr. White replied, "but before you go, do you have plans for tomorrow?"

"Why?"

"Because I thought if you weren't doing anything tomorrow, you might want to drop in for a while at our Youth Centre."

"Yes," said Mr. White, pointing to a large wooden structure across the street. "It's a place where kids can come Thursday evenings and Saturday afternoons, when they want to get together, or just want to come and unwind. We have a small basketball court along with a large craft room. There's lots of other stuff there, too. Mrs. Miller and I run the centre Saturday afternoons so, if you want to come, I'd be there to show you around."

"Who's Mrs. Miller?" asked Jason, trying not to appear too interested. "Is she another teacher?"

"No," he replied, "Beth Miller is a volunteer and a good friend of mine. I couldn't run the place without her support. She's a busy lady and I don't know how she manages to find time to give us a hand, but I'm glad she has. You should meet her. Beth's an amazing lady."

"Doesn't she have a husband and kids to look after at home?" Jason asked. He couldn't imagine his mother working as a volunteer.

"Oh sure, she has a family. In fact, in addition to her husband, she has four teenagers at home, but that doesn't stop her from also holding down a full time job as an Industrial Accountant, as well as finding time to work at the centre. Like I said, she's quite the lady."

"Doesn't her husband mind her gallivanting about?" Jason asked skeptically. "I mean, doesn't he want her to be home when he gets home?"

"Well, first off, I wouldn't say that Beth 'gallivants' around, and to answer your second question, no, Louis doesn't mind her working-- not as an accountant or as a volunteer down here with us. In fact, whenever he has the time, he comes down and gives us a hand."

Jason looked at his teacher, trying to see if Mr. White was pulling his leg. This Mrs. Miller didn't sound like any women he knew. Oh sure, some of the teachers at his school were women, but Jason always assumed that they worked there because their families need the money. Other than them, the only other women Jason knew were his mother and grandmother. And, they didn't work or volunteer their time, anywhere. Intrigued, he asked his teacher, "Does Mrs. Miller get paid for helping you?"

"No. I told you, she's a volunteer. We don't get paid but," and he winked at Jason, "we have lots of fun."

Interesting, very interesting, thought Jason, turning and walking away.

Kids were already getting on the bus when he arrived, but this time, Jason waited his turn, taking care not to push anyone, as he made his way to the back of the bus. All the way home, he thought about his conversation with Mr. White. *Youth Centre huh? I wonder what that Mrs. Miller is really like?* He tried to picture her and came up with a tall, heavy lady-- sort of a cross between Mrs. M, his Language teacher, and Arnold Schwarzenegger. The image definitely didn't look anything like his mom! Besides, his mom wouldn't work as a volunteer. His dad wouldn't allow it.

Maybe, his dad would let her work if they needed the money, but, so far, that had never happened and Jason didn't think that his mother would ever have to go to work. And, as for her volunteering somewhere, under the present circumstances, that was out too. He recalled the time he had asked her to come with his class as a chaperone on one of their field trips. Before she could even reply, his dad had butted in and said no, that she was too busy at home to go gallivanting around the country side with a bunch of kids. End of discussion.

Jason had never again asked her to come as a chaperone on a school trip. The parents who accompanied them were always other kids' parents, never his own.

CHAPTER XI

Jason sensed the change in the house the moment he walked through the door. Taking off his jacket, he heard Nicky in the kitchen, giggling and squealing with happiness, and Becky singing in the living room. Pounding on the piano, her voice echoing throughout the house, Jason listened to his younger sister as she sang: "This old man, he played one...." It took a few minutes for him to realize the reason-- his dad wouldn't be coming home tonight. When he spotted his mother coming out of the bathroom, Jason followed her into the kitchen.

She bent down and tickled Nicky under the chin and his little brother's face broke into a delighted grin. Jason smiled, too. It was nice seeing his mom happy for a change. He hadn't realized it before, but when she smiled, she was really pretty. He would have liked to have continued to watch her, unobserved, but when she left Nicky, she saw him standing in the doorway.

"Hi, how was school today?" she asked, giving him a smile.

Her smile made Jason look at her in a new light. She seemed so young-- so alive. And, her words were soft. They seemed to whisper, like willows rustling in an evening breeze. Seeing her like this made him wish his dad would never return. When he had gone, he had taken all the tension and all the other bad feelings with him, leaving behind only peace and happiness.

"Well?" she said, waiting for him to reply.

"Oh," he answered, "school was okay. Boring as ever. But, I survived."

"You weren't on the bus," said Becky, coming up behind him. "I thought maybe you ran away again."

"Hush Becky," his mom scolded. "Jason isn't going to run away again."

Jason glared at his sister and she stuck her tongue out at him. That did it. No one was going to stick their tongue out at him and get away with it. He stepped forward, shaking his fist in her face.

"Stop it!" Both of you," said his mother, stepping in between them. "Let's just try and get along for a change, shall we? Everything's going great, so try not to spoil it."

"Dumb kid," said Jason, defending himself. "Why doesn't she mind her own business for a change?"

"Please, Jason...," his mother pleaded.

Jason didn't want to be the one to shatter the tenuous peace around him, so he resisted the urge to go over and wipe off the smirk on Becky's face-- with his fist.

"Supper's ready," said his mom, "so if you guys are hungry, go wash up and put Nicky in his highchair. I'll put the stuff on the table." She went over to the stove and came back with a tray piled with fish and chips.

"Can I sit in Dad's place?" Jason asked, plopping Nicky into his chair and ignoring his mother's suggestion about washing up.

"I wish you wouldn't," she replied softly.

A strange look had come across her face and Jason felt like kicking himself. Why had he asked to sit in his dad's place? He didn't really want to sit there in the first place. He glared over at Becky. It was her fault. If she hadn't made him angry, he wouldn't have asked. "Sorry," he muttered, taking his own seat at the table.

They ate supper early that evening. In fact, it was only a little after 4:30 when he forked the last piece of fish off his plate and popped it into his mouth. With his father gone, their whole rigid routine had relaxed-- they ate what they wanted-- when they wanted.

I wish we could do this more often, thought Jason, as he pushed back his chair and drank the last of his milk.

He was stuffed and couldn't remember the last time he had eaten so much or been so hungry. Usually, he had to force himself to eat, but tonight, he had finished off two platefuls of fish and chips and could have eaten more, if there had been any left. And, it appeared that the rest of his family shared his appetite, because when he looked at the tray, only a single French fry remained.

Nicky was having a great time with his French fries and ketchup. It appeared to Jason like his little brother was more interested in seeing how much of a mess he could make, than in eating. His face, hair, and arms were covered with red, sticky globs of ketchup. And somehow, he had even managed to get ketchup on the back of his shirt. Jason sat there, wondering how he could have achieved this seemingly impossible feat.

He looks like he's been in an accident, thought Jason, as he watched Nicky happily mash his fish into a pulp. *I guess he must be full, too.*

Jason was about to leave the table and go to his room when he remembered the Youth Centre. "Hey Mom," he said, "my Math teacher asked if I'd like to come to his Youth Centre tomorrow afternoon. Can I go? Before she could reply, he glared at Becky and said: "That's why I missed the first bus, stupid. Mr. White kept me after school."

Instead of being sorry that she had wrongly accused him of trying to run away again, it seemed to Jason like his sister was just itching for a fight. She stuck her tongue out at him again and giggled.

Boy, thought Jason, *Let Dad go away for a day, and these women think they own the place. No respect at all.* "Someday, Becky," he muttered softly, so that his mother wouldn't hear, "you better watch out. I won't forget."

"What's this Youth Centre?" his mother asked.

Jason ignored his sister's silent taunting and hurried to explain. "It's a place where kids can get together and have some fun. Mr. White and another volunteer run it every Thursday and Saturday." He walked over to his mother's chair and stood looking down at her. "Mr. White stopped me after school and told me all about it. I thought that I might like to go and check it out."

A guarded look came over his mom's face. "Is that all you two talked about? Just about this Centre?" she asked nervously. "I mean, you didn't say anything... you know... about what happened?"

It was the first time his family had made any reference to his running away and subsequent punishment, except for Becky tonight. Jason felt a deep, burning anger erupt inside of him. "No, he replied harshly, "I didn't say anything about Dad. Give me a break, Mom! I'm not that stupid."

"I don't think you're stupid, Jason," she said. "I just worry about you lately, and... you know what a temper your father has. I don't want you to get into any more trouble."

Jason shuffled his feet, his eyes never leaving her face. "I won't get into any more trouble," he mimicked. Can I go, or can't I?"

"Oh Jason, I don't know. What would your Dad say?"

"Come off it, Mom. You and I both know what he'd say. He wouldn't let me. But, he's not going to be home until Sunday night and I'll be going tomorrow. Dad won't find out, if no one tells him." He turned his head and glared at Becky. This time, instead of sticking her tongue out at him, Becky slowly shook her head.

"No, I won't tell," she quietly replied.

"See, Mom, there's nothing to worry about. Dad will never know."

"Well..., I guess it'll be okay... but make sure your chores are done before you go. I just hope your Dad doesn't decide to come home early...." Her voice trailed off. She frowned.

"He won't. Don't worry," Jason assured her. He picked up his plate and walked over to the sink. "Know something Mom?" he said over his shoulder. "I think you worry too much all the time, about what Dad's going to say." He headed towards the basement steps, but his mother stopped him.

"Your old room is ready," she said. "I hope you're going to like it."

Jason knew he should have been prepared for this moment, but he wasn't. He walked over to the staircase and stared up at the landing. The thought of climbing those steps and returning to the scene of his punishment sickened him. His room flashed before his eyes. The broken furniture, the torn clothes, Pookie mutilated. How could he go back in there, without, once again, reliving those terrible hours?

I can't do it, he thought, turning away and once more, heading towards the basement steps.

His mother blocked his retreat. She came to him and said: "It's okay, Jason. Your room is as good as new. I even bought you a new clock-radio. Go on...."

Becky had joined them and Jason didn't want her to think that he was afraid. That he was a coward. He forced himself to climb the stairs... one step at a time... until he reached the landing. He looked down. His mom and sister were watching him. He started down the hallway like a man being led to his execution. He walked-- his body shaking -- his hands trembling. Finally, he reached the door to his room. Sweat poured down his face.

He turned the doorknob and walked inside.

His mind could have accepted the destruction; it couldn't accept this.

Everything had been replaced. Nothing of the damage remained.

A new bed was standing where his old one had been. A new night table held the new clock-radio his mother had mentioned. The tattered curtains were gone and in their place, crisp, new curtains hung in front of the window. The door to his closet was open and Jason saw a row of new clothes hanging from the rod stretching the length of the closet.

Jason couldn't accept this new sterile environment. This wasn't his room. It was as if he was intruding on someone else's domain. That he was the stranger in these strange alien surroundings. He blinked, trying to make this facade disappear. But, when he looked again, the newness stretched before him. His eyes roamed over the room once more. The dresser, night table, bed, and book case-- they weren't his. It was too new.

Too different. *Pookie wouldn't believe this, either.*

Jason sadly walked over to his night table. He sat on his bed and ran his hand over the varnished surface, trying not to think about how Pookie had died. It was too painful.

His raccoon would never be coming back; would never share his dreams with him; would never share his sorrows. Depressed, Jason talked to himself. "Pookie wouldn't like it here, anyway," he said aloud. "Pookie's glad he's not around to see this shit. He's gone-- but I'm still here." He buried his face in his hands and sobbed.

"I don't care!" he cried out in anguish. "Pookie should be here, too. I miss him. I don't want to stay here alone." His tears streamed down his cheeks, as Jason vented his feelings. His little raccoon should be sitting on top of his night table. That's where he belonged -- not in some stupid paper bag, stuffed into the back of his closet.

He raised his head. That's when he spotted it-- sitting on the lower shelf of his bookcase.

Jason was flabbergasted, and stared with loathing at this intruder.

Mom... he thought. *Mom must have bought it!* Jason reached over and picked up the new stuffed raccoon, stroking its soft grey fur. It was slightly larger than Pookie and its fur was soft and fluffy, not worn and scruffy like Pookie's. Pookie had a number of bald spots and the rest of his body was somewhat threadbare, too, as a result of the frequent hugging he had endured over the years.

Jason glared into the impostor's big, brown eyes, and thought he saw it wink at him. He hated it! "You're not Pookie!" he screamed in rage, hurling it across the room. "You'll never take Pookie's place; never! Do you hear me? Never!" The walls seemed to echo his words.

How could Mom have done such a terrible thing to me? he ranted silently. *Did she think that if she just went out and bought a new raccoon, everything would suddenly be okay? Was that it? Well, she was wrong! If Dad killed me, Mom, would you go out and buy a new Jason and set him in this new room and think that everything's okay now? Well, maybe you should have?*

Jason jumped off his bed and ran over to where the stuffed animal lay. He gave it a vicious kick, sending it flying across the room. It landed underneath his window and he hurried over and picked it up by the tail. With his free hand, Jason pushed open the window and hurled the impostor outside, an unvoiced scream trapped in his throat: *Get out of here, you lousy fake!* He thought he had shouted again, but only his inner ears rang with unuttered fury. Jason stood rigidly, his fists clenched, watching the raccoon as it fell to the cement below. When it hit the ground and bounced into the gutter, Jason's lips twisted in a smile of satisfaction that did not light his dull eyes. He slammed shut his window and went back to his bed, stretched out, and stared up at the ceiling. He was thinking about how he was going to get even with his mother, when he heard his door open. Becky came in and walked over to the bed.

"Hi, Jason," she said happily, looking around his room.

"What the hell do you want?" he snarled. "Hasn't anyone ever told you that you're supposed to knock before coming into someone's room?"

"I'm sorry," she apologized. "I only wanted to talk to you. I wanted to see if you liked your room. And I thought I heard you hollering a few minutes ago." She nervously chewed on her fingernails, waiting for him to reply.

"Oh," he answered sarcastically. "I thought maybe you came in here so that you could stick out that fat tongue of yours at me."

"I'm sorry. I didn't mean to make you mad."

"Well, you have. So talk, and get the hell out of here."

Becky sat down on the edge of his bed. "What's the matter with you?" she asked, her blue eyes wide and somber. "Ever since you came back, you never talk to anybody and you won't play with me anymore. You're always mad-- even at Nicky, sometimes. Don't you like us anymore?"

Jason fought to keep from exploding. His sister's accusations infuriated him. Who the hell did she think she was, coming in here and telling him that he was always mad? If he got mad, he had a lot of good reasons. He felt like picking her up and throwing her out the window, too. There wasn't anything wrong with him; it was them-- always on his case. Always doing something to make his life miserable. He didn't have a problem before she came into his room.

Becky didn't seem to realize how close she was to joining the raccoon on the cement outside and prattled on about how she had helped fix up his room. "See," she said, pointing to the bookcase, "I picked that out myself. Mom let me."

"Get lost, Becky, he muttered, his teeth clenched together. "Just get the hell out of here and leave me alone. If I have a problem, it's because I have to put up with you. You're always bugging me. Now, if you're finished, get out. Now!" He made a motion of getting up.

Becky looked heartbroken. She slowly backed away and her eyes filled with tears. "Jason?" she pleaded, but he ignored her and rolled on his side, his back to her. When he heard the door close, he turned over. His sister was gone.

Jason thought about his sister, wondering why she had to come in his room when he was so angry.

It's her own fault if I got mad. Maybe after this, she'll leave me alone. He clasped his hands together on top of his chest and tried to forget about the events that had occurred the past few minutes. Gradually, his anger began to evaporate and he was able to think about other things.

I wonder if that Youth Centre is really such a great place? His thoughts raced with suspicion. Maybe his teacher had lied just so that he could entice him into coming. Maybe he had been set up.

Why had he bothered to ask his mom if he could go tomorrow, when he had no intention of falling into Mr. White's trap?

I don't belong at some stupid kids' place, he thought. I'm different than they are. They're just a bunch of sissies. I'm a man. Why had he told his teacher that he would come tomorrow?

Jason wondered what Mr. White would say if he failed to show up-- especially after he had sort of promised him that he would come and at least see what it was all about.

Maybe if I go once, he'll be satisfied and get off my case. I don't have to stay long, or do anything while I'm there-- just look around and then come home. Yes, he decided. *It'll be better for me to go for a while and check it out. That way, Mr. White will leave me alone.*

CHAPTER XII

Jason was up and dressed the following morning before the rest of his family. Usually, Becky always beat him downstairs Saturday mornings and he would find her plunked in front of the television watching cartoons. But not this morning. When Jason came downstairs, he found himself alone. He went into the kitchen and fixed some breakfast: cold cereal and toast.

When he had finished eating, he cleaned up his mess and gathered up the garbage bags from beneath the sink and in the bathroom. Outside, he stuffed the plastic bags in the trash cans behind the fence, and went to the garage to get the lawnmower.

It was early and the grass was still covered with dew, making it difficult to cut, and Jason had to continually stop, unplug the machine and clean the blades and inner housing before he finally finished. He stopped the engine and surveyed the lawn, trying to see if he had missed any patches. It looked alright. He pushed the mower back into the garage and went inside to wash up.

He went to the bathroom and scrubbed his hands, trying to get off the green stains. When only a few green smudges remained, he decided that the rest of the green would have to wear off. He went in the kitchen to find his mom. But, no one was around. Wondering where everyone was, he glanced at his watch. It was 10:30 a.m.

They must be up by now, he thought. He was about to go upstairs when he spotted a piece of paper stuck to the fridge. He walked over and read:

Jason

I've taken Becky and Nicky shopping. Have a good time at
your centre. Your breakfast is on the stove.

Love, Mom

Guess she didn't know that I've already eaten, Jason thought, going
over to the stove and lifting up the lid on the frying pan. Three dried-out
pancakes stared up at him. They might have tasted good a few hours ago,
but they didn't appeal to Jason now.

"We should have a dog; he grumbled, as he carried the pan over to the
garbage can and let the leftovers drop into the container. He went back
to the fridge and read the note again. His mother hadn't mentioned when
they would be coming back.

"Boy," he said aloud, staring at the note in front of him, "you sure
know when dad's not here. Everybody takes off." he thought that he
should let his mom know that he had left, so he turned over the paper and
scribbled a short message on the back.

He went up to his room to change.

When he came down, he knew that he still had an hour to kill before
he left for the centre. He went into the living room and pulled *Moby Dick*
from underneath the sofa and began to read. When he looked at his watch
again, it was almost noon.

Time to go, he thought, closing the book and putting it back in its
hiding place. He wanted to allow himself enough time to get there early
so that he wouldn't walk into a room full of kids who would probably stare
at him. He ran to the bathroom and checked his appearance. Satisfied that
no one could find fault with the way he was dressed, Jason went to the
porch and slipped on his runners and his jacket. He locked the house and
strolled down the sidewalk towards the bus stop.

When he arrived at the centre, all his plans of getting there early and
missing the crowd scattered like gust-blown leaves. A group of kids were
already standing outside the door, and Jason had to walk through the
gauntlet in order to get to the front door. The kids parted to let him pass.
He saw them stare at him in curiosity and his cheeks burned.

I shouldn't have come.

But, it was too late for him to change his mind. He couldn't stand the thought of facing them again. Throwing his shoulders back, Jason grabbed the door handle and went inside.

He stood just inside the door and looked around. "Okay, Mr. White," he muttered, "it looks like you've got yourself a captive audience. Now what?" When he couldn't see his teacher anywhere, he walked over to a bench and sat down. The same bunch of kids that he had seen outside were now in the room with him and he watched as they split into smaller groups and spread out in the room. They were laughing and talking as they greeted each new arrival. Jason wished that he could be part of their group, instead of sitting on the sidelines like a bump on a log.

Why am I always on the outside, looking in? he asked himself, wistfully. It would be nice to belong somewhere.

Just then, he heard his name being called. He looked up and saw Mr. White coming across the room.

"Jason... ah... there you are. I was hoping you'd be able to come today."

Jason waited until Mr. White was standing beside him before he replied. "Of course I came. I said I would, didn't I?"

"Well, I can't say I took you too seriously," his teacher said, cheerfully. "You did have a lot of things on your mind."

"Well, I'm here."

"And I'm glad that you are. Have you had a chance to look around?"

"Not much. I just came in, but this must be the large room you were talking about, yesterday," Jason replied. He scanned the room, his eyes pausing on the basketball court a few seconds, before he returned his gaze to his teacher's face. "It looks okay," he said.

His obvious lack of interest didn't seem to disturb his teacher in the least. "Come," he said to Jason, "There's lots more to see besides this room. I'll show you around- if you want."

"Sure," replied Jason.

Feigning indifference, Jason followed him as they toured the facility. His teacher gave a running commentary as they passed from one area to another. "Over here is the basketball court."

I can see that for myself.

"And in this room," said Mr. White opening the door, We have a pool table and other games."

135

I don't like to play pool. It's a stupid game, Jason thought, giving the room a quick glance and then backing out.

"Over here is our kitchen and down that little hallway," Mr. White pointed. "is the washrooms." Jason gave the kitchen a disinterested look.

I've already eaten, thank you.

"Oh, you have to see this," his teacher said, leading Jason to another door. "I've saved the best for last." He ushered Jason inside the room. "This is our craft room. Mrs. Miller's domain."

Jason looked around, trying to find the famous Mrs. Miller. He was curious to see what this woman actually looked like. He couldn't see her and he didn't want to ask where she was in case he gave Mr. White the impression that he was interested in her. So instead, he fixed his attention on a boy who was sitting at one of the tables. He had a bunch of stuff in front of him and as far as Jason could tell, the boy was building something. But he couldn't see what. Jason was just about to ask his teacher what the boy was building, when a girl came running up to them to tell Mr. White that he was wanted on the phone.

"Excuse me, Jason. I'll be right back. Why don't you look around 'til I get back.

Jason nodded, his eyes glued on the boy. What was he building? Jason could see pieces of wood, cloth and paper, spread out in front of him. As if in answer to his unspoken question, the boy held up a wooden frame. Something clicked inside Jason's head. He recognized that shape. The kid was building a model plane!

As if drawn by invisible hands, Jason found himself propelled forward, until he was standing across from the boy. He was intrigued. He had never before seen anyone building such a large model plane from scratch. Open-mouthed, he stood watching the boy's work. The boy didn't look up.

"We call this our mini-airport hangar," said Mr. White, coming up behind him.

Startled, Jason jumped. He had been so interested in watching the boy work, that he hadn't heard his teacher approach.

"Sorry," said Mr. White. "Didn't mean to startle you." He moved over and stood beside the boy. "But, like I was saying, a lot of kids have built some great model planes here. Take Paul here for example," Paul looked up and smiled. "He's built some beautiful models. Mrs. Miller is willing to teach anyone who's interested, how to build his own model." He ruffled Paul's hair and pointed to the table. "See all that stuff? Just basic materials. No fancy kits, here. But, from what I've seen come out of this room, the kids who have built their plans the old-fashioned way, have done a super job."

"Gee, that's great," exclaimed Jason enthusiastically. All his reserve flew out the window as he stared at the material in front of him.

"Do you build models, too?" his teacher asked. A shadow passed over Jason and his sudden enthusiasm was gone.

Jason hesitated. He could see the broken pieces of his model scattered across his floor. "I used to," he replied, his voice shaking, "but I don't anymore. My Dad says it's a waste of time."

"Well, I don't want to contradict your father, Jason, but, on that point, I'd have to say I don't agree. I think building these planes takes a lot of skill and hard work. In fact, I've seen kids spend six months on a model, before it was finished to their satisfaction."

"Six months?" said Jason, incredulously. The longest he had ever spent on a particular model was three weeks.

"Yes," Mr. White affirmed. "Ask Paul, here. He'll tell you that you can't build one of these overnight."

Paul looked up, nodded his head in agreement and went back to work.

Mr. White continued. "Paul had been working on that plane in front of him for over a month, and it'll be a long time yet, before it's ready to have the cloth stretched over the body."

How do you do it?" Jason asked. "I mean, how do you know what you're supposed to do next?"

Mr. White turned to Paul. "Should I explain it to him, or do you want to tell him?" he asked.

"You go ahead," said Paul. "I need to finish shaving this tail piece before I can go on to something else."

"Okay," Mr. White replied. "Paul has a manual to work from. It helps him to take one step at a time but it doesn't do the work for him. He has to do that himself. We have lots of manuals for various types of planes," he said, waving his hand in the direction of the shelf. "Over there. It's a shame that you don't build them anymore, considering how interested you appear to be. But, I won't push you. If you change your mind, just grab a manual and elbow a spot at the table. Mrs. Miller will give you a hand to get started."

"Thanks," said Jason, sitting down in the chair and watching Paul work. "Would it be okay if I stayed here and watched for a while?" Then, he said to Paul, "I won't get in your way.

"By all means," said his teacher. "If Paul doesn't mind you watching?" He looked at Paul.

Paul looked up and grinned. "Sure you can watch."

"Before I go, Jason, I just want to say one more thing to you." His teacher came over to him and stood looking down at him. "While you're at the Centre, you can pretty much do as you like, as long as it doesn't infringe on someone else's rights. The whole idea behind this place was to give kids a chance to get to know each other, away from school or home, and have fun. So, it's up to you. Feel free to watch or participate; the choice is yours."

Jason watched Mr. White walk towards the door. He called after him. "Mr. White, can you wait up for a minute?" His teacher stopped in the doorway and Jason hurried over to him.

"Mr. White," he asked, "before you go, can I ask you a question?"

"Sure. What is it?"

"Well, I know you'll probably think this is dumb, but does Mrs. Miller really know how to build model planes? I mean... you weren't teasing me, were you?"

"No. I wasn't teasing you. Mrs. Miller is a terrific instructor. Ask any of the kids here-- ask Paul-- he'll tell you. But, why do you ask?"

"Oh, no particular reason." Jason felt embarrassed and hoped his face wasn't turning red. "I was just curious. That's all. It seems like a strange thing for women to be able to do. I've never heard of a woman building model planes before."

"Well, Jason," he said, "I'll let you in on a little secret. Never underestimate Beth Miller's capabilities. That woman has more hidden talents than anyone I've ever met. She can probably best me in almost anything, except arm wrestling, and even then, I'm not sure, because I'm afraid to try." He smiled to himself and then looked at Jason. "Anything else you would like to know?" he asked. Jason shook his head. "Well then, I'll see you later." He left the room.

Jason walked back over to the table where Paul was sitting. He sat across from him and waited for Paul to say something. But, Paul didn't look up. Instead, he appeared to be concentrating on the manual on the table in front of him. It was as if Paul didn't know he was there. Jason watched him pick up his model and run a tape from the nose to the tail. Then, he picked up a knife and carefully shaved a fraction of a centimeter off the tail section. Jason sat there, watching him for over a half an hour before Paul set down his plane and looked up from the table. But, Jason hadn't minded. In fact, he was glad that Paul hadn't spoken to him; hadn't broken the peacefulness surrounding them. Paul flashed him a grin. "What's your name?" Paul asked.

"Jason."

"Well, Jason. As you already know, my name is Paul. And, in case you've been wondering why I've been ignoring you, I haven't. It's just that I'm at a tricky stage right now, and I don't want to screw up. Why is it that the instructions always make everything look so easy when in fact, the actual doing is hell? Hope you didn't mind?"

"No," Jason lied. Even though he had enjoyed watching Paul work, he had started to think that maybe Paul didn't want him around. He was glad that the misunderstanding had been cleared up. Paul's easy manner made him feel comfortable. He asked Paul about his model and told him that he had never seen anyone build this type of model before. He smiled and asked, "I hope you don't mind me watching?"

"Not at all," Paul replied. "Be my guest." He flipped the manual over and showed Jason the cover. "This is what it'll look like when I finish," he said.

Jason scanned the magazine. "Pretty nice," Jason replied, admiringly.

Paul opened the manual again and turned back to the page he was working on. "No matter how many times I read this instructions, I can never get my pieces to fit right the first time I try to put them together. So far, I've never managed to finish a plane without asking for Mrs. Miller's help. He smiled at Jason and added, "I guess I must be a slow learner, or something."

"Have you built a lot of planes?" Jason asked.

"Yes... well... no, not a lot, but I've built three since I started coming here. Maybe a person has to build at least four before he gets the hang of it."

"Is it hard?... I mean... building a plane from a book with just wood, cloth and glue to work with?"

"No, it's not too difficult, once you get started," Paul said. Then added, "And if you follow the directions properly." he chuckled.

"Where are your other planes?" asked Jason, looking around the room in case he had missed them.

Paul followed Jason's eyes. "They're not here. The first plane I built I gave to Mrs. Miller, because I figured she deserved it. She did most of the work. And, my second plane is hanging up in Mr. White's office at his school."

Jason decided to go to Mr. White's office Monday, after school, and see Paul's plane. "What about your third plane? Where is it?"

"That's a secret," Paul replied, giving him a mysterious smile, "unless you come here and build a plane on your own-- then, I'll tell you."

Paul's evasiveness aroused Jason's curiosity. He wanted to ask him more about the fate of his third model, but he didn't want Paul to think that he was prying. So, he changed the subject. "Did Mrs. Miller really help you build your planes?" he asked.

"Yes. Why?"

"Because Mr. White said she was the instructor in here, and I thought he might have lied to me. Well..., maybe not lied, but...."

"No, he didn't lie to you. She really does know how to build model planes and," he added, "she can do lots of other things, too."

"Like what?"

Paul scratched his head, thought a few moments, and then replied, "Well, for instance, she's pretty good at video games. The last time I played a computer game with her, she nearly beat me."

Still skeptical, Jason asked, "What else can she do?" Mrs. Miller was starting to sound like some sort of super-woman, and he didn't want to be fooled into believing that she was something more than she actually was. After all, she was still a woman.

"She can build other types of models besides planes," said Paul. "When I first came here, she was helping a kid build a four-foot sailboat. You should have seen it when they finished. It even floated!"

Jason didn't know how to respond to Paul's last admission and grew quiet. He picked up the manual and pretended to read. Paul returned his attention to his model. Jason put down the manual and watched him. He found that he had enjoyed talking to Paul. Paul's easy, laid-back manner put Jason at ease and for once, he wasn't having trouble talking to someone his own age.

Paul broke the silence when he said: "You never did say whether or not you build planes, too. Here I've been telling you how everything is done and maybe I'm talking to an expert." He slapped his forehead. "Boy, would that make me feel like a real dummy."

"No, I'm no expert," Jason replied, secretly glad that Paul believed that he could be. "And," he added, "I don't build model planes... at least... I don't anymore. But, I used to a long time ago."

"Too bad," said Paul. "Well, you could start again. It would be nice having someone to work with. We could even form our own company: Paul Andrews and Jason-- Hey, I don't know your last name."

"Winters."

"Paul Andrews and Jason Winters: Aeronautic Engineers."

Jason was almost swept away by Paul's enthusiasm, envisioning their names on the side of a large metal hangar. Then, he remembered. He wasn't coming back here after today. "That sounds like a great idea, but--"

Paul cut him off. "It is a great idea," he said.

"But, if we're going to be partners, you better go over to the shelf and get yourself a manual. I'll help you get started on a plane."

Jason didn't know what to say. He knew that the smile on Paul's face would disappear when he refused his offer. Maybe Paul would think that he didn't like him or something like that. What then? He liked Paul, but he had to tell him. "Paul, don't get me wrong. I think it would be great being your partner but I don't think I'll be coming back after today." He saw the disappointment on Paul's face and hurried to explain. "If you promise not to tell Mr. White, I'll tell you a secret."

"I promise."

"Well, I only came today to get Mr. White off my back," said Jason, fiddling with scrap of cloth in his hands. "I didn't think that he'd leave me alone until I came here at least once."

"I see."

"You're not mad?" Jason asked.

Paul threw back his head and laughed. "Who me? Mad? No way. I'm glad that I'm not the only one that "old ironsides" sucked into coming here," he chuckled.

Jason was confused. "'Old ironsides... sucked in'... I don't get it."

"Let me try and explain," said Paul laying his model down on the table, folding his hands, and staring across the table at Jason. "It's kind of a long story, but if you've got the time, I think I can tell you-- that is, I can tell you, if I cut out most of the fine details and just give you the bare facts."

Jason was tempted to check his watch to see if it was almost time for him to go home, but he didn't. Nothing would have prevented him from hearing what Paul had to say about Mr. White. "I've got the time," he said.

"Okay. Here goes. Back a couple of years ago, my parents weren't getting along very well, and my Dad pulled out and left Mom to raise my sister and me by herself. Well, Mom was pretty upset being left to raise us kids without much money and a stack of bills to pay-- that kept building up. She was working in a Day Care Centre, but it wasn't enough to make ends meet, so she took a part-time job in the evenings.

"I always thought that my old man would come back and everything would be okay, but I guess life doesn't work that way. He moved in with another woman and, except for a couple of short visits after he first left, none of us have seen him since. Besides, when he moved in with that woman, Mom applied for a divorce. That settled it as far as I was concerned, because I knew he wouldn't be coming back. Not even if he wanted to.

"About the time of the divorce, I hit the streets. You have to understand, I was pretty shaken up. The psychologists called it 'Insecurity' but anyway, I started going out at nights after Mom left for work, and sometimes, I didn't come back for two or three days."

"Where'd you go?" Jason asked, totally caught up in Paul's story.

"All over. Slept on park benches or at some of my friend's places. But, getting back to what finally happened. Mom tried to get me to stay home, but she was never around to stop me from going out, and I wouldn't have listened to her, anyway." Paul paused for a second, took a deep breath, and continued. "Yeah," he said, reflectively, "Mom tried.... Anyway, it wasn't long before I started hanging around with a bunch of older kids. I don't know why they let me tag along; maybe it was because I was like some sort of mascot to them. Well, one thing led to another, and, to make a long story short, one night I got busted by the cops for a B and E."

"'B and E'?" Jason asked, unfamiliar with the term.

'Break and Enter."

"Oh."

"That's okay," said Paul, smiling at him. "If I lose you on any of these technical terms, just jump in and ask. I don't mind."

"Thanks."

"Anyway, getting back to my story. The rest of it's history now. I ended up in juvenile court and, because of my age, the judge figured I'd have a better chance at being rehabilitated and put on probation, than I'd have if I was locked up in a juvenile detention centre. I have to tell you, now, I'm glad that he did decide I was worth saving, because I spent four days in a D.T. Centre, and I didn't like it. I was scared!"

"You're on probation?" Jason asked in an awe-filled voice. No one he knew had ever been on probation.

"Uh huh," replied Paul, "but, I'll be clean, come this January. And now, I'll tell you about 'Old Ironsides.' He cleared his throat and began. "The courts assigned me a Probation Officer or if you prefer-- Counsellor-- and I have to report to her once a week. Her name is Mrs. Linow. Well, she thought that I could benefit from also having what they call a 'Friendly Visitor. Paul tried to explain to Jason. "A 'Friendly Visitor' is someone who looks out for you. I guess the best way to explain it would be to say that he's sort of like a Big Brother or an Uncle At Large-- only, he's been trained to help you if you have problems. Mr. White is my Friendly Visitor.

"He's the one that got me involved in coming here every week. Thought that it would be good for me to have some kind of hobby and mix with kids my own age. I tried to talk him out of it. But, you know Old Ironsides... he doesn't take no for an answer.

"So he made you come here," Jason replied sympathetically.

"No, he didn't make me," Paul corrected. "Mr. White just strongly suggested that I come here."

'Too bad."

"Naw," Paul grinned. "It's been good for me. I like coming here. It's fun. For the first time in my life, it seems like I have people who believe in me; who really care whether or not I screw up or do a good job. And, not just about building models, either."

Paul's story fascinated Jason. Despite all that he had gone through, it appeared to Jason that Paul had found something that had helped him come out a winner. Jason wished that he knew what it was, because Paul didn't sound like a kid that had screwed up; that had gotten into the trouble with the law and had almost been sent to jail. Paul looked like a person who had regained control of his destiny and was now, happy with life. Envious, Jason asked, "What sort of things did they teach you?"

"Oh, you know," Paul replied modestly. "Things like the difference between right and wrong."

Seeing Jason's puzzled expression, he tried to explain. "I'll give you an example. Most of us think we know what's right or wrong and, for the majority of things, you know, like stealing, we do know it's wrong. But, I'll tell you, Jason, there's a lot of grey areas in between that I never knew about before I met Mr. White and Mrs. Miller."

"What are `grey areas'?" Jason asked.

"Well...," Paul paused, trying to think of a way he could explain it so that Jason would understand. "We all learn things from our parents that might not be right. Take my old man, for instance.... Every time something would go wrong, or he thought someone was giving him a hard time, he would explode, and look out everybody! I learned to stay out of his way until he got it out of his system. Because, when he was mad-- no one was safe. Well, while I was learning to stay out of his way, I was also learning that it was okay to lose my cool anytime things didn't go my way. Well, he was wrong," said Paul softly. "I was wrong... boy was I wrong."

Jason thought he saw a tear in the corner of Paul's eye and was glad that it wasn't him who was spilling his guts to some stranger.

I don't think I could do it, Jason thought, watching Paul pull out a kleenex from his back pocket and blow his nose, before continuing with his story.

"Mr. White taught me that no one can make me angry, and if I get mad at someone, it's because my expectations don't match up with what the other person expects. For instance, suppose my Mom wanted me to take out the garbage because she's tired and wants to rest. Well, I might not want to, because I'm also tired. So, what happens now?

"She feels that she has the right to ask and I feel that I have the right to refuse. Conflict, right? So where do we go from here? If I get mad and refuse, it's because I feel I have the right to refuse. But, if she insists, it's because she thinks she has the right to ask. Well, the long and short of it is that we may be both right. But, we still may have to *compromise.*

"It was hard for me to accept the fact that, in life, you have to learn how to compromise. But, Mr. White taught me that there are few situations in life that fall in the 'black and white' category. That means that there is only one solution to a problem and when it comes to a conflict situation, if you don't win, then you feel that you have lost." Paul's voice took on a serious note as he stared across at Jason and said: "But did you know that in an argument, you and your opponent can both come out winners? The key is to compromise.

"And," he added knowingly, "you don't use anger to solve your problems. You're responsible for your own feelings. No one can make you mad and you have no right to take out your anger on someone else because they don't agree with you. Mr. White says that I can't blame other people for the way I think or how I handle my problems."

Jason still didn't understand what "expectations" had to do with getting angry and felt that he had somehow missed the main point of what Paul was trying to tell him. "Are you saying that it's wrong to get mad?" He frowned, confused.

"No, not at all." Paul laughed. "That would be silly, because we all get mad sometime or another, but, what I am trying to tell you is that it's wrong to make others suffer because they don't agree with you, or because you're angry. For example, if you have a bad day in school, you have no right to come home and break something or hit someone, just because you're in a bad mood. They're not responsible for you being mad."

"I think I can understand that," said Jason. "But, what if adults do it-- is it okay, then?"

"No," Paul replied emphatically. "That's where I got screwed up. I saw my Dad strike out whenever he got mad, and I thought that I could do the same thing. Well, he was wrong! And, sometimes I hate him for screwing up my life."

Paul stopped talking and reached for his instruction manual. Jason knew Paul had finished his story. But, Jason's mind was in a turmoil. He thought about the things Paul had said, and he thought about the boy on the swing. Had there been another way? Some of the things Paul talked about made sense, but he didn't agree that it was always wrong to make someone suffer when you were angry.

If you didn't teach people their place from the start, they would walk all over you. His grandpa said so. No one would respect a coward.

Jason wanted to tell Paul how he felt, but he didn't know how he should begin-- or how, he could say that he didn't agree with some of the things Paul had said, without implying that Paul was a wrong about life.

"Well?" Paul asked, breaking the silence.

"Well, what?" said Jason, wondering why Paul had put down his manual and was now, staring at him intently.

"Well, aren't you going to tell me I'm full of shit? That you don't believe me when I say you're responsible for your own behavior when you get angry?"

Jason sputtered trying to deny that he had any such thoughts. What was Paul, anyway? Some kind of mind-reader? He blushed.

Seeing Jason's discomfort, Paul leaned over the table and laid his hand on Jason's wrist. "Hey, it's okay. I understand. Don't feel guilty for thinking that I'm wrong. I had those same thoughts when Mr. White first started telling me this stuff. I thought he was full of shit because I knew better. I had learned from my dad and the guys in my gang, that you used whatever you had to, to ensure that you came out the winner in a fight. If you were bigger and tougher, then other people would be afraid of you and wouldn't stand in your way. Well, that way of thinking works-- for a time...."

"What do you mean 'it works for a time'?" Jason asked. Paul's hand continued to rest on Jason's wrist.

"What I'm trying to say is that... if you use violence to solve your problems, you're going to have to be prepared to pay the price-- sometime. And, there is a price. Oh, I know that you might get away with it for a while, but you'll lose in the end. Either you'll end up in court like I did and maybe even jail, or those you care about will grow to hate and despise you. Remember you can force people to do what you want, but you can't force them to like doing it-- or to love you either. I guess what I'm trying to tell you is that you have to earn people's love and respect. You can't beat it out of them."

It was as if Jason had on blinders all his life and they had now been take off exposing him to the light. He blinked. Like a house of cards, he saw his life begin to crumble before him, and he fought to reinforce the walls before they completely collapsed under this new philosophy. "You... you didn't go to jail?" he stammered.

"No..., but only because there were people out there who felt that I was worth saving; that with a little help, I might amount to something. They took the time to teach me something- something worthwhile knowing. I don't want to end up in a reform school... and I don't want to hurt anyone, anymore."

Jason didn't want to talk about it any longer. He needed time to be alone so that he could think about these new ideas. "Thank you for sharing your life with me," he said quietly. "It must have been hard telling me about your past."

"Yeah," said Paul thoughtfully. "I don't like to talk about it. It's over now and I want to forget it ever happened. It's nothing to be proud of, that's for sure. But, for some reason, you reminded me of the way I was, when I first came here. Not that we have the same problems, but it's the way you acted-- kind of hostile and definitely anti-social."

Taken aback by Paul's honest appraisal, Jason smiled sheepishly. "Do I really look hostile?"

"Not now, but you did when you first came into the room."

"I thought that you were so busy working on your model, you'd forgotten I was here. Remember... I'm the guy who sat across from you for half an hour, before you even looked up."

"I wasn't ignoring you," said Paul looking him straight in the eye. "I just thought that you needed time to unwind, before you'd want to talk with anyone-- including me. Was I wrong?" he added, smiling.

Jason smiled back. "I don't know what to say."

"You don't have to say anything. Just call me Dr. Freud," Paul laughed, as he stood up, stretched, and settled back down in his chair. He took a piece of wire, twisted it into the shape of spectacles, and set them on his nose. "Now, young man," he said feigning a thick foreign accent and peering over top of the wire frames, "tell me all your problems."

Paul's ridiculous appearance, along with the serious look on his face was the funniest thing Jason had ever seen. He doubled over with laughter. "Who's Freud?" he managed to gasp between spasms.

"Oh, he's one big-shot psychiatrist that I found out about when I was receiving counselling. My social worker had his book on her bookshelf in her office. If you plan on coming back, I'll tell you about some of the things that I read about him. Do you think you'll be back?"

Jason thought about his dad. Even if he wanted to come back, would his father let him? He looked across the table at Paul. "Yes," he replied softly, "I'll be back."

"Good! So, now that I've managed to bore you for most of the afternoon with my sob story, how about you? Ever been in trouble?"

Jason didn't know where to begin. He still had qualms about telling Paul everything about his life, but he didn't mind sharing some stuff with his new friend. But, where to start? That was the question. He thought for a few minutes, and then said, "My life is nowhere near as exciting as yours. The worst trouble I've been in, was when I ran away from home."

"I know," said Paul, "I recognized you from your picture in the paper."

It unsettled Jason to find out that Paul was already aware of some of the details of his past, and he asked, "Why didn't you say something, if you knew?"

"Because it was none of my business, and if you felt like telling me about it, you would."

"Oh," said Jason. He was having difficulty handling Paul's open, frank manner. "I guess I should thank you for not bringing it up. It's still hard for me to talk about it."

"No thanks necessary," Paul replied. "Go on with your story. You ran away...."

"Ya. I got mad at my parents and then I got in trouble at school. It just seemed that things kept piling up, until I couldn't take anymore and I split."

"What happened when you got home?"

Jason shuddered. "God, I was in trouble," he said, his voice trembling. "My Dad has a real temper when he's crossed and man, was he mad at me when I returned."

"That's rough," Paul sympathized. "I once used to know a kid who's dad would come home drunk and beat the shit out of him. I felt sorry for him. He was always coming to school covered with bruises until, one day, a woman from a Social Services Agency came to the school and took him away."

"Did they do anything to his dad?" asked Jason, excitedly. "I mean, did they punish his dad for hurting him?"

"No, not that I remember... maybe. I never saw that kid again, so I don't know what happened. But, I did hear a couple of teachers talking about him awhile later, and they mentioned something about him being in a foster home in another part of the city."

Jason was beginning to draw a parallel between the kid Paul was talking about, and his own family. He didn't think that he would like to end up in a foster home. He tried to shift the conversation back to safer ground by asking Paul about his counsellors. "When you went for counselling, did they make you talk about your parents?"

"No," Paul answered. "And I thought that was kind of funny, too. I was expecting my Probation Officer to give me a big lecture, but she didn't say a word about my past mistakes. She talked with me about my future. And, it was the same with Mr. White. I was expecting him to say something, but he didn't. Instead, he showed me around this place and introduced me to Mrs. Miller. She got me interested in building model planes. Then, after that, I was coming here every Saturday to work on my plane. Before long, we were talking about life in general and things just sort of came out. It wasn't planned; it just happened."

"I thought that your probation officer could make you answer her questions," said Jason.

"Jason... Jason... Jason..." Paul sighed in exasperation. "I hate to say this, but I think you've been watching too much T.V. Nobody, not even a psychiatrist can make you talk, if you don't want to."

"But," Jason protested, "I heard they sometimes use truth serum on you, if you don't co-operate." He didn't want Paul to think that he was totally ignorant on the subject.

"Jason!" What am I going to do with you?" Paul chuckled. "You make them sound like they're working for the Gestapo, instead of just trying to help."

"Well, I don't think that they can help someone, if that person is already crazy," said Jason, wishing Paul wouldn't laugh at him.

"You've lost me."

Jason tried to explain. "My Dad says that anyone who goes to see a shrink is nuts. I know I sure wouldn't want to have to go see one."

"Well, speaking from personal experience, I'd say your dad's wrong about counsellors. Look at me," he said to Jason, straightening up in his chair. "Do I look crazy to you?"

Jason shook his head.

Paul continued: "I had a lot of help over the past two years before I finally got my head screwed on straight. But, I don't think I'm nuts."

No, Jason thought, looking at him, *Paul certainly didn't look like someone who had lost all his marbles.*

"I've had some pretty good counsellors," said Paul, "especially after I got into all that trouble. I will admit some of the things that they get you to do seem a bit strange at the time, and you sort of feel like you're nothing but a guinea-pig, but they can help you, if you let them."

"What kind of things do they make you do?" Jason asked, his interest now thoroughly aroused.

"Oh..., they give you tests and they're always asking about your feelings and why you think a certain way."

"They give you tests?" Jason asked.

The look of surprise on Jason's face made Paul smile. "The tests aren't like the ones we get at school," he explained. "The tests my counsellors gave me were designed to show what type of personality I have. They can also measure whether or not I have any dysfunctional thinking habits."

Paul had lost him again. "What in the world are 'dysfun--'"

"Dysfunctional thinking habits," Paul repeated. "That's when you've learned bad ways of thinking about life. Let me see.., I'll try and think of an example." Paul cocked his head and stared out the window a few seconds before turning back to Jason. "Okay, I think I got it now. Let's suppose that you've learned to over-generalize nearly everything. That means that whenever something happens to you, you see it as a pattern. Let's say you make a few mistakes. Well, if you over-generalize, then you tell yourself that you're 'always' doing something wrong. In other words, you tend to put yourself down or-- someone else. This type of bad thinking habit does not accept events as a single occurrence." Paul winked at Jason. "My social worker says that it raises hell with your self-esteem."

Jason wanted to ask Paul what self-esteem meant, but the tests Paul had mentioned, fascinated him more. "Have you ever failed any of these tests?" he inquired.

"No... yes... maybe, I'm not sure. They don't really tell you if you passed or failed them." Paul thought for a moment and then added, "But maybe they told my Mom. I think she'd have told me, if she knew, though."

"I don't see much point in writing a test, if you never get to find out if you passed it or not," said Jason. "It seems kind of stupid to me."

"Me, too."

Having won this last point, Jason decided it was time to drop the subject and talk about more serious matters. "What type of plane do you think I should start with?" he asked.

"It doesn't really matter a whole lot," Paul advised, "because Mrs. Miller will help you if you run into any difficulty."

"I'm going to go look at some of the instruction manuals," said Jason, getting up and heading towards the shelf. He leafed through the pile and brought back half a dozen magazines. For the next fifteen minutes, they both sat quietly looking through the manuals. Then, Paul set down the manual he was looking at and got up from the table. He walked around the end and pulled up a chair beside Jason.

"Where do you go to school?" he asked.

"Just over there," Jason said, pointing out the window to the large brick building across the street.

"That's handy."

"Not really," Jason replied, "because I have to take the bus to get to it. It takes me about thirty-five minutes to get to school. How about you?"

"I go to a Catholic Separate School about four blocks from here."

"You're Catholic?" Jason asked.

"Yeah, I guess so. Mom is. We're not what you call 'practicing Catholics,' but Mom figures that maybe if I got some religion in my life, it would help straighten me out. So, *Voila!* She up and enrolled me in a Catholic School."

"Has it helped? I mean, getting religion?"

"I don't know whether it has helped," Paul shrugged, "but it hasn't hurt. At first I hated it there. None of the kids I knew went to a Catholic school and I was embarrassed to tell them I was going to one."

"Does it still bother you?"

"No, not anymore. Besides, it's kind of fun. The teachers are okay and I met some neat kids, so I get along."

"I like my school too," said Jason. He stared out the window at his school. "It's kind of strict, but I don't mind." He was thinking that it would be fun if he could switch schools and be with Paul. However, he didn't think his dad would go for such a suggestion. In fact, Jason was sure his dad would have a fit if he even mentioned it to him.

I guess I better leave well enough alone, he thought, turning his attention back to the manuals in front of him. *I can meet Paul here.*

It was past four o'clock before Jason got up to leave.

He promised Paul he would be back the next Saturday, and the two of them made plans to get him started on his own model airplane.

While riding the bus home, Jason spent his time thinking about Paul and the Centre. Listening to Paul, Jason realized that he hadn't thought about his own problems all afternoon-- not even once! Sure, he had told Paul about running away, but they hadn't dwelled on it, and their conversation had moved on to other things. He couldn't remember ever being this happy in his entire life. Maybe having Paul for a friend was going to make life worth living.

I wish next Saturday was tomorrow, he thought, as he stepped off the bus and headed down the street towards his house.

At peace with the world, Jason stopped to pet a black and white kitten sitting on the sidewalk. He smiled when it began to purr and rub against his leg.

If things could only stay like they were today, I would never ask for anything else, he thought, leaving the kitten and strolling up the sidewalk to his house.

Jason was barely in the door when Becky ran up to him to tell him he was late and everyone had already finished eating. He was glad they hadn't waited for him.

"Hi, Mom! I'm home," he called out.

His mother came hurrying out of the living room. "Jason, I was getting worried. We were going to wait supper for you, but Nicky was hungry and--"

He cut her off. "Hey, Mom, it's okay. You don't have to apologize and I'm glad you guys didn't wait. Don't worry, I can fix myself something to eat. I'm not helpless, you know."

His mother gave him a strange look.

For a second, Jason thought that she was going to come over and feel his forehead, so he tried again. "It's okay Mom, I'm not sick." He smiled at her. But, when she continued to stare at him without answering, he began to get worried. "Is something wrong?" he asked.

"No... nothing's wrong... I... I'll warm up supper for you."

Jason followed her into the kitchen and sat down at the table. His mom kept glancing over her shoulder at him, and he wondered why she was acting so odd. She took a casserole out of the oven and set it on the table. Then, she went back to the cupboard. When Jason saw her open the cupboard door and take down a plate, he rushed over to her and, taking the plate out of her hands said: "Mom, I can get my own dishes. You don't have to wait on me. I'm not a cripple, you know."

There! She did it again-- gave him that same strange look. Jason didn't understand why she kept looking at him so funny. Women! Who could figure them out?

"What's in here?" asked Jason, lifting the lid off the casserole.

"It's called a 'Shipwreck,' she replied. "I bought a new cookbook today and thought I'd try out a new recipe." She sat down across from him and watched him scoop out a large serving onto his plate.

"Smells good. I'm starved!"

"Did you have a good time today?" she asked.

"Yeah, it was okay."

"What did you do there? You were gone a long time?"

"Not much," he replied. "Just sat around and talked with a kid." He had already decided not to mention his new friend to his family, and hoped his mother wouldn't question him further.

"That's nice," she said. She got up and went to the fridge. When she came back, she was carrying a glass and a carton of milk. "Here," she said, setting it down in front of him. "Have something to drink."

"Thanks." Jason was relieved that his mother seemed satisfied with his explanation. Hungry, he picked up his fork and dug into the food on his plate. He saw that his mother was still staring at him, but he ignored her.

Supper was delicious and he was ravenous.

CHAPTER XIII

Jason continued to go to the Centre every Saturday and after the first few times, he felt comfortable being around the other kids. They no longer stared at him and he started to feel like he belonged, like he was part of their group. But he wasn't interested in joining them in a game of basketball, because his only interest was the craft room. Once there, he would go over to the cupboard and collect the materials he would need to work on his model.

He had met Mrs. Miller and she wasn't anything like he had imagined. She was a tiny woman with dark brown hair and had the bluest eyes Jason had ever seen. Her ready smile, coupled with her genuine interest in helping him select and build a model plane, put him at ease almost immediately. Now it seemed like they had been friends for ages, instead of having met only a few short weeks ago.

Sometimes he couldn't make it to the Centre because his dad would come up with last minute chores for him to do. It was during these times that Jason would become bitter and felt like rebelling. He wanted to tell his dad to go to hell; that he was going anyway, but he didn't dare. All he could do was wait impatiently for the next Saturday to arrive, while he dreamed about his model plane and what it would look like when it was finally finished.

It had been difficult for him to convince his dad to allow him to go to the Centre every Saturday. In fact, it had taken Jason three days to think up a plan that would persuade his father that it would be in the best interests of the family to let him go. He had rehearsed his speech for hours, before he actually broached topic with his father.

*   *   *

Three days after Jason's first visit to the Centre, and after his dad had returned from his trip, he had worked up enough nerve to talk with him about it. He was stretched out on the sofa, the newspaper propped up on his chest, when Jason walked into the room. He went over to him and stood by his feet.

"Dad, can I talk with you a moment?" he asked.

"Go ahead," his dad answered from behind the paper.

"D...ad," he stuttered. This was no good! How would he be able to tell his dad about the Centre, if he couldn't keep his voice from trembling? He cleared his throat and tried again. "Dad, my Math teacher thinks that it would be a good idea if I came every Saturday afternoon to a special class he's running for students having trouble with their math. He's going to set up a classroom in a building across from my school. Can I go?" Jason put his hand behind his back and crossed his fingers.

"So, you need help in Math, hey? I always told you that if you spent more time on your homework and less on those dumb models you're always building, you wouldn't need extra help to pass your subjects."

Jason felt like shouting at his dad that he wasn't spending any time at home building models and that the ones he had build were no longer in existence. So how could his dad accuse him of wasting time? He fought to keep the anger out of his voice and when he spoke again, his voice was soft and respectful. "I really do need the extra help. I don't want to fail Grade 7 this year."

That had gotten his Dad's attention.

His dad lowered his newspaper and stared up at him. "No son of mine is going to fail a grade!" he exclaimed, fixing Jason with a baleful glance, before he picked up his paper and started reading again. "For Christ's sake!," came his voice from behind the newspaper. "What would people say?"

Jason tried to ignore his father's rising anger, and quickly ran through the details of Mr. White's proposed program, before his dad cut him off.

"It's only once a week," Jason protested, "and like I said, I could use the extra help. And," he added, "I can do my homework there, too. That way Mr. White can check it to see if I'm on the right track."

"You-- spend your Saturdays doing homework?"

His eyebrows rose in disbelief. "That's a laugh. I don't believe you."

By this time, Jason was running out of arguments and was on the verge of panic. Did his dad know he was lying, or was he merely suspicious? Jason knew it was risky, but he had to play his last "Ace" because, if he couldn't return to the Centre, it wouldn't matter if his dad caught him in a lie. Life would be over for him, anyway. He sucked in his breath and said, "If you don't believe me, ask Mr. White. He'll tell you that he's going to be tutoring some of us kids every Saturday afternoon."

Jason's dad lowered his paper again and looked at him. Jason nervously waited for his response. Slowly, the scowl disappeared from the corner of his dad's mouth, and Jason knew his father was beginning to relent. "Please, Dad," he begged.

"Well," said his father, "I guess it'll be okay, but I better see some improvement in your grades, or else!" he shook his finger at Jason. "And, I don't want you leaving this house until all of your chores have been done. Understood?"

Jason was overjoyed, but he tried not to show it. "Yes, Dad," he replied soberly. "Thanks."

"Fine. Now, if you're done bothering me, I'd like to finish the paper. I've had a hard day, you know," his father said, bringing their conversation to a close.

Jason didn't need to be told twice to leave. He couldn't wait to get out of there. When he was out of the living room, he raced up the stairs to his room. Once inside, he stopped and rested his head on his door. His heart was pounding against his chest, and he stood trembling, the sweat dripping off his forehead into his eyes. God, it had been close! He wondered what he would do if his dad took him up on his offer and did phone Mr. White. It was no use worrying about it now, because it was too late for him to change his story.

*   *   *

It seemed to Jason that, for once, God had listened to him because his father never did call Mr. White, and Jason continued to go every Saturday to meet Paul at the Centre. By now, they had become close friends and Jason enjoyed talking with him, while they both worked at the table on their models. And Jason also enjoyed talking with Mrs. Miller.

He had met her on his second visit to the Centre and he know that he was going to like her. She had come over to where they were sitting and introduced herself.

"Hi guys," she said, looking over Paul's shoulder at his model then she had looked at Jason. "And you must be Jason," she said, reaching across the table to shake his hand. "Mr. White told me you would be here today. My name's Beth Miller and I'm supposed to help you boys learn how to build model planes." She ruffled Paul's hair. "Well, maybe not Paul, because he's almost as expert by now, but I'll help you if you run into any difficulty." She picked up the instruction manual in front of Jason, flipped through a couple of pages and set it down again. "I don't know how much I actually help around here, or get in the way, but I try... oh yes... no one can accuse me of not trying, hey Paul?"

"Don't you believe her," Paul grinned. "She knows everything about everything."

"Thanks, Paul, for the vote of confidence but, as much as I hate to admit it, there's a lot I don't know."

"But you know how to build planes," said Jason, "and Paul says you're an expert," he added, his voice filled with admiration.

"Again, I have to say I think Paul's exaggerated my abilities in that department," she replied. "However, my specialty is model planes. But, I'm no expert." she smiled at Jason and asked, "I hear that you're going to build a model plane, too."

"I'd like to try," Jason replied, shyly.

"Well then," she said, "Judging from the look in your eye, I'd say that you're going to give Paul a run for his money as to who finishes their plane first."

"But, Paul has been working on his for two months," Jason protested, "and I haven't even started yet."

"Doesn't matter," she said, a mischievous glint in her eye. "You have that look of dedication, and I'm sure that you'll catch up to him in no time."

"Hey, you two," Paul interjected, "quit ganging up on me. And you-- Mrs. Miller-- I'm surprise at your sudden lack of loyalty." He laughed. "Boy, let a new kid come on the block and -- poof-- good old Paul is cast aside. I'm crushed." He laid his head on the table and pretended to weep.

"There, there little one," consoled Mrs. Miller "I haven't forgotten about you."

Paul threw his head back and laughed. "Good!" he said. "Then what are we waiting for? Let's get started."

Jason didn't find it hard to fit in; the three of them soon formed a happy trio, as they worked together that afternoon. It was the beginning of many pleasant afternoons, where they would tease each other and laugh at the corniest jokes. When Mrs. Miller had left them that afternoon to go help Mr. White in the office, he was sorry to see her go. But, before she had left, they had picked out a bi-plane for him to build, and he had spent his remaining time reading the directions, anxious to get started.

Saturdays became his salvation from all his troubles at home. When he was at the Centre, Jason forgot about his dad and concentrated on the task before him. Under his careful administrations, his bi-plane began to take shape and he was filled with pride whenever he looked at it.

And, if he was hurting when he arrived at the Centre, Paul always seemed to know and would tease him and tell funny little jokes, until Jason's mood improved and he was able to forget about what had upset him before he arrived.

In fact, it was during these times he really learned to value Paul's friendship. Whenever he was sad or depressed, Paul would crack one of his infamous jokes like: "What did the grape say when the man stepped on him?... Nothing, he just let out a little wine." Then, Paul would laugh uproariously and Jason would find himself smiling, too. He couldn't help but be cheered by his friend's constant bantering. And before long, Jason would be happily working at the table. Soon, Jason began to depend on Paul to help him survive the bad times he endured at home. He still found it difficult to talk to Paul about his family, and if his dad beat up on Jason's mom, Jason would clam up completely. But, Paul seemed to understand.

In fact, his friend seemed to take his silences in stride and would go on chattering and joking, as if nothing was the matter. And, after a while, there wouldn't be anything the matter. Jason would find himself relaxing and would go get his stuff down from the shelf and would join Paul at the table.

Jason remembered the time one of their conversations had gotten around to his parents. He was about to finally tell Paul about his dad, when suddenly, his father's image loomed up in front of him and Jason found himself momentarily speechless. The awful specter was shaking its finger at him.

When Paul saw him go white and start to tremble, he frowned with concern. "What's wrong? Are you okay?"

Jason couldn't respond. The frightful image was still dancing before his eyes. Finally, a few seconds later it was gone. Jason sat back in his chair, exhausted from fear. He didn't tell Paul about his father-- he couldn't. He was too afraid that the monster might come back. Jason ignored Paul's concerned remarks and reached for his manual. He pretended to read. Without another word, Paul sat down in his own chair and went back to work.

How could he explain the fear that erupted inside him every time he thought about talking to someone about his father? Jason didn't think Paul would understand and would think that he was being foolish. However, sometimes Jason thought that he may have underestimated Paul's insight because after that particular episode, his friend had looked at him sadly and turned away. Jason was glad when a short while later, Paul was back to normal, larking around and acting like nothing unusual had happened.

*   *   *

Now, almost three months later, Jason still hadn't breached the silence surrounding his family. He talked about a lot of things with Paul, and with Mr. White and Mrs. Miller, too, but he never mentioned his dad to them.

A lot of things had happened during this time, the most important being that he was nearly finished his plane. Mrs. Miller said that it was because he spent all his time at the Centre working on it and he had to agree, but it was the only thing he liked to do. Every time he looked at his model he would nearly burst with happiness. He was forever picking it up and turning it around to admire it. Paul was please, too, and often told him what a fine job he was doing on it. In Jason's eyes, the plane had evolved into a thing of beauty and he was responsible for that beauty.

Today, when he arrived, Paul was already in the room waiting for him. Jason went over and lifted his plane off the shelf, holding it up so he could admire it again. Paul came up behind him and stood beside him.

"I think that maybe, just maybe, Mrs. Miller was right when she said that you had a natural talent for this sort of thing," Paul said, reaching out and running his finger along the wings of Jason's plane.

Jason was flattered by Paul's comment, but he tried not to let it show and modestly asked, "Do you really think so?"

"Yes, as much as I hate to admit it, I have to say that you're better at building planes than I am. And," he added, "You know it too so don't try and act so modest."

"Thanks," Jason whispered, overcome by his friend's kind words. "You've done a great job, too."

Paul went over to the shelf and picked up his model. Except for the decals, it was complete and Jason knew Paul was very proud of the job he had done on it. They carried their planes over to the table and set them down side by side.

"Are you going to build another one?" Paul asked.

"I sure am. I've never had so much fun."

"I'm glad to hear that," said Paul, visibly relieved. "I was afraid that after you finished, you might decide not to come back any more."

"Are you kidding?" exclaimed Jason, gripping Paul's shoulder. "I like it here, but most of all, I like you. We're friends. Whatever made you think I wouldn't come back?"

"Well," Paul replied slowly, "I know things aren't going too well for you at home, and I just thought... well, you see, I've never had a real close friend before, and I didn't want to lose you." The last part of his sentence came out in a rush of words and he stood with his mouth half-open, waiting for Jason to say something.

Jason looked at him and smiled. "I'll always come to see you here," he said, thinking about all the fun times they had shared. Coming to the Centre had been the best thing that had ever happened to him. He not only got to build model planes again, but he had also made the best friend in the world. And, in addition to all this, he had improved his grades at school, too.

His marks had steadily improved and he knew that it was because he paid attention in class and always did his homework assignments. Sometimes though, he wished that he had given his dad a different excuse for coming to the Centre, but things had worked out well for him, so he couldn't really complain.

When he had brought home his last report card, all his grades had showed some improvement and his math mark had risen by 16%. His dad's only comment was, "It's about time!", but Mr. White had come over to him after class and congratulated him on his effort. His teacher must have told Mrs. Miller, because the next time Jason came to the Centre, she came over to him and gave him a big hug, telling him how pleased she was that he was doing so well in school. Jason had never been so embarrassed in his entire life and to make matters even worse, Paul kept threatening him the whole afternoon that he too, was going to give Jason a big hug!

It was also the Saturday that Mrs. Miller had helped him mount the wings on the body of his plane. For two hours they worked together, fitting the wings into their respective slots and applying glue to hold them in place. While they worked together, Mrs. Miller related bits and pieces of her own childhood to them.

She had grown up with five older brothers and had been the only girl in the family. She was also her dad's favorite and so, whenever he took her brothers over to the field to play football, she went with them. Her dad taught her how to play football and much to her brothers' dismay, she always got to play quarterback. "Yes," she told Jason and Paul, "My Dad said I had a great right arm and that I was destined to become the best quarterback of all time."

"Did you?" Jason asked.

"Did I what?"

"Did you become the best quarterback of all time?" asked Jason seriously. By now, he was ready to accept anything anyone said about Mrs. Miller as fact. And, if she said she could do a particular thing, there was no way that Jason was going to think otherwise. He had never met another woman like her and, now that he had gotten to know her, anything was possible, where she was concerned.

She laughed at the serious expression on his face and reached over and ruffled his hair. "Oh no," she replied. "When I turned sixteen, all thoughts of being a football star flew out of my head and I turned my attention to trying to attract boys, instead of tackling them."

"Yuck!" Jason exclaimed, a look of disbelief on his face. "You gave up being a football star for boys? That's crazy!"

Mrs. Miller laughed. "Well, as ridiculous as it might sound to you guys, I wanted a boyfriend." When she saw Paul smirk and exchange glances with Jason, she chuckled. "Just wait 'til you get older," she warned, "you'll understand."

"Still...," said Jason; unconvinced that she had made the right decision.

"I know," she conceded graciously, "I may have made a mistake. But, when I finished school, I thought that I would probably make a better living as an Accountant than as a football player- Star or not. Besides, I don't get as many bruised shins doing accounting."

They all laughed at that, and Jason tried to picture Mrs. Miller in a football helmet, a pigskin gripped under her arm, running down the field with a pack of opposing players hot in pursuit.

"Go for it Mrs. Miller," he whispered, as he watched her approach the goal posts. "You can make it!" She scored a touchdown and he cheered.

"What's with you?" Mrs. Miller asked in astonishment.

Jason grinned sheepishly.

"What were you cheering about?" Paul asked. "Come on-- share it with us."

Jason had no other choice but to come clean. "Okay, okay," he laughed. "I was just imagining Mrs. Miller all decked out in her football gear, running down the field towards the goal posts. I guess I got carried away in my daydream, because she made a touchdown and I cheered."

Instead of teasing him, Mrs. Miller appeared to be flattered. "Why, thank you for the compliment. I'll have to tell my Dad what you just said, because sometimes he thinks that I've gone soft."

They continued to work on his plane, and the topic of conversation switched from football to baseball and, finally, to hockey. Jason told them that his favorite team was the Calgary Flames and that someday, he was going to go to the Saddledome to watch them play.

"Not me," said Paul. "I don't care if I do live in Alberta. My favorite team is the Pittsburg Penguins."

"Boo!" said Jason, pretending to glare at him. "They only win because they have Crosby. Take him away and they're history." Jason was somewhat annoyed at Paul's lack of loyalty to the home teams. Whoever heard of a Albertan rooting for the Pittsburg Penguins? But he didn't want to hurt his friend's feelings, or destroy the happy mood around him by taking a stand, so he kept his thoughts to himself. However, he couldn't resist telling Paul that Calgary was going to whip Pittsburg in the playoffs.

"Maybe so," Paul replied slyly, "but the odds are still in my favor. Care to make a little bet?"

"Sure," said Jason. "What do you want to bet?"

"Oh...," Paul replied, "Let's see now. How about something that won't cost us any money, but will let the loser know he's backed the wrong team. Hmm." Paul looked at the model in his hands, deep in thought. Finally he looked up and said: "I got it. Let's say the loser has to clean up the craft room and put everything away for three Saturdays. What do you say about that?"

"You're on!" Jason exclaimed excitedly. "I'm just glad that you're already so good at cleaning up, because you'll be the one doing it after the playoffs."

Paul laughed. "We'll see who does the cleaning up around here. Don't be so sure. I just hope you remember where everything goes, when you lose the bet."

"Okay, you two," said Mrs. Miller. "Now that you have turned the Centre into a gambling casino, I want to ask both of you a serious question. What do you guys plan on doing when you finish school? How about you Jason? Are you planning to go to university?"

"Yeah, I guess so, 'cause my Dad says I can either become a doctor or a dentist, like he is."

"Those are both interesting and challenging professions," she replied, "but what I want to know is, what do *you* want to be, not what your dad wants you to be?"

Jason was bewildered. "I don't understand," he said. "I told you. Dad wants--"

"I know," she interrupted, "that your dad expects you to follow in his footsteps. But, what I'm asking you is, what *you* would like to do with *your* life, if *you* had the choice?"

Jason didn't know how to answer her question. He had always taken it for granted that he would be what his father wanted him to be. Period. His future career had already been decided upon and he had never questioned his dad's decision. He sat there thinking for a while and then, replied: "I suppose I'll be whatever Dad wants me to be. I don't have any choice in the matter because Dad has already decided that I'll either be a doctor or a dentist. He's already set up a fund for my university education."

Mrs. Miller frowned. "I don't know," she said, "but I don't think it's a good idea to let someone decide your whole future for you. You should have some say in that decision."

"Yeah, Mrs. Miller's right," said Paul; his voice held a note of authority. "Nobody is going to tell me what I'm going to be, because I've made up my mind already. I'm going to build planes-- real one-- and nobody is going to stop me!" he added emphatically.

Jason was surprised at the determination in his friend's voice. He looked at the set expression on Paul's face and wondered, What's the big deal? *What was so important about making up your own mind when it came time to choose a career?* Until now, he had never even questioned his dad's right to make that decision for him.

Paul's last disclosure signaled an end to their conversation. Nobody said anything for a few minutes and then, Mrs. Miller got up to leave. She turned to Jason and handed him the tube of glue. "I think you should be able to do the rest yourself," she said. "But, before I go, I just want to say one more think about what we were discussing. It's important for a person to set his own goals in life and work to achieve them. Your dad can help you make a decision, but he isn't going to be the one who has to do the work for you." She gave him a meaningful look. "So," she added, "be sure you want to become a doctor or a dentist, before you enroll in university."

When she left, Paul turned to him and said, "You know something, Jason, I think she's right. I think you should be the one to decide what you want to do when you grow up. I've found that grownups can really screw up your life, if you let them make all your decisions."

"Yeah, I guess you're right," Jason agreed. But, he didn't need Paul to remind him of that because he was already thinking about future career possibilities.

Mrs. Miller had opened a whole new world for him and now, that world stretched before him. Even before she had left the room, Jason's mind had been churning out various options. He had already rejected over a dozen possibilities. It was as if Mrs. Miller had given him permission to daydream and now, his mind refused to think of anything else.

What should he be when he finished school? *Good question! I could be a truck driver or a cop. No. Not a cop, cause Dad would never forgive me. He's going to be made enough about me not becoming what he wants without finding out I'm going to be a cop. Maybe a teacher.... Mr. White's a teacher and he seems to like it. I bet it's boring, thought Jason, rejecting the idea. I don't want to have to teach a bunch of kids who don't want to learn.*

The more careers he examined, the more rejections he came up with. Nothing seemed suitable as a lifelong occupation. It wasn't long before he felt he was running out of choices. *What's left?* he wondered, as he worked on his model.

Jason had just finished painting the fuselage, when he thought of a new exciting prospect. He now knew what he was going to be. He was going to be a Marine Biologist.

In the front office of his school stood a large aquarium, filled with an assortment of brightly colored goldfish. Every morning when Jason arrived at school, he would take time to stop at the tank and watch the fish, until it was time for him to go to his locker and get ready for class. He liked fish; liked the way they glided gracefully through the water, stopping occasionally to look at him with their large, round eyes. He wished he had his own aquarium, so he could stock it with angel fish. Yes, fish were neat, and it would be great if he could get a job working with them. Excited, he said to Paul, "Well, I've decided. "I'm going to work with fish when I grow up. I'm going to be a Marine Biologist."

"That's different," Paul replied. "Whatever made you decide to do that?"

Judging from his friend's expression, Jason knew that a full explanation was in order. He explained to him about the fish in the school aquarium, and how he had liked fish ever since his parents had taken him to Sea World in Vancouver a few years ago. "When I watched a guy ride on the back of a Killer Whale, I imagined that it was me," he said letting his mind take him back in time....

Jason could hear the crowd cheering as the man rode the giant beast around the outdoor aquarium. Suddenly, his memory shifted, and now, it was he who was on the whale's back, riding through the water. Jason could feel the whale's muscle's ripple beneath his thighs and trembled with excitement. Gripping tightly Jason hung on for dear life as the whale leaped out of the water. The sale spray stung his eyes when they came down with a splash drenching the audience. He could have ridden the whale forever, except that his reverie was broken by someone calling his name....

"Jason... yohoo.... Jason, come back, come back, wherever you are."

A hand was being waved in front of his eyes, and Jason snapped back to reality. Dazed, he tried to focus and realized that the hand belonged to Paul. "Sorry," he mumbled, trying to rid the cobwebs from his mind. "I guess I must have been daydreaming. You see, there was this whale...." When he saw the worried look on Paul's face, he felt foolish that he had been caught fantasying. He apologized again.

"That's okay," Paul said, "but it must've been some daydream. I've been trying to get your attention for the last five minutes."

"Guess I really let my mind wander this time," Jason admitted.

"I wish I could block out the world like that," said Paul, shaking his head in wonder. "There was no way that I could get through to you. If I could do what you do, I'd use it whenever Mom starts to nag at me."

"Yeah, it's great," said Jason, but his voice lacked conviction. "Sometimes though, it can be pretty scary."

"Scary?"

"Yah. I've grown so good at daydreaming that sometimes I think there'll come a time when I won't be able to find my way back to reality." It was the first time Jason had shared his secret with anyone, and even though it was Paul he was talking to, he still felt a little nervous about disclosing his ability to escape from life.

Jason was relieved when Paul, after considering Jason's disclosure for several minutes, finally said: "That would be scary alright. But, I still think it's a good way to shut out the rest of the world, when you need to escape for a while. So, tell me, why do you think that someday you won't be able to get back?"

"I don't know...," Jason confessed. "It's just that, when I blank out my mind and concentrate on the darkness, I find I don't want to come back. It's like an invisible force is trying to close the door, so I can't return." Jason put his hands on the table and stared across at his friend. "Paul, what would happen to me if someday the door closed before I got back, and I was locked inside my mind forever?"

Paul rested his chin in his hands, and stared back at Jason. He thought for a few minutes, before he replied. "Gee, Jason, I don't know. Perhaps you'd die...." His voice trailed off and Jason saw his friend close his eyes and shudder.

"I thought that, too," said Jason softly. "That's why I try not to stay-- out-- too long. But, don't you think that even if I did get locked in my mind, my body would still stay alive, waiting for me to return?"

"Maybe," Paul replied, his eyes still closed. "But I wouldn't count on it. Besides, I don't know what good it would be for you to have your body stay alive, if your mind was somewhere else. Maybe you shouldn't do it anymore; or if you do, you shouldn't stay away too long or go too far."

Jason could see that his friend was genuinely worried about him, and he was sorry that he had upset Paul. He tried to allay Paul's fears by agreeing to take his advice. However, Jason knew that he wouldn't stop daydreaming or escaping to the grey room. He couldn't. He needed this method of escape to get away from his father. That he would be lost anyway, if he had to face his dad without having a safe place to flee. "Don't worry about me," he said to Paul. "I'll be careful; I promise."

"Good," said Paul, wiping the perspiration off his brow with his shirt sleeve. "Because, I wouldn't want to lose you."

Jason tried to ease the tension that now filled the once happy room. "Oh, you can't get rid of me that easy," he joked. "Haven't I told you? I'm going to be around forever."

"That suits me just fine," Paul replied, "and now that you've rejoined the land of the living, it's time you gave me a hand cleaning up this mess. You haven't won that wager yet, you know."

"Sure," Jason laughed. He picked up his model and carried it over to the shelf. When he returned to the table, Paul had already put their materials into the box and was wiping off the table. Jason walked over to him, and laying his hand on Paul's forearm, said, "Don't worry about what I just said to you. I'll be okay-- really."

Paul placed his hand over Jason's and smiled. "I know you will," he said seriously. "Because, if I ever see you drifting too far away, I'm going to tie a string around your ankle and yank you back. I won't let you get lost." He turned away and Jason thought he heard him mutter under his breath, "I won't let you die."

"Thanks...," Jason called after him. He was overcome by Paul's obvious concern for his well-being. No one, except for Pookie, had ever cared for him before or been as kind and understanding.

When Paul came back from the sink, Jason said to him, "I'm glad we're friends."

"So am I," Paul replied. "So am I."

CHAPTER XIV

Two weeks later, Jason finished his model and proudly stood in the middle of the craft room holding it up for Paul to admire. The silver decals on the four-foot long wings shimmered under the overhead lights. To Jason, the plane was the most wonderful thing he had ever owned. His voice swelled with pride when he said to Paul, "Isn't it beautiful!"

Paul ran his fingers over the smooth silk wings and agreed. "I couldn't have done any better," he conceded graciously. "You should be very proud of yourself."

"I am."

"Now that you've finished, what are you going to do with it-- take it home?"

"No," Jason replied. He had asked himself that same question many times and still hadn't come up with an answer. The only thing that he knew for sure was that he wouldn't take the plane home.

"Well, you have plenty of time to decide," said Paul, unaware of Jason's dilemma, "because first, you have to show it to Mrs. Miller and Mr. White. But, even before that, we have to take it for a spin."

"Take it for a spin?"

"Yeah," Paul replied, walking over to the table and sweeping his arm along the length of it, clearing off the remaining scraps of wood and cloth into a garbage bin. When he had finished, he walked to the end of the table and stood waiting for Jason. "Okay," he said, cupping his hand into an imaginary microphone, "This is control tower speaking. Runway one is clear for takeoff. Please proceed on green flag." He picked up a piece of green silk off the floor and slowly waved it back and forth.

Caught up in Paul's game, Jason walked to the opposite end of the table and set down his plane. He pretended to give the propeller a spin. "Pilot to control tower. We are ready for takeoff."

"We acknowledge: please proceed," said Paul, stepping aside and leaving the runway clear for Jason's maiden flight.

Jason started off slowly, pushing the plane along the table, and then speeded up until he was running along-side his plane. When he came to the end of the makeshift runway, he gripped the plane tightly and soared upward into the air. He circled the table twice before returning for the landing. When he had successfully landed and rolled to a stop a few feet from Paul, he radioed the control tower. "Test flight completed; all system A-OK." He picked up the plane and came over to where Paul was standing. He sat down on his chair, his plane cradled in his lap.

"Well, I guess you earned your wings," said Paul, pulling up a chair beside him. "I guess I have," Jason replied modestly, his eyes fixed on the plane in his lap. "It was great Paul; just great!" I wish it was real," he added wistfully.

"I know what you mean. When I finished my first plane, I wanted to climb inside and actually fly away."

They spent a few more minutes admiring the model and then Paul asked, "If you're not going to take it home, what are you planning on doing with it?"

The future of his plane was no longer undecided. While running alongside it, Jason had come to a decision. "I'm going to give it to Mrs. Miller," he said and then added, "just like you did with the first plan you built."

Paul didn't say anything for a few moments and Jason thought that his friend was going to ask him why he wasn't going to take it home, instead. But, when Paul finally spoke, all he said was, "That's a good idea. I know she'll like it, because she's been admiring it ever since you first started to put it together."

"You really think she'll like it?" Jason asked, filled with trepidation. He didn't know what he would do if Mrs. Miller rejected his gift.

Paul was about to answer when the object of their discussion walked into the room and joined them at the table. She looked at the plane in Jason's lap, and then looked at him. "Well, I see that you're finally finished," she said, gently picking it up and examining it. "You must be very proud of the job you've done. I can't remember seeing a better example of superb craftsmanship."

Jason visibly swelled from the generous praise being given him by Mrs. Miller. However, he didn't want Paul or her to know how much her praise meant to him, so he brushed her words aside and assumed an air of indifference. "Thanks," he said quietly and then, as if it were an afterthought, added, "I'd like you to have it, if you want it."

"Jason are you sure?" she asked, moved by his generous gesture. "I'd love to have it, but you've put so much work in it that I thought that you'd want to take it home and hand it in your room."

Jason closed his eyes and was once again transported back in time. *He was standing amid the rubble that had once been his room. He saw the boy in the mirror bend down and pick up pieces of what had once been his model planes. The boy opened his hand and let the broken plastic drop to the floor....* Jason blinked twice and looked up at Mrs. Miller. "No," he said softly, "I don't want to hang it in my room. I want you to have it."

Jason watched as she held up the plane and scanned the undercarriage. She smiled. He was glad she wasn't able to see into his mind, wasn't able to see the bits of broken plastic lying on the floor like so many broken dreams.

"Well then," she said, "if you're sure you don't want to change your mind, I'd be thrilled to accept your gift." She set the plan on the table, came over to him and gave him a hug. "Thank you. Thank you very much," she whispered hoarsely, tears in her eyes. "Wait 'til I show your plane to Mr. White. He'll be green with envy."

Jason relaxed; the crisis was over. He was glad that she had accepted his gift without any further comments. *Maybe she somehow knew why I didn't want to bring it home, he thought, giving her a speculative look. But, how could she know; how could anyone know the truth?*

They followed Mrs. Miller out of the room and over to her office. Every few feet, she would stop to admire the plane. When they reached her office, she pointed to a spot on the ceiling directly over her desk. "I'm going to hang it right there," she informed them. "That way, every time I look up, I'll be able to admire it."

It was the first time Jason had ever been in her office and while he was looking around, he spotted a large, single-engine plane hanging over her filing cabinet.

Paul saw him staring at the plane. "It's mine," he announced proudly. "That's the very first plane that I built."

The two boys looked at each other and smiled.

Unaware of the silent communication taking place between them, Mrs. Miller continued to chatter about how great her office was going to look when Jason's plane was hanging over her desk. "As long as I remember to duck," she said, trying to gauge the distance from where the plane would hang to the top of her head.

Jason and Paul left her bustling around trying to find a hammer and the roll of wire that she swore was always in the bottom drawer of her desk- until she needed it. Then, it would mysteriously disappear never to be seen again.

They went back to the craft room and Jason went over to the shelf. When he came back to the table, he had a stack of instructions manuals tucked under his arm. He set them down on the table and began to absentmindedly leaf through them.

"Going to start another one right away?" Paul asked.

"I guess so," Jason replied, but his voice lacked conviction. "Nothing else I like doing here," he added, his arm sweeping the room.

"Don't be depressed," Paul tried to console him. "I know it was hard for you to give it away, but you're going to build more; lots more."

Jason gave him a sad smile. "yah," he replied. He knew Paul was only trying to cheer him up, but he wished his friend would leave him alone for a while.

Why did I have to give it away? he thought dejectedly. *How come Mrs. Miller can like it and not you, Dad? Why?*

Jason would have continued to question the injustices in his life, but Paul interrupted his thoughts. "Hey!" Paul exclaimed excitedly. "I've got a terrific idea. You're good at building planes-- real good. So, why don't we form a partnership when we grow up? Then, we could work together and open our own airplane-building business."

"That sounds great, Paul, but I can't. I have other plans. Remember the Marine Biologist....?"

"Oh yeah... sorry... I forgot. Do you really plan on becoming a Marine Biologist?"

"Yes."

Paul was disappointed that Jason didn't share his enthusiasm over the suggestion they become partners. "Well, I guess that settles that."

"Yeah, I guess it does."

"Mrs. Miller was real happy you gave her your plane," said Paul, changing the subject. "I think you should give yourself a pat on the back for your generosity."

Jason wished Paul would just forget about his plane and quit praising him for his generosity. He wasn't used to all the flattery and it was starting to get on his nerves.

Paul was about to say something, but when he looked at Jason, he closed his mouth and stared out the window. It was as if he had read Jason's mind. After a few minutes, he got up, walked over to the shelf, and came back with his plane. He still had some finishing work to do on it, and Jason knew that if Paul had wanted, he could have completed it over three weeks ago. Sometimes, Jason got the impression that for some strange reason Paul was deliberately stalling.

It appeared to Jason that Paul spent more time watching him work this past while, than he did working on his own model. When he mentioned it to him, Paul only smiled and continued to watch. "Maybe," he said mysteriously, "but remember, I've already built three other planes besides this one. This is your first and it's special. When it's done, you shouldn't have to share the glory with anyone else... at least, not for a while."

Jason didn't know what Paul was getting at, and even now, as he watched Paul paint, he still wondered at the meaning behind his friend's words.

A little while later, Paul put his paint brush in a jar and looked across the table at Jason. "You never did have any intention of taking your plane home, did you?"

"No," Jason softly replied, "I never did." For a minute, Jason thought about concocting some story rather than tell Paul the truth, but he didn't want to lie. Jason was curious to know how Paul had come to that conclusion. "How did you know?" he asked.

"I figured it out from what you didn't say."

"Huh?"

"Well, for one thing, you never once mentioned how proud your parents were going to be when you brought it home to show them."

"You're right there," agreed Jason. "My Dad wouldn't have been impressed. He thinks building models is stupid and that I'm wasting my time."

"I thought as much."

Now it was Paul's turn to watch him and Jason shifted uneasily in his chair. Paul's persistent stare began to unnerve him. It was as if Paul was waiting for him to explain. Jason couldn't. He couldn't talk about his father to Paul or anyone else. Grabbing a manual from the pile, Jason opened it and lifted it up so that his face was concealed behind it. He pretended to read.

"Don't get me wrong," said Paul, reaching across the table and pushing the magazine away, exposing Jason's face. "I'm not trying to make you feel guilty and I'm not trying to force you to talk about your dad. I understand why you gave Mrs. Miller your model. I also know why you didn't want to take it home. I've never taken any of my planes home either."

"Why not?"

"Because nobody at home would appreciate them."

Jason didn't respond to his friend's open admission. Instead, he stared down at the manual he was holding and hoped that Paul would take his silence to mean that he agreed with him.

His friend didn't appear to mind his reluctance to verbally agree with him, because Paul continued: "The way I see it, I spend weeks pouring my heart and soul into building these planes, and my family just doesn't give a damn. Maybe my Mom wouldn't say I was wasting my time, but she still wouldn't understand. She'd probably say, 'That's nice dear,' and wouldn't know, or probably care, that I slaved for weeks to build that plane. And, you can bet your life, neither Mom nor my sister would take time to really examine it closely... or tell me that I did a great job!"

Jason was relieved to find that Paul understood his problem perfectly and found himself vigorously nodding his head in agreement. "You're right on," he said. However, Jason knew that his problem would not be one of just appreciation for the work that he had done, because his dad didn't know he was building models. His father thought that he was spending his Saturdays doing Math. If he ever suspected the truth.... Jason shuttered.

"Come," said Paul, "No use us moping around here all afternoon feeling sorry for ourselves. I want to show you something."

Jason followed him out of the craft room and across the main room to a door just off the main entrance.

"Behind this door," Paul explained, "are stairs leading up to a large meeting room. Remember? When you first came here, you asked me what I did with the third plane that I had built and I told you that if you stayed and built one of your own, I'd tell you?"

"Well, you've finished your plane and I'm going to show you where my plane is hanging. Follow me." Paul opened the door and they began to climb the stairs. When they reached the top of the staircase, Paul felt along the wall until he found the light switch. He flipped it on. Then he led Jason down a short corridor and into a room at the end of the hall. It was dark inside the room and Jason couldn't see anything. He was just beginning to wonder if Paul knew what he was doing, when Paul reached over and flipped another switch.

Light flooded the room and Jason found himself staring up at the ceiling in amazement. There were planes-- dozen of them-- all suspended from the ceiling by invisible wires. Speechless, all Jason could do is stare up at them, his mouth open. The draft from the open door set the planes in motion and they began to slowly turn on their pivots. "Are these all yours?" Jason asked in awe.

"No. I wish they were, though," Paul replied, his voice filled with reverence. He pointed to a plane on Jason's right. "See that one? That one's mine."

Paul joined him. "You can see why I was so impressed with your plane," he said to Jason. "That's the third plane I built and it's still not as good as your first one."

"It's beautiful!" Jason was still dazzled by the splendor hanging overhead. He stepped back to admire Paul's aircraft.

"Thanks." Paul's eyes glowed from the praise.

"Who built all these?" asked Jason.

"Kids like us. The Centre has been operating a long time and lots of kids have built model planes over the years."

"But why are they here? Why didn't they take them home?"

"Why didn't you? Why didn't I? Who knows? Maybe they felt like we do and were afraid to take them home. I don't know....

"But where are these kids now?" Jason asked. So far, ever since he had first come to the Centre, only he and Paul had made use of the craft room to build model planes.

"They're gone now," Paul replied. "Maybe they've grown up and are too old to come to the Centre anymore."

Jason's eyes swept across the ceiling. "They're terrific," he murmured.

"I thought you'd like to see them. No one comes up here unless the adults who run this place have a meeting or something like that; nobody that is-- except me. And now you. I love it here."

"But why didn't you show me this room before?" Jason asked. He wondered how his best friend could have kept this wondrous place a secret all these weeks and hadn't said anything to him.

"Jason," said Paul, trying to explain. "This room means a lot to me and if you had no intention of staying, or you weren't really interested in building model planes, then you wouldn't have appreciated this room. And," he added, "that would have spoiled some of its attraction for me."

"I understand," said Jason and he did. If the roles had been reversed, Jason would have been reluctant to show this room to anyone else. Staring up at the planes, he wasn't even sure that he would have shared this secret now.

Paul headed for the door. "We better go now, before someone decides to come looking for us."

Jason walked over to the door and they both stood there a few more moments staring up at the ceiling. "My next plane, Paul is going to hang in this room," said Jason with quiet resolve.

Paul didn't answer him, but Jason knew that he understood how he felt. Together, they walked down the steps and went back to the craft room. They took their places at the table but they didn't speak to each other. Neither of them wanted to destroy the special feeling that the room had generated by talking.

They stayed this way, each of them doing his own thing, until the feeling passed. Jason leaned back on his chair, his mind on the secret room. "Paul, are all the kids that come here like us? You know-- do they all have problems?"

Paul took his time before answering. "No...," he replied. "I don't think so... some, yes... but not everybody. Why?"

"Because I thought that maybe they were pressured into coming here-- like us."

"I doubt it," replied Paul. "Besides I like coming here." "Me, too." said Jason. "But, I thought that maybe this place was only for kids who had problems."

"I don't think so." Paul picked up his paint brush and turned his attention to his model.

The subject was dropped. Jason picked up a manual and began to read. He was pretty sure by this time that he had selected his next project. He was still reading when Mrs. Miller joined them.

"Hi boys," she said, pulling up a chair and sitting down. "I got Mr. White to give me a hand to hang up your model," she said to Jason. "Those two planes sure add life to my little cubbyhole."

Jason grinned. Without saying anything, he handed her the manual he was holding and pointed to the picture on the front page. "I'm going to start on this one."

"Phew," she said. "That's going to be a first for this place. No one that I know has ever built a rocket before. I can see it now. There goes the ceiling and we just had it repainted last fall," she laughed.

Paul came over and looked at the picture. "Don't worry," he said, "it shouldn't make a very big hole and we can always cover it up with a picture or something."

"Thanks, Paul," she said squeezing his cheek. "Thanks for those very encouraging words." She turned to Jason. "All I have to say, Jason, is go for it. I think it's a great idea and I'll say like they do in the movies, 'Dare to go where no man has gone before.'"

CHAPTER XV

Even after Jason had helped Paul clean up their mess and had left the Centre for home, he couldn't quite contain the excitement he felt over building the rocket. Riding on the bus, he hummed; he fidgeted in his seat; he craned his neck to stare out the window at the clouds overhead. He tried to remember what the rockets in the movies he had seen looked like. His was going to be nicer-- much nicer! *I'll have to pick out a name for it* when I finish building it, he thought happily, his mind running through a list of possibilities. *Maybe I'll call it Enterprise II. That would be a good name.*

His good mood lasted until he walked through the front door and saw Becky run out of the kitchen, crying. His sister passed him and ran upstairs. Her face was flushed and she cast him a despairing look as she raced away.

Oh shit! Dad's at it again, Jason thought, quietly removing his shoes and tip-toeing towards the stairs. Maybe he could make it to his room without being seen. His foot barely touched the bottom step when he heard his father shout at him.

"Jason!"

Jason froze like a startled rabbit-- afraid to turn around.

"Where the hell have you been?" his dad screamed.

Jason forced himself to turn around and face his father. He was standing a few steps away, his face contorted with rage. Jason tried to gauge the reason behind his dad's anger, but he was too afraid and his mind went numb. He couldn't think. His voice shook as he whispered, "Down at the Centre."

His answer seemed to only serve to infuriate his dad even more. "Down at the Centre!" he yelled, coming over and grabbing Jason by the scruff of the neck. "You're always at that damn place! What's the matter with you? Don't you have enough to do around here, that you have to bugger off every Saturday? If you don't, I can soon rectify that in a hurry!"

"No, Dad... I mean... yes, Dad, I got enough to do here," he squeaked. Frightened, Jason shifted from one foot to another, trying to figure out how he was going to survive his dad's rage. He knew it was only a matter of time before his dad started swinging. Jason didn't want to be around when that happened.

"Get upstairs and get washed up for supper," his dad snarled, giving Jason a shove. Jason sprawled on the floor. "But remember," he warned, standing over him, "I'm not through with you yet."

Jason picked himself up off the floor and cast his father a backward glance to make sure another blow wasn't forthcoming. He bolted up the stairs and ran to his room. Only when he was safe inside, did he give in to his fear. Whimpering like a hurt animal, Jason walked over to his bed and sat down. He began to cry. Everything had been going good up until now. What had he done to make his dad so mad?

Unable to find an answer, Jason gave up trying and stretched out on his bed. He thought about his rocket, instead. He stared up at the ceiling and tried to imagine what his rocket would look like when it was finished and suspended from the ceiling in the mystery room. He could still hear his father shouting downstairs. He turned on his radio, trying to drown out the noise. His thoughts turned to the discussion Paul had with him about getting angry and making others suffer for it.

My counsellors should be here, listening to Dad, Jason thought scornfully. Or, is it that it's wrong for everyone else to kick the shit out of somebody, but it's okay for Dad?

The more he thought about what Paul had told him, the more convinced Jason became that these "rules" didn't apply to his father. There was nobody around to tell him that it was wrong-- No one would dare! Jason cursed his dad and wished his father would just drop dead and leave them alone.

"Jason...! Jason! Get your ass down here right now! Do you hear me?"

Jason scrambled off his bed and ran out of his room. When he reached the kitchen, he heard his dad scream at his mother-- scream about the Centre. Jason hurried to sit down at the table. He watched his father stomp around the kitchen, kicking at anything that got in his road. He came over to where Jason was sitting.

Where the hell were you?" his dad demanded. "If you think this family is going to wait supper for you, you better think again. It isn't bad enough that you're never home anymore, now you think you can start coming in whenever you like. Well, I'm sick and tired of you wasting time with that God-damn teacher of yours. If you weren't so stupid in the first place, you wouldn't need any special "tutoring." He slammed his fists down on the table. "From now on, Linda, I want that boy to stay home where he belongs. Dammit anyway! You're turning these kids into a bunch of little tramps-- like you."

When his father had pounded on the table, Jason knew that unless he did something soon, he would succumb to the fear that had been building inside him since he first heard his dad shouting. He tried to keep himself from shaking by clasping his hands tightly together and drawing in his elbows 'til he was now sitting as motionless and frightened as the rabbit in his memories. It was time for him to escape!

He concentrated-- tried to call the darkness to him-- but, this time it didn't seem to work. No matter how hard he tried, he couldn't escape the noise around him. With his dad's cruel taunts ringing in his ears, Jason tried again. Sweat beaded on his forehead and his breathing became labored, as he struggled to overcome the barrier that would allow him to escape reality to the safety he knew waited beyond. Finally, Jason could feel his self begin to fade away.... His dad's voice faded out and became a faint echo the deeper he descended into the darkness. Jason embraced the blackness-- the silence-- as one would embrace an old friend. Mechanically, his hand lifted his fork from his plate to his mouth, but he didn't taste the food. He couldn't-- he was gone!

Before he had completely slipped away, Jason saw his father raise his hand and slap his mother across the face. But the violent act had no effect on Jason because the only thing that mattered now to Jason was that he reached the end of his journey. The grey room awaited him. He was speeding further and further away, when he saw the boy in the mirror reach out to him. Jason took hold of the outstretched hand and they continued the journey together....

Gradually, the darkness began to be replaced by light and Jason knew they were near their destination. When they reached the room, the boy led Jason inside and over to the staircase. They boy started to climb the steps and beckoned for Jason to follow. Jason stood at the bottom watching the boy get smaller and smaller as he climbed higher and higher. Jason was tempted to follow him but held back, his hand gripping the rail and his left foot on the first step. He was plagued with uncertainty. What would happen to him if he climbed those steps and disappeared? Would he be able to come back? Would he die? Something inside him warned him that the latter was a distinct possibility. The boy had stopped and was waving at him, wanted Jason to join him. Jason thought about Paul and his warning. "Where's your string, Paul? "Where's your string now?" he whispered, and the sound reverberated in the emptiness surrounding him....

Jason had no idea how long he stood there looking up at the boy, before he finally turned and walked towards the little door leading out of the darkness.

The next thing he knew, he was back in the kitchen, still sitting at the table, but his return was greeted by silence. Gone was the screaming-- the shouting. Confused, Jason shook his head, opened his eyes and blinked, trying to figure out what had taken place while he was gone. He was alone at the table. His mother was busy washing pots in the sink but other than her, no one else was in the kitchen. Jason stared down at his empty plate, wondering if any of them were aware that he had been "gone."

Fatigued from the effects of his journey into the darkness, Jason made no effort to leave his place at the table. He watched his mother work. It had been close this time-- he knew that. Never before had he wanted to climb the staircase to see what lay beyond. But this time, it had been different. This time he didn't want to come back. The boy had offered him a permanent means of escape and he had turned it down. Why? Was it Paul's warning that had prevented him from taking that first step? He didn't know.

Right now, all he wanted to do was go to bed. He was exhausted and had to force himself to get up from the table and walk across the kitchen.

Like an old man, he shuffled towards the stairs. Slowly, putting one foot in front of the other, he managed to climb the staircase and go to his room. He went inside and closed the door behind him.

It was two weeks before his father finally relented and let Jason return to the Centre. During this period of time, Jason was so depressed he could barely stand to go through the motions of living. At home and at school, he fell into his old routine of avoiding his classmates and teachers alike. If he couldn't go to the Centre and work on his model, he didn't feel like life was worth living anymore.

He tried not to let his desperation affect his performance in school, though. He didn't want any more hassles. His homework was still done on time and he was prepared whenever a teacher asked him to answer a question in class. But when he wasn't busy working on his homework, he kept to his room. Alone, he would let his imagination soar and take him beyond his walls into new exciting worlds that lay outside his room.

Only then, did he feel completely free and uninhibited. He would climb into the cockpit of his bi-plane and soar into the sky, swooping through the clouds to attack the enemy below. He would peer over the side, raking the ground with his eyes, trying to spot enemy movement. Often, when he bought the plane lower to the ground to get a better view, he would be fired upon. Laughing, he would maneuver through the heavy anti-aircraft fire, easily avoiding the shelling behind directed at him. With the white puffs of smoke exploding around him, he would yell down at them: "You can't catch me. I'm too smart for you." Only when he was sure that he had showed them how easy it was for him to make fools of them, did he pull back on the throttle and lift into the air, heading for home.

However, even though he was able to easily stay out of his enemy's reach, his escapades were not completely without cost to him. Every time he had safely landed, exhaustion would sink in and he'd be so weak that he wouldn't be able to lift his head off his pillow. He would have to lie there until his strength returned. And, when he was finally able to move, he would bury his face in his hands and beseech God to do something that would get his father to relent and let him go back to the Centre.

During this period of his life, Jason would also use his plane to help him escape at school and he easily avoided Mr. White's questioning glances by climbing into his plane and soaring away until he was lost in the clouds.

One time Mr. White had tried to corner him in the hallway, but Jason had ducked into the boys' washroom and, after that, his teacher had made no further attempts to detain him. Jason knew that he should be glad that he had eluded Mr. White so easily, but he wasn't. Instead, he was left with a feeling of being totally isolated in his own world-- the world he had created.

Jason was preparing to spend another Saturday afternoon in his room, when he heard a soft knock at his door. "If that's you, Becky," he said, "leave me alone. I don't want to be bothered right now."

"It's me," his mom said, opening the door and stepping inside his room. "I just came up to tell you that I talked with your Dad last night and it's okay for you to go back to the Centre this afternoon, if you want."

"Want!" exclaimed Jason, jumping up off his bed and hurling himself into his mother's arms. "Of course I want to go. Thanks! Thanks a lot." He gave her another hug and then rushed out of the room and downstairs. He put on his shoes and coat and ran down the street to the bus stop. He couldn't wait to get there and see Paul!

When he arrived at the Centre, he ran up the steps and threw open the door. Mr. White was standing in the middle of the room and Jason waved at him as he quickly made his way over to the craft room.

"Welcome back," his teacher yelled after him.

"Thanks," Jason called back, not bothering to stop. He had to see Paul; had to see if anything had happened during his absence. Paul was standing in front of the shelf when he came through the door. Jason ran over to him and threw his arm around Paul's neck. "I'm back," he said, grinning from ear to ear.

"So I see," said Paul coldly. He brushed off Jason's arm and walked over to the table.

Jason was crushed. "I'm back," he repeated, his voice cracking with suppressed emotion. Wasn't Paul glad to see him? Weren't they friends anymore?

Paul turned and stared at him, his expression unreadable. "You could have called."

Hurt by his friend's coldness, Jason withdrew to the opposite end of the room and stood silently looking out the window at his school across the street. What right did Paul have being mad at him when it wasn't his fault? He turned to face Paul and said sadly, "Dad wouldn't let me come and I couldn't call you 'cause I don't have your number."

"I know that, dummy," said Paul breaking into a wide grin. He came over to where Jason was standing and gave him a shove. "I was only giving you a hard time. Don't take everything so seriously," he added, throwing his arm around Jason's shoulder. "I missed you, too."

Jason almost collapsed with relief. He had to sit down before he fell down. *Thank you, God*, he whispered to himself. He didn't know what he would do without Paul's friendship and even thinking about it made him feel sick to his stomach. He waited for Paul to ask him why his dad wouldn't let him come, but Paul just stood smiling down at him.

Jason didn't want to tell him about his parents fighting or about the many trips he had taken in the bi-plane. *He wouldn't believe me, anyway*, thought Jason, staring up at his friend. He didn't want Paul to think he was joking about his ability to fly the plane, or worse yet, think that he had lost his mind while he was away, so Jason put any thoughts of sharing his secret with Paul, out of his mind. Instead, he smiled back at his friend and said: "I missed you."

"Well, I missed you, too. Don't mind me staring at you. I just can't believe that you're really here, sitting in front of me. I was afraid that you were never coming back again."

"Don't be crazy."

They continued to stare at each other for a few more minutes without speaking. Then, Paul went back to the shelf. "Let's get to work," he said, handing Jason his instruction manual and picking up their box of materials. Paul set the stuff down on the table. "Before we start," he said, "I've got to go take a leak. Don't go away; I'll be right back."

As soon as Paul had left the room, Jason got up and followed him out of the room. However, he didn't stop at the bathroom, but instead walked over to the door leading up to the secret room. He checked to see if anyone was watching him, before quickly opening the door and climbing the stairs. He didn't bother to turn on the lights and had to feel his way until he came to the room at the end of the hallway. Silently, he opened the door and stepped inside.

The room smelled musty and Jason crinkled his nose as he stood in the darkness peering upwards. Even without the lights, he was able to see the grey outlines of the planes overhead, as they slowly turned on their wire strings in the silent room.

The same feeling of awe washed over Jason as he stared up at them. "Someday," he whispered, "I'm going to take a ride in all of you." He reached up and gently touched the plane handing over his head. It gently swayed back and forth and he stood watching it move, as if he had been hypnotized. The plane seemed to be beckoning to him to climb in and, if he dared, together they would travel to new and wondrous places that even in his mind, Jason had never dared go before.

Jason could have stayed there for hours but he knew that if he didn't return now, Paul would come looking for him. On his way out, he stopped in the doorway and cast one more glance up at the ceiling. "I'll be back," he whispered to them, "I'll be back."

CHAPTER XVI

By the following Saturday it had snowed, and Jason had to plow through the deep drifts that now covered the sidewalk in front of the house. The air was crisp and cold, and he pulled his toque down over his ears as he waited for the bus.

I hope it's warm in the Centre, he thought, clapping his mittens together to keep his fingers from freezing. By the time the bus finally arrived, he didn't think he'd ever get warm again.

But once inside the warm vehicle, Jason started to thaw out and his fingers began to tingle. He stomped his feet on the floorboard, trying to get some feeling back into his toes and thought that maybe he should have taken his mother's advice about wearing his winter boots instead of his runners. When the bus pulled up at his stop, Jason was reluctant to leave the warmth and shivered, as he stepped back out into the frigid air.

Today, no one was standing outside as he ran up the steps, and he thought that he would find everyone inside. However, when he went in, the place looked deserted and for a second he thought that he might be early until he checked his watch. Nope, he was on time, but where was everyone else? He was busy hanging up his coat on a hook when he heard footsteps behind him.

"Hi Jason," said Mrs. Miller, coming over to him. She stopped by the door. "Burrr..., it's cold out there," she shivered.

Jason laughed. "Yeah, it sure is. But I'm glad that it snowed. It means Christmas isn't too far off."

"Yes, I guess only a couple weeks left before the fat man makes the scene."

He gave her a strange look. Then it suddenly dawned on him who she meant. He chuckled. "Yeah," he agreed, "I can hardly wait." He changed the subject by asking: "Where is everyone? I thought when I got here that maybe you guys had decided to shut it down today because it was so cold outside."

"No. If we say we're going to be open, then we're open," she replied. "I think, though, that the cold weather will keep a lot of the kids away today."

Stay away from the Centre, just because it was a little bit cold outside? To Jason, that was a ridiculous excuse. He shook his head. "Naw," he informed her, "I don't think so. It's not that cold outside."

"Well, I hope you're right or we're going to have the place to ourselves today."

That wouldn't be a bad idea, thought Jason, as long as Paul showed up.

He was just beginning to imagine all the neat things that they could do here alone, when Mrs. Miller interrupted his thoughts.

"Say, I forgot to ask you if you've started on the rocket yet? You haven't asked for my help, and I thought that you must either be doing just fine without me, or you've abandoned the idea altogether."

"No," he replied. "I haven't changed my mind. I already started carving out the frame last week, but it's going to take me a long time before I'm finally finished this model. Each piece of wood has to be soaked and bent to the right shape."

"Well, remember, if you need any help, give me a shout," she answered. "I like to help, but only if I'm needed. I don't want to butt in where I'm not wanted."

"You don't interfere, Mrs. Miller," Jason protested. "I really appreciated all the help you gave me on my plane."

"Why thank you. But you can take most of the credit there. You did a fine job."

"Thanks."

"I'd like to stay and talk with you," she told him, "but I have to get some paperwork done before Mr. White arrives. If I get everything done, I'll stop in later to visit you. Okay?"

"Sure." Jason watched her until she disappeared inside her office, before going to the craft room. He spread out his materials on the table and began to work on his rocket, while he waited for Paul to arrive.

While he worked, Jason thought about Mrs. Miller. Their relationship had deepened over the past few months into mutual friendship. He recalled the time that he had spent an entire afternoon alone with her, talking and working on his model. Paul had stayed home sick with the flu and as much as Jason missed seeing his friend, he had been glad to have Mrs. Miller for company.

She had casually asked him about his family and he had told her about Nicky and Becky. But, when she asked about his parents, his happy mood had vanished.

*   *   *

"What does your husband do for a living?" Jason asked, trying to get the topic of conversation on to safer ground.

"Oh, Jack is a professional chef. He cooks for one of the major hotels downtown," she answered proudly.

"That's a wimpy job for a man," said Jason without thinking, and then blushed when he realized what he had said might have hurt her feelings. He looked up sheepishly.

But instead of being offended by his remarks, Mrs. Miller's expression never changed, as she replied, "I don't think being a chef is a wimpy job." Jason was ready to sink into the floor. How could he be such a klutz? But then she continued. "Jack's a great cook-- much better than I'll ever be. In fact, two years ago, he won two gold medals for his creations in an international competition in Europe." Her eyes grew misty and she smiled as she remembered that day. "Yes, I was so proud of him that I cried at the closing ceremonies. And," she added, "I'm still proud of him."

Trying to redeem himself and also impressed by the fact that Mrs. Miller's husband had won two gold medals for his cooking, Jason said,

"Gee, I didn't mean to call him a wimp. Imagine? Food Olympics! Is it hard? I mean, does he have to work hard to be a chef?"

"Yes," she replied, her voice taking on a serious tone, "it takes years of practice and education to become a world-class chef."

"But," Jason persisted, "I thought that cooking was a woman's job. I'm not trying to put your husband down," he quickly added when he saw Mrs. Miller frown, "but I find it strange that he'd want to be a cook, when he could've been a doctor or a lawyer, or maybe, even a truckdriver."

"Jack never wanted to be any of those things," she replied softly, and Jason could tell from her voice that she wasn't upset with him. "All he ever wanted was to be a chef and he's succeeded. But tell me, why do you think that cooking is strictly a woman's job?"

Jason didn't know how he was going to answer her question without telling her about the things his grandpa and dad had said about women and their role in life. He decided to take the easy way out. "I don't know," he replied indifferently, "I just think it is. Men are supposed to work and bring home the money and women are supposed to look after the house and do the cooking."

"I don't agree with you, said Mrs. Miller. "I know lots of women who work and contribute to the family income and their husbands help around the house. Take me, for example. I've worked for most of my married life, not because we're desperate for money, but because I find it challenging and I like my job. And," she added, "Jack has always encouraged me in my efforts, as well as helped out around the house. He has also helped to raise our children. We never had separate roles, just because I'm a woman and he's a man."

Jason sat there, silenced by the force of her arguments. All the old rebuttals that he would have once used, he know didn't seem to apply to Mrs. Miller. In fact, even he found them to be shallow and invalid now. Unsettled by the direction the conversation had taken, Jason tried to hide his discomfort by pretending to read from his instruction manual.

"Your Mom doesn't work, does she?" Mrs. Miller asked.

Jason didn't want to tell her that all his mother did was stay home and look after the house. Especially now, after he had just finished listening to Mrs. Miller's spiel on women. Ashamed, he thought of inventing an exciting career for his mother so she would sound more glamorous instead of being the drab creature that she was now. But, when Jason looked up and saw her watching him, he knew he couldn't lie to her. "No," he replied softly, "Mom's just a housewife." *Why couldn't Mom have an exciting life like you do?* Jason wondered waiting for Mrs. Miller to agree with him that his mother wasn't a very important person. He was surprised when he heard her exclaim:

"Don't you ever let me hear you refer to your mother as `just a housewife'! Being a housewife and mother is one of the toughest jobs going. And," she added sternly, "It takes more brains than you've apparently given her credit for! Jack and I raised four kids and I know that I couldn't have done it without his help. I think your mother deserves a gold medal for staying home and raising you kids."

Even though he was being taken to task for his beliefs, Jason didn't get defensive or angry. He was glad that his mother's role was considered such a worthy one. He had never known that before, and now it wiped away the guilt he was feeling. "I'm sorry," he apologized, I didn't--"

"That's okay," she smiled. "It's not always easy for men to accept women as equals in our society. You're not the only male to think that women should be kept in the house. I just hope that when you get married, you will always treat your wife as an equal partner, because if you don't I don't think your marriage is going to be very happy. Without mutual respect and admiration for each other, couples soon drift apart. Especially," and she cast him a meaningful look, "if one of them tramples on the rights of the other."

"Rights?" Jason asked, not comprehending what Mrs. Miller was talking about.

"Yes rights," she replied. "I'm talking about the things each partner in a marriage has the right to expect. For instance: A person has the right to expect to live without fear of being threatened or hurt; the right to be involved in major decisions concerning the family; the right to be treated with respect and caring; and the right to continue to develop to their full potential, regardless of their sex."

"I don't think I'll ever get married," Jason responded, his voice serious. "It sounds too complicated for me."

Mrs. Miller laughed and patted him on the back. "We'll see," she said to him kindly. "Give you a few more years and you might think a lot differently."

After he left that day, Jason thought about the things Mrs. Miller had said to him. He couldn't figure her out. Every time he thought that he had finally fitted her into an acceptable role, she blew him out of the water, like she had today. It wasn't just that she didn't fit any of the roles he knew women should fit into; she wouldn't allow herself to be placed in them. When he tried to compare her with his mother, he couldn't. They were worlds apart. What made Mrs. Miller different than his mother?

Jason tried to picture his mother working as an accountant or even as a volunteer at the Centre, but the image was so foreign that he was forced to reject it. His mom could no more fill Mrs. Miller's role than Mrs. Miller could fill--

That was the difference! He had found the key.

When he tried to picture Mrs. Miller in his mother's place, he saw what it was that made them so different. *It was his dad!* It was like a load of bricks had come crashing down on top of his head. Why hadn't he seen it before now? It was his dad who made his mother appear so different than Mrs. Miller. But how? And, why?

The answer to these two questions escaped him, and he was still trying to figure out what it was that his dad did, that made his mom "less" of a woman than Mrs. Miller, when he reached his front doorstep. Was it because his dad hit her, or was it because she was afraid of him? Or was it both?

His mother was sitting on the floor in the living room, playing with Nicky. Jason felt a twinge of guilt as he watched them play, unaware that they were being observed. Okay, so his mom didn't work; so what?

She's as good as Mrs. Miller, he thought. *And she's smart too. She's not just a dumb housewife.*

His early disloyalty to her now weighed on his mind, and he tried to think of different ways that his mother was better than Mrs. Miller. He wasn't able to let the issue drop and it stayed with him throughout the evening and even after he had gone to bed.

Sure, she's not like you, but she isn't a bad mom. Only different, he thought, drifting off to sleep.

* * *

When Jason heard Paul's voice, he put the memory of that day aside and ran out of the craft room to greet his friend. They spent the afternoon working together and talking about Christmas. By the time they shut it down for the day and prepared to leave, Jason was filled with excitement as he thought about Christmas.

And, when he woke the next morning, Christmas was still on his mind. It was only two week away and he wondered what he'd get this year. It always seemed to him that what he wanted, and what he got, were two different things. He had tried many times to bridge this gap by selecting inexpensive items out of the catalogue, in case it was the price that was causing the problem. But, after a time, he was sure that couldn't be the case, because many of the gifts he did receive were far more expensive than what he has asked for-- only they were always things that weren't on his list.

Then he had thought that maybe he was asking for too many things. So last year he had pared down his list until only three items remained: a model airplane kit, a skateboard, and a school jacket. But what did he end up getting? A chemistry set, a new pair of skates (he hated skating), along with a bunch of other stupid stuff he would never use. *What the hell did my parents expect me to do with a lousy chemistry set? I should have made a bomb and blown up the house,* he thought angrily. *Would've served them right!*

Thinking of Christmas reminded Jason that he hadn't had a chance to look at the Christmas catalogue. He hadn't even seen it anywhere in the house.

It has to be here by now, and I know who's got it. I bet Becky has it in her room.

Every year since he could remember, he'd have to search around the house for the Sear's *Wishbook* only to find that his sister had gotten to it first and, if he wanted to look at it, he'd have to search her room until he found where she had dropped it. Well, not this year. He wasn't going to search for it. He would just go to her room and demand that she find it and turn it over to him. Angry, he got out of bed and stomped down the hall towards his sister's room.

No one else was up and so he quietly opened her door and slipped inside. Becky was sitting up in bed reading "his" catalogue! Before she had a chance to hide it from him, Jason ran over to her and snatched it out of her hands.

"Jason!" she cried, reaching out, trying to retrieve it. "Give it back."

"Shut up!" he hissed. "Do you want to wake up Mom and Dad?"

She fell silent. "But, Jason," she protested, "I had it first."

"You always `have it first,'" he reminded her, "but now it's my turn. I haven't even had a chance to look at it once since the mailman dropped it off here."

"I was going to give it to you when I was finished," she replied whining.

"Oh, sure you were. And when would that be... next Christmas?"

"No...," her voice trailed off when she saw the sneer on his face. "I only wanted to look at the dolls."

"Dolls!" he exclaimed. "You've kept the catalogue for the last two weeks so that you could look at *dolls*? What about me? Don't I get a chance to look at what I want for Christmas, or do you expect me to look at your stupid dolls, too?"

"No."

"Well then, why don't you use your imagination for a change and ask for something really exciting?"

"Like what, Jason?"

"Oh, I don't know right off hand." His eyes shot to her shelf and he stared in disgust at the rows of dolls lining the shelves. "You could ask for a battery-powered truck or even a... football. Just don't always ask for dolls."

"But I like dolls."

"So what? You can learn to like other things, too. Maybe if you didn't always act like a girl, Dad would start treating you differently."

She looked puzzled as she asked, "What do you mean-- treat me differently?"

How could he explain to her what he meant, when he didn't fully understand everything himself? The conversation he had had with Mrs. Miller about women came into his mind. He had come to the conclusion that his dad didn't like women and that was what made his mom different than Mrs. Miller. Mrs. Miller's husband sounded like he liked his wife and so he allowed her to work outside the home and help down at the Centre. So, if Becky quit acting like her mom, then, as he saw it, she wouldn't get in trouble as often with their dad. Maybe if she started acting more like a boy....

These were the things that Jason wanted to tell his sister, but he could see from her expression that she wouldn't understand. He shrugged, "I can't explain it, Becky, but all I know is you shouldn't act like Mom."

"What should I act like, Jason?" she asked, more confused than ever.

"I don't know. But, don't always act like a girl. At least, not around Dad, because it won't work with him."

"But why?" she persisted.

"I told you. I don't know. Just don't." He tucked the catalogue under his arm and left her room.

Back in his own room, Jason sat on the edge of his bed, slowly flipping through the catalogue pages, stopping whenever something interesting caught his eye. He had no idea what he wanted for Christmas until a picture on page 312 caught his eye. There it was! There, on the page in front of him, was the perfect Christmas gift. If he could have this gift for Christmas, he wouldn't ask for anything else-- ever! Jason studied the picture and then turned to the information section on the right-hand side of the page and read:

Gha-19792 - HF: 15 Gallon Starter Aquarium complete
with pump, air-filter, gravel, charcoal, fish food...

Jason couldn't tear his eyes off the page and the picture of the aquarium, filled with fish, made him sigh with anticipation. He tried to imagine how the tank would look when it was filled with water and sitting on top of his dresser. Taking the catalogue with him, Jason walked over to his dresser and carefully took everything off the top. This was where his aquarium would sit... right up here, so he could watch his fish swimming when he was in bed.

His mind churned out a dozen other details that would have to be considered. Where would he buy his fish? What type of food should they have? Slowly, he solved each of these minor problems and now, only one major problem remained: How to convince his parents that he needed this aquarium for Christmas?

He heard a noise downstairs and knew his mom must be up. *Maybe if I hurry, I can get downstairs and talk to her before Dad or Becky come down,* he thought excitedly. He threw on his clothes and ran downstairs to the kitchen. His mother was standing at the stove. "Hi Mom," he said, coming over to stand beside her. "What's for breakfast?"

She was surprised to see him. "You're up early for a Sunday morning," she said, giving him a brief smile. At that moment, a pot began to boil over and she quickly reached over to turn down the heat. She stared at the mess on the stove. "Does that answer your question?" she asked, staring at the porridge dripping on the stove."

"Yeah," he replied. "Do you want me to get the dish-rag?"

"It's okay, I have it here somewhere," she said, moving the toaster aside and lifting the cutting board.

Jason waited until she had cleaned off the stove before he broached the subject of his aquarium. "Mom, what do you think the chances would be of you and Dad buying me an aquarium for Christmas?"

It looked to Jason like his mother was seriously considering his request, because she stood there, seemingly lost in thought, while he waited he waited expectantly for her reply. Finally, she asked, "Why do you want an aquarium?" She paused for a second and then added, "You know how your dad feels about pets."

"But Mom," he pleaded, "Fish aren't really pets... I mean, they don't run around the house or mess on the floor. And, I'd take care of them. I'll keep them in my room and feed them myself. You wouldn't even know they were in the house and--"

"Jason," she interrupted, "I don't think it's a good idea to ask for a fish tank. You don't want to upset your father-- not with Christmas only two weeks away, do you?"

"No," he answered, shaking his head, but neither did he want to be put off so easily, so he tried a new tactic. "It's not for me; not really. I'm studying fish for a school project and I need an aquarium if I'm going to get a good mark on my assignment. You don't want me to fail, do you?"

The look his mother was giving him made Jason think that maybe she wasn't fooled by his lie. When she continued to eye him speculatively without saying a word, Jason began to squirm. "Really, Mom," he added, hopefully. "It's the truth."

"Well... I don't know," she said reluctantly.

"Please, Mom?" he begged. "I'll ask him myself, if you'll put in a good work for me. Please...."

"Okay," she relented, "but if he says no, I don't want you to mention it again. Like I said, it's almost Christmas and I don't want any trouble.

"Promise," he said, crossing his heart and smiling at her. *Dad won't say no*, he told himself. *He can't!*

"Nervously, Jason waited until his family had finished breakfast before he brought up the subject. He wiped his sweaty palms on his jeans, took a deep breath, turned to his father and asked, "Dad, if you and Mom haven't bought my Christmas present yet, could you buy me an aquarium for Christmas?"

His father gave him a strange look, as if he didn't quite believe what he had heard. Quickly, Jason cut in before his dad could reply. "It's not for me. I need it so I can study fish for my science project at school. You see, I got this great theory that fish can be taught to respond to certain sounds and...."

"You never told me that you were working on a science project involving fish," said his father skeptically. "When did this all start?"

Jason wasn't prepared for his dad's sudden interest in the details of his imaginary science project. Afraid that he wouldn't be able to pull it off, Jason tried to keep his voice from trembling when he replied: "Oh, we all got to choose our own projects to work on a few months ago," he said, flicking a crumb off the table, trying to give the impression that he found the whole topic slightly boring-- and that he needed the fish and tank for scientific purposes only. "I know how you feel about pets," Jason conceded, "but when I got back to school after I was away-- that time-- all the good projects had already been taken, and I was left with the fish." From the look on his face, Jason thought that his dad was beginning to weaken, so he drove his final point home. "Since I have to do this project, I thought you and Mom could save some money if you bought me the aquarium as a Christmas present."

"Well, we'll see," his father said as he pushed away from the table and strode over to the cupboard. He poured himself another cup of coffee.

"Thank you," said Jason respectfully. He was having difficulty containing his excitement and hoped his dad would dismiss them soon so he could go back to his room and look at the catalogue again. This year, he was going to get his wish; this year he was getting his aquarium.

Unable to wait any longer, Jason asked, "Can I be excused?"

"Yes."

Jason got up to leave.

"Before you hide yourself in that room of yours," his father added, "I want you to go out and shovel the walk."

"Yes, Dad."

Jason shoveled the walk like a man possessed. The snow fairly flew off the end of his shovel as he hurried to finish so he could get back to his room and... to the catalogue. When he was satisfied that his father could find no fault, he put the shovel away and went back inside.

He raced up the stairs to his room. Throwing open the door, he let his excitement spill over. "I'm getting fish for Christmas!" he exclaimed. "Can you believe it, Pookie? This year Dad's going to buy me what I want?" He was so happy that it took him a few seconds before he realized that Pookie was no longer around to share his happiness with him. His good spirits sagged and he walked sadly over to his night table and stared at the empty spot that Pookie had once occupied. "I wish you were here," he whispered to his absent friend, "because you'd have liked to sit and watch the fish, too."

For the rest of the week, Jason could hardly wait for next Saturday to arrive. He wanted to see the expression on Paul's face when he told him that he was getting an aquarium for Christmas.

When Saturday finally did arrive, Jason ran all the way from the bus stop at his school to the Centre. He burst through the door and, not bothering to take his coat and boots off, ran to the craft room. "Hey Paul," he shouted through the doorway, "Hey Paul, wait till you hear my news!"

Paul jumped up when he heard Jason shout. He ran over to Jason, concerned by his friend's flushed appearance. "What's up?" he asked, listening to Jason pant, trying to catch his breath. "You win a lottery or something?"

"Oh, better than that," Jason gasped. "Guess what I'm getting for Christmas?"

"Gee... how should I know? It must be something pretty special, though. I've never seen you so worked up before."

"Guess?" said Jason, barely able to keep himself from blurting out his good news.

Paul affected an air of deep concentration. "Let's see," he said. "Could it be... no... hmmm..., maybe... naw, not that. All right. I give up."

"Come on, Paul," said Jason impatiently, "Just take a guess!"

"Okay... okay... keep your shirt on. I'm thinking. I know! You're getting... a new pair of pajamas." He laughed, enjoying Jason's exasperated expression.

"Be serious!" Jason pleaded. "Try and guess."

"Okay," said Paul, "but there's so many things you might be getting, that I don't know where to begin. Is it a computer?"

"No, it's not a computer. It's better than a computer."

"Better than a computer, hey? Then I can't guess unless it's something like a motorcycle and I know you're too young to get your license."

"Guessed wrong again," Jason boasted triumphantly. "I'm getting an aquarium for Christmas. My Dad said so."

"You're kidding?"

"No, it's true," said Jason, pleased that Paul was properly impressed with his disclosure. Jason went on to describe all the features his new tank would have. "And Paul," he said reverently, "this is going to be the best Christmas of my whole life. I can't tell you how happy I am. Ever since Dad said he'd get me my tank, I've been walking around in a daze, almost bursting from happiness."

"You're sure lucky," Paul agreed. "I already know most of the stuff I'm getting." Seeing Jason's puzzled expression, he explained: I peeked. I know I'm getting a couple of plane models, a basketball hoop and some new clothes. I'm afraid nothing as exciting as your present. But tell me, how did you talk your parents into it? I remember you saying that your dad doesn't like pets."

Jason hesitated, unwilling to confess to Paul that he had had to lie before his dad agreed to buy him an aquarium. He was afraid of what Paul would think of him. Knowing he had to say something, Jason decided to leave out the part about his fictional science project. "I just asked them for an aquarium this year and they said they'd buy me one."

"That's great! I wish my parents... well at least my Mom... listened to me when I asked for a computer this Christmas. She nearly blew a gasket!"

"That's too bad," Jason sympathized. "Well, maybe you'll get one for your birthday."

"I doubt it. No money."

"Oh." Jason knew from some of the things Paul had told him, that Paul's family seemed to always be short of money. But Paul never tried to hide the fact and it appeared to Jason that his friend didn't think money was all that important. Jason knew that his own family was never short of money, but it seemed to matter a great deal to his father. Comparing his situation to Paul's Jason found that it strange that his father placed so much emphasis on the importance of money and constantly strived to make more and more, when Paul's family was content to barely make ends meet. It didn't make any sense to Jason.

For the rest of the afternoon, Paul helped him work on his rocket. They had made a pact where they would help each other whenever they could so that they wouldn't have to ask for Mrs. Miller's assistance. They wanted to impress her with their skill.

"Do you know that the Centre is having a Christmas party here next Saturday?" Paul asked, cleaning up his place at the table.

"No, I didn't." Jason replied, his interest aroused by Paul's comment.

"Didn't you read the poster on the front door?"

"What poster? I didn't see any poster." Then Jason remembered his headlong rush up the steps and through the door. "I guess I didn't stop long enough to see it," he confessed.

"Well, it's going to be fun. I was talking with Mrs. Miller before you came and she told me that they're going to have a party with food and games and... guess what?"

"What?"

"Santa Claus is coming to hand out the presents?"

"We get presents?" Jason's eyes widened with surprise.

"Yeah, we usually exchange with someone," Paul explained, "but Santa Claus also gives each kid a special gift from Mr. White and Mrs. Miller. Want to exchange gifts?"

"Sure. That sounds great."

"Are you telling me that Santa Claus is coming here next Saturday?" Jason studied Paul's face to see if he was being serious. He had fallen for Paul's practical jokes too many times in the past to be easily fooled again.

"Yup, the fat man himself is coming here, so you better be good. Paul laughed. "If you don't believe me, just ask Mr. White... or Mrs. Miller. They'll tell you."

Jason was at last convinced that Paul was telling the truth. "No, he said, "I believe you. That's going to be neat. I haven't visited with Santa

Claus since I was a little kid and Mom took me to see Santa in one of the malls."

"Personally," said Paul assuming an adult voice, "I think I'm a little old to believe in Santa Claus. And besides, I have it from a good source that Mr. White is going to play that role this year."

"Oh quit being such a stuffed shirt," said Jason, poking Paul in the ribs. Paul giggled. "I think it's great. I never expected a Christmas party."

Paul moved out of his reach. "Don't get me wrong," he said, "because I think it's going to be a lot of fun, too. It's just that I didn't want you to think that I still believed in Santa Claus, that's all."

"Don't be silly. I know that."

Jason helped Paul clean up. He hummed to himself as he bustled around the room putting everything back in its place. How was he going to last out the rest of the week when he had so much to look forward to? In addition to getting his aquarium Christmas morning, he also had the Christmas party the day before!

At last, everything was neat and tidy, and they walked together to the front entrance.

"Have a good week and I'll see you at the party," said Paul, gently cuffing Jason with his mitten.

"You sure will!" Jason exclaimed, returning the gesture and smiling at Paul. "You have a good week, too."

They left the Centre together. When they reached the end of the sidewalk, they parted company.

"See you later," Paul called over his shoulder.

"Ya. Take care." Grinning with barely-contained excitement, Jason raced toward the bus stop.

CHAPTER XVII

From the following Monday, right through to Saturday, Jason ate, slept and thought: *Aquarium!* His happiness spilled over at school-- much to the amazement of his classmates, who had never seen him so animated before. He whistled and hummed, while he strolled down the hallways and went to his classes. Whenever he passed Mr. White in the hallway, he would wave and, if he had the time, stop and talk to him.

At home, Jason played with Nicky and even shocked his sister, by asking her if she wanted him to come upstairs and play dolls with her. The look on her face had been priceless and he smiled whenever he thought about it. He could still see her standing there, her mouth open, staring at him like he'd lost his mind. "Jason, are you sick or something?" she asked in astonishment.

Even his mother was astounded by his behavior, especially when he volunteered to get the Christmas decorations out of the garage and offered to help decorate the house. When he finished hanging up the wreath on the outside of the front door, he ran back into the house and gave her a big hug.

"Why, Jason," she said, smiling at him, "I can't remember the last time you hugged me!"

Embarrassed, Jason shrugged and grinned back at her. "It's almost Christmas," he said "and I know this is going to be the best Christmas of my whole life. I just know it."

"I hope so, honey," she said, reaching for a box of ornaments so she could get started on the tree. "Here...," she said, handling him a small box. "If you're not busy, can you stick the angel on the top of the tree?"

"Sure, no trouble," Jason replied, taking the small silver and gold angel out of the box. He walked over to the tree standing beside the fireplace. A faint pine smell filled his nostrils and he breathed in deeply, trying to absorb this sure sign of Christmas. He pushed the footstool over to the tree and climbed on it, balancing on one leg, while he leaned over and positioned the angel on the treetop. "There," he called down to his mom, "I'm done." He jumped off the stool sucking his fingers, trying to get rid of the sticky pine sap on his hands.

The only one who didn't seem to share his good mood was his father. He didn't take part in any of the preparations and Jason thought that his dad was getting more and more edgy, the closer it came to Christmas. Finally, even his own good mood started to be affected by his dad's anti-social behavior. Jason began to grow apprehensive.

He acts like Scrooge, Jason thought, when he saw his father go into the living room without even glancing in the direction of the tree.

Jason tried to stay out of his way and made sure his chores were done on time, so his father wouldn't have to get after him. Jason didn't want him to get mad now, thus jeopardizing his chances of getting the aquarium he so badly wanted for Christmas.

At last it was Saturday, the day of the party had arrived and when Jason woke up, he got up out of bed immediately. He could hardly believe that today was Christmas Eve and his long period of waiting would be over tomorrow morning. He hopped around his room. "Tomorrow's Christmas, tomorrow's Christmas," he sang. *I can't wait any longer,* he thought excitedly. *I can't wait...*

Everything he did that morning was done in a hurry. He dressed in a hurry; gulped down his breakfast in a hurry (he couldn't even remember what he ate); and he did his chores in a hurry. In fact, he was moving around the house so quickly, that his mother told him to slow down because all his energy was starting to give her a headache. Finally, it was time for him to leave for the Centre. But, before he left, he ran over to where his mother was sitting and gave her a quick peck on the cheek.

Then he grabbed Becky and swung her around the kitchen, chanting, "Christmas is coming! Christmas is--"

"What's all that racket in there?" His dad's voice roared from the living room.

Jason shut up and ran for his coat.

"Have a good time, dear," his mother called after him.

"Thanks. I will," Jason shouted back, slamming the door behind him.

Everything was in full swing when he reached the Centre. The big hall was teeming with kids milling around, chatting happily about the stuff they wanted to get for Christmas. Jason heard Christmas carols being played on the piano and he looked around until he spotted Mrs. Miller at the piano, with two kids sitting beside here, pounding the keys. When they began to play, "Deck the hall..." he joined the rest of the crowd in singing at the top of his lungs.

"This is great," he whispered to himself when the song had ended. He walked over to the coat rack and saw that everyone had thrown their jackets and boots on a pile behind the door. He took off his coat, threw it on top of the heap and kicked off his boots in the corner, then joined a group of kids standing beside a long table in the center of the room. As he drew closer, he saw that the table was the one he and Paul used to build their models on. But as his eyes wandered over the abundance of food covering the surface, Jason didn't mind sacrificing his workbench, just for this once. His mouth watered at the assortment of cakes, cookies, nuts and candies laid out before him. He reached towards the food, planning to sneak a piece of Christmas cake, when a hand grabbed his wrist.

"No so fast. I caught you red-handed," It was Paul. "If anyone's going to snatch a piece of cake, it's going to be me first," he said, reaching over Jason's hand and picking up a large piece of cake. He popped the whole piece in his mouth.

"Hey, no fair!" Jason protested, shoving him aside and grabbing a piece, too. He followed Paul's example and crammed the cake into his mouth, munching contentedly.

They looked at each other and laughed. They looked like pocket gophers, with their cheeks filled to bursting.

"Merry Christmas," mumbled Paul, showering Jason with crumbs.

"Merry Christmas to you, too," Jason replied, returning the favor.

At last, when they had managed to swallow the last of the cake, Jason was able to speak properly. "Where did all this stuff come from?" he asked Paul.

"Oh, didn't you know... every year Mrs. Miller's husband bakes all this stuff for us. He's a professional chef, you know."

"Yeah, I know," said Jason quietly, regretting more than ever his remark about Mrs. Miller's husband being a wimp.

"Come," said Paul, grabbing Jason by the arm. "Let's go look at the tree."

Jason had never before seen such a large Christmas tree indoors and he stood back, admiring it. From its top branches to its bottom, the tree was covered with bells, tinsel and lights. "It's beautiful," he murmured.

"Forget the tree," Paul ordered, "Look at all the presents."

Jason looked beneath the tree. The floor around its base was covered with dozens of gaily wrapped boxes. "Wow!" he exclaimed, dropping to one knee to get a better look.

"Looks pretty good, doesn't it?" said a voice behind him.

Jason turned his head and saw Mrs. Miller standing beside Paul. "Yeah" he replied dreamily, "it looks just great."

She smiled at their sticky faces. "Merry Christmas."

"Merry Christmas," they replied in unison.

"I see from your faces that you've already sampled some of the baking." Paul and Jason looked at each other and grinned. "Well," she continued, I don't know whether or not it's safe to leave you two so close to the presents. Remember," she said, shaking her finger, "Santa Claus is watching and he knows who's been naughty or nice."

The two boys giggled and then Paul said soberly, "Us... peek? Why Mrs. Miller, how could you even think such a thing?" He spread out his hands. "See... nothing. Honest. We were only looking."

Her eyes twinkled. "Sure you were," she chuckled, "Just remember.... I know you two." Then, she asked, "Is the food good?"

"Was what good?" Jason asked, and then remembered the cake. "Oh, yeah. It was great! Your husband is a good cook." He wiped his mouth with his sleeve.

"Thank you, Jason," she said, "Thank you very much. I'll have to tell Jack what you said."

"Do we have to wait 'til Santa Claus comes before we eat?" asked Paul, his eyes on the table.

"No, I don't think so," she answered, "but I think we should wait 'til most of the kids get here before we turn you guys loose. I'll remember to stay out of the way so that I don't get trampled in the stampede."

They laughed and chatted a few more minutes about all the food they were going to try and stuff down, before the conversation returned to the Christmas presents under the tree.

"Is there one for me?" Jason asked.

"There sure is," Mrs. Miller affirmed. "Somewhere in the middle of that pile is a present with your name on it."

"How about me?" Paul butted in, "I hope you haven't forgotten about me." His eyes scanned the gifts trying to pick out his present.

"Of course there's a gift for you, Paul," she said. "We wouldn't forget to bring a gift for our star model builder."

Paul beamed under her praise and his happy face made Jason smile. "I'm getting an aquarium for Christmas," Jason informed Mrs. Miller.

"That sounds like a super gift," she said. "You must be pretty anxious for tomorrow morning to arrive."

"I am," said Jason enthusiastically. "I can hardly wait."

"Well, you don't have long to wait now," she said. "How about you, Paul? What did you want for Christmas?"

"Oh, I don't know," he replied, "I wanted a computer but they're pretty expensive, so I'll settle for a new basketball hoop and some models." He winked at Jason and Jason winked back.

"It sounds like you two are going to have a real special Christmas," she said to them. "I have to admit that I'm also having difficulty waiting to see what I'm going to get tomorrow morning. In fact, if my husband and kids didn't watch me like a hawk, I'm sure that I would be tempted to peek." She put an arm around each of them. "I'm so proud of you guys," she said, giving them a squeeze.

"Thank you," Jason stuttered. He wasn't used to having a woman, other than his mother, hug him but it felt so good, that he wished she would do it again.

"I'd like to stay," she said, "but, I have to go help Santa get ready, so you boys just enjoy yourselves."

"We will," Paul called after her. He turned to Jason. "Follow me," he said, "I have something that I've been dying to show you." He led Jason into the craft room and sat him down in a chair. Then, Paul walked over to the counter and came back with his knapsack. He opened the buckles and reached inside. He pulled out a wrinkled brown bag. "Here," he said gruffly, handing the bag to Jason. "Merry Christmas."

Jason wasn't expecting a gift from Paul and the thought that his friend had spent some of his small allowance on him, brought a tear to his eye. He took the bag from Paul's hand and set it on his lap. "Thank you, Paul." He sat there staring at the bag, wondering what Paul could have bought him.

"Well, aren't you going to open it?" Paul asked impatiently. "But whatever you do, don't shake it," he advised.

"Okay," Jason said, slowly untwisting the top of the bag and peering inside. He was startled to find two large, round eyes staring back at him. "What is it?"

"Take it out and you'll see," said Paul, grinning from ear to ear. "I hope you like it."

Jason reached inside the bag and pulled out a smaller bag filled with water. Inside that bag, a large orange and red-goldfish was swimming around. "Oh...," he gushed. He was so excited by Paul's gift that he found it difficult to speak. "Oh Paul, he's wonderful. Thank you."

"You're welcome. I would have bought you two, but they're pretty expensive, and I still had to buy my sister a present."

"He's perfect," said Jason, turning the bag around to admire the fish. "I know you wanted to get angel fish," said Paul, "but, until you do, he can live in your aquarium. The man at the pet store said he'd live a long time. Maybe three years if he doesn't get sick."

"I'm going to call him 'Moby Dick,'" said Jason, beaming with satisfaction.

"That's a strange name."

"Yeah, I know, but I have a book about a whale named Moby Dick," Jason explained. When he had returned to his new room, Jason had taken the book out of its hiding place under the chesterfield and now had it hidden in between his mattresses.

"Okay, if you say so," said Paul, "but he doesn't look like a whale to me."

They continued to talk about the goldfish and Paul told him how he had to run all the way from his house to the Centre so "Moby Dick" wouldn't freeze to death before he arrived.

Although Jason hadn't expected a gift from Paul, he had gone shopping and now, pulled out a crumbled package from his hip packet. "I bought this for you," he said, handing the gift to Paul. "Merry Christmas."

"Thanks, Jason." Paul slowly unwrapped the gift and now it was Jason's turn to wait impatiently for him to finish. He wanted to see Paul's face when Paul saw what he had bought him. "I'm sorry it got so squashed," Jason apologized. "I didn't want to bring my pack, so I just shoved it in my pocket."

"That's alright," Paul replied, "but I guess you'll have to pack Moby home inside your coat or he'll never survive."

"Don't worry; I will."

Paul tore off the remaining paper and was left holding a small, stainless-steel carving knife. He turned it over in his hand. "This is perfect," he said, smiling up at Jason. "Thanks a lot. Now I can do some work on my model at home."

"I'm glad that you like it," said Jason modestly. He hoped Paul wouldn't ask him if it was expensive. The knife had cost him his last three week's allowance but Jason didn't want Paul to know this. Now, seeing his friend's happy face, Jason knew that it had been worth every penny he had spent.

Paul slipped the knife into his shirt pocket and stood up. "Leave Moby on the counter," he told Jason, "and let's go join the others. We don't want to miss Santa Claus."

Jason laughed and jumped up. "No way!" He put Moby back in the paper bag and set it on the shelf, then followed Paul out of the room.

They maneuvered through the crowd until they were standing back at the table. They each picked up a cookie and were about to take a bite when they heard a familiar sound echo through the room.

"HO, HO, HO!" the voice shouted. "Merry Christmas!"

"It's Santa!" the kids screamed, surging forward. Jason was swept forward and found himself directly in front of the man dressed in red. He smiled when he saw the familiar face of his teacher, now covered with a fluffy white beard. And, when he spied Mr. White's stomach, he broke into gales of laughter. His teacher's usually slim figure had entirely disappeared, to be replaced by a bulging middle that extended over a large black belt.

He must have three pillows stuffed in there, Jason thought, grinning, as he watched "Santa" waddle over to the tree and throw down a huge brown sack crammed to the top with presents. *He's a good sport. I don't think I could dress up like that, even if it is almost Christmas-- not in front of everyone!*

"HO, HO, HO," Santa hollered again, giving everyone a huge smile. "Have all of you been good boys and girls?"

A resounding "YES!!!" shook the room, as the kids surged forward again and in seconds, Santa was surrounded by the happy group; all trying to be the one to get the closet to him. Jason was no exception. He found himself pushing forward until he was standing right next to the jolly man dressed in red.

"Well then," said Santa, "if you're all ready, would one of you like to drag my bag over here so we can get started."

Like a shot, Jason reached the bag first and pulled it across the floor to Santa's feet. He reluctantly let go of his burden and stepped back into the crowd. Excited, he watched Santa reach into his sack, pull out a gift, and call out a name. The lucky recipient rushed forward to receive her present.

Name after name was called out and Jason continued to wait patiently for his turn. He was mortified when some of the girls climbed up on Santa's lap and gave him a kiss. He elbowed Paul and snickered. "I hope he doesn't expect a kiss from me."

Paul giggled. "Yeah, can you imagine us sitting on his knee?"

Jason was about to make another comment, when he heard Santa call his name. In his excitement, he forgot all about any reservations he might have had in his hurry to get to Santa. The kids in front parted to let him through and he made his way over to where Santa was sitting. He had planned to casually saunter up when his turn came-- not act like a little kid-- but, he couldn't carry out this charade now. He reached Santa and threw his arms around his neck. "Merry Christmas, Santa."

"Well, if it isn't Jason. I'm glad you could come to our Christmas party," said Santa, returning his hug. He reached inside his bag and pulled out a gift. Looking at it in surprise, he said, "What do we have here? Well, bless my soul. I think this gift has your name on it." He handed the gift to Jason.

Jason's hand trembled as he took the present from the mittened hand. "Thank you," he gasped in delight and turned to leave. He spun around and threw his arms around Santa, hugging him tightly. He whispered in his ear, "Merry Christmas and thank you, Mr. White."

"Ho, Ho, Ho. Merry Christmas to you, too, Jason."

For a moment, they stared into each other's eyes and Jason smiled at him.

"Oh, I almost forgot," said Santa, reaching deep inside his coat pocket. "I have another gift for you from Mrs. Miller." He handed a small box to Jason.

'Gee, thanks," said Jason.

"You're welcome, Jason. Just make sure that you have a very Merry Christmas this year and we'll see you in the New Year."

"Sure thing!" Jason replied. Clutching a gift in each hand, he ran back to where Paul was waiting.

"What took you so long?" Paul inquired. "I wanted to watch you get your present from Santa but with this crowd, it was impossible for me to get close enough."

Jason thought about the hug he had given Santa. That was almost as bad as sitting on Santa's lap! He was glad that Paul hadn't been able to get closer; hadn't seen him act like a complete fool. Especially after they had made fun of everyone else!

"Did Santa give you everything in his sack?" Paul asked, staring at the gifts Jason was holding.

Jason didn't answer. Instead, he stared around the room, savoring his happiness; wanting it to last forever. Everything seemed too good to be true and he wondered if perhaps he had unwittingly slipped into a glorious daydream. If he had, then he never wanted to come back. He felt a tug on his sleeve.

"Oh Jason...," a voice whispered in his ear. "Come on Jason, you're not going to drift off to 'that place' again. Are you?"

Jason turned his attention to Paul. His friend was staring at him, a worried look on his face. "No, I'm not daydreaming," Jason said, "but I wish I were. This is almost too good to be true. I think this is the best Christmas I have ever had."

"Good," Paul sighed with relief. "Now, can we get down to serious business-- like, what did you get?"

"I don't know," said Jason, looking at the parcels in his hands. "I haven't opened them yet."

Exasperated, Paul's hand flew to his forehead and he stared up at the ceiling, a pained look on his face. "I can see that," he said, "but what I want to know-- is *when* do you plan on opening them? We haven't got much time left before we head for home."

Jason laughed. "Right now!" he said, ripping the paper off the first gift he received, exposing a small cardboard box. He carefully ran his thumb nail along the flap, cutting the tape, and opened it. Inside, was a miniature sunken ship-- the kind especially made to go inside an aquarium! Speechless, Jason could only stare at the tiny ship in his hand.

"Do you like it?" Paul asked. "I told Mr. White that you were getting an aquarium for Christmas and that I was going to give you your first fish. I guess he decided to get something along the same line."

Jason inspected the little ship from stern to prow. "I can't believe it," he said admiringly. "It's so-- so perfect." In his mind, Jason could already visualize what the ship would look like when it was resting on the gravel in his tank.

"You have another gift," Paul reminded him.

"Oh, Yah. I forgot." Jason carefully placed the little ship back in its box. "This one's from Mrs. Miller," he informed Paul. He tore off the wrapping paper. When he had completed that part of the operation, he was again left with a small paper box. Quickly, he opened it and looked inside. He gently lifted his gift out of its box and set it on his knee. It was a tiny treasure chest and when he opened the lid, he saw that the little chest was filled with an assortment of plastic pearls, coins and chains, all painted to look real."

"Gosh, that will look good in your aquarium, too," said Paul, bending down to get a better look inside the chest.

"It sure will," Jason agreed. "I can see my aquarium now. I'll put the ship on the gravel in the middle and this little chest can sit in the corner beneath a plastic plant and--"

His planning was cut short when Paul's name was called.

"Hey! It's my turn."

Jason watched Paul run over to Santa. Most of the crowd had already received their gifts and had spread out around the room. Jason was able to watch his friend as he went over to Santa and was given his gift. Jason saw him bend down and whisper something into Santa's ear. Mr. White raised his head and looked in Jason's direction. He smiled. Jason waved and smiled back.

By the time Paul returned, he had already unwrapped his present and was proudly holding a package containing a complete set of model paints, along with a set of drafting pens. "This is terrific!" He thrust his present into Jason's hands so that he could admire his gift. "But," Paul added, looking perplexed, "how did they know what I wanted?"

Jason gave him a sly grin and said, "You're not the only one who talked to them about Christmas presents for certain people."

"Gee, thanks."

"Don't mention it," Jason said. He would have added that he hoped Paul would now be able to do a lot of the time-consuming work on his models at home, but just then a voice shouted: "Come and get it! There's still lots of food here!"

"Let's go!" said Paul. "No use in letting all that good food go to waste."

"You're on!"

They ran into the craft room, set their gift on the shelf, and ran back into the room, shoving their way up to the table.

"Here goes," Jason stuffed a whole mincemeat tart into his mouth. "Hmmmm, gooood," he mumbled, reaching for another.

"That's disgusting!" Paul exclaimed as he, too, tried to jam a whole piece of cake into his mouth.

They ate until they were afraid that if they tried to stuff in one more crumb, they would burst. Stuffed and happy, they made their way over to a vacant spot by the wall and sank down on the floor, where they contentedly watched some of the other kids put their coats on, getting ready to leave.

"I don't know how they can eat and run," Paul groaned. He patted his full stomach. "I can barely move."

"Serves you right for eating three pieces of cake and a dozen tarts," was Jason's retort.

"Look who's talking! It wasn't me who got into a contest with Mrs. Miller on who could crack and eat the most walnuts in a minute."

"Don't talk to me about food," Jason groaned. "I don't think I'll ever eat again."

"Well, if I can get this body to move, I'm going to go over and talk with Mrs. Miller and Mr. White. See them...?" said Paul, pointing across the room. "They're sitting over there by the tree."

Jason struggled to his feet. "You have no mercy," he said to Paul, as he followed him across the room. Mr. White was now dressed in his regular clothes and looked like he had suddenly lost about fifty pounds. "I see Santa's left," he said to his teacher. "He must be getting ready for his long trip tonight."

"I guess so," Mr. White replied wearily. "I don't envy his job. Exhausting work."

"Well," said Jason, "if you see him again, would you thank him for me for the ship and treasure chest? They're just what I wanted."

"Yeah," Paul joined in, "Thanks him for me, too."

"I will," Mr. White smiled. "We're glad you guys liked your gifts." He turned to Mrs. Miller. "Aren't we, Beth?"

"We sure are," she said happily. "And it's funny that you two came over because we were just talking about you. We were wondering what plans you two had for the holidays?"

Paul spoke up first. "My cousin Bill is coming to visit, with Aunt Judy and Uncle Ben. Bill is almost my age and we'll probably fool around. Go to a movie. Maybe go skating. Things like that."

"How about you, Jason?" Mrs. Miller asked.

"I don't know what I'll be doing. Probably spend a lot of time setting up my aquarium. Did you know that Paul bought me my first fish? I've called him 'Moby Dick.'"

"That's quite an impressive name for a goldfish, all right," Mr. White said. "For your sake, I hope he doesn't grow as big as his namesake."

Jason laughed. He tried to imagine what the little bug-eyed fish would look like, should he grow that big. "He better not or I'll need a new tank."

"It does sound like you two are going to have a lot of fun," Mrs. Miller remarked. "You are planning on coming back after Christmas, I hope?" She looked first at Jason, then at Paul.

"We sure are," said Paul. "You can't get rid of us that easy!"

"Me neither," Jason added. "I have to finish my rocket."

"Yes," said Mr. White, "Mrs. Miller told me that we might end up with unexpected air conditioning this winter."

They continued their playful bantering for a while longer, before Mr. White got up to leave. "I've got to get home and wrap a few last-minute presents," he explained.

"And I have to get home and finish getting everything ready for Christmas dinner tomorrow," said Mrs. Miller.

"Isn't your husband going to cook dinner?" Jason asked.

"Oh no," she smiled, "I always cook Christmas dinner. Maybe I'm just being sentimental, but I always insist on cooking the turkey."

"It's okay, Mrs. Miller," said Jason. "You don't have to explain. I wasn't thinking that you should be the one to cook Christmas dinner because it was a woman's job."

"I know you weren't, Jason," she replied softly.

"Am I missing something?" Paul asked, giving them a strange look. "What are you two talking about?"

Jason winked at Mrs. Miller, then turned to his friend. "You didn't miss anything," he said. "It's just that we once had a conversation about cooking, that's all."

"Cooking!" exclaimed Paul in disbelief. "What in the world made you talk about cooking? You plan on becoming a chef or something? You told me you wanted to be a marine biologist."

"Don't get excited, I *a*m going to be a marine biologist," Jason said to him. "But," he added, "there's other important jobs as well, and I know it takes a lot of brains to be a good cook."

Paul's obvious confusion made Mrs. Miller chuckle. "You got something against men becoming chefs?" she asked Paul mischievously.

Jason knew that Paul had been caught off guard by Mrs. Miller's last comment. He was enjoying his friend's discomfort.

"No...," Paul answered slowly, "I don't have anything against men cooking. Even I like to fry hamburgers, and once I made a cake all by myself." He glanced at Jason, daring him to make some sarcastic comment about his admission.

Jason kept quiet. But he could just picture Paul standing in front of the cupboard, wearing an apron stirring a bowlful of cake batter. The whole scene reminded him of the Swedish Chef on the *Muppets Show.*

Paul looked at him suspicious. "What are you smiling at?" he demanded.

"Oh nothing," Jason replied innocently. "Just daydreaming again."

"Well, it's time for us to get going, so quit your dreaming and let's go get our stuff," said Paul, still trying to figure out why Jason was smiling.

"That sounds like a good idea," Mr. White nodded, "I'm going to help clean up here and I'm heading home, too. You guys have a very Merry Christmas and we'll see you next year."

"Merry Christmas," they answered together. Paul and Jason walked over to the craft room and went inside. Paul picked up the bag with Moby Dick and handed it to Jason. "Better shove him inside your coat," he advised. "It's probably still pretty cold outside."

"I will," Jason said. "As soon as I put my coat on, I'll place him right next to my heart."

"Well then, what are we waiting for-- let's go," said Paul, heading out the door.

"I'm right behind you. Lead the way." Jason started to follow Paul out of the room but stopped at the doorway. He turned and glanced around the room. "I'll be back," he whispered. He ran to catch up with his friend.

They put on their coats and boots and were about to leave when they spotted Mrs. Miller coming out of her office. She also had her coat on and was heading their way.

"Merry Christmas!" they shouted.

"And God bless everyone," Paul added, opening the door and stepping outside. When Jason joined him on the step, Paul turned to him and said, "You're not the only one who reads books you know. I got that saying from Dicken's *Christmas Carol.*"

I'm impressed," Jason teased, smiling at his friend. "But there's my bus! I've got to run. Merry Christmas and I'll see you after the holidays," he called, running towards the waiting bus.

"Merry Christmas," Paul called after him. "See you next year."

CHAPTER XVIII

Jason was disappointed to find that Christmas Eve at home was a lot different than Christmas Eve had been at the Centre. No one, except for Becky, seemed to share his happiness and even she acted rather subdued at the supper table.

It was difficult for Jason to keep his exhilaration to himself when he was so close to getting the object of his desire. He wanted to tell his family all about the party and the gifts he had received, but he remained silent. How could he tell them about the party without revealing the truth about the Centre? So, throughout the meal, Jason kept his good spirits under wraps and watched his family. He was keenly aware of every subtle shift in mood and hoped things would improve before tomorrow morning. Because, although his parents seemed more relaxed then he had seen them for a long time, Jason knew that something was bothering his father. His dad didn't look very happy.

Jason was still stuffed from the party and had difficulty feigning an appetite. As he slowly chewed his food, he thought about his trip home. With "Moby Dick" safely tucked inside his coat, Jason had enjoyed his ride on the bus. His fellow passengers were all in a Christmas mood, smiling happily. The bus driver greeted each new arrival with a resounding, "Merry Christmas!" When the bus stopped to let him off, Jason plowed through the snow, enjoying the crunching sound beneath his feet. He stopped every few feet to admire the brightly lit houses along his block with their strings of Christmas lights and their shimmering Christmas tree inside. *Christmas is a wonderful time*, he thought happily *and tomorrow is going to be even better!*

"What did you learn today?" his dad asked casually.

Immediately on guard, Jason wondered if he had somehow found out about the party. Jason had cautiously entered the house and, without taking his coat off, had snuck upstairs and hid his fish in his room. His dad couldn't know about "Moby Dick," could he? Jason glanced at his dad's face and then returned his attention to the food on his plate. His dad didn't appear to be suspicious-- just curious. Jason thought that there might not be any harm in telling him part of the truth, so he said, "I learned how to do a new math equation and then afterwards, Mr. White had a small Christmas party for us."

"That's nice," his dad replied disinterestedly. He rose from the table and walked into the living room. "Where's the paper, Linda?" he called over his shoulder.

Jason watched his mother go to the closet and get the newspaper off the top shelf. As much as Jason wanted to avoid talking about the party for fear that he might accidentally reveal the true nature of the Centre, he couldn't help but feel a little bit disappointed that his father wasn't at all interested in hearing about his afternoon.

It would have been nice if I could have told him about my gifts and all the food they provided for us, he thought sadly. *I could have shown him my goldfish.*

When he had reached his room, Jason had set the bag with his fish inside, on his bed and had gone down to the kitchen and got a jar. He filled it with water and brought it back to his room, then plopped "Moby Dick" into his new temporary home. He swam happily around inside the jar and Jason had carefully carried him over to the dresser and set him down on the spot he had cleared off for his aquarium. "Tomorrow, you get a new home," he grinned.

But now, as he stared at the doorway leading into the living room, Jason wondered if his father would have been interested, anyway. He sat quietly at the table while his mom and sister finished picking up the dishes. When everything had been cleaned off and put away, he asked them if they wanted to go into the living room and sing a few Christmas carols.

"That sounds like fun," said his mother.

"Can we sing, 'You better watch out, you better not cry'?" Becky asked, running out of the kitchen and over to the piano.

"Sure," Jason called after her. He waited until his mom was ready and they went into the living room together.

His mother sat down on the piano stool and picked up a song-book.

"Will Dad mind the noise?" Jason glanced worriedly over at his father.

His mother looked up at him, smiling. "No, I don't think so," she replied. "After all, it is Christmas Eve."

Jason peered over at the stack of presents under the tree. "Mom, when we're done singing, can we open just one gift tonight?"

Now it was his mother's turn to cast a glance at the reclining figure on the sofa. "You know how your Dad feels about that," she said softly. "We all better wait for tomorrow morning."

"Yeah," he agreed, dismissing any further thoughts he might have had with regard to getting his aquarium early. His dad didn't allow it last year, so why should he relent now?" "I can wait," he whispered to himself.

Becky was standing beside the piano stool and for a minute, Jason looked at her, wondering where he was suppose to stand. Where was his place? He wanted to stand next to his mother. It seemed to him that he was always on the outside, looking in. Any other time, he would have probably pushed his sister aside, but he didn't want her to start complaining-- not tonight. He went and stood beside her.

"How about you, Nick?" his mother called over to his dad. "Would you like to join us and sing some carols?"

Jason saw his dad look in their direction and shake his head. "No," he answered, "I'm busy, but you go ahead."

Why is he always busy when we ask him to something with us that's fun? Jason thought, watching his dad turn his attention back to the newspaper. *He's never too "busy" to take time to bawl us out when he's mad or kick the shit out of us if we do something wrong, so why is he so busy now?*

Angered by his father's indifference, Jason looked around the room. The tree; the decorations; the glowing light from the fireplace-- it was all so beautiful. How could everything look so good and feel so wrong? Something very important was missing.

It reminded Jason of a play and they were all actors, each playing a role. Only no matter how much they rehearsed, their roles kept changing until finally they were meaningless. He looked at his mom and saw her frown as she turned the pages of the songbook. Suddenly, he felt sorry for her. She shouldn't have to be the one to play the part of the jester-- the fool-- trying to force gaiety into a home where there was none.

"Let's sing 'The First Noel,'" Jason suggested, determined that she should not have to act the part alone.

"Becky!" his dad shouted.

Everyone jumped!

"Yes?" Becky whispered, frightened.

"Becky, I told you to keep an eye on Nicky!" he said, glowering.

Jason looked around and spotted Nicky sitting under the tree, happily ripping the wrapping paper off one of the gifts.

How did he get over there so fast? Jason wondered. When he had come into the living room, his mom had set Nicky on the floor beside the piano stool....

"Well, don't just stand there. Go get him!" his dad ordered, the sharp edge of his voice slashing through their earlier merriment.

Becky hurried to comply. She rushed over to Nicky, picked him up, and carried him back to where Jason was standing.

His dad continued to glare at her across the living room. "You better keep an eye on him," he warned. "If I see him in there again, no Santa Claus for you."

"Here," said his mom, reaching out her arms, "Give him to me."

Becky handed Nicky over to her mother and she sat him down beside her on the stool.

"You stay with Mommy," his mother chaffed softly, then turned to Jason and Becky. "Okay, everyone, let's sing 'The First Noel,'" she sighed and began to play the piano, but her fingers were spiritless and her shoulders sagged with an air of defeat.

Jason no longer felt like singing. The last remnants of the good feelings he had brought home with him had now completely disappeared and he was left feeling cold and empty. Angry at his father, he glared at the song sheet in front of him.

And I thought this year was going to be different. Boy, how could I have been so stupid as to think that anything has really changed.

His mom began to sing and he forced himself to join her. It wasn't long before he realized that he and his mother were the only ones who were singing. He looked at his sister and saw that she was just standing there, staring off into space. Her lips weren't moving. He sidled up to her and jabbed her in the ribs with his elbow.

"Sing!" he hissed. Startled, her eyes flew to his face and he snarled again. "Go on, sing."

Softly, her voice trembling, she began to sing.

They sang three more carols before their father hollered at them to shut it down and go to bed. Jason didn't need to be told twice. He walked stiffly out of the room and went upstairs.

Once inside his room, he walked over to "Moby Dick" and stood in front of the jar, watching the fish swim round and round blowing bubbles as its mouth slowly opened and closed. "I bet you're hungry, hey fellow?" Jason said. Up to now, he hadn't given any thought to how he was going to feed his new pet. "Don't worry," he told it, "I won't let you starve."

He went over to his bed and reached underneath for the Christmas catalogue. Quickly, he thumbed through the pages until he came to the page describing his aquarium. "Ah, just as I thought," he muttered, reading the information again. He walked back to his dresser, the catalogue in his hand. He lifted it up and pointed to a pertinent section of the description. "See here," he said shoving the catalogue up to the jar, "It says that this tank comes with a can of goldfish food. So, as Dad always says, 'You'll just have to tighten your belt.' Tomorrow morning, I'll give you lots to eat."

It seemed to Jason that his fish understood what he had said, because it appeared more contented now that it knew food was on the way. "Everything's going to be okay if you can just hand in there until tomorrow morning," Jason promised. "Dad can't spoil this Christmas for us. I won't let him. I'm going to get your aquarium and then, he can go to hell!"

Moby stared back at him and Jason felt his anger subside. It was almost like his fish was chiding him for his anger.

"Okay... you don't have to look at me that way," Jason said to his fish. "I guess I shouldn't let Dad get to me, but it's not easy to stay in control when he's always on my case. You don't have to worry though, because

I won't let anything happen to you; like what happened to Pookie." He tapped the glass with his fingers and Moby swam over and looked at him. "I'll take care of you, I promise," said Jason softly.

Jason left his fish and went to the bathroom. He brushed his teeth and got ready for bed. But before he switched off his light and climbed into bed, he checked on Moby Dick once more, to see if he was settled in for the night. "See you in the morning," Jason said and turned off the light.

Alone in the dark, Jason's mind filled with thoughts of tomorrow morning. His wait would at last be over and he'd finally get his aquarium. He wished that he had the nerve to sneak downstairs after everyone was asleep and take a quick peek. "I can wait," he murmured sleepily, "I can wait...."

It was six o'clock when he woke up.

Jason lay in his bed, listening to see if he could detect any movement downstairs. Nothing. More waiting! He was sure that if his mom and dad didn't get up soon, he wouldn't be able to stop himself from going downstairs and opening his gifts. He weighed the pros and cons of such an action. His dad would get mad-- he knew that, but what would his dad do? That was what Jason was more concerned about.

Maybe he'd take away my aquarium, Jason thought, filled with apprehension. *That would be terrible!*

The risk was too great. He decided to wait.

Two hours passed before he finally heard someone moving out in the hall. He heard the toilet flush. Jason threw off his blankets and jumped out of bed. He ran to his door and opened it a crack. He saw his father come out of the bathroom and head downstairs.

"It's Christmas! Yippee!" Jason exclaimed, hopping around his room, bursting with excitement. He ran over to his dresser and opened a drawer. He grabbed a pair of jeans, and then ran over to his closet to get a shirt. He opened the door and pulled one off the hanger, making sure that he didn't step inside the closet. Ever since that day he had found Pookie's torn body on the floor, Jason had kept the promise he had made to himself and never went inside his closet again.

When he was dressed, he ran over to his fish, wished him a Merry Christmas, and then ran out of his room and down the stairs. He heard his parents in the kitchen and burst through the doorway, shouting: "Merry Christmas everybody!"

His mom and dad were at the table, drinking coffee. His mom looked up and smiled. "Merry Christmas, Jason," she said, getting up and giving him a big hug.

Jason returned her embrace and waited, expectantly, for his father to return his greeting. But his father remained silent, as if he were deep in thought. He watched his dad get up and walk over to the window, his coffee cup in his hand.

His dad pushed the curtain aside and peered over at the thermometer mounted on the window ledge. "It dropped to -15o last night," he said, letting go of the curtain. He walked over to the coffee pot to get a refill.

His dad's behavior bothered Jason. *Who cares how cold it is outside?* he thought, disgruntledly. *It's Christmas. It's supposed to be cold!* Jason couldn't understand why his father wasn't excited about Christmas; why he didn't have any Christmas spirit? His dad was treating today like it was any other ordinary day.

"Well, it's not any ordinary day," Jason wanted to shout. *Today, I get my aquarium and you can't ruin that!*

"Jason, would you get Nicky out of his crib and bring him down for breakfast?" his mom asked. "And give Becky a call," she added. "Tell her that breakfast is almost ready."

"Sure!" Jason ran upstairs and pounded on Becky's door. "Get up!" he yelled, "It's Christmas!" Then he ran to his little brother's room. The door was open and Nicky was standing in his crib, rattling the bars, and jabbering away to himself. "Come on," said Jason, scooping him out of the crib and throwing him up on his shoulders. "It's Christmas time and Santa came last night," Jason informed him.

Nicky screamed with delight. "Horsie," he hollered, pulling Jason's hair.

"Ouch!" Don't do that!" Jason scolded. "That hurts, you know."

Jason galloped twice around Nicky's room, imitating a bucking horse, while his little brother hung on to his neck for dear life. "I'm getting an aquarium," Jason gasped. "Aren't you happy for me, Nicky?"

His little brother laughed and when Jason turned his head and looked up, Nicky was bobbing his head. Jason wasn't sure if Nicky was happy for him or he was just enjoying the piggy back ride. "Better be careful," Jason warned him. "If you're not good, you'll get a lump of coal in your stocking."

Jason galloped out of his brother's room and down the hallway, stopping once more in front of his sister's room. Her door was open and her room empty. "Guess she must have heard me," he said to Nicky, "so let's get downstairs and get at those presents!"

But when Jason got downstairs, he found out that his dad expected everyone to eat breakfast before they would be allowed to open their gifts. Jason put Nicky into his high chair and quickly sat down in his own place. He wolfed down his food, gave his face a quick swipe with his napkin, and sat waiting for the rest of them to finish. Becky ate almost as quickly as he had, and they waited for their father to set down his knife and fork. They knew from past experience that he would then allow them to attack the pile of gifts under the tree.

As soon as his dad laid his cutlery on his plate, Jason jumped up from his chair. "Can we go open our presents now?" he asked excitedly.

His father stared at him. "I guess so," he shrugged. His voice sounded hollow and lacked enthusiasm.

Jason raced Becky to the tree and sat amongst the presents, his eyes scanning the pile, trying to see if there was a large box with his name on it. His dad came in and sat next to him on the footstool. Jason waited impatiently for his mom to join them. Finally, she came in carrying Nicky. She set him on the floor next to his father.

"Can I play Santa?" Becky asked.

"Don't be ridiculous!" his dad exclaimed. "Whoever heard of a woman Santa Claus? Jason can hand out the presents."

Becky bowed her head and slowly moved over to where her mother was standing. She hid behind her. Jason felt sorry for his sister.

Why can't she be Santa? he thought angrily. *What's the big deal, anyway? Women can do lots of other things, so why can't Becky be Santa Claus; at least just this once?* He felt like telling his dad that he may as well let her play Santa, because he sure didn't want the job. Not now. He sat there, lost in thought, until his father nudged him with his foot.

"Well come on, get with it," he ordered.

Jason didn't want to anger his father, so he picked up the nearest gift and read the tag. "This one's for you, Mom," he said, handing his mother a box.

"Thank you." She took the gift from his hands and set it down beside her.

Jason made sure that he had given each of them a gift before he looked around for his special present. Behind the tree was a large box. It was about the right size. Jason maneuvered through the stack of presents and pushed the tree branches back so he could read the label. It had his name on it! Quickly, he hauled the box out from behind the tree and set it in front of him. He knelt down and began tearing off the paper.

There it was!

The picture on the outside of the box was identical to the picture of the aquarium in the Christmas catalogue. Jason felt that he was going to expire from happiness. All his dreams had come true. He was so engrossed with getting the rest of the paper off, so he could open it, that he didn't hear his father speak to him. It was only when his father spoke up again, that Jason quickly looked up.

"Jason!" his father said sharply. "If you're going to hand out the gifts, then I suggest that you get at it."

"Oh sure," Jason replied breathlessly, "I'm sorry. It's just... you see... it's my aquarium. Thank you! Thank you so much."

"Don't thank me," his dad corrected, "thank your mother."

The caustic tone of his dad's voice caused the hair to rise on the back of Jason's neck.

"You know how I feel about animals in the house," his dad continued. You only got that tank because your mother's been whining about it for the past two weeks." He shifted on the stool. "Now get on with it," he ordered. "Pass out the rest of the gifts. You have other presents besides that dumb aquarium."

Jason ignored him and stood up. He walked over to where his mother was standing. "Thank you, Mom," he said softly. Tears filled her eyes. "It's the best Christmas present I have ever gotten," he said, gratefully. I love you, Mom."

His mother sniffed and wiped her eyes. "You're welcome, Jason," she replied, squeezing his cheeks between her palms. "Merry Christmas."

"I'm waiting..." his dad said angrily.

Jason hurried back to the tree before his dad could finish his sentence. He quickly handed out the remaining presents, setting his own gifts behind his aquarium box. Then he sat down and pried the metal staples out of the top of the cardboard box.

"Aren't you going to at least open your other gifts before you start fooling around with that tank?" His father's sharp tone sliced at Jason's enthusiasm.

Although he didn't know the reason behind his father's anger, Jason didn't want to further upset him by failing to comply with his suggestion. Disappointed, he pushed his aquarium aside and picked up a long, flat rectangular box. He read the label: TO: JASON FROM: DAD

"Thanks, Dad," he said, turning it over, trying to guess what was inside.

"Well, just don't sit there, open it," his dad insisted. "I'm not sitting here all day!"

Jason quickly tore off the wrapping paper and opened the box. Inside was a rifle and two boxes of shells. Bewildered, Jason stared at his dad's gift. Why had his dad bought him a gun? What was he supposed to do with it. He didn't even like guns. Reluctantly, he lifted the rifle out of the box, running his fingers along the smooth, wooden stock. "It's nice, Dad," he lied. "But, what's it for?" he asked staring up at his father. His father frowned and Jason quickly added, "I mean... what am I supposed to do with it?"

"What does anyone do with a gun?" His father's voice snapped with sarcasm. "You use it!"

"I know that, Dad... but... where?" Jason had never seen any place in the city where he could use a gun-- at least not a real gun-- like the one he now held in his lap.

"You'll use it when we go hunting," his dad said.

Jason didn't want to argue, but now he was more confused than ever. "But Dad, I don't know how to hunt."

"Then it's time you learned!" his dad shouted, waving his fist in the air. "You're never going to amount to anything, if you don't start acting like a man-- start learning the things that a man needs to know if he's going to be a success in life. But oh... I forgot... my son is more interested in playing

225

with some stupid fish than in learning how to become a real man!" He got up off the stool, walked to the fireplace, and spit. The glob landed in the ashes and Jason saw a tiny puff of ashes rise into the air. His dad turned around and stared at him. "Hell," he continued, "If I had known how you were going to react to the gun, I'd have bought you a doll instead. That way, you could have played with Becky. You don't know how to appreciate a real gift." His lips sneered with contempt.

Jason was desperate. He wasn't prepared for his dad's sudden display of anger. "No, Dad," he pleaded, "I like the rifle. Honest."

"Sure you do," his dad retorted. "You're so interested in that rifle that you can't wait to put it down so you can go back to playing with your aquarium."

His dad walked over to him and snatched the rifle out of his hands. He stomped across the living room and stood by the chesterfield, the gun clasped tightly in his hands. He waved it in the air. "You're all alike," he shouted, hatred blazing in his eyes.

Jason shivered. The room was now deathly quiet, all eyes were fixed on his father. When his dad sat down, the gun cradled in his lap, Jason continued to stare at him until he saw his dad close his eyes.

Everything's going to be okay, Jason tried to reassure himself. *Dad's just a little upset but he'll get it over pretty soon.* He turned his attention back to his aquarium, trying to ignore the tension that now filled the room. Carefully, he pulled open the lid and removed the packing from the box before gently lifting out the glass tank. He set it on the floor and reached inside for the instructions.

It doesn't matter if Dad's mad at me because I don't like that dumb rifle, he told himself. *I got my aquarium and that's all I care about.*

It was easier for him to eliminate his dad's anger in his mind, than it was in actual life. His hands shook and he had difficulty reading the operational directions for his fish tank. He tried to concentrate, but a nagging thought kept popping into his head. Everything that had happened to him this past couple of days, until his run-in with his dad, had been good things. Yesterday, he had gone to a party. He had Moby Dick and his other presents, and today his wish had come true. He had his aquarium. However, from past experience, Jason knew that life didn't turn out this way. His wishes had never come true in the past, so why should it be different now? He felt a stab of fear take root deep inside him.

Trying to rid himself of the dark and gloomy thoughts that were now filling his mind, Jason thought about his tank and how good it was going to look when it was all set up and sitting on top of his dresser. He chided himself for always looking on the dark side. What did he have to be afraid of?

I have everything I want, he thought. So what if things haven't worked out in the past? It's different now. Why should I look for ghosts where there are none?

His little pep talk helped him overcome the awful premonition he had that disaster awaited him. He began to feel better. Now, he was able to smile at Becky, as his sister happily pushed her new doll carriage across the living room, pretending that she was taking her doll for a walk to the store. His mother had received a new Kitchen Centre and was busy trying to fit the pieces together. Nicky was sitting in the middle of the room, happily tearing pieces of wrapping paper to shreds.

Jason looked across the room at his father. His dad was still sitting on the couch with the gun resting on his knees, his eyes still closed.

Jason picked up the can of fish food from inside the aquarium and was about to go upstairs and feed Moby, when his dad spoke to him.

"Bring me a box of shells," he ordered.

Jason pushed a bunch of crumpled paper off the gun box and reached inside. He picked up one of the boxes of shells and walked slowly over to his dad. He handed him the box of bullets.

Jason watched as his dad opened the box, dropped some of the shells into his hand, and proceeded to load them into the rifle. Slowly, his father transferred one cartridge at a time into the cartridge chamber in the rifle.

"That's how you load it," his dad said, shoving in the last bullet. He cocked the gun and aimed it at a plate sitting on the mantel.

Jason's mother came hurrying over to them. "Nick, do you think it's safe?" she inquired fearfully. "I don't think you should have a loaded gun in the house." She wrung her hands.

"When I want your opinion, I'll ask for it!" he snapped.

Once again, everyone in the room stared at Jason's dad. When Jason looked at his family, he could tell that they were as frightened as he was by his dad's unexpected actions. As Jason watched his father aim at different objects in the room, he wondered what was going to happen next?

"Now, this is a real nice little piece," his father said admiringly, running his right hand along the barrel. "It's a semi-automatic so, with a little practice, it should be easy for you to pull down a deer next fall." He took aim at the little Christmas angel on top of the tree.

"But Dad," Jason pleaded, "I don't want to kill anything. I like deer. I've fed them grass at the zoo. They're pretty. They have big brown eyes..." Jason was repulsed at even the thought of killing one of them. If it was to look at him... he knew he wouldn't be able to pull the trigger. No even if his dad ordered him to shoot.

"Big brown eyes, my foot!" his dad shouted, glaring at him. "You'll kill anything I tell you to kill." He swung the rifle around and Jason ducked, narrowly avoiding getting smashed in the teeth. The action served to break the hypnotic hold his dad seemed to have had on him, and Jason jumped back and ran over to his mother.

His dad jumped up and in less than three strides, was standing, towering over Jason. He grabbed Jason by the shoulder and said coldly, "This is how I want you to spend your time." He waved the gun in Jason's face. "Not playing with fish or down at that damn Centre all the time!"

Suddenly, he released Jason, swung the gun up to his shoulder and fired!

The bullet blasted through the glass walls of the aquarium, showering the room with fragments of broken glass!

In disbelief, Jason saw his dream disintegrate in front of his eyes. A glass splinter struck his cheek and his hands flew to his face. When he lowered them, they were covered with blood. In shock, he let the blood drip freely down his cheek, as he slowly walked over to inspect what was left of his aquarium.

All that remained of his beautiful dream was a broken pile of glass at his feet. Without a word, Jason bent down and started to pick up the broken pieces, carefully setting each one in the box that had held his aquarium. His mother and sister joined him and together, they cleaned up the mess.

Jason wondered why his mother was crying, when he himself... felt nothing. He was empty inside. *This can't be happening to me. Hey God!* his mind screamed in pain. *Where are you now? Why did you let this happen? What's the matter? Was it that I was too happy-- that I didn't deserve to be happy? Is that it? Tell me, God, am I such a terrible person that you couldn't let me have one lousy little fish tank? Or, is it because you're going to teach me a lesson, too?* If that were the case. Then Jason was sure that God must be laughing at him now, because he had been taught a lesson-- a very valuable lesson. Anger burned white-hot inside of him, consuming him 'til all he could see was a red haze in front of his eyes.

He heard his father speak to him: "I'm sorry, Jason," he said. The gun just went off..." Jason looked at him, his eyes filled with hate. "Now don't get upset," his dad hastily added. Maybe it's all for the best. You're too old to play with fish..."

Jason continued to glare at his father. Never in his life had he hated anyone as he hated his dad at this moment. He wanted to tear the gun out of his dad's hands and kill him! Wanted to wipe the smirk off his face, once and for all. It would be so easy. Just lift the gun up, aim, and blow him away, like he had blown away the aquarium.

He could actually visualize the bullet leaving the barrel of the rifle, travelling through the air, and entering his dad's skull right between his eyes. He saw the blood spurt out and laughed at the look of astonishment that came over his dad's face before he slumped to the floor. He stood up.

His mother tried to hug him, but Jason shook her off, and continued to stare into his father's eyes. For the first time in his life, he saw his dad's eyes waver and then look away. Jason watched him slowly walk over to his chair and sit down, his eyes on the floor. He leaned the rifle against the wall and picked up a magazine.

The need for revenge filled Jason's heart and he walked over to the gun and picked it up.

"Here, let me show you how to use it," his dad said, reaching for the gun.

Jason jerked the rifle away and stepped back. "No thanks, Dad. You've already shown me how it works." he sneered.

"Look son, I told you I was sorry. What more do you want?"

"I want you dead!" Jason screamed, lifting the rifle up to his shoulder and aiming it at his father. "And," he added, his voice shaking, "I never want to call me 'son' again."

"Hey there!" his dad recoiled in surprise. "What the hell do you think you're doing? Don't point that thing at me!" He started to rise from his chair. Jason cocked the rifle and his dad sat back down again.

"Don't move," Jason cautioned. "Don't even think about trying to take this away from me." He felt his finger grow warm on the cold metal trigger and smiled.

"Look, you crazy little bastard. This has gone far enough. Don't you know that the gun is loaded?" He paled, pointing to the cartridge chamber.

"I know," Jason purred. He felt better now; felt more in control now, then he had ever felt before. He continued to smile at his father. "I'm going to blow your fucking head off," he said calmly, "and I'm going to enjoy watching you die."

His dad's face went a sickly white and he trembled. For a moment, Jason was tempted to throw down the gun and run away, but he'd gone too far this time-- it was too late to turn back. Besides, he knew what would happen to him if he ran away again. No, there were no "grey areas" here. He had a job to do and he knew he'd pull the trigger.

"Look, Jason," his dad tried to reason with him. "You're crazy, but we can get you help. Just put the gun down and we can talk about it. You don't want to kill me. For Christ's sake! I'm your father."

Jason turned his head and glanced at his mother. In the split second that their eyes connected, he was able to read her mind. Why, she wants me to pull the trigger, he thought in surprise. She wants him dead, too. This can't be happening; this can't be happening to me!

"See here, Jason," said his dad. "I've had enough of this nonsense. If you don't give me that gun, right now, I'm going to call the cops and have them take you away."

"You're going to do shit!" Jason replied coldly, his eyes returning to his dad's face. "You call the cops? That's a laugh! I thought that Mom was the only one who had to call the cops when you were done beating on her?"

"Look here--"

"No, you look here! I'm the one holding the gun. I'm the one in charge now, and you aren't calling the cops or anyone else." Jason saw the anger in his dad's eyes become mingled with fear. "But don't worry," he jeered, "They will be called-- after I've killed you. Besides, even if I let you call them, what would you say? Do you want everyone to find out what a bastard you really are? Because, I'd tell them, before they took me away. Then, everyone would know our family secret. Wouldn't they, Mom?" He glanced in her direction. He saw her slowly nod her head. He turned back to his dad and adjusted the height of the barrel until it was aimed between his dad's eyes.

"Please, Jason," his father begged. "Let's talk this over...."

Jason felt his finger tighten on the trigger. Just a little more pressure and it would be all over. His pleading had no effect on Jason. But... something else made him hesitate about pulling the trigger. He wanted his dad dead, but what would his teacher say? Better still, how would he explain what he had done to Mrs. Miller-- to Paul? Would they understand why he had to kill him? Would they understand that his dad deserved to die? Would Paul understand? Sure, Paul was on probation, but he hadn't killed anyone.... Now confusion beat at his resolve. *I bet Mrs. Miller would think that I never learned anything from our talks.*

Their many discussions now filled his mind. He had spent a lot of time with her, discussing many things besides how to build models. They had talked about life and the difference between dreams and reality. Was all this only a dream-- a nightmare-- or was he really standing in the middle of the living room, pointing a gun at his father's head?

I wish you were here, Mrs. Miller, so you could tell me what I should do now. You always know what's right and wrong. But right now, I don't seem to be able to tell the difference.

Is it wrong to kill my dad because he smashed my aquarium, or is it right for me to shoot him because he deserves to die?

Jason turned his head to look at his mother. But this time, his mom dropped her eyes and stared at the floor. *Why can't you be like Mrs. Miller and tell me what I should do?* he wondered. Why don't you smile all the time or laugh sometimes? *Why can't you help me find out who I really am because right now, I don't know. I need you to help me out of this mess. How can I do what's right, if you can't teach me the difference between right and wrong. I saw you looking at me. You wanted me to pull the trigger. Wanted me to kill him. Can't you understand? I need you.*

When his mother didn't look up, Jason's thoughts returned to Mrs. Miller. He recalled the time they had talked about marriage. She had explained to him that the purpose of a marriage wasn't to see how miserable you could make your partner's life. Marriage was supposed to bring out the best in two people. There should be love and understanding and yes... respect.

Yes, he thought sadly, turning back to his father, *I finally know what respect really means.*

Respect wasn't something that could be demanded. You couldn't use threats or fear to get respect. Respect has to be earned and freely given or it wasn't respect at all. It was fear and forced compliance. But, most important of all, Jason had learned, was that *before a person could get respect, he had to be worthy of it.*

Dad's not that kind of person, Jason suddenly realized, watching the man in front of him who seemed almost a stranger cringe and beg for mercy. *Even you-- Grandpa-- were wrong! What's the use of being Number 1, if people end up hating you-- if you end up alone? I wouldn't trade being Paul's friend for all the power in the world. I wouldn't want him to be afraid of me.*

Jason knew he still didn't fully understand everything Mrs. Miller had tried to teach him-- especially when it came to the different roles men and women were expected to play in life. However, he was certain of one thing-- the way his dad treated his mother wasn't right! And, he also now knew that other families didn't live like this. Why was his family different? What had gone wrong...?

The answer washed over Jason in a sudden flood of understanding: *You didn't have to be tough and mean to be a man.* Mr. White had taught him that. *In fact, he finally knew with bell-like clarity, if you were a real man, you didn't have to always go around trying to prove it to everyone-- by making them suffer. Real men know who they are. They like themselves and therefore, they can afford to be gentle and kind to others. And... the first step in learning to like and trust other people was to like and trust yourself.*

Dad's not a real man!

With this astounding realization, Jason's anger flickered, then died. He searched his father's face to find something-- anything-- that would show him that his dad was genuinely sorry for what he had done. But all Jason saw in his father's face was-- fear!

His dad was afraid of him! At first, Jason thought that he must be mistaken, because he had never before seen his father afraid of anyone or anything. It gave Jason a queer feeling. Seeing his father this way didn't give him any pleasure. His father looked broken and defeated.

Jason wanted to shout at him; wanted to make him tell him why he had forced him to do such a thing. *Why did you screw up my life?* he silently condemned. His finger relaxed on the trigger and he lowered the gun.

"I've changed my mind, Dad; I'm not going to kill you."

He heard his dad exhale and the sound seemed to fill the room.

"I'm sorry, Mom, said Jason.

His dad stood up and reached for the gun but Jason quickly stepped back and raised the rifle back to his shoulder. "Don't try it," he advised.

"I knew you wouldn't pull that trigger." Now it was his father's turn to jeer; once more, in control. "It takes guts to kill someone and you're all a bunch of cowards," he accused, his disdainful eyes sweeping across the room.

His father's last remark didn't anger Jason. In fact, it made him smile. "Don't push it, Dad," he said calmly. "The only reason that you're still alive is because Mrs. Miller wouldn't understand. You got that? She wouldn't know why I did it."

"Who the hell is Mrs. Miller?"

"Oh," Jason replied, "just somebody I know, but I'm afraid you'll never get a chance to meet her." He lifted the gun a little higher. "But don't worry," he continued, "you wouldn't like her anyway. Not that it matters a whole lot; nothing matters anymore." He smiled. "Now if you guys will excuse me, I'm going up to my room. I don't want any of you to follow me or to try and open my door." He rubbed his cheek against the smooth, wooden rifle's stock. "If you do, I really will shoot and I won't miss. This I can promise you."

No one moved as Jason backed out of the living room and over to the staircase. He put the back of his foot on the first step and slowly backed up the stairs, never taking his eyes off his family, crowded in the doorway, watching him. When he reached the top, he rested by the landing. His head was spinning and he knew he needed time to think; time to be alone. He was about to walk the rest of the way to his room when he heard his dad shout.

"Who the hell does that little bastard think he is? Imagine-- pulling a gun on me! Well, he's not going to get away with it. Do you hear me,

Linda? I'm calling the cops! They can come and get him. Maybe when he finds himself locked up in a cell for a few years, he'll find out just how good he had it here."

Jason heard his mom begging his dad not to call the police; heard her tell him that he didn't mean to point that gun at him.

"Didn't mean it?" He shouted incredulously. "He knew what he was doing. I saw it in his eyes. The little bastard was going to kill me."

"But Nick, he's only twelve years old...."

Jason turned and walked down the hallway to his room. "Don't beg, Mom," he whispered. "It's no use. He won't listen anyway. He's never listened to us before and now... it's too late."

He opened his door and went inside, quietly closing it behind him.

Now, what do I do? he wondered.

CHAPTER XIX

Jason felt old-- older than time itself. Like a clock winding down, he moved jerkily across his room and sat down on the edge of his bed. He laid the rifle on his pillow. His body slumped forward and he buried his face in his hands.

Slowly, he began to rock back and forth moaning softly. "Someone help me!" he cried out. "I'm scared."

But, he knew, there was no one who could help him now.

He rested his elbows on his knees and began to sob. Loneliness welled up inside him. He didn't try to stop his tears. He felt too weak to fight any longer. Why should he? He was alone, trapped in his room forever.

It was an effort for him to raise his head and look around his room. He was surprised to see that nothing had changed: that everything was the same... except for him. He had changed; he was different than he was before.

In fact, he knew he would never be the same again.

He tried to stand, but his knees buckled and he collapsed back onto his bed. Reaching over, he picked up his pillow and buried his face in its softness.

"You won't send me away, Dad," he moaned. "You won't send me away. I showed you who was in control. I saw you. *You* were the one who was afraid. You were afraid of *me!*"

Jason waited for his dad's apparition to appear as it had so many times in the past when he had tried to defy his father. But this time, it never materialized.

Jason spoke to the empty space usually occupied by his father. "What's the matter, Dad? You too much of a coward to come up here and finish me off? Or, maybe you're scared I'll finish you off this time. Is that it?

"I could have done it, you know. I wasn't afraid. In fact, it would have been so easy. All I had to do was squeeze the trigger a little harder and *poof*... you'd have been dead!"

Jason shook his head. He didn't want to dwell on what had just occurred downstairs.

"I think I'm losing it," he said aloud. "Nothing's the same anymore. My bed is new; my clothes are new; even the planes I built are new." He looked up at his bare ceiling. "Everything in here is new, except me! I'm old. Too old."

Jason rolled up his sleeves and looked at the skin on his arms. "I know what happens to people when they get old," he said. "They get wrinkles and then they die!" He was surprised to see that the flesh on his hands and arms was still smooth; still free of the telltale signs of old age.

He stared up at his goldfish and asked. "Do I look old to you, Moby?"... "No? Well, it's only a matter of time. There's no escaping it."

His fish stared back at him, its bug-eyes full of understanding. Jason pushed himself up off the bed and stumbled over to his dresser. He gently picked up the glass jar and set it on his night table.

"I'm sorry about your new home," he said to the goldfish. "I didn't mean to break my promise to you. You see... it wasn't my fault. Dad gave me this gun and.... Hey, don't look at me like that! I didn't kill him. And, you're not the only one who has lost his home. Look at me! See this bed? This is not my real bed; my real bed got broken, too. And... nobody's sending you to jail!"

The fish continued to stare at him and from the way it opened and closed its mouth, Jason knew that it was speaking to him. He leaned over and put his ear against the glass. "Ya," Jason replied, "I'm sorry, too." His fish spoke again. "No, I can't explain what happened," said Jason wearily, "You wouldn't understand, anyway. It wasn't my fault."

Jason didn't want to talk anymore and turned away. He walked over and leaned against his dresser. He felt drained; tired to the point of exhaustion. He pushed, using the last of his energy to move the dresser across the floor and over to his door. He gave it a final shove to ensure that it was jammed tightly against the door.

"Merry Christmas and God bless everyone!" he giggled, sinking on his knees to the floor.

Why don't I feel anything?

His body felt numb and emptiness consumed him. He wondered why he didn't at least feel hatred or sadness for the injustice that had brought him to this state.

Maybe I'm crazy, he thought, gripping his dresser and pulling himself up. *That's it. It's finally happened. I've really lost my mind this time.*

He began to wave his arms-- slowly at first-- then faster and faster until he rose to his feet and the momentum sent him careening around his room. Hopping from one foot to the other, he began to chant: "They're coming to take me away. They're coming to take me away. They're...."

The last of his energy spent, Jason collapsed on his bed and curled up in a ball. He thought about Paul. *Would Paul want a friend who was crazy?* His vision blurred and he closed his eyes. When he opened them again, he could clearly see Paul sitting at their table, working on his model. Jason watched him carefully run his knife along the edge of a piece of wood, shaving a quarter inch off each end. Paul frowned and picked up his instruction manual.

"It's okay," Jason said. "You haven't screwed up. Just take a little more off the far end and it should fit perfectly."

Paul looked up and smiled at him. For a second, Jason thought that Paul was going to say something to him, but then his friend bent his head, his attention once again on his model.

"Hey Paul," Jason called out, "we really built some great planes, didn't we?"

When Paul didn't reply, Jason tried again.

"Look Paul, I just want to tell you that I'm glad we're friends. I want to tell you that I almost ended up on probation, too. Or even worse! It was awful! I almost--"

Before Jason could finish his sentence, Paul's image began to fade away, "Wait...," Jason called after him, "This is important." But it was no use. Paul was gone and Jason was once again alone in his room.

Disappointed that his friend had vanished before he could tell him what had happened, Jason felt better when he looked up and saw Mrs. Miller standing beside his night table. She was dressed in blue slacks and had on a white ruffled shirt.

"Hi, Mrs. Miller. How did you get in here?" He glanced over at his door to make sure that it was still tightly secured. He waited for her to say something to him, but she, too, remained silent. "What's wrong with you guys?" he shouted. "Why won't you talk to me? I didn't do anything wrong. I didn't kill him."

Jason stared at her, trying to force her to say something-- anything-- to him. He reached for her and was startled when his hand passed right through her.

"Are you a ghost?" he asked fearfully, but before he could get an answer, she began to disappear, too. "Don't go," he begged. "Not yet." The image appeared to steady slightly, and Jason quickly continued, "I just want to thank you for not letting me shoot him, even if he deserved to die. You know that don't you?"

No, he thought. *How could you when I never told you all the terrible things he's done to us-- to me.*

"The reason I didn't pull the trigger," he explained to the shadowy figure, "was because you wouldn't have understood why I killed him.

"Did I ever tell you that I like the way you laugh? Well, I do. Mom doesn't laugh very much. And... I just want you to know that I think you're a great teacher, too. I didn't believe Paul and Mr. White at first, when they said you knew how to build model planes. But, I do now."

Her image was almost completely gone and he shouted at the retreating figure. "Thanks for everything. I had lots of fun with you guys."

"Hey, where'd you come from?" Jason asked, surprised to see Mr. White now standing beside his dresser. "I don't know how all of you are getting in here, but I'm glad you came." He was slightly perturbed though, that his friends could come into his room unobserved. He said to his teacher: "Did you know that Paul and Mrs. Miller were here just a few minutes ago?"

By now, Jason was getting used to his friends not saying anything and it didn't bother him as much when his teacher didn't reply. Jason watched him walk across the room and come over to where he was sitting. When Jason felt a hand softly ruffle his hair, he smiled. The familiar gesture made him remember all the good times he and Mr. White had shared at the Centre.

"Know something?" Jason said to his teacher. "You're all right. Paul likes you, too. He told me. He said that you're the best thing that ever happened to him.

"And, I like you, too." Jason smiled up at his teacher. "Remember the time you challenged Paul and me to a contest on who could make a paper plane the fastest? Well, you didn't stand a chance because Paul and I are experts, you know." Jason laughed at the memory of his teacher vainly trying to fold his paper into the proper shape-- under pressure. Mr. White had thrown up his hands in frustration.

Jason saw his teacher slowly glide over to the window-- where he stood-- looking out.

"I'm glad you had the time to talk with me about all that other stuff, too. Because, I learned a lot about life from you. Hell... oops... sorry, I didn't mean to swear. I was just going to say that I bet my dad could learn a lot from you, too. Did I ever tell you about my Dad?" His teacher didn't reply. Jason continued. No? Well, never mind, it doesn't matter now.

"I guess I won't be coming back to the Centre anymore... Dad's sending me away. Would you do me a favor? Would you give my rocket to Paul and ask him to finish it for me?"

While Jason watched, his teacher slowly began to fade, until at last, he too, had disappeared. Jason looked around, hoping that his friends would decide to come back. When a few minutes had passed and none of them had reappeared, Jason felt that they had abandoned him to await his fate-- alone.

"I'm scared, Mrs. Miller," he whimpered. "Really scared!"

Jason looked wildly around his room, trying to see if his teacher was hiding somewhere. "I'll be back, Mr. White!" he called out. "Dad can't keep me away!"

Slowly, Jason rolled over, dropped his feet over the edge of his bed and pushed himself into a sitting position. He stood up, walked over to his closet and opened the door. He looked in the mirror, trying to find the boy who lived behind the glass.

"Where are you?" he asked, trying to see beyond his own reflection.

He waited for the boy to appear, but the only thing he could see in the mirror was his own image, staring back at him.

"I need you," he cried. "Don't you understand? I don't want to be alone!" After a while, Jason knew that it was pointless to keep beseeching the boy to come to him.

Jason left his mirror and walked into the closet. He reached up to the top shelf and his fingers closed around a small brown paper bag. He lifted it out of its hiding place and clutched it tightly to his chest. He backed out of the closet and went over to his bed.

Hesitantly, he opened the bag and stared inside. He was hoping for a miracle; some act of God that would have made his stuffed raccoon whole again. He had prayed that when he opened the bag he would find Pookie the way he had been when he had left him that fateful morning. Jason needed him; needed him to understand how he was feeling. Pookie didn't need any explanations. He would know! Pookie would soak up his tears without condemning, offer love where there was no love.

But, as Jason stared at the inside of the bag he realized that no miracle had taken place. The sight of Pookie-- torn from limb to limb-- broke Jason's heart. He began to sob uncontrollable.

"Why couldn't God have fixed you?" he blubbered. "Why did he have to let you die?"

Gently holding the bag containing the remains of his friend, Jason pulled back his covers and climbed into bed. With his free hand, he pushed the rifle aside and laid his head on his pillow.

One by one, he removed the furry pieces and set them on his chest. When the bag was empty, he scooped up the small pile of fur and pressed it under his chin.

He talked to his raccoon. "Well old fellow, it looks like we both have had the stuffings ripped out of us. I couldn't save you then, but I know what to do now. You don't have to worry anymore, because everything's going to be okay. I promise."

He rubbed his chin in the soft fur, while he thought about his family.

I never told you Becky, but I really do like you, even if you are a pain sometimes. I didn't mean to shake you that time. I was scared. You'd have been scared, too, if you had to go out in that hall with Mom and Dad screaming at each other.

And Mom, thanks for helping me pick up the broken glass. I know you couldn't stop him and I'm not mad at you. I wish you'd talk with Mrs. Miller. Maybe she could help you, too. I think you'd like her, if you met her. I know you would. You have to learn to laugh and be happy like she is, or you'll end up as mean and small inside as Dad.

Jason thought about his little brother and how he had run down the hall this morning with Nicky clinging to his hair.

What's going to happen to you? he wondered. Are you going to end up like me? Just remember, if Grandpa tries to tell you that you have to make people afraid of you to be in control, don't listen to him. Please Nicky, don't listen... because it's not true... none of it is true. If you don't believe me, go ask Mr. White. He'll tell you.

Jason eyes filled with tears and he pressed his face into Pookie's tattered remains as he thought about what had taken place downstairs between his father and himself. He forced himself to look about his room, whispering softly to himself:

"I didn't mean to point the gun at you.... I was angry. You get angry-- lots of times. Why didn't the cops ever come and take you away? Remember the time you hurt Mom and she had to leave and take us to that Place? You didn't get sent to jail for hurting her... and you hurt her really bad. I remember. Why didn't they come and get you for that? Why are they coming for *me*?"

Jason's head dropped to his chest and he closed his eyes, trying to make his mind blank. He squeezed Pookie tighter and small pieces of stuffing dropped to the floor. As if aware that he, himself, was as tattered and falling apart as Pookie, Jason opened his hands and let the remaining pieces of the raccoon fall from his fingers. The soft stuffing made no sound as it landed on the hardwood floor at his feet. Slowly, Jason opened his eyes and looked down. There were no more tears, no more time even for tears for the time had come and gone. The time was now.

His face was blank, unreadable, as though he no longer dwelt within his own skull, as though he had fled elsewhere. Jason looked at the bits of black and white material at his feet and then his eyes moved over to the bed, coming to rest on the rifle. He walked over to the bed and picked up the gun, running his hands down the barrel. The metal felt cold-- like he did.

"I wonder if Mrs. Miller sews?" he murmured, as he bent down to pick up one small piece of fur near his foot. He held it a moment and then let it drop.

He placed both hands on the rifle and leaned toward the muzzle. Taking careful aim, his finger gently squeezed the trigger.

THE END

Printed in the United States
By Bookmasters